## Also by Barbara Delinsky

*A Woman's Place*

*Shades of Grace*

*Together Alone*

*For My Daughters*

*Suddenly*

*More Than Friends*

*The Passions of Chelsea Kane*

*A Woman Betrayed*

# THREE WISHES

### a novel

# *Barbara Delinsky*

Simon & Schuster

SIMON & SCHUSTER
Rockefeller Center
1230 Avenue of the Americas
New York, NY 10020

SIMON & SCHUSTER and colophon are registered trademarks
of Simon & Schuster Inc.

Designed by Sam Potts

Manufactured in the United States of America

1   3   5   7   9   10   8   6   4   2

Library of Congress Cataloging-in-Publication Data
Delinsky, Barbara.
Three wishes : a novel / Barbara Delinsky.
p.   cm.
I. Title.
PS3554.E4427T48   1997
813'.54—dc21                              97-15217
                                                    CIP
ISBN 0-684-84507-5

# Well-Wishes

## A Personal Note from the Author

I've always been a wish maker. I wish at the sight of evening's first star, on pulling the long end of the turkey wishbone, in secret notes written on birch bark and tossed onto a campfire, and, of course, over birthday candles. Some of my wishes are general and constant, most notably for good health and happiness. Others are more specific.

On the occasion of the publication of this book, I offer three of the latter. First, anniversary wishes to Steve; I vote for another thirty years. Second, graduation wishes to Andrew and Jeremy; may you each find deep satisfaction in whatever field you choose to enter. Third, wedding wishes to Jodi and Eric, with the sweetest dreams of good health, happiness, and—I can't resist—true love always.

I've made other wishes this year. Thanks to my agent, Amy Berkower, and my editor, Laurie Bernstein, many have already come true. You both know what's left. We'll wish together.

# chapter
## one

It wasn't the first snow of the season. Panama, Vermont, lay far enough north to have already seen several snow-dusted dawns. But this wasn't dawn, and these flakes didn't dust. From early afternoon right on into evening, they fell heavy and fat and wet.

Truckers stopping at the diner complained of the roads growing slick, but the warning carried little weight with locals. They knew that the sun would be back, even an Indian summer before winter set in. Snowfall now was simply frosting on the cake of another wildfire fall, thick flakes silencing the riot of colorful leaves, draping a plump white shawl on the town green's oak benches, on marigolds that lingeringly lined front walks, on a bicycle propped against an open front gate.

The scene was so peaceful that no one imagined the accident to come, least of all Bree Miller. Winter was her favorite season. There was something about snow that softened the world, made it make-believe for the briefest time, and while she wasn't a woman prone to fancy—would have immediately denied it if accused—she had her private moments.

She didn't bother with a jacket. The memory of summer's heat was all too fresh. Besides, with locals wanting to eat before the weather worsened and with truckers bulking up, the diner had been hopping, so she was plenty warm without.

She slipped out the door, closing it tight on the hum of conversation, the hiss and sizzle of the grill, the sultry twang of Shania Twain. In the sudden hush, she ran lightly down the steps, across the parking lot, then the street. On the far side, she flattened her spine to the crusty trunk of a large maple whose amber leaves hung heavy with snow, and looked back.

The diner was a vision of stainless steel and neon, rich purples and greens bouncing off silver, new and more gallant through a steady fall of snow. Gone were little items on her fix-it list—the scrape Morgan Willis's truck had put on a corner panel, a dent in the front railing, bird droppings off the edge of the roof. What remained was sparkling clean, warm, and inviting, starting with the diner's roadside logo, concentric rings of neon forming a large frying pan with the elegant eruption of FLASH AN' THE PAN from its core. Behind that were golden lamps at each of ten broad windows running the diner's length and, in booths behind those lamps, looking snug and content, the customers.

The diner wasn't Bree's. She just worked there. But she liked looking at it.

Same with Panama. Up the hill, at the spot where East Main leveled into an oval around the town green, snow capped the steel roofs of the row of tall Federals and beyond, white on white, the church steeple. Down the hill, at the spot where the road dipped past the old train depot, snow hid the stains that years of diesel abuse had left and put a hearty head on the large wood beer stein that marked the Sleepy Creek Brewery.

Panama was ten minutes off the highway on the truck route running from Concord to Montreal. Being neither here nor there was one of its greatest strengths. There were no cookie-cutter subdivisions, no planned developments with architect-designed wraparound porches. Porches had been wrapping around houses in Panama since the days of the Revolution, not for the sake of style but for community. Those porches were as genuine as the people who used them. Add the lack of crime and the low cost of land, and the town's survival was ensured. Bright minds sought haven here and found inspiration. The brewery was but one example. There was also a bread company, workshops producing hand-carved furniture and wooden toys, and a gourmet ice cream factory. Native Panamanians lent stability. Newcomers brought cash.

Bree drew in a snow-chilled breath, held it deep in her lungs, let it slowly out. The occasional snowflake breached the leaves overhead to land in an airy puff on her arm, looking soft, feeling rich, in those few seconds before melting away. On impulse, she slid around the tree trunk to face the woods. Here, the snow picked up the diner's lights in a mystical way. Drifting leaves whirled about, forest fairies at play, Bree fancied. From nowhere came childhood images of carousels, clowns, and Christmas, all more dream than memory. She listened hard, half expecting to hear elf sounds mixed in with those of nocturnal creatures. But, of course, there were none.

*Foolish Bree. High on snow. Time to go inside.*

Still she stood there, riveted by something that made her eyes mist and her throat ache. If it was wanting, she didn't know what for. She had a good life. She was content.

Still she stood there.

Behind her came a fragment of conversation when the diner door opened, and the subsequent growls, muted by billowing flakes, of one big rig, then a second. By the time the semis had rumbled out of the parking lot, cruised down the hill, and turned toward the highway, the only sound left was the cat's-paw whisper of snow upon snow.

The diner door opened again, this time to a louder "Bree! I need you!"

Brushing tears from her eyes, she pushed off from the bark. Seconds later, she was running back across the road, turning her head against the densest of the flakes, suddenly so desperate to be back inside, where everything made sense, that she grew careless. She slipped, fought for balance with a flailing of arms, landed in the snow all the same. Scrambling up, she brushed at the seat of her black jeans and, with barely a pause to shake her hands free of snow, rushed inside, to be met by applause, several wolf whistles, and a "Way to go, Bree!"

The last was from a trucker, one of the regulars. Another round of applause broke out when she wrapped her icy hands around his bull neck and gave an affectionate squeeze on her way to the kitchen.

Flash, the diner's owner and executive chef, met her at the swinging door. A near-full gallon of milk hung from his fingers. "It's bad again," he said, releasing the door once she was inside. "What're we gonna do? Look of the roads, no delivery's coming anytime soon."

"We have extra," Bree assured him, opening the refrigerator to verify it.

Flash ducked his head and took a look. "That'll be enough?"

"Plenty."

"Seventeen's up, Bree," the grillman called.

The diner sat fifty-two, in ten booths and twelve counter stools. At its busiest times, there were lines out the door, but bad weather slowed things down. Barely thirty-five remained now. LeeAnn Conti was serving half. The rest were Bree's.

Balancing four plates holding a total of twelve eggs, twelve rashers of bacon, six sausages, six slabs each of maple nut and raisin toast, and enough hash browns to crowd everything in, she delivered supper to the men in seventeen, the booth to the right of the door. She had known the four all her life. They, too, had

gone to the local schools and stayed to work in the area, Sam
and Dave at the lumber mill three towns over, Andy at his family's tackle store, Jack at the farm his father had left his brother
and him. They were large men with insatiable appetites for early-
evening breakfast.

The Littles, two booths down, were another story. Ben and
Liz had fled a New York ad agency to run their own by way of
computer, fax, and phone from Vermont. Along with seven-year-
old Benji, five-year-old Samantha, and two-year-old Joey, they
hit the diner several times a week to take advantage of Flash's
huge portions, easily splitting three orders of turkey, mashed
potatoes, and peas, or biscuit-topped shepherd's pie, or American
chop suey. They were currently sharing a serving of warm apple
crisp and a large chocolate chip cookie.

At Bree's appearance, the two-year-old put down his hunk of
cookie, scrambled to his feet on the bench, and opened his arms.
She scooped him up. "Was everything good?"

He gave her a chocolaty grin that melted her heart.

"Anything else here?" she asked his parents.

"Just the check," said Ben. "That snow keeps coming. Driving
won't be great."

When Joey squirmed, Bree kissed the mop of his hair and
returned him to the bench. At the side counter, she tallied the
check, then put it on their table and set to cleaning the adjacent
booth, where the drivers of the newly departed big rigs had been.
She cleared the dirty dishes, pocketed her tip, wiped down the
black Formica, straightened shakers, condiment bottles, and the
small black vase that held a spray of goldenrod. She set out new
place mats, oval replicas of the frying pan from the logo, with
the regular menu printed in its center. Specials—"The Daily
Flash"—were handwritten on each of two elliptical chalkboards
high behind either end of the counter.

She moved several booths down to Panama's power elite—
postmaster Earl Yarum, police chief Eliot Bonner, town meeting
moderator Emma McGreevy. Before them were dishes that had
earlier held a beef stew, a pork chop special, and a grilled chicken
salad. All three plates, plus a basket of sourdough rolls, were

empty, which was good news. When sated, Earl, Eliot, and Emma were innocuous.

Bree grinned. "Ready for dessert?"

"Whaddya got?" Earl asked.

"Whaddya want?"

"Pie."

"O-kay. We have apple, peach, and blueberry. We have pumpkin. We have strawberry rhubarb, banana cream, maple cream, maple pecan, pumpkin pecan, lemon meringue—"

"Anything chocolate?" Earl asked.

"Chocolate pecan, chocolate mousse, chocolate rum cream—"

"How about a brownie?"

She might have guessed they were headed there. Earl was predictable.

"One brownie," she said, and raised questioning brows at Emma. "Tea?"

"Please." Emma never had anything but tea.

Eliot played his usual game, letting Bree list as many ice cream flavors as she could—Flash owned part of Panama Rich and stocked every one of its twenty-three flavors—before ordering a dish of plain old strawberry.

Working around LeeAnn, the grillman, the cook, the dishwasher, and Flash, Bree warmed the brownie and added whipped cream, hot fudge, and nuts, the way Earl liked it, and scooped up Eliot's ice cream. She served a chicken stir-fry to Panama's only lawyer, Martin Sprague, in the six spot at the counter, and pork chops and chili to Ned and Frank Wright, local plumbers, two stools over. With carafes in either hand, she topped off coffees down the row of booths, then worked her way along the counter.

At the far end sat Dotty Hale and her daughter, Jane. Both were tall and lean, but while Dotty's face was tight, Jane's was softer in ways that had little to do with age. Not that Bree was impartial. Jane was one of her closest friends.

LeeAnn had her elbows on the counter before them. In contrast to the Hales, she was small and spirited, with short, spiked blond hair and eyes that filled her face. Those eyes were wider than ever. "Abby Nolan spent the night *where?* But she just *divorced* John."

"Final last week," Dotty confirmed, with the nod of a bony chin. "Court papers came in the mail. Earl saw them."

"So why's she sleeping with him?"

"She isn't," Jane said.

Dotty turned on her. "This isn't coming from *me.* Eliot was the one who saw her car in John's drive." She returned to LeeAnn. "Why? Because she's pregnant."

LeeAnn looked beside herself with curiosity. "With *John's* child? *How?*"

Bree smiled dryly as she joined them. "The normal way, I'd think. Only the baby isn't John's. It's Davey Hillard's."

Dotty looked wounded. "Who told you that?"

"Abby," Bree said. She, Abby, and Jane had been friends since grade school.

"Then why'd she spend the night with John?" LeeAnn asked.

"She didn't," Jane said.

"Were you there?" Dotty asked archly.

"Abby just went to talk," Bree said to divert Dotty's attention from Jane. "She and John are still friends. She wanted to break the news to him herself."

"That's not what Emma says," Dotty argued. Emma was her sister and her major source of gossip. "Know what else she says? Julia Dean got a postcard."

"Mother," Jane pleaded.

"Well, it's *fact,*" Dotty argued. "Earl saw the postcard and told Eliot, since he's the one has to keep peace here and family being upset can cause trouble. Julia's family is *not* thrilled that she's here. The postcard was from her daughter in Des Moines, who said that it was a *shame* that Julia was isolating herself, and that she understood how upset she had been by *Daddy's* death, that they *all* were, but three years of mourning should be enough, so when was she coming home?"

"All that on a postcard?" Bree asked. She didn't know much more about Julia than that she had opened a small flower store three years before and twice weekly arranged sprigs in the diner's vases. She came by for an occasional meal but kept to herself. She struck Bree as shy but sweet, certainly not the type to deserve being the butt of gossip.

"Julia's family doesn't know about Earl," Jane muttered.

"Really." Bree glanced toward the window when a bright light swelled there, another eighteen-wheeler pulling into the parking lot.

"And then," Dotty said, with a glance of her own at that light, "there's Verity. She claims she saw another UFO. Eliot says the lights were from a truck, but she insists there's a mark on the back of her car where that mother ship tailed her."

LeeAnn leaned closer. "Did she see the baby ships again, the squiggly little pods?"

"I didn't ask." Dotty shuddered. "That woman's odd."

Bree had always found Verity more amusing than odd and would have said as much now if Flash hadn't called. "Twenty-two's up, LeeAnn."

Bree stayed LeeAnn with a touch. "I'll get it."

She topped off Dotty's coffee and returned the carafes to their heaters. Scooping up the chicken piccata with angel hair that was ready and waiting, she headed down the counter toward the booths. Twenty-two was the last in the row, tucked in the corner by the jukebox. A lone man sat there, just as he had from time to time in the last seven months. He never said much, never invited much to be said. Most often, like now, he was reading a book.

His name was Tom Gates. He had bought the Hubbard place, a shingle-sided bungalow on West Elm that hadn't seen a stitch of improvement in all the years that the Hubbards' health had been in decline. Since Tom Gates had taken possession, missing shingles had been replaced, shutters had been straightened, the porch had been painted, the lawn cut. What had happened inside was more murky. Skipper Boone had rewired the place, and the Wrights had installed a new furnace, but beyond that, no one knew. And Bree had asked. She had always loved the Hubbard place. Though smaller than her Victorian, it had ten times the charm. She might have bought it herself if she'd had the nerve, but she had inherited her own house from her father, who had inherited it from his. Millers had lived on South Forest for too many years to count and too many to move. So she contented herself with catching what bits of gossip she could about restoration of the bungalow on West Elm.

None of those bits came from Tom Gates. He wasn't sociable. Good-looking. Very good-looking. Too good-looking to be alone. But not sociable.

"Here you go," Bree said. When he moved his book aside, she slid the plate in. She wiped her palms on the back of her jeans and pushed her hands in the pockets there. "Reading anything good?"

His eyes shifted from his dinner back to the book. "It's okay."

She tipped her head to see the title, but the whole front looked to be typed. "Weird cover."

"It hasn't been published yet."

"Really? How'd you get it?"

"I know someone."

"The author?" When he shook his head, the diner's light shimmered in hair that was shiny, light brown, and a mite too long. "Are you a reviewer?" she asked.

He shifted. "Not quite."

"Just an avid reader, then," she decided. Not that he looked scholarly. He was too tanned, too tall, too broad in the shoulders. Coming and going, he strode. Flash bet that he was a politician who had lost a dirty election and fled. Dotty bet he was a burned-out businessman, because Earl told of mail from New York. LeeAnn bet he was an adventurer recouping after a tiring trek.

Bree could see him as an adventurer. He had that rugged look. His buying a house in town didn't mean much. Even adventurers needed to rest sometimes, but they didn't stay put for long. Panama bored men who loved risk. This one would be gone before long.

It was a shame, because Tom Gates had great hands. He had long, lean, blunt-tipped fingers and moved them in a way that suggested they could do most anything they tried. Bree had never once seen dirt under his nails, which set him apart from most of the men who ate here, and while he didn't have the calluses those men did, his hands looked well used. He had cut himself several months back and had needed stitches. The scar was nearly two inches long and starting to fade.

"I just finished the new Dean Koontz," she said. "Have you read it yet?"

He was studying his fork. "No."

"It's pretty good. Worth a shot. Can I get you anything else? Another beer?" She hitched her chin toward the long-neck on the far side of his plate. "You know that's local, don't you? Sleepy Creek Pale. It's brewed down the street."

His eyes met hers. They were wonderfully gray. "Yes," he said. "I do know."

She might have been lured by those eyes to say something else, had not the front door opened just then to a flurry of flakes and the stamping boots of four truckers. Shaking snow from heads and jackets, they called out greetings, slapped the palms of the men in seventeen, and slid into sixteen, which meant they were Bree's.

"Nothing else?" she asked Tom Gates again. When he shook his head, she smiled. "Enjoy your meal." Still smiling, she walked on down the line. "Hey, guys, how're you doin'?"

"Cold."

"Tired."

"Hungry."

"A regular round for starters?" she asked. When the nods came fast, she went to the icebox on the wall behind the counter, pulled open the shiny steel door, and extracted two Sleepy Creek Pales, one Sleepy Creek Amber, and a Heineken. Back at the booth, she fished a bottle opener from the short black apron skimming her hips and did the honors.

"Ahhhhh," said John Hagan after a healthy swallow. "Good stuff on a night like this."

Bree glanced out the window. "How many inches would you say?"

"Four," John answered.

"Nah, there's at least eight," argued Kip Tucker.

"Headed to twenty," warned Gene Mackey for the benefit of a passing, predictably gullible LeeAnn.

"*Twenty?*"

Bree nudged Gene's shoulder. "He's putting you on, Lee. Come on, guys. Behave."

"What fun is that?" Gene asked, hooking her waist and pulling her close.

She unhooked his arm. "All the fun you're getting," she said, with a haughty look. "I'll be back to take your order *once* I'm done scraping down plates."

"I'll have my usual," T. J. Kearns said fast, before she could leave.

"Me, too," said Gene.

John pointed at himself and nodded, indicating beef pot pie topped with mashed potatoes and gravy, served with hunks of bread for dunking and whatever vegetables Flash had that day, buttered.

Kip was eyeing the specials board. "What's he got up there that I want?"

Bree knew Kip. "Brook trout," she said in a cultured way, "sautéed in butter and served on a bed of basmati rice, with sun-dried tomatoes, Portobello mushrooms, and broccoli."

Kip sighed his pleasure. "One up, right here. Thanks, doll."

Panama lay in hill country. Come the first of November, sand barrels sat on most every corner, trucks carried chains, and folks without four-wheel drive put on snow tires. But this wasn't the first of November. It was the ninth of October, and the snow was coming heavy and fast. By eight, only a handful of stragglers remained.

Armed with a laptop computer and her own serving of trout, Bree slid in across from Flash. He was reading the newspaper, alternately sipping coffee and pulling at one of two sticky buns on his plate, no doubt his dinner. She never failed to be amazed that a man who was endlessly artful when it came to creating meals for others had such abominable eating habits himself.

"You're missing good trout," she said.

"I hate bones."

"There aren't any bones. Not in your trout."

"That's what we tell the customers," he said, without looking up, "but I never know for sure if I get them all out, and the fear of it would ruin my meal. Besides"—he looked up then—"there aren't usually any sticky buns left after five. Why are there today?"

Bree opened the laptop. "Because Angus, Oliver, and Jack didn't make it in"—and wisely so, since the three were in their eighties and better at home in a storm.

"Flash?" asked LeeAnn. She shot a look at the last man at the counter. "Gav says he'll drive me home, since I don't have boots or anything, but he can't hang around till we close." Her brows rose.

Flash shot a look at Bree. "Ask her. She's the one who'll have to cover for you."

Bree shooed her off. "No one else is coming in. Not tonight. Go."

LeeAnn went.

"She skips out early too often," Flash said. "You have a soft heart."

"Yours is softer than mine, which is why you didn't say no first. Besides, she has kids at home. I don't."

"Why not?" he asked.

Bree pulled up the supply list. "I think we've been through this before."

"Tell me again. I especially like the part about needing a man to have kids, like you couldn't have any guy who walked in here. Know what turns them on? Your disinterest."

"It isn't disinterest. It's caution."

Caution sounded kinder. Disinterest was probably more to the point. The men who passed through the diner were just fine for conversation and laughs. They gave appreciative looks to her hair, which was thick, dark, and forever escaping whatever she tied it with, and her body, which was of average height and better toned than most. What they liked most, though, was the fact that she served them without argument and, more, that she knew what they wanted before they said it. Her father had liked that, too. She had been his cook, his maid, his tailor, his barber, his social secretary . . . the list went on and on. In the days following his death, she'd had her very first taste of me time. Now, three years later, it was still both novelty and prized possession.

"Caution. Ahh. Well, that is you, Bree. Cautious to a fault. Have you hired someone to get you a decent heating system, or are you still getting estimates?"

"I'm still getting estimates."

He glanced at the snow. "Time just ran out."

"Give it a day. Sun'll be back."

"You're only postponing the inevitable. Last winter you were racing over here half frozen. Why wait? You have money."

"I have money for a new car. That's first on my list. Heating is second."

"That's crazy."

"Why? I have a woodstove in the kitchen and quilts in every room. I can stay warm whether the furnace works or not. But I can't go anywhere without a car." She tapped the laptop's screen. "We have to talk about getting a new milk supplier."

"No."

She softened her tone. "Stafford's local. We both want to support him, but his deliveries are late more often than not, and lately a full quarter of what he brings is bad. Think back two hours. You were in a panic."

"I was tired, is all. Stafford's working the kinks out."

"He's been working the kinks out for two years, but they aren't going away."

"Give him a little longer," Flash said. He flipped up his paper and resumed reading.

Bree didn't know whether to laugh or cry. Oh, yes, Flash was softhearted, a sucker if the truth were told, though that was a good half of the diner's charm. He was an artist. Try as he might to look like a trucker in the black jeans, purple T-shirt, and bill cap that were the diner's uniform, he couldn't pull it off. Even without the long mane spilling from the hole in the back of his cap, he had too gentle a look, and that was even before he waved off the difference when one of the town's poorest came up short on cash at the end of a meal.

Not that Bree was complaining. Had her boss been anyone else, she would still be waitressing, period. But Flash wasn't hung up on formalities. She was good with numbers, so he had her balance the books. She was good with deadlines, so he had her pay the bills. She worked with the people who printed their place mats, the people who serviced the drink machines, the people who trucked in fresh eggs, vegetables, and fish.

Hungry, she dug into her trout and broccoli. Focusing on the computer screen, she plugged in the week's expected deliveries, noted shortages that had arisen, set up orders to be placed as soon as she hooked the computer to the modem in the back office. Flash was a softie there, too. That modem had been installed within twenty-four hours of her saying it might be nice.

The sound of spinning wheels drew her eye to the window, where a truck was heading out of the lot. After a minute, the tires gained traction, the sound evened out, and taillights disappeared in the thickening snow.

By eight-fifty, the last of the diners had left, fifty-two places had been wiped down and set for breakfast, dishes had been washed, food put away, the grill scraped. Minutes after Flash officially called it a night, the staff was gone.

Bree was pulling on her jacket when he said, "I'll drive you home."

She shook her head. "Driving is slow. It'll be faster if I walk." Tugging up the leg of her jeans, she showed him her boots. "Besides, you live downhill, I live uphill. No need backtracking in weather like this."

But Flash was insistent. Taking her arm, he guided her out the door.

The world had changed dramatically since Bree's earlier foray into the storm. With the exception of bare pavement where others of the staff had parked and just left, everything was pure white, and colder, far colder than before.

"It's too early for this," Flash grumbled as they approached his Explorer. While he dug behind his seat for a scraper, Bree started on the windows with the sleeve of her jacket. When he took over with the brush, she climbed inside. Leaning over the gearshift, she started the engine and, once the windshield was clear, turned on the wipers.

Since the parking lot had last been plowed, another several inches of snow had fallen. Between those inches and what had been left around cars that were parked, the lot was ragged. Flash gunned his engine to back the Explorer over the pile of snow at its own rear, then shifted into drive. The Explorer jolted its way to the street.

Bree stared hard out the windshield. As far as she could tell, the only thing marking the road was the slightly lower level of snow there. The headlights of the Explorer swung a bright arc onto East Main. Flash accelerated. His tires spun, found purchase, started slowly up the hill. They hadn't gone far when the spinning resumed. The Explorer slid sideways. He braked, downshifted, and tried again.

"Bad tires?" she asked.

"Bad roads," he muttered.

"Not if you're going downhill. Let me walk. Please?"

He resisted through several more tries, shifting from drive to reverse and back in an attempt to gain traction, and he always did, but never for long. The Explorer had barely reached the first of five houses that climbed the hill to the town green when, sliding sideways and back this time, he gave in.

Bree pulled up her hood and slid out. "Thanks for trying. See you tomorrow." Shutting the door, she burrowed into her jacket and started up the hill.

At first, with the Explorer coasting backward, its headlights lit her way. When Flash turned at the diner's driveway and came out headfirst, the lights disappeared. Moments later, even the sound of his engine was gone.

In the silence, Bree trekked upward. The snow on the road wasn't deep, rising only to the top of her boots, but she had the same problem the Explorer had. With the drop in temperature, the thin layer of packed snow left by the plow had frozen under the new-fallen stuff. She kept slipping on the steepening incline.

Tightening her hood, she tucked her hands in her pockets and plodded on. When she slipped again, her arms flew out for balance, hands bare and cold. She wished she had gloves, wished it even more in the next instant, when she lost her footing and landed wrist deep in the snow. Straightening, she shook herself off and went on. One more slip, though, and she trudged to the side of the road. The snow was deeper there, well past her calves, which made the walking harder but safer.

Head bowed against the steady fall of snow, she leaned into the climb. She had walked the same route for years, barely had to lift her eyes to know where she was. One foot rose high after the other to clear the drifts. By the time she passed the last of the houses, her thighs were feeling the strain. She felt instant relief when the road leveled off at the top.

Turning left, she started around the town green under the gaslights' amber glow. There were no cars about, just snow-shrouded shapes in driveways. Wood smoke rose from high chimneys to scent the air. Snow slid, with a rush and a thud, down tall steel panels from roof to ground.

The curve of the road took her past the Federal that housed the bank, with smaller offices above for the town's lawyer, realtor, and chiropractor. The one beside it housed the Chalifoux family, the one beside that the Nolans, the one beside that the library. Farther on, in a more modest house, lived the minister and his family. At the end of the oval, spire high, large green shutters and doors finely edged in snow, was the church.

The wood fence circling the churchyard had disappeared under the snow, as had the split-rail one around the town green. But the green wasn't to be missed. A true common area, it had recently been host to sunbathers, picnickers, and stargazers. Now the limbs of maples, birches, and firs hung low to the ground under the weight of the snow, transforming stately trees into weepers.

The sound of an engine broke the silence. At the opposite end of the green, a pickup coasted down from Pine Street and cruised slowly around the oval. When it reached Bree, it stopped.

Curtis Lamb rolled down his window. "Just comin' from work?"

Bree raised an arm to shield her eyes from the snow. "Yeah."

"Want a lift?"

But Curtis lived downhill, not far from Flash. She smiled, shook her head, gestured toward Birch Hill, just beyond the church. "I'm almost there. You go on."

Curtis rolled up his window. The pickup went slowly forward, turned right at the bank, and started down East Main.

Bree resumed the hike. She was making good time now, was actually enjoying the snow. It was cleansing, coming so soon after summer's sweat.

Another engine broke the stillness, with a growing sputter. Bree guessed the vehicle was climbing Birch Hill. Its headlights had just appeared when a second pickup swooped down Pine, far off to her right. It was going fast, too fast. She watched it skid onto the oval, regain traction, and barrel toward her end.

Eager to be out of its way, she quickened her step. At the corner, she turned onto Birch Hill. The car climbing it—a bare-bones Jeep—was twenty feet off but approaching steadily, so she hopped from the street into the deeper snow at the side.

The pickup kept coming. Alarmed by its speed, fascinated in a horrified way, Bree stopped walking. The pickup looked to be dull blue and old. She figured that whoever was driving was either drunk, inexperienced, or just plain dumb.

"Slow down," she warned. At the rate it was going, it would surely skid when it turned. And it was going to have to turn, either right onto Birch Hill or left around the oval. If it went straight, it would hit her head-on.

Suddenly frightened, she moved. Running as quickly as she could through the deep snow, she started down Birch Hill, but it was an ill-timed move. Seconds after she passed the Jeep, she heard the crunch of metal on metal. Then the Jeep was skidding back, sliding faster than she could run and in the god-awful same direction.

Its impact with her was quieter. She felt a searing pain and a moment's weightlessness, then nothing at all.

# chapter
# two

The first hit sent the Jeep skidding sideways and back. When the pickup tried to swerve away, it skidded into a broadside hit that crushed the Jeep against a stone wall. On the rebound, the pickup ricocheted back to the center of the road and sailed off down the hill.

Tom Gates didn't see that. He had only one thought in mind. Heart pounding, he rammed his shoulder once against the Jeep's door, realized that it was too damaged to open, and scrambled over the gearshift to the passenger's door. When it wouldn't budge, he raised his feet, kicked out the glass, and tumbled through. He grazed the edge of the stone wall on his way to the snow but was on his feet in an instant, racing back over the wall and around the Jeep.

He searched the road and saw nothing. He fell to his knees beside the Jeep, searched underneath, ran to where it met the wall, and, putting everything he had into the effort, moved the Jeep enough to see that no one was trapped there, not even down by the tires.

Frantic, he looked around. He was sure that someone had turned the corner seconds before the pickup hit him. He had hit whoever it was. He was sure of that, too.

He had just spotted a dark lump in the snow when a light came on in the house deep in the yard. "Anyone hurt?" Carl Breen hollered.

"Yeah," Tom hollered back. "Call an ambulance."

He stumbled to his knees by the inert shape, reached out to touch it, paused. What to do without causing greater injury? The legs looked normal, no grotesque angles there, but an oversize jacket hid everything above. Crouching over the head, he saw a face, which meant that whoever it was wasn't suffocating in the snow, assuming that whoever it was hadn't died on impact. At least he saw no blood in the snow.

"Hey," he said urgently, "hey. Can you hear me?"

A hood covered half of the face. When he loosened its strings and eased it back, recognition was instant. No matter that her normal coloring had gone ashen. If the fineness of her features hadn't given her away, stray wisps of dark hair would have.

Tom closed his eyes and rocked back on his heels. It was Bree, sweet Bree from the diner.

"Christ," he whispered, coming forward. He touched her cold cheek and pulled the hood up again to protect her face from the falling snow. He felt her neck for a pulse, though his own was pounding so hard he didn't know whose he perceived. Her skin under her clothing was warm, though. Taking hope from that, he pulled off his jacket and spread it over her.

That was when he saw her hand, little more than a small band of knuckles at the end of her sleeve. It was cold and limp. Taking it gently, he rubbed it to warm it up.

"Bree?"

She didn't move, didn't moan, didn't blink.

He slipped a hand inside the hood and put it to her cheek. "Can you hear me, Bree?"

A beam of light swung past him, then returned. Squinting into it, he saw Carl Breen trudging through the snow. His wool topcoat flapped over wash-worn pajamas. He had a southwester on his head and unlaced galoshes on his feet.

The beam of the flashlight shifted to Bree. "Is she dead?" Carl asked.

"Not yet. Did you call?"

"Ambulance is on its way."

"How long will it take?"

"Good weather? Ten minutes. This weather? Twenty."

"*Twenty?*" Tom cried. "Christ, we need something sooner than that."

Carl was bending over, lifting the edge of her hood. "What was she, coming from work?"

"Twenty minutes is too long. She can't lie here that long."

"Won't have to. Chief's on the way. Travis, too. He's a paramedic. Need a blanket?"

"Yes." While Carl plodded back to the house, Tom kept one hand around Bree's and the other on her cheek, so she would know that someone was there.

"Christ, I'm sorry," he murmured. "Ten feet up or back, and I'd have missed you." He leaned close, looking for movement. "Are you with me, Bree?" He didn't know what he would do if she died, couldn't conceive of living with that. Being a self-centered bastard was one thing. Causing someone's death was something else entirely.

"Hang on, baby," he murmured, looking at the road, rocking impatiently. "Come on, come on. What's taking so fucking long?"

Carl returned, unzipping a high-tech sleeping bag. "My

grandson's," he explained, and shook it out over Bree. Squatting, he said, "Quite some noise, that crash. What happened?"

Tom shot another glance at the street. "Where are they?"

"Chief was down Creek Road when I called. He'll be coming up East Main." He shone his flashlight on Tom's face. "You're bleeding." Tom pushed the light away, still Carl saw fit to inform him, "Your face got cut."

Tom felt nothing but fear. Again he searched Bree's throat for a pulse, sure he felt one this time, though it was weak. Slipping his hand inside the hood, he cupped her head. "They're almost here, Bree. Help's almost here."

Miraculously, then, it was. In what seemed the best thing to have happened to Tom in months, the headlights of the Chevy Blazer that served as a cruiser for Eliot Bonner, Panama's police department, preceded it by seconds around the corner. Travis Fitch followed close in his own car. Both vehicles pulled in at either end of the Jeep, doors opening in tandem, drivers running through the snow in the crisscross of headlights.

Travis, in his early thirties and beanpole long, wore dark pants and a dark hooded jacket. Eliot was a bit older, a bit shorter, a bit heavier. In his plaid jacket and orange wool cap, he looked more like a hunter than a police chief, which, given Panama's minimal law enforcement needs, wasn't far off the mark.

Though Tom shifted to allow Travis access, he kept the back of his fingers against Bree's cheek. "She hasn't moved," he said, giving in to traces of panic, "hasn't opened her eyes or said anything."

Travis was feeling around under the coverings.

The police chief hunkered down beside Tom. In a gravelly voice to match his beer belly, he said, "Jeep's a mess. What happened?"

Tom was watching Travis, wondering if he knew what he was doing. "A truck hit me. I hit her."

"Must've done it real hard, to throw her so far. Where's the truck?"

Tom twisted to look down the road. It was nowhere in sight.

Swearing softly, he twisted back to Bree. "What do you feel?" he asked Travis.

"Neck's okay. Spine's okay. I think the problem's inside."

"What do you mean, inside?"

"Stomach, or thereabouts. Somethin's hard."

"She's bleeding internally?"

"Looks that way."

"Who was driving the truck?" the chief asked.

But Tom couldn't think about the truck yet. "Can she bleed to death?" he asked, as Travis worked his way down Bree's legs.

"She could," Travis said. "Nothing's broken down here, leastways nothing I can feel."

"How do you stop the bleeding?"

"I don't. Surgeons do." He re-covered Bree and pushed to his feet. "I'm calling ahead. They'd better get in someone good." He loped back through the snow to his car.

"Where will they take her?" Tom asked Bonner. He didn't want Bree to die, did not want Bree to die. For the first time in seven months, he wished he were back in New York. There, she would have had top doctors, no questions asked. Here, he wasn't so sure.

"There's a medical center in Ashmont," Bonner answered.

There certainly was. Tom had been there. It had been just fine for stitching up his hand, but Bree hadn't been cut by a saw. "She needs a *hospital.*"

"She needs fast care," the chief replied. "No chopper's taking off in this snow, so she's going to Ashmont. They'll get a surgeon up from Saint Johnsbury. If he sets off now, he'll reach Ashmont by the time she's ready."

"Does Ashmont have operating rooms?"

Bonner screwed up his face. "Hell, man, we're not hicks. Our operating rooms may not be as state-of-the-art as yours, but they get the job done. We don't like dying any more'n you do, y'know."

Tom straightened. He wasn't the helpless type. Yet what he felt now ranked right up there with what he had felt all those months before, standing alone at his mother's graveside with nothing to do but grieve. "Someone has to call her family."

"Well, there isn't any of that to speak of," Bonner advised, "not for Bree. Her mother left her when she was a baby. Her father raised her, but he's been dead three years now. There weren't any sisters or brothers. No husband. No kids."

That surprised Tom. He had watched Bree work. She had always seemed so self-possessed, so grounded, that he had assumed she had the solid backing of family. He pictured her with a husband and a child or two, maybe a mother or sister to help with the kids while she worked. He had envied her that, had envied her for belonging.

Bonner rose. "Flash is as close to family as she has. I'll give him a call."

He set off just as Travis returned. "The ambulance is three minutes away. No sense my moving her. They'll have a long board."

Tom sat on his knees in the snow. He touched Bree's neck, her forehead, her cheek, wanting to do something and feeling hamstrung. He brushed snow from her hood, for what good that did. She had been at the wrong place at the wrong time. So had he.

Desperate for someone to blame, he looked skyward. The clouds were a dense night gray, still heavy with snow. "It's October, for Christ's sake. When's this supposed to stop?"

Carl, who continued to hold his flashlight on Bree, said, "Weatherman says morning."

"Yeah, like he said this was gonna be rain."

"Difference of a few degrees, is all."

Tom might have said what he thought of that if the ambulance hadn't circled the town green just then. Its engine was all business, giving it away even before it pulled around the corner, red and white lights flashing, and ground to a halt.

Leaning over Bree, Tom felt a fast relief, a sharp fear, and something almost proprietary. He talked softly, telling her that help had come, that she was going to be all right, that she shouldn't worry about anything. He wasn't pleased when the ambulance crew hustled him aside, or when one of them threw a blanket around him and poked at his face. He was most bothered when they wouldn't let him ride with Bree.

"I'm all she has right now," he argued, acutely aware of the "right now." Bree might not have family, but she had friends. He had seen the way she had with people. Flash would be only the start. Once word spread that she was hurt, friends would rush to her bedside, and he would be the outsider, the villain of the piece.

The grasp Eliot Bonner took of his arm said it was happening already. "We need to talk, you and me. We'll follow in the cruiser. Unless," he added dryly, "you were a doctor back in the city." The ambulance doors closed. "You never did say what you were."

Soon after Tom had come to town, the police chief had stopped by. "Offering a welcome," he had said, with a too wide smile, and a welcome might have been part of it. Tom wasn't so untrusting as to deny that. But the bottom line had been curiosity about Panama's newest resident.

In the ten minutes that they had spent talking on the front walk, Tom had been vague. More than anything, he had wanted anonymity, and he still wanted it. But having been involved in an accident in which one of Panama's own was badly hurt, he was in a precarious position. He might have a history of lying to friends and family—worse, of lying to himself—but he knew better than to lie to the law.

"I'm a writer," he said.

Bonner sighed. "Ah, jeez. Another writer. Searching for inspiration, am I right?"

"Not really." There was so much else for him to seek before he sought that.

"Then what?"

Tom didn't answer. He had come to Panama to distance himself from the arrogant, self-absorbed man he'd become. He had wanted time alone to think, to soul-search, to look inside and see what bits of decency were left—all of which was self-indulgent, none of it remotely relevant to what had happened that night.

For the first time, watching the ambulance pull away, he felt cold. There was some comfort in the thought that Bree had his jacket—though he wondered if they had tossed it aside to work on her. He pictured her in a neck brace, strapped flat, being hooked up to monitors and IVs. He prayed she was holding her own.

The chief ushered him toward the Blazer. "You're shaking. Not goin' into shock on me, are you? Better get in."

The offer was for the passenger's side, rather than the backseat, which was the good news. The bad news was that shaking was the least of it. Climbing in was a challenge. Tom's body was starting to hurt.

Bonner eyed him from behind the wheel. "You okay?"

"I'm okay." The paramedic had given him gauze for his cheek. Pressing it there, Tom waved Bonner on after the ambulance. It was already out of sight, gone too fast with Bree.

The Blazer took up a slow, safe, frustrating pace through the snow. "So. What happened?"

The shaking increased, radiating outward from his belly.

"Gates?"

Tom forced himself to think back, but things were fuzzy. "I was coming up the hill toward the green."

"Slippin' around, were you?"

He didn't remember slipping around. "Not particularly. The Jeep holds the road."

"Why were you out?"

There hadn't been any special reason. He had been restless, even lonely. He had been thinking how different his life was, at that moment, from what had gone before. There had surely been regret, surely self-pity. "I just felt like being out."

"Were you drinking?"

Tom slid the man a long look. "You leaned in close when you reached the scene. Did you smell booze on my breath?"

Bonner smirked. "Nope. Just coffee."

"You saw me at the diner. I had one beer with my chicken. Bree asked if I wanted another. I didn't. LeeAnn poured the coffee. I had two cups." The wipers pushed snowflakes from side to side. Peering out between them, Tom envisioned himself in a tunnel of light formed by the Blazer's headlights. The eeriness of it gave him a chill. "Where's the ambulance?"

"Up a ways. So. You had your coffee, then you left. What time was that?"

"Eight, give or take." His left side ached. He changed position to ease it, still he felt the Blazer's every shift. "I went home, stayed half an hour, then left."

"To go joyriding in the snow."

"Not joyriding." He hadn't felt any joy, hadn't felt any joy in too long to remember. "Just riding."

"Where?"

"Around town. Out toward Lowell. Into Montgomery. Like I said, the Jeep holds the road."

"So you wanted to see how good it was in the snow?"

"If you're asking whether I was pushing to see how fast I could go before spinning out, I wasn't. Come on, Bonner. You looked at tire tracks back there. Did it look like I was weaving coming up the hill?"

"Nope."

"As soon as the truck hit, I was gone. It was like being at the wrong end of a bulldozer, pushed sideways into the wall."

"When did you first see the truck?"

Tom took a deep breath and swallowed it fast when he felt pain. Bruised ribs, he guessed, plus cuts on his hands from fleeing the Jeep, plus God only knew what up and down his left side, where the truck had hit him hard. But all that was nothing compared to what had happened to Bree.

"Gates?"

Squeezing his eyes shut, he struggled to re-create those lost seconds. Finally, he sighed and looked up. "All I remember is the headlights closing in."

"What kind of truck was it?"

"I don't know."

"Color?"

Again he tried to recall. "It wasn't a big truck. More likely a pickup. Color? Black, maybe? Hell, I couldn't see much in the glare of the lights. Take a look at my Jeep, though. It'll have paint in the scrapes."

"I looked. The truck was maroon."

"What about the tires?"

"Consistent with a pickup, but bald. When did you first see Bree?"

"I didn't see her. Not directly. I was aware of passing a dark shape just before the truck came around the corner, but it didn't register as anything more than a shadow, maybe a lamppost. I didn't know it was a person until I heard the thud. *Felt* the thud." He felt it again, and again, and again. He doubted he would live long enough to forget it. It raised the hair on the back of his neck. "How much longer till we're there?"

"Not long. So you don't have any idea who was driving the truck?"

Tom expelled a frustrated breath. "If I knew, don't you think I'd say?"

"Beats me. I don't know you much."

"Trust me. I'd say."

"Yeah? Funny that you would. Most guys would be clamming up around now."

"Only if they have something to hide. I don't. That guy hit me. You studied the scene. You know that. There wasn't a hell of a lot I could have done differently."

"Still, you're city. I'd have thought you'd be yelling and screaming for a lawyer."

"I *am* a lawyer." He hadn't intended to say it, but there it was.

Bonner sent him a guarded look. "I thought you said you were a writer."

"I am. I write about law."

"Ah, *jeez*." His head went back with the oath. "Another one lookin' to be the next Grisham."

"Actually," Tom said, because he figured Bonner would run a check on him and find out anyway, and then, of course, there was his damnable pride, which survived despite months of trying to kill it, "I was writing before Grisham ever did."

"That's what they all say."

"I was published before Grisham ever was."

The chief paused. "That so?" Cautious interest. "Have I read anything of yours?"

*While the Jury Was Out.* One look at the chief and he had his answer. "Lucky I have a common name, huh? I've been here seven months, and no one's figured it out. Christ, they will now," he muttered, refocusing on the road. "How much longer?"

"Not much. Why the secret?"

"It's been a rough few years. I needed downtime. I needed to be someplace where people didn't know who I was."

"Why's that?"

Taking aim at that damnable pride, he said, "I ran into trouble."

"Legal trouble?"

"Ego trouble."

He stared out the window at the outskirts of Ashmont. Small frame houses came closer together now, lights on here and there. The Blazer fell in behind a plow that was spewing sand and slowed to give it space.

Tom felt a surge of impatience. "Pass him."

"Not me. I'd rather be safe than sorry. I'd think you would, too. You don't need two accidents in one night. So. You got famous and bought into the hype."

Tom lifted the gauze from his cheek, glanced at it, put it back. "Something like that."

"Weren't there movies, too?"

"Yeah."

"Are you loaded?"

"Not now."

"Poor?"

"No." Tom looked at Bonner. "If she doesn't have insurance, I'll cover her bills."

"That's nice and generous, thank you, but Bree won't have any part of it. She's an independent sort. Besides, don't feel guilty. If you hadn't been where you were, that truck would've hit her directly, and it was bigger than you."

"So if she dies, she'll be less dead?" Tom asked. "Besides, it isn't guilt."

"Then what?"

*Redemption* was the word that came to mind, and it didn't sound right. But he did know, for all he was worth, that this time he couldn't turn his back.

The Ashmont Medical Center was small and relatively new, a two-story brick building at the end of a long drive curving back behind the old stone town hall. Tom remembered the parking lot as being neatly landscaped, but the peaceful feeling he remembered, from things green and flowered, was gone. Halogen lights on the snow turned the scene a garish yellow.

There was a small emergency entrance at the side of the building. The ambulance stood there, empty. Within seconds of the Blazer's pulling up behind it, Tom was out. He pushed through the door and approached the nurse at the desk.

"Bree Miller?" he asked, though he knew at a glance that she wasn't there. The emergency area was negligible. Each of three cubicles was open and quiet. That meant she was either upstairs or in the morgue.

He was tied in knots envisioning the latter scenario, when the nurse rounded the desk. She was a competent-looking sort, less laid-back than the typical local. "You must be the other injured party. I was told to watch for you."

"His name's Tom Gates," Bonner said. "He needs stitching. Check his ribs. And his hands."

Tom wasn't being touched until he had some news. "How is Bree?"

"She's upstairs."

"Is she alive?"

"Yes."

He released a small breath. "Is the surgeon here yet?"

"No, but he's close."

Ignoring protests by both the nurse and his body, he strode toward the elevator, spotted the stairs on the near side, and slipped through the door. Minutes later, he approached the second-floor nurses' station. "I'm looking for Bree Miller," he said. He saw a slew of patients' rooms, what looked to be a kitchen, a supply area, an open lounge, and a lot of closed doors.

This nurse was younger and gentler, but focused. Rising to meet him, she reached for the gauze he still held to his cheek. "Were you in the accident, too?"

"Yes, but I'm fine."

She was studying the gash on his cheek. "This has to be stitched. How'd you get past Margo?"

"I just went. Tell me more about Bree, and I'll go back. Where is she?"

"If I tell you, you might head that way, and if you do, you'll contaminate everything they're trying to keep sterile."

Tom backed off. "Okay. Just give me an update. Has she regained consciousness?"

"Not that I know of."

"The paramedic at the scene said she was bleeding internally. Did the EMTs find anything else?"

"Bruises, but bleeding's the first worry."

"My blood type is A. Will that help?"

"No. She's B. We have some here, and a list of donors. We've already called in a few."

Things were bad, then. Tom felt weak. "How many doctors are here?"

"Normally, one. We called in another of our own. The surgeon coming from St. Johnsbury makes three."

"Have your two ever done anything like this?" He knew he sounded snobbish, but refused to take back the question even when the nurse looked vaguely annoyed.

"Yes," she said. "Doctors here know everything and do everything. They're better rounded than city doctors. They have to be." She took his arm. "I think you should go back downstairs."

He held his ground. "Where can I wait afterward? I want to know how she is the minute they're done. I want to talk to the surgeon."

"You're shaking."

He had been trying to ignore that, but he kept hearing that *thud* again and was feeling sick. "Wouldn't you be shaking if it was your car that hit someone?"

"Yes, but there's nothing you can do for her right now," she said, pleading now. "The doctors are working on her, and you can't be there. So let Margo patch you up. Please?"

What with cleaning, stitching, and X-raying, Tom was downstairs for an hour. During that time, the doctor from St. Johnsbury arrived and Bree's surgery began.

When Tom finally made it back upstairs, Flash O'Neil was in the waiting room. The police chief must have filled him in on the details of the accident, because other than a quiet "You okay?" he didn't ask questions.

It was nearly midnight. Tom lowered himself onto a vinyl sofa and sat, first, with his head low against dizziness, then, as time passed, with his eyes closed and his legs sprawled stiffly. Any movement in the region of the operating room brought him up straight, but news was scarce. He sat forward again, then back, shifted gingerly, stretched out. Had he been a religious man, he might have prayed, but it had been years since he'd done that. After his mother died, he hadn't felt worthy, and before, well, he hadn't felt the need. He had been his own greatest source of strength, his own inspiration, his own most blind, devoted, and bullheaded fan.

So here he was.

Somewhere around one, Flash began to talk. He had his elbows on his knees and his hands hanging between, and was studying the floor, looking lost. "Bree was the first person I ever met in Panama. I heard the diner was for sale and came to see it. She waited on me and my wife, sold us on the town with that friendly way she has. After we bought the place, we had to close down a month for renovations. Bree was the only one who said she'd wait out the month and work for us when we reopened. She did more than wait. She was right there with us, making suggestions during the renovations—you know, things that people around here would like that we didn't know, not being from here. She and Francie—my wife—they got along fine."

Tom had never seen a wife. "What happened to Francie?"

"She left. Proved to be a *real* flash in the pan," he muttered. "Not Bree, though. She's worked for me for fourteen years now. I oughta make her a partner."

A nurse ran down the hall from the operating room. Tom came to his feet.

She held up a hand, shook her head as she passed, and disappeared. A minute later, she returned carrying an armload of supplies, but she had no more time for him then. It was the young nurse from the station who came to report, "It's going slow. She lost a lot of blood."

Again Tom felt the frustration of not being in New York, and while part of him knew that the going might have been just as slow there, it was small solace.

"I started to drive her home," Flash said, with more emotion now, "but the hill was so bad I gave up. If I'd stuck with it, this wouldn't have happened."

Tom made a disparaging sound. "It wasn't your fault."

"So whose fault was it?"

"Whoever drove that truck."

"So who drove it?"

"How the hell would I know?"

"You were there. It was your car that hit Bree. What were you, asleep at the wheel?" The words were barely out before Flash held up a hand. "Sorry. I'm scared."

Tom knew how *that* was. "Are you and Bree together?"

Flash made a sputtering sound. "Nah. She won't have me. She likes going home alone. Says she needs it after a day at work. But, man"—he gave a slow head shake—"she's my right hand at the diner. If anything happens . . ."

"It won't," Tom said.

"How do you know?"

"I just know."

"How?"

He opened his mouth to answer, and closed it again. One part of him feared Bree's dying as much as Flash feared it, but there was another part, a part that said the accident had happened for a reason and that her dying right now wasn't it.

True, that kind of thinking wasn't logical, and he was a logical guy—cold, calculating, and shrewd, his father had accused him of being, before turning his back on him for good. Maybe his father was right. With regard to family and friends, Tom had been cold, calculating, and shrewd.

Not so professionally. He had been creative and caring in his defense of clients, creative and caring in the construction of a plot. And he definitely had an imaginative streak. *Something* had to explain the eeriness he had felt when passing through the tunnel of light that the Blazer had carved in the snow. He felt that eeriness still, felt it deep in his tired bones.

While Tom waited for news with his eyes closed, his legs braced, and his arms cradling his bruised ribs, down the hall in the operating room, Bree watched with fascination as five skilled professionals tried to restart her heart.

# chapter three

"Wake up, Bree. Time to wake up."

Bree struggled to open her eyes. It was a minute of starts and stops, and what seemed a great expenditure of energy, before she succeeded.

"That's it. You can hear me, can't you?"

She nodded, more a thought than an act, and tried to look around. The woman who had spoken was pale green. Beyond was a room that was dimly lit, cool, and sterile, totally different from where she had been seconds before. That place had been bright and warm. The memory of it brought a wisp of calm.

"She's awake?" asked another voice, this one male, and for a minute she thought it was *his*. But this face had features. The other had been too bright to see.

So how had she known it was male? And how had it smiled? Or had she only imagined a smile?

"Hi there, Bree," came this new one again. "Welcome back." The voice was familiar, but nothing else.

"Do I know you?" she asked in a whispery croak.

"I'm Paul Sealy, one of the ones who've been working on you for the last five hours."

She tried to moisten her tongue, but her whole mouth was dry. "Where am I?"

"In the recovery room. How do you feel?"

She felt confused. Sad, like she'd been someplace nicer and didn't want to be back. But happy to be here, too.

"Any pain?"

Maybe, in her midsection, but it was more dull than excruciating. The thoughts that came and went were harder to handle. She kept picturing herself on the operating table, kept *seeing* herself there, as if she had left her body behind and was rising to a gentler place. If she didn't know better, she would have thought she had died and gone to heaven. But this clearly wasn't heaven. So she'd been sent back down to earth. Which was a *really* weird idea.

Far easier to stop thinking and just drift off to sleep.

That first day passed in groggy spurts. She dozed and woke, dozed and woke. There were questions about comfort and pain, much poking and prodding, an overall jostling when she was wheeled down the hall to her room. Doctors and nurses hovered. More than once, she fought through a private fog to tell them that she would be fine, because she knew that she would be. She wasn't sure how she knew, but she did.

That was the only certainty she had. Between the lingering anesthesia and the drugs they gave her for pain, she was confused about where she was and why she hurt. She was confused about who was with her, seeing familiar faces one minute and new faces another, and each time she remembered what had happened in the operating room, she was confused about what was real and what was dream.

Sleep continued to be a lovely escape.

By the second morning, the effects of the anesthesia had worn off and she was awake enough to respond to the nurses attending her. Yes, her stomach hurt. No, she wasn't dizzy. No, she wasn't nauseated. Yes, she was thirsty.

None mentioned the surgery. She guessed that they were leaving that to Paul Sealy. By the time he showed up, it was late morning, snow was dripping past her window from the roof under a repentant October sun, her mind was clearing, and she needed feedback.

Standing by her bedside, with his hand in the pocket of his lab coat, he told of the tearing in her abdomen. "There was extensive bleeding. We had to find its source and stop it, then piece you back together again. It was touch-and-go for a while."

In a scratchy voice, she asked, " 'Touch-and-go'?"

He softened the words with a smile. "We lost your pulse for a bit."

"I died?"

"Not exactly. We kept you going until your heart started back up on its own."

"You used electric shock." It wasn't a question, but the doctor didn't realize that.

"Actually, we did. It's the most effective thing in situations like yours."

"How long was my heart not beating?"

He waved a hand. "Not long enough to cause any damage."

But Bree wanted to know. It had seemed an eternity that she had watched them work on her, and then there was the upward floating, and the bright light, and the sense of total and utter well-being. "Seconds? Minutes?"

"Your brain was never without oxygen," he said, which didn't answer the question, so she tried a different angle.

"How many of you were working on me?" She had seen five.

"There were seven—three doctors and four nurses."

"At the time when my heart stopped?"

He thought back. "No. There were five in the room then—Jack Warren and I, two nurses, and Simon Meade, up from St. Johnsbury."

Simon Meade. The tall one in the dark-blue scrubs. The one who had applied the paddles that shocked her back to life. It had taken more than one application.

"I felt those shocks," she murmured. It had been at the very end. She had been at peace with herself and the world, totally happy, then, *whap!*

The doctor smiled. "Patients often say that, but it's actually only the thought of the procedure that hurts. You were completely anesthetized."

"I felt them," Bree insisted, but softly, because there was a chance he was right. What she thought she had seen didn't make sense. Maybe it was her imagination. She was heavily medicated. Maybe she was pulling images from the past. After all, she had watched *ER*. She knew what went on in operating rooms.

She also knew about near-death experiences—hard for an avid reader not to, what with so many books and magazine articles on the subject. So maybe what she had thought was real was nothing more than the power of suggestion. Maybe she had dreamed it up, after all.

But the dream wouldn't be dispelled. It penetrated her discomfort in bits and snatches, in ever greater detail as the day progressed. Friends stopped by to say hello, only to be hurried along by the nurses. Flash was one of the few who were allowed to stay.

He arrived late in the afternoon, with a platter of goodies from the diner. Bree was awake, but a long way from eating anything solid. Her stomach hurt. Her whole body hurt—cheek, arm, hip, legs. The last thing she felt was hungry. Thirsty, yes. Hungry, no.

"Not even one little cookie?" Flash pleaded. "I brought the shortbreads just for you. You love them."

"*You* love them," she said, in a raspy voice, and grimaced against the pain of movement when she reached toward the cup on the bed table. "I'm so dry. Help me, Flash. I can't reach that cup." When he moved it closer, she fished out several ice chips and put them in her mouth.

"What have we here?" Flash asked on his way to the window. A bubble bowl on the sill was filled with flowers, exquisitely arranged. "Pink geraniums, purple somethings, white crocuses. And lots of local ornamental grass. From Julia Dean. That's so nice." He returned to the bed. "I talked with the doctors. Another five days here, they said, and you'll be home. A couple of weeks at home, and you'll be back at the diner. Jillie's filling in while you're gone, and if you don't feel like waitressing after that, she'll stay on. You can just sit in the office and manage the place. I'm paying you either way. You don't have to worry about a thing."

Bree wasn't worried. She hadn't thought about what would come after, was still trying to figure out what had come before. "I died on the operating table."

"No, you didn't. Your heart stopped for a few beats before they started it up again. That's not dying."

But she wasn't being put off. Flash was one of her best friends. She needed to tell him what had happened. "I knew when it stopped. I felt things."

He looked skeptical. "What kinds of things?"

"Lightness. Out-of-my-body kinds of things. I went through the ceiling."

"So did I when Eliot told me about the accident. I knew I should have driven you all the way home. If I had, you wouldn't be lying here now. Whoever was driving that truck is in deep shit."

He wasn't listening. Frustrated, Bree closed her eyes. But a greater need forced them open again. "What do you know about near-death experiences?"

"As much as I want," he said, with a snort that said he didn't think they were real. "When we die, we die. I don't believe in heaven or hell."

He didn't believe in God, either. He had told her that more than once, and while she didn't agree with him, she respected his feelings. She also respected the fact that he had a graduate degree in art history from Columbia. He wasn't dumb.

"What if I said I'd had a look at heaven?" she asked.

"I'd say it's the medication talking. They have you on morphine. That's strong stuff."

She gave a tiny head shake. "It's not the medication."

"No? Listen to you. Your words are slurred. It's the medication."

Possibly. Still, she saw that scene and felt that light, felt the *benevolence* of it. "I don't usually believe in things like this."

"Damn right you don't," Flash scolded. "Verity does. Do you want people laughing at you the way they laugh at her?"

"But I see this so *clearly,*" she pleaded.

"I'm telling you, it's the morphine and, if not that, the anesthesia. It'll pass." With more fear than humor, he added, "It better. I need you with your feet on the ground. You're the sane one, Bree. Don't flip out on me, huh?"

Bree wasn't flipping out. He was right. She *was* the sane one.

But each time she closed her eyes, she was back in the operating room, hovering over the table, then rising, rising, and then there was that light. As confused as she was about what was real and what wasn't, she couldn't deny the calm that flowed through her each time she thought of that light.

And there was more to the experience. She hadn't told Flash the half of it. More returned with each wakeful stretch, much of it sketchy still, but exciting, baffling, even scary, if what she thought she had heard was true.

Dusk fell. Bree dreamed about the operating room again, dreamed of hovering above it and looking down. This time she saw a mole on the nape of the neck of one of the nurses.

She awoke convinced that it wasn't a dream at all. She *had* seen a mole in the operating room that night. But how, if she had been unconscious? There was only one way.

Shaken, she forced her eyes open. The only light in the room was the dim glow of a corner lamp. It was a gentle light, less harsh than the overheads, but reassuring. She wouldn't have wanted to wake up to total darkness and wonder which world she was in.

She lay without moving for a while, trying to separate pain from other needs, deciding whether she wanted to act on any and, if so, how. First priority, easiest to meet, was water. Her mouth was still abominably dry.

She had barely reached for the overhead bar, in an attempt to sit up, when the chair in the corner came alive. Her eyes widened on the man who approached. Uncommon height, tapering body, light-brown hair long grown out of a stylist's cut—no mistaking his identity.

He poured fresh water into the cup from the pitcher beside it, flexed the straw so that she could drink more easily, and slipped an arm behind her. "Don't use your stomach muscles. Let me do the work."

She stared at him, wondering why he was there but too dry to ask. And he was right. She felt less pain when she let him take her weight. With her upper body raised just enough, she drank, paused, drank again, then whispered, "Why am I so dry?"

"It's from the anesthesia. The IV pumps in fluids, but it doesn't seem to make a difference."

"Actually, it does," she remarked, because the bathroom was second on her list.

"Ah." He set the water back on the table. "I think, for that, maybe a nurse."

"No. They had me up before. If you can just help me across the room." She moved the covers aside and got her legs over the edge of the bed, though not without the kind of pain that had her taking quick, shallow breaths.

"Can I carry you?"

"No," she gasped. "I need to walk. Not only for the stomach. The rest of me is stiffening up not doing anything."

He eyed her swollen cheek. "The rest of you is bruised, too. The only thing that'll cure it is time and rest." He looked away, looked right back. "I'm sorry, Bree. If there'd been any way I could have avoided hitting you, I would have."

She had known that, from the moment Eliot had told her about the accident. Tom had always struck her as a decent sort. He was respectful at the diner, and he left great tips. Besides, she remembered how the accident had happened and knew that he had been in the Jeep, not the pickup. From the look of his own face—a cruel line of stitches beneath a dilly of a shiner—he hadn't escaped unscathed. Yet here he was. *The* Thomas Gates.

Hard to take in, that little twist. Had she felt better, she might have been awed, but tackling celebrity status wasn't high on her list just then. Nor was talking books. Prioritywise, her body was calling the shots.

Holding the mass of bandages that covered her stomach, she inched to the edge of the bed and, with his help, shifted her weight to her feet. It was a long minute of unsteady breaths before she could straighten enough to walk.

He supported her with one arm, guided the IV pole with the other while she shuffled forward. By the time she was finished in the bathroom, she couldn't get back to bed fast enough.

Tom helped her in, got the IV business straight, covered her up. "There's Jell-O in the kitchen," he said. "Will you tell me when you want some?"

She nodded, eyes already closed, and sought memory of the light to ease her pain.

She must have dozed, because when she opened her eyes again, the wall clock's small hand had moved from nine to ten. A nurse was checking her bandages, taking her vital signs, adjusting the IV drip, administering pain medication. Bree tried to look for a mole, but the light was too dim, the angle wrong. The woman had barely vanished into the night hush of the hall, when Bree remembered Tom.

Her eyes flew to the chair in the corner, and there he was. Slouched low, with his head against the back of the chair and his fingers laced over his middle, he looked decidedly unfamous. The book in his lap suggested he planned to stay awhile.

At first she thought he was sleeping. His eyes were hooded, his body was perfectly still. Then his mouth moved in the touch of a smile.

She hadn't seen him smile before. He was usually serious and withdrawn. But his smile was something, even just that touch. It reminded her of those great hands of his, which she now pictured poking at a word processor. That made her think of the kind of life he must have led before coming to Panama, which made her think of the kind of people he must have known, which made her think that she was *nothing* by comparison, which made her wonder why he was glued to the chair in her room.

Since she didn't want to think it was guilt, she didn't ask. "How'd you get the nurses to let you stay?" she asked instead.

He stretched. "I convinced them that if I can be a help to you here, there's less work for them."

"Do they know you write books?"

There was a brief, thick silence, then a wary "I hope not. Who told you? Eliot?"

"Yes."

"I'd rather you forget it. I didn't much like the man who wrote those books. I was trying to put distance between him and me."

"Was it working?"

"I don't know. My life is different here, that's for sure. Not being known helped."

"I won't tell."

"You're not the problem. Eliot is. One word to Emma, and Dotty will know, and once Dotty knows, the world knows." He sniffed in a long, loud breath. "But that's fine." Setting the book aside, he pushed himself out of the chair. "It had to happen sooner or later. How do you feel?"

She hurt. But she was also thinking that her mouth felt like sand and that something smooth, cool, and moist would feel good. "Did you mention Jell-O?"

"I did. Name your wish—strawberry, cherry, or lime."

Name your wish. Weird. "Cherry."

"Bathroom first?"

"Please."

He helped her there, then helped her back. He fluffed the pillow and turned it, held the water for her, settled her in. She was grateful to rest while he went for the Jell-O, but drew the line when he offered to feed her. So he cranked up the head of the bed and retreated to the chair while she ate.

It was slow going. Her hand was shaky, her whole arm ached. She felt weak, despicably weak, and reminding herself of what she'd been through didn't help. What did help was thinking about the light. It gave her strength.

She wanted to tell Tom about it, wanted him to say that she hadn't imagined anything, that near-death experiences did happen, that the light and all the rest was real. But she would be mortified if he was skeptical, too, especially now that she knew who he was.

So she finished her Jell-O, let him crank down the head of the bed, closed her eyes, and drifted off.

She awoke slowly, didn't open her eyes, didn't move, just thought—about the light first, because she had been dreaming of that, then about the silence of the night, then about her stomach. During one of the doctor's checks, she'd had a glimpse of what was under the bandages. The incision was huge, actually two crisscrossing cuts. Granted they were a small price to pay for life, but they weren't pretty.

She had seen those incisions when they were wide open. They hadn't been pretty then, either. Hard to believe that that body had been hers.

So maybe it hadn't been. Maybe she had conjured the scene from a movie.

Only those had been strands of *her* hair escaping the cap on her head, and she had heard the people around her chanting, "Come on, Bree, hang on . . . you can do it, Bree."

It had been *so real*. She *wanted* it to be real. She had never been in the presence of anyone as cheerful and loving and good as that being in the light. The high of being with him was like nothing she had ever felt smoking Curtis Lamb's homegrown pot, and Curtis Lamb's pot was good.

With a sigh, she opened her eyes. They went first to the clock, which read two, then to the man who sat in the chair, reading. Still there. Amazing.

*Tell him, Bree.* He'll laugh. *So what?* So he's Thomas Gates!

At the silent sound of his name, Tom looked up and saw that she was awake, propped his cheek on a fist, and smiled, and suddenly it didn't seem fair that he was who he was and that she should care whether he laughed at her or not. It didn't seem fair that, even banged up, he looked good. It didn't seem fair that she was out of his league.

"Aren't you tired?" she grumbled, more accusation than question.

"No. I slept most of the day."

"You don't have to stay here. The accident wasn't your fault."

"That's not why I'm here."

"Then why?"

It was a minute before he said, "Because this beats sitting in the snow waiting for an ambulance, or sitting outside an operating room waiting for the doctors to come out."

She forgot her pique. "You were here then?"

He nodded.

Cautious now, she asked, "How much did they tell you about the surgery?"

"Enough," he said, in a way that said it all, and it was like an invitation, only she couldn't get herself to accept.

*But why not?* she asked herself. *Forget who he is. One Panamanian winter, and he'll be gone. What does it matter if he thinks you're nuts?*

She closed her eyes and listened for the turning of pages to suggest he had gone back to his book, but there was none. Finally, without opening her eyes, she asked, "Did they tell you my heart stopped?"

"Oh, yeah."

"Scary, huh?"

"*Oh*, yeah," he said, with feeling.

Then, because in order to write the way he did he had to be worldly, and because something about dying and being reborn told her to take the risk, she opened her eyes and said, "Do you believe in near-death experiences?"

He was silent for a time, sitting with the book in his lap and his ankle on his knee. "I don't know."

"Do you know anyone who's had one?"

"No. But that doesn't mean anything." Setting the book aside, he pushed up from the chair—gingerly, she thought, but she promptly forgot it when he approached the bed and asked, "Did you have one?"

She looked for mockery, saw none. "Maybe. I don't usually believe in things like that."

"Neither do I. But that doesn't mean anything, either. Sometimes seeing is believing."

"Oh, I saw," Bree drawled, emboldened by his encouragement. She felt suddenly heady, but her tongue was dry again.

Tom slid her up, held the straw to her lips. After turning her pillow, he lowered her to its fresh, cooler side. Then he sat down on the spare patch of bed by her hip. "Tell me what you saw." He seemed genuinely curious.

Buoyed by that, she said, "First, I heard. I heard them say they'd lost a pulse, and I heard their fear. Then it was like something sucked me out of my body and up, and I was looking down on what was happening. They did CPR. There were two of them working on that, and one monitoring my signs, and another shooting me with adrenaline, only my blood pressure kept falling, and I wouldn't breathe on my own. They were getting really scared; I could hear it in them. Only *I* wasn't scared"—and she felt a wave of calm now—"because I was with this . . . thing, and it was *so nice.*" She didn't know where she found the strength to talk, but the words kept coming. "It didn't have arms I could see, but its arms were open in welcome. It was strong but gentle. And powerful. It could do whatever it wanted—miracles, I swear. Maybe what happened to me *was* a miracle. I don't know. I only know that I was with this very bright being. It was visually bright and smart bright, and pure and kind and sweet, and it *loved* me."

She closed her mouth on the rush of words, afraid that she had gone too far.

But Tom looked intrigued. "What happened then?"

"Do you think I'm losing it?"

"No."

"This is pretty bizarre."

"Tell me what happened next."

"They applied electric shocks. They had to do it twice. Each time, it jolted my whole body. It really *is* like you see on TV, only it's not so much fun when it's your own body down there. It was awful to watch, awful to *feel.*"

"You *felt* it?" he asked.

"Only the last time. Before that, I was with this person, this being, and I was happy and peaceful and *relieved.*"

"Relieved. Why?"

She wasn't sure. The word had just popped out. "Relieved to be there, I guess. Maybe relieved to know that *there* existed. Was it heaven?"

"I don't know. Did you see anything beyond this being?"

Shaking her head, she reached for water.

He held the cup and put the straw to her mouth. "What did it look like?"

After several sips, she let the straw fall away. "Light. It was nothing but light. It didn't have a face, but it smiled and was beautiful, and it spoke." She frowned. "There wasn't any voice. I just . . . felt its thoughts."

"What was it thinking?"

"I'm not sure I can find the words," she said, holding back for the first time. This was the newest part of her recollection, potentially the silliest. Self-consciousness kept her from risking sounding like a fool to this virtual stranger, who was a handsome one at that. She may have nearly died, but she had a little pride, after all.

He returned the cup to the bed tray.

Whispering, she asked, "Are you leaving now?"

He shook his head. "I'll stay awhile."

"You don't have to. I'll be going back to sleep. I won't need anything until morning."

"Then I'll just read." He left the bed and crossed to the chair. Easing into it, he stretched out and crossed his ankles.

He was wearing running shoes. That was the last thing she noticed about him before she closed her eyes, but it wasn't the last thing she thought. The last thing she thought was that she didn't care if he *was* driven by guilt: no one had ever spent the night sitting by her bedside before.

It was the pain that did it. After sleeping for nearly two hours, she woke up feeling awful. Tom was beside her in an instant, ringing for the nurse, then running to get her when she didn't come fast enough.

The morphine brought instant relief. It also enveloped Bree in a dull haze that lowered her inhibitions. Alone with Tom again, with him sitting on the side of the bed like he was her very best friend, she said in a molasses-thick voice, "There's more to the story of the being of light."

"More?"

"More bizarre. I keep hearing something he said. Thought. Whatever."

"What was it?"

"Three wishes. I have three wishes." Her voice was slurred, but the words came anyway. "I died. Only it wasn't my time. So I was sent back with a gift. Three wishes before I die again. Like a reward."

"To make up for the accident?"

The being of light hadn't said. "Maybe." She waded through the haze in search of other possibilities. "Or to make up for my mother. Or my father. But my life's good. So maybe it's just *because.*" She closed her eyes. With an effort, she opened them again. "This part's harder to believe than the rest."

"Why?"

It took a minute of pushing her thoughts past the morphine before she recalled. "Wishes lie ahead. The rest, the bright light and all, is past."

"So there's no way to prove whether the bright light was real, but there is a way to prove whether the wishes are or not."

"Ex*actly.*"

"Do you want them to be?"

She frowned. "I guess." She wasn't sure. But she didn't know why.

"Only guess? Aren't there things you'd wish for?"

"Yes." Something nagged at the back of her mind.

"So?"

Then she remembered. "Three wishes before I die again." Was that the message she had received, or were the drugs confusing her? She looked at Tom. "I guess I'm a little worried about what happens after the third wish." She watched his face for understanding. When nothing came, she continued. "It's like this. It seems like I've come back to use the wishes, but if that's true, does it also mean that once I've used the third one, my time will be up? Will I have to go back?"

His eyes widened and his chin came up. "Ah. I see what you mean."

That chin was slightly square, slightly stubbled. She stared at it until Tom waved a hand before her eyes. Then she blinked, took a sleepy breath. "It's okay." Her voice was distant. "They're probably not real anyway." Seeing something after the fact, she frowned and lifted the hand he had waved. His palm was covered with barely scabbed cuts.

When she looked questioningly at him, he said, "Getting out of the Jeep."

She looked at his cheek. "That'll leave a scar."

"It'll add character. I can use that."

Her eyelids were growing heavy. "Maybe I'll wish for no scar for you."

"Don't you dare."

"Then no scars for me."

"You wouldn't waste a wish on that, would you?"

"Maybe not." Her lids drifted shut. Whether it was the thinking of the being of light, or being with Tom, or floating on a morphine high, she felt peaceful. "Maybe I can use only two. Save the third up. Know what I mean?"

"That's a thought."

Smiling, she gave herself over to whatever it was that felt so good.

Bree was sleeping when Tom left. The morning nurses had just arrived, the sun was newly up, and he was desperate to ease his own aches with a long, hot bath and a long, firm bed. First, though, he needed information.

He drove home in the car he had rented the day before. Snow still lay on the roadside, but two days of melt under sun and mild air had thinned it considerably. Limbs that had fallen under the weight of the snow had been moved aside. Fall foliage had reemerged. The roads themselves were wet but clear, the spatter under the tires a steady *shushhhh* through his open window.

West Elm was off Pine Street, two miles up from the town green. The houses here were farther apart than the ones in the center of town, and hidden from each other behind evergreen shields. That was the first thing Tom had liked about the bungalow. The second was the modesty of it, the third its difference from his earlier homes.

He turned into the driveway along ruts widened by melt and climbed out in time to hail the newsboy, who was pedaling his mountain bike through the slush on the road. The paper he carried wasn't a local. Panama wasn't big enough for that. This one was out of Burlington and had local news at the back.

Tom fished a dollar from his pocket.

The boy stopped, straddling the bike. "They told me you're s'posed to subscribe."

"I swore off newspapers when I left New York."

"So why do you keep flagging me down?"

"I just need a fix now and then." Specifically, he wanted to see if there was mention of the accident and, if so, his identity. He tucked the dollar in the boy's pocket. "The Johnsons are on vacation. This is for theirs."

Folding the paper under his arm, he slogged back to the car and drove on to the carport. Entering the kitchen, he kicked off his sneakers, dropped the paper on the table in passing, and took the stairs two at a time. There were three bedrooms on the second floor of the house. The only room whose door was open was the one with his king-size bed. He opened the door at the end of the hall and went in.

This was the room he had designated as his office when he had moved to Panama seven months before. He could count on both hands the number of times he had been in it since then, and it showed. Unopened cartons stood exactly where the movers had placed them. Walls and windows were bare. The only color to speak of came from a pair of overstuffed briefcases that lay on the handsome mahogany desk behind which he had once practiced law.

He unzipped one of the briefcases, removed a laptop computer, plugged it in, and booted it up. While it hummed on its own through obligatory openers, he rubbed his aching side. He bent over the desk, realized that his body wouldn't take that for long, dragged over the chair, and adjusted the angle of the laptop. The first thing he saw was that he had mail.

No surprise there. Weekly messages came from his agent like clockwork.

He debated passing it by; but there was always the chance that someone else wondered how he was.

Clicking into his mailbox, he found one, two, three messages from Nathan Gunn, sent in, yes, each of the last three weeks. He didn't have to read them to know that Nathan wanted another book. The plea was always the same.

At least Nathan cared enough to keep contact. No one else did, for which Tom had no one to blame but himself. Friends who had once E-mailed him regularly had deleted his name from their address books months before.

That bothered him, but the self-pity that usually followed the thought didn't come. Closing the file, he logged on to the Internet, typed in NEAR-DEATH EXPERIENCES at the blank, and clicked on Search.

# chapter
# four

Tom read dozens of personal recountings of near-death experiences. He read excerpts from books, comments from researchers, transcripts of interviews. He read until he was bleary-eyed and too tired even for the hot bath his bruised body craved. Leaving his clothes in a heap, he crawled into bed and fell into a dead sleep until noon, and the only thing that brought him awake then was the pain of inadvertently turning onto his left side.

He took the bath and a painkiller, fell back into bed, and slept until early evening. Then it was hunger that woke him. He hadn't eaten since he had woken at roughly the same hour the day before, scarfed down several slices of leftover pizza, and driven to the hospital.

Leftover pizza wouldn't do it this time. After a hot shower, he headed for the diner.

The roads were clear and dry. The only evidence of the storm that had hit three days before was the lingering sogginess of the earth and the occasional patch of unmelted snow. The air was warm, the foliage vivid even in twilight. It was the kind of sweet October night Tom had dreamed of when he moved north, the kind of night when he might have walked through his yard to the brook and followed it upstream, sat on a moonlit bench, and done the kind of connecting with himself that he needed to do. It was the kind of quiet night when he would have been able to hear his innermost thoughts, had he not been preoccupied with Bree.

The diner was doing a brisk Sunday business. Every booth was taken, with two parties of four waiting and only one empty place at the counter. Tom preferred the privacy of a booth, but he was too hungry to wait, too anxious to be on his way to the hospital. He eased through the eight standing just inside the door and was halfway to the empty stool when the hum of conversation dimmed. In its place, loud without it, were the slap of burgers on the grill, the clink of dishes in the kitchen, and Vince Gill sounding lonely and sad.

Tom wasn't a novice at being in the spotlight. He had been a star quarterback in high school and college, the stroke of his crew boat in law school, an articulate champion of the poor working out of the public defender's office, an equally articulate, often flamboyant savior of the rich as a private practitioner of increasingly national prominence. As a writer, he had been followed by the spotlight from his very first sale, which had made *Time, Newsweek,* and *People* magazines, to the very last, when an argument that had taken place at Lutèce between him and his publisher, coincidentally his lady of the moment, was reported in some detail on *Inside Edition.*

At the time, believing that even bad publicity was good, he

hadn't been bothered. But this was different. This spotlight invaded the space that he was trying to put between himself and the past.

He didn't know these people well. They were the kind of small towners for whom he had carelessly signed books at malls, the kind who wrote him letters care of his publisher and received form letters from his publisher in return. The old Tom would have seen them as nothing more than a vehicle for his own adulation. That Tom would have looked around the diner with a grin, hitched his chin in recognition of the attention, held up a falsely modest hand, and said, *My thanks, folks, but please, go ahead and eat.*

The new Tom, the one who didn't know whether the sudden silence reflected his past fame or the fact that his car had been the one to hit a woman these people loved, kept his eyes straight and walked forward. He was nowhere near as confident as he looked when he slipped onto the stool. With brief, unreturned glances at Frank Wright on his left and Martin Sprague on his right, he studied the menu on his mat, then looked up at the chalkboard's specials.

Flash entered his line of vision. He was wiping his hands on a towel, but his eyes quickly went past Tom to the booths behind. His voice followed, loud with meaning. "You folks waiting for something?"

There were several grunts and an inarticulate word or two. Anything more was lost when the surrounding conversation resumed.

Flash gave Tom a dry look. "Walk in here with a shiner like that, and that's what you get. How're you feeling?"

"Arthritic," Tom said. Then, because Flash seemed Bree's closest friend, and because she was Tom's major concern, he asked, "Have you seen Bree today?"

"A little while ago. She's hangin' in there. She said you spent the night. Said you were a help. That was good of you."

"It was the least I could do."

"How did she seem to you?"

"She was uncomfortable."

"I mean mentally," Flash said, more hesitant now. "Did she seem confused?"

"Not terribly."

"Did she say anything much?"

Tom knew what he was getting at. What he didn't know was whether anyone other than Flash knew Bree's thoughts. With Frank at his left elbow and Martin at his right, both ignoring his presence and surely listening to his every word, he chose those words with care. "She mentioned what she had been through. I thought she was coherent."

"You did?"

Tom nodded and, when Flash looked relieved, asked, "How's the veal?"

"Tender and light."

"I'll try it. With a tall ice water."

Flash seemed to want to say more. After a look down the counter, though, he wiped his hands again and disappeared into the kitchen.

The grillman called out an order for LeeAnn, who passed Tom without a glance. Frank finished his blueberry crisp, dug money out of his pocket, and studied the check. Martin forked up American chop suey to a steady beat.

Tom studied the diner's reflection in the stainless steel over the grill. He picked out faces he knew—Curtis Lamb and John Dillard, a boothful of local truckers, Sandy and Jack Swartz with little Tyler, the trio of Earl, Eliot, and Emma. People were looking at him, no doubt about that. He guessed they were talking about him, too. Once, he had craved the attention, so he deserved the discomfort it brought now. Be careful what you wish for, his mother had always said. She was right about that, too.

Frank put a handful of money on the counter and left. Jillie delivered a pizza to the man two stools over and breezed back past Tom to the kitchen. LeeAnn strode by with an armload of dirty plates and not a word.

Tom was feeling like a pariah by the time Flash set down a glass of water and said, "I hear your Jeep was totaled."

"The axle's gone."

"Are you getting another?"

"Jeep? No. I want something heavier."

"Self-protection?"

For sure, Tom thought, and said as much with a look.

Flash moved on. In the stainless steel, Tom watched the occupants of one of the booths slide out and head for the door. LeeAnn had barely reset the table when a new foursome slid in.

Martin Sprague ran a napkin across his mouth. "Hear you're a lawyer," he said, without looking at Tom.

Tom would have denied it, had there been any point. "I was."

"Not much need for lawyers in Panama."

"I didn't come here to practice."

"That's good. I do what has to be done."

Tom imagined that he did. Panama was hardly infested with crime. Since he had come, the only offense he had heard about was the case of a four-year-old child stealing a handful of artificial flies from the tackle shop. Martin Sprague might be getting along in years, but Tom guessed that the legal needs in a town like this were tame enough for him to handle. "Are you the only lawyer here?"

"Not enough work for any others."

"What type of things do you do?"

"Nothing you'd be interested in," Martin said, and raised a sharp voice. "LeeAnn, where's my check?"

Tom took a drink of water, set down the glass, ran his fingers up and down its sides. The cuts on his palms were beginning to scab. The cool felt good.

Martin moved away the instant LeeAnn gave him his check, and waited for his change by the cash register at the end of the counter.

Eliot Bonner slid onto the stool on Tom's left.

Tom shot him a look. "You're brave. Everyone else hurried off when I came. Is it the writing that did it, or the accident?"

"Both, I'd guess. No one thought twice about you when you didn't make noise. Now you stand out. Panama's like a boat. You up and rocked it."

"Yeah, well, I didn't do it on my own. I have a totaled Jeep and a battered body to prove it." And then there was Bree. "Any luck tracing that truck?"

"Nope. I talked with local departments. Talked with the state police. I was hoping one or the other would have caught someone driving stupid that night. There were a couple of other accidents and an arrest or two, but nothing involving a pickup. Hard to believe, what with so many trucks around here. Lucky, maybe." He smirked. "Bree says it was blue, you say black, your Jeep says maroon."

"Trust the Jeep," Tom advised and might have made a remark about physical evidence holding up in court, if his veal hadn't come just then. He began to salivate instantly. It looked and smelled as good as anything he had had in New York. Of course, he might have salivated over stale meat loaf, he was so hungry.

"There are a dozen people in town with maroon pickups," Bonner said. "Every one of them's got alibis. None's got dents consistent with what happened."

Tom decided that Flash hadn't been bragging without cause. The veal was tender and light, the Madeira sauce pleasantly mild. He chased a second mouthful with helpings of new potatoes and grilled asparagus.

"What about maroon pickups in neighboring towns?" he asked as he ate.

"We're working on it. Bree said not to bother. Said she's alive and that's all that matters."

Tom put his fork down. "It is, assuming whoever was driving that pickup got enough of a scare to change his ways, but that's a big assumption. He probably didn't even know I hit Bree, probably thought he'd just hit another car. He's probably out there telling himself, No sweat, car's insured, no one's the worse for the wear." Tom realized how angry he was. "Who's to say the next time he careens around in the snow he won't hit a bunch of kids and kill one or more outright?"

"Told her that myself."

"He must have been stoned or drunk. How else could a human

being do what he did and then just drive away? Hell, she nearly died."

Bonner squinted up at the stainless steel. "I heard she did. Heard she died on the table. Heard she made it to heaven, before someone sent her back. She tell you about it?"

Tom wanted to say that what Bree told him was privileged information, only they weren't lawyer and client. He wasn't quite sure what they were—friends, maybe—but whatever, he wasn't betraying her. "Heaven?" he echoed. "Did she tell you that?"

"Nah. My cousin works with Paul Sealy. Bree told Paul."

Bree had told Paul, who told his coworker, who told Eliot, who would tell Earl and Emma. Emma would tell Dotty, who would tell anyone else in town who cared to listen.

Tom was angry on Bree's behalf. "Did Bree tell Paul in confidence?"

"Who knows. Look, it's no big thing. She won't sue Paul, any more'n she'll press charges against whoever was driving that truck. If you ask me, it's a lot of hokum, this near-death business, but I don't blame Bree. She had a scare. She earned the right to hallucinate. I just don't want someone having a *real*-death experience because I didn't catch the bastard the first time around." He pushed himself off the stool, straightened the belt under his belly, cleared his throat. "So. I hear you've been on Larry King."

Tom stared at him, then beyond. Conversation was abruptly down again. Half the diner was looking their way.

With a thanks-for-nothing look at the chief, he returned to his veal.

"More than once," Bonner went on. "He musta liked you."

"He liked what I did," Tom muttered, jabbing at his food with his fork. "I wrote about incendiary cases. It made for an easy show."

"What about Barbara Walters?"

Tom snorted. "You've done your homework."

"It's my job. I'm all Panama's got. So. How'd she treat you? Did she put you on the spot? She can be a tough one sometimes.

Course, that's what people like about her. Boy, she's been at it for a long time now. How'd she look in person?"

Tom raised a piece of veal, pondered it, returned it to his plate. Whoever in the diner hadn't known who he was before this would know now, and it wouldn't stop there. It was only a matter of time before the whole town knew.

So let them know something else, he decided. With a resigned sigh and a meaningful look at the faces turned his way, he said loudly and to the point, "I bought a house in Panama because it seemed like the kind of place where people respected each other, the kind of place where I could go about my business without being questioned about the past. I chose Panama because I wanted privacy, and because it was far away from New York." Though his gaze settled on Bonner, his voice was a warning for the rest. "If I wanted to tell the world I was here, I'd have taken out an ad in the *Times*. If the media track me here, I'm gone. Am I getting through?"

Miraculously, he finished his dinner. No doubt stubbornness was part of it, since his hunger had left with the mention of Larry King. It wasn't that he had a gripe with the man, or with Barbara Walters or any of the others who had interviewed him. The majority of those interviewers had simply asked the questions Tom's publicist had fed them. They were questions Tom had helped formulate, each designed to show yet another flattering side, and he hadn't felt a bit of guilt doing it. That was how the game was played. He had left those interviews walking on air, totally enamored with himself, sold on the flattery.

Thinking back on it made him sick to his stomach. But he needed food if he planned to stay at the hospital again, and he most definitely did plan to stay. He felt good when he was there, felt decent and different and right. So he finished the veal, drank two cups of coffee, ordered desserts to go, and left.

When Tom started high school, he was five feet eight, which would have been a fine height for a fifteen-year-old if he hadn't wanted to play football. He had come off a summer of painting houses during the day and playing ball at night, so he was tanned and fit, but he lacked the bulk that the older players had.

"You're scrappy," his mother pointed out when she caught him moping around on the eve of tryouts.

"That doesn't matter. I won't make it. I'm too small."

"Smallness is a state of mind," she said, as she puffed up every cushion in the living room except those on which he was slouched. "Walk onto that field with your head high, and you'll look a foot taller. Look the coach in the eye, and he'll think you're more solid. Carry yourself like a quarterback, and people will see you as one."

It worked. He played backup to a senior quarterback that freshman year, then starting quarterback for his remaining three years. By the time he graduated, he was six four and strong. Though he no longer needed pretense, the lesson in projecting confidence was ingrained.

It stood him in good stead now. For the third night in a row, well after visiting hours ended, he walked into the medical center past the nurse at the desk, swung into the stairwell, climbed the stairs, and strode down the second-floor corridor to Bree's room as though he had every right in the world to be there. No matter that the nurses on duty were new and that his battered face made him look like a thug. Then again, perhaps they knew exactly who he was and didn't dare stop him. Whatever, no one looked twice.

He was the one to blink when Bree was nowhere in sight.

Bree sat in the dark of the deserted lounge at the far end of the hall. The music drifting from wall speakers was classical, soft and soothing, exactly what she needed. Her room had grown oppressive. Even now, well after the last of her friends had left, she could still hear them telling her that they missed her, that they wished her a speedy recovery, that any out-of-body visions would end once her mind cleared.

The thing was that her mind was perfectly clear. She had slept most of the morning, had cut back on pain pills, and if anything, her memory of that time in the operating room had sharpened. She didn't tell her friends that. They weren't inclined to listen, and she didn't have the strength to make her case. Sitting here, with the mild night air whispering in through half-open windows, she found it hard to believe that a major snowstorm had hit three days before, much less that she had died, gone to heaven, and returned.

It was all at the same time crystal clear and totally unreal. Unreal that it had snowed so hard so early in the season. Unreal that she had been at just that spot on Birch Hill at just that moment. Unreal that she had watched the goings-on in the operating room. Unreal that she felt the calming force of that bright light still. Unreal that silent Tom from the diner was Thomas Gates of national renown.

Thomas Gates. Unreal.

Shifting gingerly in the wingback chair, she started to raise her legs to tuck her cold feet beneath her. When the soreness in her abdomen wouldn't allow for the movement, she settled for layering one foot over the other and burying her hands in the folds of her robe.

She knew about Thomas Gates. Being a fan of his books, she had read articles on him. Many hadn't been flattering. He wasn't supposed to be very nice.

Odd, but the Tom Gates she knew seemed perfectly nice.

Releasing a breath, she put her head against the back of the chair and closed her eyes. She remembered those articles in detail. Thomas Gates was reputed to be callous and conceited, but she hadn't seen either trait in him, and as for being the womanizer the articles implied, he hadn't womanized in Panama. He hadn't come on to her as had other men in the diner, hadn't leered or teased or touched her in inappropriate ways.

Footsteps came from the hall, and suddenly he was there. Thinking she might have imagined him, she blinked, but he remained.

She hadn't wished him there. She was being careful not to make wishes accidentally. But she was inordinately pleased that he'd come.

"Hi," he said. Backlit as he was, she couldn't see his face, but his voice was gentle, smiling.

Her heart beat a little faster. She smiled back. "Hi."

"Walk all the way down here yourself?"

"Uh-huh." Dryly, she added, "It took everything I had."

He made a show of looking around. "No more IV. That's progress."

"Uh-huh. I had solid food for dinner. Chicken."

"Bet it wasn't as good as Flash's."

"No. But that's okay. I was full after two bites." She felt revived now that he had come. "Want to turn on a light?"

"Not if you prefer the dark."

"I don't."

He slipped a hand under the shade of a nearby lamp. The soft light that filled the room made him real, in an unreal sort of way. He was gorgeous, with his tousled hair and his athlete's build, and he was *there*.

"I didn't think you were coming," she said.

"I promised I would. You just slept through the promise."

No. She had heard. Then she had wondered if she had simply dreamed it up because she wanted it so much. "I thought you might go home and think about it and decide I was loony."

"If you are, then so are a hell of a lot of other people." He lowered a leather knapsack from his shoulder at the same time that he lowered himself to a chair. The knapsack settled on the floor between his knees. He unstrapped the top and pulled out a folder that was a solid inch thick. "Printouts from my computer. They're personal accounts of other people who have experienced what you did."

Bree's heart beat even faster than before. She looked from the folder to Tom and back. She didn't know whether to be more pleased that there were others like her or that Tom had made the effort of seeking them out.

The first took precedence. Taking the folder from him, she put it on her lap and covered it with a proprietary hand. Cautiously, she asked, "Did you read them?"

"Every one."

"What do they say?"

"Much of what you do," he answered gently. He had his elbows on his thighs. His hands dangled between. "An accident or a medical crisis occurs. The victim is conscious of leaving his body, rising up above it, and looking back down. Sometimes it happens at the scene of the accident, sometimes in an operating room. He sees people working on him, hears their voices. Then there's the light. It's always very bright. It's always benevolent. It conveys a sense of well-being. It speaks without actually talking."

"It *did*," Bree breathed, delighted. She hadn't realized how alone she had felt until she suddenly felt less so. "What else?" She put her fingertips together in front of her mouth and tried to contain her excitement.

"There's a lot of the same uncertainty that you feel. The person knows he's had an out-of-body experience, but he's still not sure."

"Exactly."

"He knows people don't believe him, but he can't forget what happened. He's afraid to talk about it. Some people hold it in for years—twenty-five, by one account."

"Oh, my. But I know the fear that person felt." She reversed her feet, putting the bottom one on top. "Did anyone else mention being promised three wishes?"

Tom gave a quick head shake. "That doesn't mean anything. No two accounts I read were exactly alike. One person said that the air around the being of light was purple. Another passed through a tree during his experience and woke up covered with sap. Another left his body and floated around the city for a while before waking up in the hospital. Another tried to open a door while he was out of his body, but couldn't. Some remember feeling a sense of belonging when they're with this being."

Bree had, now that she thought of it.

Tom went on. "Lots of people report being sucked out of their bodies and up through a dark tunnel. The bright light is at the end of that tunnel. Some of them report hearing a buzzing or jangling noise. Some say they fought it, fought the noise and the light, fought being sucked up."

Bree shook her head. She hadn't experienced anything like that. There had been nothing to fight. She had simply been in her body one minute and out of it the next. Once she was with the being of light, she wouldn't have fought anyway. That being had been compelling. If anything, she had been sad to leave it.

"Some people say they were given a choice and made a conscious decision to return to life. Others believe they were returned to life for a reason. Being granted three wishes is a reason."

"But no one else mentioned getting wishes?" she asked, knowing that the concept would be more credible if it had happened before.

The small lines that furrowed his brow did nothing negative. Black eye and all, he looked great.

"No one else mentioned getting wishes," he said. "One person mentioned coming back to take care of a sick parent, another coming back to be with a lover, but neither mentioned it as a response to a wish. There were reports from people who said that they had done things wrong and were being given a second chance, and reports from people who said that the being of light showed them what hell looked like, so they were reformed. Some specifically said they'd been to heaven. They wrote about seeing dead relatives and friends."

"I didn't," Bree said, and was grateful for it. She might have liked to see her father, but if the dead congregated, he would have been with his parents, and they were dour people. Their presence in a room put a damper on everyone and everything. It would have surely dulled the luster of the being of light. She was glad that had remained unspoiled.

Of course, it was still possible that the being didn't exist. "What do you think?" she asked Tom. "Was it real, what happened to me?"

Again those small creases touched his forehead. He frowned at his palms, let them fall to his thighs, and met her gaze. "I don't know. Your claim is certainly more plausible than some of the others. Take young children having near-death experiences. Kids of three or four, even seven or eight, are imaginative. They're wide open to the power of suggestion. And I have a hard time believing near-death experiences reported by people who acknowledge that they were either stoned or drunk at the time. I also have a hard time believing the stories written by people whose lives were unstable to begin with. They may be prone to hallucinating. Same with a person who suffers a severe head injury.

"Then there are those people who report a cataclysmic awakening. They're walking down the street and—wham—they suddenly see something or know something or feel something that may or may not have to do with God. I wouldn't call that a near-death experience. An epiphany, maybe. Same thing with people who recover from a serious illness and report having seen Saint Peter and the pearly gates. Serious illnesses naturally spawn thoughts of mortality, which naturally spawn thoughts of religion."

Bree shook her head. "Not in me. My dad was a Congregationalist, but I'm not much of anything."

Tom smiled and sat straighter. "So then there are people like you. They're well-adjusted adults. They're intelligent. They may or may not be religious, but they're good people. They aren't hopped up or soused, they're in accidents not of their own making, and somewhere along the line their hearts stop. Medical personnel verify it and reverse it. These momentarily dead return to the world of the living with stories that are so much alike that it gives you chills. These people come from all walks of life. They don't know each other. They may or may not have ever read an account of a near-death experience, still the experiences they report have eerie similarities." He blew out a breath. "Hard not to believe people like that."

Bree felt suddenly lighthearted. "You're very convincing."

"When you sum it up, it *is* convincing. The only theory I found at all plausible made the argument that the end of life is like the very beginning, that things come full circle, that there are parallels between the birth process and near-death accounts. The dark tunnel that some people claim they're sucked into at the moment of death is like the birth canal. The bright light is what the delivery room must seem like to the newborn after the dark of the womb. Same with the noise. The implication is that at the moment of death, or just prior to death, the human mind reverts in time to the moment of birth."

"Then what I saw were memories?" She shook her head again. "Babies aren't given three wishes. Besides, I saw a mole."

"A mole."

"On the neck of one of the nurses who was in the operating room that night. She was bending over me, and it was on the back of her neck. How could I have seen it there if I wasn't above her?" Bree held up a hand. "Okay. I know. Maybe she was in the recovery room when I woke up, and I saw it when she turned away from me, and I'm just confusing the two locations. But there was only one nurse in the recovery room—I asked—and she wasn't in the operating room during the time my heart stopped, and besides, she doesn't have a mole. I checked."

"Have you checked the OR nurses?"

"One. She didn't have a mole. The other has long hair. She only puts it up when she's in the operating room." Bree tucked her hands inside each other on the folder. "I should just come out and ask her about it, but I feel silly." At times, she felt silly, period. "Word's already going around town. What if the whole near-death thing is bogus?" She reversed her feet again, rubbing them together to generate heat. Flash had brought her robe, which was fleece, large and warm, but he hadn't thought to bring slippers. The hospital provided foam ones that were barely better than nothing.

Tom slid to the floor, shifted her feet to his lap, and began to chafe them. The warmth of it went all the way to her cheeks.

"You don't have to do that," she said.

"I want to."

"You must have better things to do with your time."

He shook his head, looking pleased.

"You're feeling guilty," she insisted, "but I told you, the accident wasn't your fault." And he was a celebrity and movie-star handsome. But did she move her feet out of his grasp? No. "This is embarrassing."

"Why? You have nice feet. Nice icy feet."

"They're always that way."

73

"My mom used to say that it's a female thing, that women's warmth is concentrated in the region of their hearts, so their extremities suffer."

Bree laughed, then hugged her middle when the movement hurt.

Tom's hands stopped. Troubled eyes went to her stomach. "I'm sorry."

"Don't be. It's fine now. But what a nice thought. You say things like that in your books, little gems of wisdom. Is that where you get them, from your mom?"

His reply was snide. "I never thought so. I thought it was all me."

"Is she still alive?"

Quietly, he said, "She died last year."

"I'm sorry."

"Me, too."

When he resumed his rubbing, it seemed more a massage, a gentle kneading that involved both of his hands and both of her feet, from the tips of her toes to her ankles.

Closing her eyes, she gave herself up to the feeling. It occurred to her that she could easily spend a wish on a permanent foot masseur, if the business of wishes was real.

She wondered if it was. No one else had ever reported being granted three wishes.

So maybe it was just her. Or maybe someone had used all three wishes and died before writing about it.

She wouldn't use the third wish, wouldn't take the risk. Then again, maybe *none* of it was real.

The massage stopped. Tom reached into his bag, pulled out a sweater, and was about to wrap it around her feet, when she said, "I'm getting tired. I'd better go back to bed."

He returned the sweater to the knapsack, pushed to his feet, and hitched the knapsack to his shoulder. Holding the folder in one hand, he helped her up with the other. He kept one arm around her as they walked.

She had made it to the lounge on her own. Aside from the bend in her middle, she was remarkably steady. Even tired, she could have made it back to her room on her own. But she let Tom help her into bed, let him straighten the covers and pull them up. She watched him put the folder on the table where she could reach it when she was ready, watched him pull a book from the knapsack.

"That thing's full of goodies," she mused.

His face brightened, rendering him devilishly handsome. She could see why he was called a lady-killer. "As a matter of fact." He reached in again and produced two take-out containers. "Pudding. One for you, one for me."

She was touched. He had brought a sweater and a book, which meant that he was staying. And now pudding.

Thinking that he might stay longer if he had *both* puddings, she touched her stomach and said, "That was so sweet of you. But the chicken filled me up. Honestly."

He set one container on the bedstand and opened the second. "Don't like tapioca?"

He put it down and was reaching for the other, when she said, "I love tapioca, but I'm stuffed. Really. You eat it."

"This one's Indian pudding."

She took a quick breath. "Indian pudding?" Indian pudding was her favorite.

He upped the ante. "There's a microwave in the kitchen. I could heat it for you."

She was sorely tempted.

"Then, once it's hot, I could raid the freezer and add a little vanilla ice cream."

That did it. "Just a very, very, *very* little."

He gave her a smile that warmed her all over. Watching him head for the kitchen, she decided that she didn't need three wishes as long as Tom Gates was around.

On Monday night, he pulled a pair of wool socks from his knapsack. They were soft, clean, and large, and clearly his, which made them more special than if he had spent a fortune on fancy slippers. They warmed her feet perfectly.

On Tuesday night, just when she was starting to feel hungry, he showed up with a meal from the diner and said, "Flash recommended the Yankee special, but the risotto sounded lighter and too good to pass up. Interested?" Was she ever, and *not* for the Yankee special. The Yankee special was a pot roast reminiscent of the kind her grandmother had made every Thursday without fail, and while Flash's pot roast was light-years better, memory had her avoiding the dish. Risotto, on the other hand, she loved.

On Wednesday night, he brought her a book. It was one of the advance reading copies his agent had sent, a legal thriller that tackled the issue of privacy and had made him think, he said, as many of the others hadn't. He thought she might enjoy it and was interested in her opinion. Would she read it? he asked. Like she would ever say no.

On Thursday night, when the walls of her room were starting to close in, he helped her steal past the nurses' station for a quick trip to the rooftop deck. Her pace was slow, but the freshness of the night justified the effort. She felt that she had never in her life seen so many stars. They seemed to fill the sky in ways that suggested a million worlds beyond.

Friday morning, a full week after the accident and an hour before her discharge, she formally met Dr. Simon Meade from St. Johnsbury. He examined her and removed her stitches. Then he drew up a chair and in a kindly voice broke the news that she would never be able to have a child. "When we reconstruct people's insides like we did yours, their bodies develop scar tissue," he explained. "It gets in the way of conception."

Bree was startled. "No children? Ever?"

"I can't say the chances are zero, but they're pretty slim. You haven't had any yet, have you?"

She shook her head.

"And you're how old?"

"Thirty-three."

"You're less fertile now than you were ten years ago. Put that together with scarring, and you have a problem."

Bree hadn't been thinking about having a child. She hadn't

been feeling desperate about it, hadn't heard any biological clock ticking. So she was surprised when her eyes filled with tears.

"I'm sorry," the doctor said. "This is the worst part of my job. The good news is that you're alive. If you'd been left lying in the snow, you'd have bled to death."

She knew that. And she was grateful. And she really *hadn't* had her heart set on having children.

Still, there was an awful emptiness, a sudden sense of loss.

"In every other respect, you're healing well," the doctor went on. "I agree with Dr. Sealy. No reason why you can't go home. Take it easy for the next few weeks. Add activity a little at a time. Listen to your body. It'll tell you what you can do."

She continued to stare at him through tear-filled eyes.

He rose from the bed, gave her hand a pat, and smiled. "I have to get back to St. Johnsbury. This is a long way to come to make rounds."

She swallowed the lump in her throat.

"Well, then," he said, "good luck to you." He turned toward the door.

"Dr. Meade?" When he looked back, she said, "What if I lie perfectly still?"

He seemed confused.

"If I lie perfectly still, will less scar tissue grow?"

"No. Scarring is a natural part of healing."

"There's no way to prevent it?"

"No."

She swallowed again, took a breath, thought of the benevolent being of light, and felt less alone. It was all right, she reasoned. So she wasn't destined to be a mother. She supposed it made sense. She hadn't grown up in a house full of kids. She didn't have a maternal role model, or even a husband. She wouldn't know what to do with a child of her own. Besides, she didn't want to be tied down, after being finally free after so long.

So fate had simply formalized what her instincts had always known.

She rubbed her eyes with the heels of her hands, took another breath, and smiled at the doctor, who lifted a hand in farewell and turned again toward the door.

That was when she saw the mole on the back of his neck.

Once the breakfast rush at the diner was over, Flash came to the hospital and drove Bree home. She didn't tell him what the doctor had said, didn't see the point, since she didn't know how she felt about it herself. All her rationalization notwithstanding, there was still an unexpected emptiness. So she pushed it from her mind.

The weather helped. The sun was bright and the air warm; the roads were dry. It was the type of autumn day she loved, the type when the smallest pile of raked leaves, heated by the sun, perfumed the air for miles. If the jostling of the Explorer as it barreled along caused her discomfort, it was soothed by the rush of the breeze past her face.

The roads grew progressively familiar. Not a thing had changed while she had been gone, it seemed. The Crowells' rusted Chevy still sat in the tall grasses of the field beside their house, the Dillards' front lawn was still filled with pumpkins for sale, the Krumps' three-year-old triplets still clustered on the big old tire that swung from the sprawling oak at the side of their house.

Everything was just as it had been prior to the snow a week before—just the same, yet different. The trees looked larger, the sun brighter, the colors richer. The smiles of the people they passed were broader, their waves higher. Even Bree's old Victorian seemed less prim as it welcomed her home.

She went up the front walk hugging the bubble bowl that Julia Dean had sent. The few flowers left in it were so feeble that Flash had wanted to leave it behind, but Bree wouldn't hear of it. Julia's arrangement had been the first splash of color she had seen, waking up in her hospital room. Then, it had seemed a link between the world she had glimpsed beyond and the earthly one to which she'd returned. Her need for that link was greater now than ever.

# chapter
# five

Tom was unsure of his place, with Bree suddenly home. Each
time he drove past her house that first day, a different car was
parked there. Talk at the diner revolved around who was sitting
with her when, who was cooking for her when, who was cleaning
for her when. Directly or indirectly, most everyone in town had
a role.

For the first time in years, he thought about his own home-
town, small and so like this one. He hadn't appreciated it then,
but he did now. Having lived in the city, having been one of
those who were too busy—or self-important—to care about a

neighbor's woes, having felt the brunt of isolation during his last few months there, he found it heartwarming to see Panama rally around Bree. A schedule was drawn up to ensure that during those first few days, at least, she was never alone.

No one asked him to take a turn. So he approached the group that surrounded Flash, making final arrangements. Jane Hale had known Bree since childhood, LeeAnn Conti had worked with her for years. Dotty Hale and Emma McGreevy, both a generation above, spoke for the town. Liz Little was simply a friend.

"I'd like to do my part," he said. "I feel responsible for her needing the help."

All six regarded him with eyes that ranged from cautious to cold—a sobering experience for a man who had once had the power to charm by virtue of simply walking into a room.

"Thank you," said Emma, with a curt smile, "but we take care of our own."

He absorbed the rebuff as his due. But it didn't stop him. "I'd like to be considered one of your own."

Emma looked at his fading shiner and the livid line beneath it. "After half a year? I think not. Besides, we don't need help with Bree. We have it all arranged."

"All but the nights," he said, when she would have closed the circle and shut him out. He had overheard enough to know where they stood. "You're still working that out. I can help."

Emma fingered the short strand of pearls that circled her neck. "You wouldn't know what to do."

"Bree says he does," Jane said in a quiet voice.

Dotty scowled at her. "What's there to do in a hospital? This is at home."

"I can help there, too," Tom said.

"Can you cook?" asked Liz.

Emma waved a hand. "No need for him to cook. We have plenty of food."

"It'd be nice if he could heat up what's there."

Emma tried shaking her head. "No matter. He can't stay with her."

Jane dared a soft "Why not?"

"Good *God*, Jane," Dotty flared, "how can you even *ask* that? He said it himself. He's responsible for putting her there."

"It wasn't his fault," offered Flash. "She doesn't blame him."

"Still," Dotty insisted, "looking at him will only remind her of bad things."

"He's famous," said LeeAnn, with a curious glance Tom's way.

Emma grunted. "More like *in*famous. Goodness, LeeAnn, Dotty's been waving those articles in front of your nose for a week now."

"Do you really want Bree to spend the night with a womanizer?" Dotty asked.

"*Alleged* womanizer," Tom corrected. "Just because the tabloids loved writing about me doesn't mean everything they said was true."

Dotty brushed his comment aside. "You can't stay with her. It isn't proper."

"Why not?" Jane asked again.

"Because . . . he's . . . male."

"So's Flash," Liz said, "and he's spending the night."

"Bree's like my sister," Flash reasoned. "I've known her for years."

"So have you," Dotty told her daughter. "You're a selfish one, wanting him there to spare you the work."

"That's not it at all. I *do* want to help. In fact, I can sleep better at her house than at ours. You wake up all the time."

"Do I tell you to get up with me? I do not. It's not *my* fault you sleep so lightly every little noise spooks you. Good *God*, Jane. I'm your mother. You complain about me, you complain about Bree . . ."

Tom saw Julia Dean watching them from a booth. She looked torn, as though she wanted to join the group but didn't dare. What with the way they weren't welcoming him, Tom didn't blame her. What with the way Dotty was going after Jane, he *really* didn't blame her.

"The thing is," he said to end the last, "you all have other things to do during the day. I don't. I can sleep all day if I want.

Look at you, Liz. You can't sleep all day. You have three young kids."

"But I love Bree," Liz said. "She house-sits with our cats whenever we go away, and she never lets me pay her for it. I owe her this."

"Me, too," Tom said, but Emma was moving on, paper and pencil in hand.

"All right. It's Liz tonight, LeeAnn tomorrow night, Flash Sunday, Jane Monday. Abby wants Tuesday night, and then we'll regroup." Throwing a smug look Tom's way, she drew a line across the bottom of the list, and that was that.

But Tom couldn't stay away. He left the diner at eight, saw two cars in Bree's drive, drove past and down the turnpike to the mall, where he rented a movie. Reversing the trip, he arrived back at Bree's shortly after nine. The two cars had been replaced by Liz Little's Suburban. Satisfied that Bree was in capable hands, he went home and put the movie in the VCR. He watched it for half an hour, before turning it off and snatching up the keys to his car.

Bree's Victorian was a behemoth of a house. It was tall and lean, made all the more so by its setting on a rise. *Staid* was one word Tom might have used to describe it, *stark* another. In the absence of a moon, not even the dim lamplight seeping from the lower-floor windows added cheer. The house felt cold. He never would have matched it with Bree.

Climbing the front steps, he crossed the porch to knock softly on the old wood door. After a minute's wait, he gave another knock. He was about to go around to the back, when the door opened.

Having fully expected to see Liz, he was startled to find Bree. She looked so waiflike in the meager porch light, with dark eyes in a pale face, framed by long, dark, damp hair, and the rest of her lost in her huge fleece robe, that something tripped inside him.

"Hey," he half whispered. "I didn't mean to get you up. Where's Liz?"

Bree's voice wasn't much louder than his, though he suspected she had sheer physical weakness to blame. "On the phone. One of the kids is sick. She's talking with Ben." She reached for his arm and drew him in, then closed the door and leaned against it.

He stayed close. "How do you feel?"

"Tired. Friends keep coming. And I'm grateful. But it's hard to say no when they want to talk."

"Go on to bed. I'll talk with Liz."

For an instant, looking up at him, she seemed on the verge of tears, and for the life of him he didn't know what to do. What he wanted to do was hold her, but that didn't seem right. So instead he simply asked, "Are you okay?"

She swallowed, nodded, and eased away from the door. He followed her as far as the bottom of the winding staircase, and then it took everything he had just to watch, instead of walking beside her or even carrying her up. But they weren't at the hospital anymore. This was personal stuff.

When she had reached the top and disappeared down the hall, he looked around. The foyer in which he stood was large and opened to an even larger living room. Furnished in dark woods with frayed fabrics, both areas looked tired. Like the outside of the house, they didn't fit Bree.

Liz Little's voice came from the back of the house. Following the sound, he found himself in a kitchen that was old but functional and clean. Liz had the telephone cord wrapped around her hand and was saying, with what sounded like dwindling patience, "On his forehead. Hold it flat on his forehead until the strip changes color." She paused. "I *know* he won't lie still, but believe me, it's easier doing it this way than the other way." She paused again. "Well, *hold* him there. Come on, Ben," she pleaded, "you're a whole lot stronger than he is. You can immobilize him for two minutes." She listened, pushed a hand through her hair, spotted Tom. She held his gaze while she said, "Yes, I'm *thrilled* that he wants me, but the fact is that I'm not there."

"Go," Tom mouthed. "I'll stay."

Liz declined his offer with the wave of her hand. "No, Ben, he doesn't specifically need me. He needs one of us, and you're there. It's good for him to know that you can take care of him as well as I can." She paused. "Of course you can. You're a great parent. Besides, wasn't that a major reason why we gave up our old jobs and came here, so you could be with the kids more?" Another pause, then a frown and a cry. "I *do* love my kids. I'd be home in a minute if I thought Joey was very sick. He was fine when I left."

When she paused this time, Tom actually heard Ben yelp.

Liz's eyes went wide. "Oh, yuck," she finally said. "All over you?" She made a face. "Okay, sweetheart, sit him in a tepid tub. I'll be there in ten minutes."

She hung up the phone and looked apologetically at Tom. "You don't mind?"

"Not if you don't." He was counting on Liz being more accepting of him than the others. She had been an outsider herself not so long ago. "Bree's gone to bed. I'll just sit around down here."

Liz rummaged in her bag. "There's enough food to feed an army," she said, with a glance at foil-wrapped bundles on the counter. "I'll settle things at home and come back."

"No need. I'm here until the next person shows up."

"That won't be until ten tomorrow morning."

"Ten is fine."

Liz came up with her keys. "The others will kill me."

"Tell you what," Tom said. "Come back at nine, and they'll never know."

She stared at him for a minute. "That's sly."

He didn't say anything.

For another minute she stared, then she opened the back door. "You really wrote those books?"

He nodded.

"How many in all?"

"Six."

"I can't imagine writing one, let alone six."

"Then we're even. I can't imagine cleaning up after a sick kid."

She gave him a grudging smile. "I'll be back tomorrow morning at nine. Thanks."

*  *  *

Tom stood at the base of the front stairs, his hand on the mahogany newel post, his eye on the landing above. He was as unsettled remembering Bree with tears in her eyes as he had been at the time. Wanting to make sure she was all right, he started the climb.

At the top, all was dark. Only when his eyes adjusted did he make out three open doorways. That a fourth was closed was underscored by a pale line of light at its base.

His knock was little more than the brush of knuckles on wood, too soft to disturb sleep if that was where she was. He listened for sound, heard none. Slowly, carefully, he turned the knob and opened the door.

The light came from a small lamp that stood by the side of the bed. Both the lamp and the bed frame were made of wrought iron. Everything else was either white—bedding, draperies, ceilings, walls, and wood—or yellow—throw pillows, lamp shades, and carpet.

The bedroom was smaller than he guessed the others in the house to be, with space for little more than a double bed, a chest of drawers, and a big old upholstered chair. But framed pictures stood on the chest, and books were stacked by the chair, and though the wind chimes hanging at the window were still, they added charm. There were no ruffles or bows, nothing showy or overly feminine. Even the flower arrangement on the dresser, a fresh one with Julia Dean's unmistakable stamp on it, was bright and honest, like Bree.

The quilt was bunched at the bottom of the bed. She lay above it, curled up with her back to the door. Her robe was dark against the sheets, her hair dark against the pillow.

Quietly, he rounded the bed, to find that her eyes were open and sad. They climbed to his and held.

When he sat by her hip and touched her cheek, she closed her eyes. Within seconds her lashes were wet.

He felt the same tripping sensation he had earlier, even stronger now, and suddenly it didn't matter that he wasn't a Panamanian, didn't matter that her needs now weren't for impersonal things like Jell-O, wool socks, or Internet printouts. It didn't matter that he might be crossing a line. He had no choice but to gather her up and let her cry.

Cry Bree did. Tom's chest was the best thing that had happened to her all day. It gave her permission to be weak for a change, made her feel that if she broke down, the world wouldn't end. Crying eased the tension that had been building in her since morning, eased the sorrow she hadn't expected to feel. It eased the confusion of coming home to a house that was the same as before, in a body that wasn't. It eased her fear of a world where anything at all could happen and leave her wondering what was real and what wasn't.

But tears were real. And Tom's chest was real.

She ran out of the first before the second left, but by then she was sleeping too soundly to notice.

LeeAnn drove to Bree's straight from work on Saturday night. By the time Tom arrived an hour later, her boyfriend was brooding on the front steps in the dark. Though Tom had seen the man numerous times at the diner, they had met formally only the week before. Gavin was the mechanic who had declared Tom's Jeep a total loss.

"What's up?" Tom asked.

Gavin grunted. "Nothin' at all."

Guessing that that was the man's gripe in a nutshell, Tom went past him up the steps and across the porch. He had barely knocked on the door when LeeAnn pulled it open, looking ready to do battle. She closed her mouth when she saw Tom instead of Gavin, and glanced uneasily past him to the porch steps.

Tom slipped into the house. "Crossed signals?"

LeeAnn was clearly peeved. "No. He knew I promised to spend the night here. He just isn't happy about it, what with my having a baby-sitter for the night. It won't help that you're here. I told *him* he couldn't come in."

"Why can't he?"

Her cheeks reddened while she searched for an answer. Tom guessed it had to do with sex.

She tipped up her chin. "If you're here to see Bree, she's eating dinner."

"I'm sorry. I didn't mean to interrupt."

"You're not interrupting me. I ate before. I'm just keeping her company." She scowled at Gavin. "He was supposed to tend bar at his uncle's place in Ashmont, but he got the night off at the last minute. I mean, what am I supposed to do? I'm already committed."

"Bree will probably be going to bed soon."

"But I have to be here in case she wakes up and feels sick."

"Do you think she will?"

LeeAnn thought about that. "No. She told me she slept well last night." The look she shot at Gavin this time was softer. "I mean, it's not like she really needs me. I didn't even have to bring food from the diner, there's so much here already." She darted a quick look at Tom. "How long did you want to stay?"

Tom shrugged. "Ten minutes, ten hours. You tell me."

She thought for another minute, then shook her head. "I shouldn't." But she looked tempted. "My ex's mother has the kids. She's probably already put them to bed. She may be asleep herself. It'd be silly to wake her." She drew her teeth over her lips. "I have to work tomorrow." She tacked on, "I could use a good night's sleep."

Tom understood perfectly.

LeeAnn alternated hesitant glances between him and Gavin. "Maybe I could go out for a little while. I mean, if you're going to be here anyway."

"Sure," Tom said, with an innocent shrug.

"I mean, what would be *really* good is if I could get some sleep and come back later."

"What time would that be?"

She dipped her head to the side in a timid shrug of her own. "I don't know. One, two. I mean, three would be really great."

"I slept most of the day, so I'll probably still be up then. I have a movie. You could watch it with me."

"Well, if you're only watching a movie, I could sleep longer," she said, confidentially now. "Like until four or five. *Six* would be *really* awesome. I mean, I could be back here by seven, no questions asked. Bree would *never* be up before seven. She isn't a morning person. She doesn't get to the diner before noon. She likes taking her time waking up."

"Then it'd be pretty safe for you to come back at seven."

"For sure." She paused, looking at him askance. "Did you really break Courteney Cox's heart, like the *Star* said you did?"

"I've never met Courteney Cox."

"That's good. Because if you broke her heart, I couldn't trust you with Bree. Bree is too nice to be hurt." A sound came from the porch. Her eyes flew there, then shot back to Tom. In a voice that held a hint of conspiracy, she whispered, "So if I tell Bree I'm going out for a couple of hours, you'll cover for me till I get back?"

Tom was glad to do it.

He had a head start Sunday night. Right about the time he was finishing off the pasta special at the diner, in short order Jillie went home sick and the grillman burned his hand. Flash, who had wanted to leave early to stay with Bree, slid in across from Tom.

"You were going over there anyway, weren't you?" he asked, in a voice low enough not to carry beyond the booth.

Tom nodded.

"Think you could stay till I get there? It shouldn't be later than ten."

It was actually fifteen minutes before ten. By ten, Flash was stretched out on the floor in front of the television in Bree's den, snoring softly.

"So much for the movie I thought was riveting," Tom remarked, though he wasn't hurting any. He took satisfaction in seeing that Bree was wide awake, looking rested and riveted indeed. Each day, her face was regaining more of its natural color, and while she still moved with care, she was greatly improved.

The den had been a welcome discovery, the only room other than Bree's bedroom with her personal stamp. Filled with a large, cushiony sofa and chairs, a low coffee table that she claimed she ate dinner on more often than not, and shelves of books, it was a room after his own heart.

Bree looked away from the movie long enough to say, "Let's give him a few minutes and see if he wakes up."

The snoring grew louder.

She leaned down from the sofa, jiggled his shoulder, and gave a gentle "Shhh."

Flash turned his head, and the snoring stopped. It resumed with a vengeance moments later.

Bree sent Tom a beseechful look, so sweet it made him laugh. "Don't look at *me*," he said. *"I'm* not the one making the noise."

"Why do men do this? Snoring in bed is one thing, but doing it in a room full of people? My father used to turn on the radio in the living room and snore to the music. It ruined it for me." She leaned sideways. "Flash!" She gave his shoulder a sharp jab. "Wake up!"

Tom felt a moment's sympathy for Flash when he bolted up, looking dazed. "What?"

"Go home," she said, with affection. "Sleep in your own bed."

He ran a hand over his face. "No. I'm okay. I'll just go in the other room and stretch out on the sofa. A few minutes is all I need."

"This is ridiculous, Flash. There's no need for you to spend the night here. There's no need for *anyone* to spend the night." She rubbed his shoulder where she had jabbed it. "The thought is sweet. But I'm so much better."

"You're still in pain."

"Much less now."

"What if it gets worse? What if you get up in the middle of the night and pass out?"

"I won't. Please, Flash? I love you for wanting to help, but what'll make me feel best is if you go home and sleep so I can finish watching this movie in peace. Besides, Tom's here."

Tom sat a little straighter, felt a little better.

Flash wasn't so happy. "That's why I have to be. Dotty would have a fit if she heard I left you two alone."

"Like he's taking advantage of me. Come on, Flash."

"I'll never hear the end of it."

"Are *you* going to tell her?" Bree asked.

"Me? Christ, no."

"Well, I'm not, and Tom won't. So please, go home to bed."

"You're kicking me out?"

"Yes!" She softened the rebuff with a gentle smile. "I'm tired of people being here all the time. I like having my house to myself."

"Tom's staying."

"Tom's different."

"How?"

Bree seemed at a momentary loss. Tom held his breath while she searched for an answer. Finally, she tipped up her chin and quite logically said, "Tom's recovering, too. He rests when I rest, so his sitting with me kills two birds with one stone. Besides, he'll leave if I ask, and he won't be hurt. Easy. No hassle."

"I'm easy, too," Flash said.

She smiled. "I know. Know what you can *really* do to help?"

"What?"

"Get them to cancel the night shift. Please?"

Bree was relieved when the stream of visitors slowed. She wasn't used to being coddled. Once, she would have wished for it with all her might. Now she found it stifling.

She liked stretching out on the sofa without making excuses for not going to bed, liked getting up without apologizing for not sleeping longer. She liked walking in the backyard without someone telling her that it was too cool or, worse, going out there with her and tainting the fresh air with human speech.

Tom understood. He was as pleased as she to sit out back on the trunk of a fallen maple and listen to the rap of a woodpecker, the hoot of an owl, the rustle of squirrels in the dry autumn leaves. When he spoke, it was in the same hushed voice she used, and he was just as good when they were inside. As he had in the hospital, he sensed what she needed without having to ask. He talked when she was in the mood for talking, opened a book and read when she grew tired, made tea when she was thirsty, made himself scarce when she needed time alone. He didn't rush to make her bed the minute she left it, didn't balk when the movie she wanted to watch began at eleven at night, and he made her a breakfast of sweet apple pie with a wedge of sharp cheddar—melted—a totally indulgent, thoroughly enjoyable treat that none of her other caretakers would have allowed.

As relationships went, it was the most unusual one she had ever had. They didn't talk about his books. They didn't talk about her tears. Many a time they sat silently, each of them reading, sharing the occasional look and smile. She knew little about him, save what she had read. She had no idea what he wanted from her or where he was headed. Still, she felt closer to him for the silence, and for all the other nonverbal things that he did. He calmed her, like the being of light she still saw in her dreams. He made her feel cared for, even loved.

Talk around town, passed on to her like little get-well gifts, with varying degrees of delight, was that he was dangerous, but she had never felt that. To the contrary. He was so perfect for her that he seemed unreal. And that was okay. Something had happened that night on the operating table, something that said life was too short to analyze things too much, something that relaxed her and made her see and do and feel things that weren't entirely sensible.

So what if Tom had a whole other life waiting for him in New York? So what if his feelings started and stopped at guilt? So *what?*

Falling for Tom wasn't sensible. But it sure felt good.

# chapter
## six

Tom made a point of eating at the diner every night before going to Bree's. He wanted to be seen as a regular there, wanted to be accepted, wanted to feel he was part of the town.

Funny. Belonging hadn't been something he had thought much about when he chose Panama. He had sought a place to hide in while he figured out what to do with the rest of his life. Panama had fit the bill, first and foremost, because it wasn't New York. If someone had suggested that he was actively seeking small-town flavor, he would have denied it. He had grown up in a small town and left at the first opportunity, thinking bigger was better.

He had to rethink that now. Panamanians seemed perfectly happy, perfectly content, perfectly intelligent and enterprising, even sophisticated in a modern, media-driven way. The town wasn't poverty-stricken. Anyone who wanted to get out could get out. That so few did said something.

He thought about it as he sat in his booth day after day, while the townsfolk mingled comfortably among themselves.

He also thought about the surprising relief he felt now that his identity was known. It was nice not to have to avert his eyes or hide behind a three-day stubble, nice not to have to fear discovery. Not that anyone here seemed impressed by who he was. Glances his way were few and far between.

He thought his ego would mind, even just a little. That it didn't was a sign of how far he had come. But then, being ignored in as close-knit a town as Panama was deliberate. It told him that people were fully aware of what he was doing, and were watching and waiting.

By the time he was into his second week of spending nights at Bree's, the waiting ended. He began having visitors to his booth.

It started simply enough, with Sam, Dave, Andy, and Jack—all local boys, Bree's contemporaries and friends—shuffling over on their way out the door. They loomed over him, four solid men made more solid by layers of November clothing and more imposing by the earnestness of their expressions.

"We hear you've been at Bree's a lot," said Andy, whose experience in sales at his family's tackle store apparently made him the designated speaker. "She's a friend of ours. We'll be checking up on her to make sure she's all right. We thought you oughta know that."

Before Tom could react, they shuffled off.

Eliot Bonner stayed longer. The following day, after eating with Emma and Earl, he slid in with his coffee cup, facing Tom. "Saw your car at Bree's again last night," he said. "Is somethin' going on that I should know about?"

No beating around the bush, Tom thought, and he said, "That depends. We played backgammon and watched TV. Are there town ordinances against either of those?"

"No. Can't say there are. So are you gonna keep going over there?"

Tom waited only long enough to make a show of giving his answer some thought. "For a while. She doesn't seem to mind."

"Maybe she's star struck."

He smiled at that. "I doubt it." Bree never mentioned his work.

"Are you planning to stay in town?"

He had given himself a year. Now he sensed he might need longer. "I have a house here. I'm registered to vote here."

"Doesn't mean a thing," Eliot said. "What keeps you going to Bree's? Is it guilt?"

"No." It might have been at first, but that was gone.

"Then what?"

He thought about the comfort he felt when he was with her. It was honest, pure, even uplifting, if he wanted to be lyrical about it. It was also addictive. He was coming to depend on seeing Bree each day.

To Eliot, he simply said, "I like Bree."

"So where's it headed?"

He was beginning to ask himself the same question. "Nowhere for now. She's a long way from being recovered."

"Nah. Knowing Bree, she'll be back here in two weeks, tops. So I'm warning you. Be careful."

"Careful?"

"What you do with Bree. She's a nice girl. Know what I mean? I don't want anything happening to her now that things are finally looking up. Boy." He shook his head. "Her father was a long time dying." He sniffed in a breath, leaned forward, confided, "He was a tough one, Haywood Miller was. Not abusive. Nothing physical. But one cold son of a bitch. The one who could have made all the difference to Bree was the mother, but she didn't want any part of either of them. If I'd had *my* way, I'd have gone after her for abandonment. Course, I wasn't the chief then. I was still working at the lumber mill, right there alongside Haywood, except for the year he was gone. It was a month after he came back before any of us knew he'd brought a baby with him. He hadn't been much of a talker before he left, but after, he was even worse. We only learned about the baby because he had to take it to the hospital when it got sick."

"Why the secret?"

"Go ask him. He was a strange bird. The miracle of it is that Bree's so normal. She's got a strength in her most people don't." He raised a warning finger. "So don't mess with it, you hear?" He sat back. As an afterthought, he took a drink of his coffee.

"How did her father die?" Tom asked.

Still holding his coffee cup, Eliot slid out of the booth. "Terminal ill humor," he said and stalked off.

Tom was finishing his own coffee when Martin Sprague took Eliot's place. The tired look that Martin always wore was even more so than usual. With his face drawn and his eyebrows lowered, he was all business.

"I think you should know that I handle Bree's legal affairs," he said, without prelude.

Tom was taken aback. Not sure how to respond, he settled for a polite "Yes?"

"So if you're broke because you spent it all," Martin warned, "don't go looking for money from her. She doesn't have any."

"I'm not broke."

"You wouldn't be the first to think she's loaded, coming from that family, but I handled Haywood's legal affairs and his father's before him, so I know. There's no money left. None."

"Was there once?"

"Once. Osgood Miller owned some of the best hardwood forest for miles around. He was good with the trees, but he didn't have an ounce of business sense. When he should've been building his own lumberyard so that he could make the most of what he cut, he was putting his money into foolish things. Most of it was gone before Bree was born. The rest went after. Haywood wasn't any better with money than Ozzie. Between them, they lost the land, the trucks, the name. The house was all Bree got, and it's a sad old pile of wood."

Tom had stopped seeing the frayed parts. Bree divided her time between the bedroom and the den, so he did, too. Both of those rooms were brighter.

"It looks okay to me," he said.

"Look closer," Martin advised, pushing himself out of the booth. "Walls are rotting, furnace is dying. She's going to have to put big money into the place before long." With a final look, he said, "So you'd best stay where you are."

If that meant staying at the bungalow and away from Bree, Tom couldn't comply. The time he spent with her was more rewarding than anything he had done in years. When she smiled, or laughed, or looked up at him with a face full of warmth, he felt like a million bucks, so much so that he started staying longer. Rather than leaving after breakfast, he lingered into the morning. Rather than waiting until nine at night to return, he began going straight from the diner. He took her for drives when she was feeling shut in, took her for walks through the backyard leaves when she wanted exercise, took her to the general store for soft-serve Oreo fudge frozen yogurt when she had a sudden sharp craving. Eliot was right. She was recovering fast.

At the end of her second week at home, he took her to the diner. Visiting royalty couldn't have received a more rousing welcome. She was escorted from booth to booth, from one seat of honor to the next. Superfluous, Tom fell into the background.

Emma found him there. "Could I have a minute, please?" she asked, and gestured toward the empty booth at the far end of the row. As soon as they were seated, she faced him straight out and said, "I'm worried about Bree."

"She's healing well."

"That's not what worries me. People are starting to talk."

"About . . . ?"

"Bree. And you."

Surprise, surprise. "Ah."

"You spend too much time with her. Her friends are feeling left out. I can't tell you how many come up to me to ask if I know what's going on."

Tom was curious. "What do you say?"

"What *can* I say? *I* don't know what's going on. What *is* going on?"

He was trying to figure it out himself. All he felt safe saying was, "Nothing sinister."

"Maybe not, but your presence is putting a wedge between Bree and her friends, and that's an awful thing to happen. One day you'll be gone, and then where will Bree be? She needs her friends. They're her family, now that poor Haywood is gone." Her eyes grew distant. She fingered her pearls in dismay. "Poor Haywood. All those years, and he never recovered." She refocused on Tom. "She was a free spirit, Bree's mother was, and he fell for her hard. When he came back without her, he was the shadow of a man."

"I was under the impression he was the shadow of a man before."

Emma frowned. "Who told you that? That's not true at all. Haywood might have been quiet, but he stood on his own two feet. He was always proper and polite. He never missed a town meeting. He went to church every Sunday."

Some of the worst scoundrels did, Tom mused.

"Poor Haywood," Emma went on, lost in it now. "He didn't have an easy time, with a mother like that. Hannah Miller was a rigid woman. She gave new meaning to the words *proper* and *polite.* Long after the rest of the women eased up, she was still wearing dresses that buttoned up to her chin. Everything around her was neat as a pin. Everything was regimented. She was the kind of woman who made the rest of us grateful for our own mothers."

"Did she help raise Bree?"

"She had to. Poor Haywood couldn't have done it on his own, what with needing to work to earn money for food. There wasn't any day care center in the basement of the church in those days.

Ozzie was dead, or just as good as dead, so the burden of it all was on poor Haywood." She shook her head. "What that woman did to him . . ."

Tom was about to ask whether she was talking about Hannah Miller or Bree's mother, when Dotty materialized at the booth. As sisters went, there was little physical resemblance between the two women. Though the younger of the two, Dotty was taller, thinner, and grayer than Emma, who never failed to look the part of town leader with her stylish suit, her light makeup, her hair that was a tad too auburn.

Their differences were exaggerated now by Dotty's scowl. "What are you telling him, Emma?"

"I'm just giving him a history lesson," Emma said, sliding out of the booth. "Don't get all ruffled up, sister."

"You're the one always telling me *I* talk too much."

"You do," Emma declared, and walked off.

Dotty glared after her, then, still glaring, turned back to Tom. "Don't ask me why we voted *her* town meeting moderator. She's been insufferable ever since."

"How long's it been?" Tom asked. He had arrived in town shortly before the last town meeting but hadn't bothered to go. He wondered if Emma's election was one of the things he had missed.

Apparently it wasn't.

"Eight years," Dotty replied, "and each one of those it gets worse. She thinks she can stick her nose into everyone else's business, sitting there with Earl and Eliot each and every day. John must be turning over in his *grave*. He wanted his wife in his home. He'd never have let her do what she does if he'd been alive. If he knew the *half* of it, he'd lock her up." She slid into the booth. Her manner sweetened. "What was she telling you?"

"She was talking about poor Haywood," Tom said.

Dotty rolled her eyes. "Poor Haywood, my foot. She always had her eye on him was her problem, but he couldn't talk his way out of a paper bag, much less court a woman, so she married John, and even *then* she kept an eye on Haywood. Did she tell you he was handsome?"

"No."

"That's a surprise. Usually it's the first thing she says. Well, he *was* handsome, I have to admit. Handsome and dull. And drab. And sour. Even *he* knew there was something wrong with his life. That's why he left that year. He went down to Boston to see about getting work there. Then he met that woman."

"Bree's mother?"

"What other? He never used her name, once he was back here. She couldn't have been more than twenty. Haywood, he was nearing forty. He happened to run into her in a sandwich shop one day, and that was all it took." She threw up a hand. "He was gone. Crazy in love. But a love like that never lasts, not between a woman so young and spirited and a man with his feet rooted so deep in New England soil. He needed to come back here to live, and she couldn't do that, so he came back alone, he and Bree." Her voice went higher. "Can you imagine turning your back on a baby that way?"

Tom, who knew well how to play devil's advocate, imagined that there might be situations in which walking away from a baby was the most compassionate thing to do, particularly when the baby had a father and a home. He didn't know enough about Bree's mother's situation to judge one way or the other.

"So what happened?" Dotty asked, sounding affronted. "People talked. They talked when he came back to town without a word as to where he'd been and what he'd done, and they talked when they learned there was a baby and no wife. They talked about that child from the time she was old enough to walk down the street by herself, and they *still* talk, when you get them going. So"—she looked him dead in the eye—"that's why what you're doing to her is wrong."

He drew his head back. "What am *I* doing to her?"

"It doesn't matter. That's my point. They'll talk if you give them the slightest cause, and she deserves better."

Tom couldn't help himself. "Maybe you could tell them not to talk. Maybe you could set an example. You know, live and let live?"

Dotty straightened. "Are you saying that *I* talk? I'm no worse than anyone else in this town. My goodness, if *I* don't talk, the others will anyway, and then all the *wrong* things will be heard." She scooted across the bench and out of the booth. "You have no call to attack me. I was only giving you friendly advice." With a righteous look, she was gone.

Jane Hale caught up with him in the parking lot when he went out to bring the car around for Bree. She glanced back to make sure they were alone, pulled her coat tighter around her with fingers whose nails were bitten short, and said in a quiet voice, "I'm sorry about my mother. She tells herself she's doing the right thing. Don't let her put you off."

Tom smiled. What Jane lacked in looks she more than made up for in gentleness. It was hard not to like her. "I won't. She only did what other people have been doing all week."

"They're worried, is all. They like Bree. So do I. She's my oldest friend. I mean, she isn't old, but we've been friends a long time."

He indicated his understanding with a nod.

She glanced back again, drew her collar up higher against the brisk air. "We became friends in first grade. She was lonely because her grandmother kept her apart, and I was lonely because, well, my mother was always right *there,* so it was better sometimes not to have friends at the house." She looked down, then behind her, then straight at him again. "I'm not complaining. My mother loves me. I wish Bree had that."

"Didn't her father love her?"

"I suppose. But he was unhappy. Maybe he wanted to be a good parent but didn't know how. Bree's mother must have been the colorful one. Bree had to get her spirit from someone, and it wasn't from him." She was instantly contrite. "I shouldn't say that, his being dead and all." She paused, then blurted, "But I remember him, and he was grim. Bree's mother was probably the most exciting thing that ever happened to him. It's like he spent the rest of his life mourning her."

"Is that what Bree thinks?"

Jane nodded. "We used to talk about it. She always wondered

about her mother. She used to imagine all kinds of things, mostly pretty things, flattering things."

"Didn't her father tell her anything?"

"Her grandmother wouldn't let them talk about her, and after Hannah died, well, I guess the course was set. Haywood got quieter and quieter and more and more dark. Bree was keeping house for him and pretty much raising herself. She started working part-time at the diner when she was fifteen, just to get away. She wanted to be with people who talked and smiled and laughed. The diner was more of a home to her than the house on South Forest." She dug her hands into her pockets. "Here I am, jabbering on like my mother."

"There's a difference," Tom said, which was as close as he would come to criticizing Dotty in front of Jane. "Did Bree's mother ever try to reach her?"

"No."

"Did Bree ever try to hunt her down?"

"No. By the time Haywood died, she'd lost interest."

Tom thought about the Bree he was coming to know. "She's remarkable to have overcome all that."

"Yes." Jane seemed suddenly less concerned about who might see her in the parking lot than about what she wanted Tom to know. "That's why people are protective of her."

"I understand."

"They're worried she'll come to depend on you and then you'll leave."

"She's getting more independent by the day."

"She may be more vulnerable because of the accident."

"Because of her near-death experience, you mean?"

Jane nodded.

"I'll keep that in mind," he said.

"Jane!" The voice was distant but definitely Dotty's.

Jane gasped. With a last, pleading look that made him envious of the loyalty she felt for Bree, she slipped off between the cars so that she wouldn't be anywhere near Tom when her mother tracked her down.

*     *     *

Flash had his say when he stopped by to visit Bree several days later. Tom had been reading in the den, while Bree napped on the sofa there. She opened unfocused eyes at the sound of the back door opening and closing. He tossed another log on the fire and motioned her to stay where she was.

"Just as well," Flash said, when Tom explained. "I have to talk to you alone." He set a foil-wrapped bundle on the counter. "Lasagna, with sausage and extra cheese. She needs fattening up."

Tom's hand went to his stomach. Several day before, it had been an extra-rich fettuccine Alfredo, a few days before that, a thick-gravied beef stew. When Bree refused to eat either, he was the one who ended up stuffed.

"It's still warm," Flash went on. "If you use it for dinner, all it'll need is ten minutes in a hot oven. Put what's left over in the fridge. It'll be even better tomorrow." Bracing himself against the counter, he looked at Tom. "I'm not here because of me. I want you to know that. I don't think you're so bad, and besides, Bree's been taking care of herself for a long time with regard to everything else, so I'm sure she can take care of herself with regard to this, too. The problem is, being so close to Bree and all, I don't hear the end of it. Half the town's on my back to learn what I can."

Tom leaned against the enamel sink and folded his arms. "I'm not sure what's left that the others haven't asked, but you're welcome to give it a shot."

"You want to make fun of us, go ahead, but you ought to know that what's happening here is highly unusual."

"My helping Bree? Isn't that what this town is about? If I weren't here right now, someone else from town would be."

"No. Bree wouldn't have had that. Remember when she told me to cancel the nighttime detail? That was the Bree this town knows, the independent-to-a-fault Bree. Her letting you hang around is not normal, and don't tell me she needs you to fetch and carry, because she's perfectly capable of doing that for herself. More*over,*" he said, with gusto, "this is the first time since I've known her that she's had a man in this house."

Tom was startled but pleased. "No kidding?"

"Don't get me wrong. She isn't some shrinking violet. She's had relationships with men. But none of those has ever stayed here one night, let alone however many you have."

"Sixteen," Tom put in.

"Christ. Are you paying *rent?*"

"No, and for what it's worth, I sleep on the sofa while she's up in her bed."

"No matter," Flash said. "Bree likes her space." He frowned. "Maybe it's different since she isn't coming to work. She has a lot of people there. Here she doesn't. So she's lonely. You know?"

Tom didn't point out that she continued to choose his company over that of others who offered to come. "Tell me. Who has she dated in town?"

"No one," was Flash's automatic response. Then, as though the temptation to be the one to tell was too much to resist, he said, "At least not since I've been here. I heard she and Curtis Lamb were a number in high school, but there hasn't been anyone local since then."

Tom waited, then asked, "That's it? Just Curtis Lamb?"

"From Panama."

Again Tom waited.

And again it was as if Flash couldn't resist. "Men are always coming to the diner from one place or another. They pass through once a week, once a month. She had a thing for a while with a trucker, and for a while after that with a computer salesman, but she never brought them back here. It was kind of a rule she had. They were both good-looking guys, too, both love-'em-and-leave-'em types. She wanted to be the one doing the loving and leaving."

"You make her sound hardhearted."

"No. She just knows how to protect herself."

"If she knows how to protect herself, why are you all so worried about me?" Tom asked.

"Because she lowered the bridge and let you in. So now people are wondering why you're still here and how long you're planning to stay."

"Ah," Tom said.

"What does that mean?"

It meant that Tom didn't know the answers. He had never felt as innocent an attraction to a woman as he felt toward Bree. Hell, he hadn't even kissed her. "Just . . . 'ah.'"

"What does *that* mean?"

"Hi, Flash," Bree said from the door. She crossed to him, slipped an arm around his waist, and kissed his cheek. "How's my favorite boss today?"

Flash glowered. "Lousy. I tried to do the payroll and screwed up the figures. I need you, Bree. When are you coming back?"

Julia Dean phoned Tom at home. She identified herself, apologized for disturbing him, then said, "I missed Bree's visit to the diner the other day. Listening to people talk about it was a little confusing. One said she looked good, another said she was pale. One said she moved like she hurt, another said no way would anyone know what had happened. You see her all the time. You'd know, more than they would. How is she?"

Tom heard genuine concern. "She's much better."

"Really?"

"Really."

She breathed a sigh of what sounded like genuine relief. "That's good. I was worried."

"She loves the flowers you send." New arrangements were delivered each week. "They have a special place on her bureau, so she can see them when she wakes up. You ought to stop over sometime. She'd like that."

Tom heard genuine pleasure in Julia's reply. "Well, she'll be back in the diner before long. I'll see her there. Will you give her my best until then?"

Tom did it again, anticipated Bree's wishes and made them come true. Just when she was itching to see the inside of the place where he lived when he wasn't with her, he invited her over.

"The house isn't much to see," he warned, pulling in under the carport, but she disagreed. Just as she had known, the bungalow had charm. The kitchen opened to a breakfast room, dining room, and screened porch, all overlooking a stone terrace. There was a large family room and a larger living room and, up one flight, three bedrooms and two baths. The ceilings were lower than hers, the wooden floor planks wider and pegged, the hearth of fieldstone and raised.

The fact that nearly every room held cartons Tom hadn't unpacked, and that he hadn't done any decorating, and that there wasn't a single family picture in sight, told her he was unsettled, neither here nor there, unsure of who he was and where he was headed. From the looks of it, he could fill a U-Haul in an hour and be gone from town ten minutes later.

That thought made her uneasy. It sent a different message from the one she usually received, one of a man who was staying right where he was. When he was with her at her house, he was committed. She had been with enough men to know.

Tom was hooked, for now at least, and so, God help her, was she.

When he took her by the hand and led her from room to room, the physical connection lessened the forlorn feeling of the house. It disappeared completely when he led her outside.

"This is what I really wanted you to see," he said, and instantly she understood. Just beyond the terrace rose the sound of the brook. It lured them across a lawn covered with dry, snapping leaves, down a slope roughened by tree roots, and over a border of pebbles. The brook itself was an undulating swath that varied in width from three feet to six, and in depth from two inches to several dozen. Fall rain, added to their one major storm and a handful of night snows, kept the current moving. Clear water sped over rocky clusters whose colors ran from ivories to mossy greens, blues, and grays. Though clouds covered the sun, the sway of dappling evergreens gave the water sparkle.

Bree put her palms together. "A magical place."

"Maybe."

"Definitely," she said, lowering herself to a large rock.

"Tired?"

"No. I just want to look."

"There's even better looking upstream a little way. Want to try it?"

She answered by pushing herself right back to her feet and leading the way. It wasn't far. The instant she turned a bend, she saw the falls. They were minifalls, really, tumbling little more than four feet, but all the sweeter for their size. Bundles of mud, sticks, and stones at either end suggested beavers at work. On the shore, perfectly set for viewing, was a bench.

"I found it the day I came to look at the house," Tom said. "Look at the worn spots on the seat. The Hubbards must have spent hours here, maybe even whoever owned the place before them. It looks ancient."

Bree ran a hand over the weathered wood in awe, then turned and fit her backside to the indentation on the left. Stretching an arm over the bench arm nearest her, she took a deep breath and grinned up at Tom.

He sat down on her right, stretched an arm over the bench arm on his side, took a deep breath, and grinned right back.

Bree took a second deep breath, then a third. She looked up at the fir fronds above them, then across the brook into the forest. The hardwoods were largely bare. What few leaves still clung to their limbs were curled there, faded and dry. Evergreens swelled around them as though freed for the first time since spring.

In that instant, she felt invincible. In that instant, she chose to believe. She was healthy, Tom was devoted, life held the promise of love and three wishes.

"I used to hate fall," she said. "I hated it when the trees lost their leaves. I always thought it was a time of death."

"You see death differently now."

"Uh-huh," she said, and unexpectedly, her throat went tight. She didn't know of another man who would let her talk, much less hear her, the way Tom did. He was special. Very, very special.

"Do you think about it much?" he asked.

Her near-death experience. "Uh-huh." She thought about it more and more as she began doing those things she had done before the accident, like driving a car, paying Flash's bills, taking walks in the woods. Everything was the same, yet nothing was.

"I would, too," he said. "I do, actually. I think about what I'd be feeling if I were in your shoes."

She spent a minute loosening the knot in her throat, then asked, "What would you be feeling?"

He took a breath that expanded his chest. "Regrets. For missed opportunities."

She didn't want to think of his other life, the one with "unsettled" written all over it. But that life was part of Tom, and she was feeling strong, feeling *invincible*. So she said, "*You* missed opportunities?"

"For the things that counted." He took a quicker, lighter breath. "I'd also be feeling hope. Like I'm just beginning the rest of my life and can do things differently this time."

The look he gave her brought the lump back to her throat. It stayed there when he threw an arm around her shoulders and drew her close.

"I'm not leaving, Bree," he said.

Wanting to believe, wanting to believe so badly, she closed her eyes. He smelled the way he looked, clean and male and outdoorsy, a Vermont man now with his wool jacket open over flannel, over thermal, over just a glimpse of warm, hairy skin. He wore his jeans low and slim, like the best of the Panamanians. Only his running shoes set him apart.

*I'm not leaving, Bree.*

Nestling against him, she felt something bright touch her eyelids. Cracking them open, she squinted up at the spot where a single brilliant ray of sun breached clouds and trees. It was only an instant before it was gone, but that was enough.

She was invincible. She was in love.

# chapter
# seven

"If you had three wishes, what would they be?" Bree asked, looking from one to another of her boothmates, Liz to LeeAnn to Jane. Her laptop was closed, several hours of catch-up bookkeeping done.

"Three wishes?" Jane asked unsurely.

"Dream stuff?" Liz asked hopefully.

"I know what I'd ask for," LeeAnn announced. "First, I'd wish for money—oh, maybe a million dollars. Then I'd wish for a yacht, I mean, like a big one with beautiful bedrooms and a crew to serve *me* food. Then I'd wish for a prince."

Jane grimaced. "A prince?"

"A real one. Doesn't have to be a major one. But real. I want a tiara."

"A tiara." Liz sighed. "That's sweet. But I wouldn't wish for that."

"What would you wish for?" Bree asked, just as Liz's Joey scampered up. He gave his mother a huge grin, squealed, turned, and raced back to the other end of the diner.

"A nanny," Liz said. "But not just any nanny. Mary Poppins, so I wouldn't feel so awful when Ben and I close the office door and go to work."

"That's only one wish," LeeAnn said. "What else?"

Liz thought for a minute. "A time-share in the Caribbean. With airline tickets there for the next fifteen years. And a beach for the kids. That's all one wish."

"What's the third?"

Liz grinned. "Thick curly hair. I've always wanted that."

Bree wouldn't have made curly hair one of her own wishes. She turned to Jane, whose thick straight hair was her single greatest asset.

"I like my hair," Jane said.

Bree laughed at the echo of her thoughts. "What would you wish for?"

"A trip to Disneyland."

LeeAnn shot up a hand. "Me, too. Make that one of mine. Disneyland with my kids."

"Not me," Liz drawled, as Joey returned. He was either skipping or galloping, hard to tell what, with his legs so small and his diaper so big. When Liz made a grab for him, he shrieked unintelligibly, whirled around, and ran off. "But I'd pay Mary Poppins to take my kids there for me."

Bree watched Joey for a fascinated minute before returning to Jane. "Why Disneyland?"

"Because I think it'd be fun. I always wanted to go." She didn't have to say that life with Dotty wasn't fun, or that Dotty left Panama only when she absolutely, positively had to. Those were givens.

"Okay," Bree said. "Disneyland. What else?"

With surprisingly little pause, Jane said, "I'd wish for a scholarship to art school."

Liz gave her a curious smile. "No kidding?"

Bree should have guessed it. Even without formal training, Jane was an artist. She designed all the church flyers and calligraphed all the town notices. Her work was such a staple in Panama that it was largely taken for granted.

"What's the third?" LeeAnn asked.

Jane swallowed. "Courage. I'd wish for courage."

No one spoke. Bree, who knew that for Jane, courage meant freedom, gave her friend's hand a squeeze. "You can wish for that," she whispered.

"Like the lion in *The Wizard of Oz*," LeeAnn crowed, then turned to Bree. "What about you?"

"Me?"

"What would your three wishes be?" Liz asked, narrowing her eyes. "Wait a minute. I recall your refusing to make a wish when you blew out the candles on your birthday cake last year. What was it you said, that wishes couldn't compete with elbow grease? So why the sudden interest in them?"

Bree shrugged and said lightly, "I don't know. An idle mind. You know. It's kind of fun to think about. No big thing, really."

"So what would yours be?" Jane asked.

"First," LeeAnn teased, "you'd wish to be back at work."

Bree glanced at the computer. "I already am." She had been in for a few hours every afternoon that week.

"You haven't waitressed yet. You'd wish for that, because you miss it so much."

"I do. I miss seeing everyone."

Flash appeared from nowhere. "Your wish is granted. I'm putting you on the schedule for light hours next week. Can you handle it?"

She was handling long walks, driving a car, doing the books. Waitressing was the next step, and a good thing it was. She feared she was becoming too dependent on Tom. "I can."

"Thank you." He stared at LeeAnn. "I need *someone* who'll work, instead of sitting around talking all day."

"I'm coming," LeeAnn said, but the minute he left, she turned expectantly to Bree.

So did Liz. "I bet you'd wish for a new car, one that would take you for miles without fading out like your old one does. If you had a new car, you could drive to California. You told me you wanted to do that."

She had wanted it once. Her father had mentioned that her mother had come from there, and Bree had imagined looking her up. But she didn't know if her mother was anywhere near California now, much less how to find out. Besides, right now there was plenty to keep her in Panama.

"What about Tom?" asked Jane, with intuitive precision. "Would you wish for him?"

"I would, if I were you," LeeAnn said.

"LeeAnn!" Flash hollered.

She shot him a look, grumbled something about wishing for longer breaks, and slid out of the booth. Joey wormed into her place and tucked his head against Liz, who cradled him close and asked, "So would you wish for Tom?"

Bree made a noncommittal face.

"You like him," Jane said.

"What's not to like?" Bree asked.

Liz was suddenly sober. "Plenty, says the grapevine. He goes through money like water. He has a wicked temper. He breaks contracts."

"The grapevine knows all that firsthand?" Bree asked. No answer was necessary. "Firsthand, I know that he's always kept his word to me. If he says he's coming over, he comes over. He's never lost his temper, never even come close. And he doesn't waste his money. I was with him when he bought his new truck. He'd done research and knew what the dealer's cost was. He was patient but firm with the salesman, so he got a great deal. Besides, I don't know what I'd have done without him these past few weeks."

"How long do you think he'll stay in Panama?" Jane asked.

Bree didn't know.

"More to the point," Liz said, "do you want him to stay? That's what a wish is about."

"I think he cares about you," Jane said.

Liz arched a brow. "He spends enough time at your house. It really is remarkable, considering who he is. Think about it. You have a world-famous author, who just happens to be gorgeous, sleeping over every night." Her brow went higher in speculation. Then she caught herself, pressed her fingertips to her mouth in self-chiding, and held them off to the side. "Not my business."

Bree looked at Joey, who was all warm and cozy, with his thumb in his mouth and his eyes half closed, and felt an unexpected pang of envy. She raised her eyes to Liz. "It's innocent between Tom and me."

"Then you haven't . . . is it . . . *can* you yet?"

"I can." The doctor had checked her out earlier that week and had rattled off all the things she could do. Sex was on the list. "But we haven't."

"Why not?" Jane asked quietly.

Liz's eyes went wide. "No chemistry?"

"There is. I think." There was. She knew. She had felt it, looking at his hands, at his long, long legs, at the sprinkling of hair she saw when he rolled back the cuffs of his shirt.

Jane gave her a look.

"Okay," Bree conceded, because Jane knew she was no nun. "That sounds odd coming from me, but what I'm trying to say is that with my being sick and all, chemistry has been low on my list."

Liz grinned. "So now you're not sick. I repeat. If you had three wishes, would you wish for Tom?"

Bree didn't know. Tom was either the best thing that had ever happened to her or the worst. He was strong but sensitive, self-sufficient but attentive, everything she wanted in a man and had never had. He was also a man whose past might easily rise up to claim him again, in which case he would be gone.

Liz and Jane weren't the only ones to warn her. Most everyone she ran into had some little confidence to share about Tom. Eliot said he was slick, Emma said he was cocky, Dotty said he was rude. Flash bet he'd be going back to New York. LeeAnn bet he'd be going back to Hollywood. Martin Sprague went so far as to say that Bree's father would die a second time if he knew she was seeing a man like that.

"A man like what?" Bree had asked.

"Shrewd. He's too smart to be sitting here doing nothing. Mark my words, he's out for something. Know what I think? I think he's writing. Wouldn't surprise me at all to see Panama as his next book, and you'd be right in the center of it, Bree Miller. Could be he's using you. Could be he's using all of us."

Bree didn't think so. She had seen Tom's house. His office had cobwebs. Okay, so there weren't any cobwebs on his computer. But he wasn't writing. At least she didn't think he was.

The thing was that the more she was warned off Tom, the more strongly she was drawn. Defending someone who had no one else was only part of it. She was good for him in other ways, ways that had nothing to do with making his bed or cooking his food, neither of which he had ever asked her to do. He was at peace when he was with her. She could see it in the comfortable slant of his shoulders, the restful ease of those wonderful hands of his, the pleasure that lit his face and made it younger and warmer—all of that a far cry from the man who used to sit with downcast eyes in his lonely diner booth.

So was it real or an act? Was he a godsend or a nightmare?

"What's wrong?" Tom asked from the bedroom door. His voice held the gentle huskiness of recent sleep.

It was three in the morning. She had woken half an hour earlier, used the bathroom, and had been shifting in bed ever since. Her movements must have wakened him.

"Just restless," she said.

"Nervous about waitressing tomorrow?"

"No. Just restless."

"Want some warm milk?"

She didn't think warm milk would do it this time, and said as much with the shake of her head. Sighing, she switched on the lamp. Then she pushed herself up, piled the pillows against the wrought-iron swirls, and sat against them.

He grinned knowingly. "Want to talk?"

"Yes."

His shirt was open, the top snap of his jeans undone, his feet bare. He looked warm from sleep, raw and appealing, as he settled cross-legged on the bed, facing her. Was she attracted to him? Was she ever!

"Why so restless?" he asked.

"Three wishes."

"Aha. That'll do it. Are you thinking that they're real?"

"No. But they're interesting to think about. I keep asking myself what I'd wish for."

"What would you?"

"I don't know. I always come up with dumb things, like a trip somewhere or a new watch or a big-screen TV."

"Those aren't dumb things."

"They're material things. I don't want to waste a wish on something material." She had decided that much after talking with her friends. Not that she faulted them. To them, talk of three wishes was make-believe, and make-believe was just for fun. "What about you?" she asked Tom. "If you had three wishes, what would they be?"

He thought about it for a while. His frown deepened. Finally, looking resigned, he said, "I'd wish to turn back the clock and redo certain things."

"What things?" she asked, but less surely. She sensed that if he answered, they would be treading new ground.

He studied the quilt for a minute. Then he raised his eyes to hers. "I've always been competitive. I was that way as a little kid. I was that way in college and law school. I was that way as a lawyer, right from the start, driven to do better and be better. I went for the best cases, even when that meant taking them from lawyers who may have been just as good but weren't as forceful. I strode my way to the top, and when I had to climb on other people to get there, I reasoned that my clients were the winners and that was all that mattered.

"When I wrote my first book, it was the same. I'd established my name as a lawyer, so I had access to the most powerful literary agent, no questions asked. We had a publicist working even before my manuscript was sent to editors. That book could have been a dud and it would have been published, we were so successful at creating hype. Some editors called in bids even before they finished reading the thing."

"That book *was* good," Bree said.

He smiled sadly. "Lots of books are good. Lots of books are *better*. So why did mine hit it big? Because I was clever. Once that book hit the top of the best-seller lists, anything I wrote that was marginally good was guaranteed to make it, too, because the hype continued to build. Success fueled success. There were reviews and interviews. There were profiles in magazines. There were publishing parties in New York and screening parties in L.A. I was," he said with something of a sneer, "rich and arrogant and famous."

Bree sat forward and took one of his hands. He studied the mesh of their fingers.

"I wasn't a nice man. Did you know I was married?"

"No."

"Not many people did. Her name was Emily. We were college sweethearts. She worked to support us while I was in law school. So how did I thank her? Once I graduated, I buried myself in the law and ignored her. Two years of that, and she asked for a divorce, and would you believe I was startled? I had no idea she was unhappy, no idea at all. That's how attentive I was."

Bree didn't know what to say.

"She remarried soon after, and no wonder. She was a great girl. She has four kids now. From what I hear, she's really happy. I'd turn back the clock with her, too."

"You still love her?" Bree didn't see how that could be. She hadn't died, gone to heaven, and returned, only to fall in love with a man who still loved his ex-wife. Then again, what did she know?

"No. It's not about love. It's about the bastard I was even after the divorce. She came to a book signing of mine once. The line was around the block when I got to the store. I saw her standing there and should have pulled her out of line and brought her inside with me. But I was all caught up in myself. I waved and walked on, like it was my due and not hers." He looked to the side. "I did things like that a lot—saw someone I knew and rather than acknowledging the relationship, treated the person like just another one of my fans. It happened in restaurants, in airports, at parties. I have a knack for condescension. I have a history of dropping people."

"Had," Bree whispered.

His eyes returned to their hands. "After Emily, I had two long-term relationships with women. The first was with a female associate who worked at my firm. We were together for three years. I dropped her when my first movie came out, because I didn't see her fitting in with a Hollywood crowd. The second was a production assistant on the second movie. She was Hollywood through and through—long legs, blond hair, blue-jeans glamour. I was with her for two years, when she started making noises about marriage." He snapped his fingers. "That was it. I was outta there. But not before I told her that if she thought she had anything that a thousand other women didn't have, too, she was nuts." He let out a disgusted burst of breath. "I was not nice at all. And *then* there's my family." The eyes that met Bree's were filled with self-reproach. "I haven't talked much about them, have I? They are my one, single greatest source of shame."

She might have denied it, might have tried to lighten his burden with empty words. But she wanted their relationship to be an honest one. This was Tom's moment of confession.

"I come from a small town in Ohio," he said. "There were six of us kids, five boys and Alice. She was the youngest. I was right above her. My father worked for the highway department, and not in administration. He plowed snow and patched roads and pitched roadkill into the back of the truck. We were working class all the way. I was the first to make it out. I got a football scholarship. Boy, were they proud of me. They treated me like a king when I came to visit. It wasn't more than once or twice a year, and then only for a few days at the most. There was always something to keep me away—spring training, a trip with my friends, catch-up studying—and they accepted that. It didn't occur to them that I didn't want to be small-town anymore, that I was separating myself from everything they stood for. My two oldest brothers got on my case once, and I let them have it, told them how hard it was trying to make it in a cutthroat world and the fact that they didn't understand just went to show how little *they* knew." He raked his teeth over his upper lip. "Only I didn't say it like that. The words I used were more crude."

He stared at her, inviting her disdain.

She said nothing.

Still staring, still daring, he said, "After I hit it big, I sent money, mostly around holiday time, usually to make up for not going out there myself. At one point, I didn't see them for two years. In the middle of that time, I actually did a media thing in Cleveland. They could've driven up in two hours, or I could've driven down. But I didn't even tell them I was coming. They found out after the fact. My mother took it hard."

Memory broke his stare, visibly taking him back. "She was a plucky lady—petite, like my sister Alice, but strong-willed. I used to think my dad wore the pants in the family. He came home from work, planted himself in that big old armchair of his, and let us wait on him. Only she was the one telling us what to bring him. She kept the house and paid the bills and made us do our homework. Long after he'd fallen asleep in that chair, she was folding laundry or mopping the floor or cutting hair." He smiled. "It wasn't until I was eighteen that I ever went to a barber." He grew quiet.

Still Bree said nothing. She would have given anything to have a mother who did those kinds of things. She would have given anything to have someone care that way.

Tom's quiet lingered, then yielded to sorrow. "I never could think of her as being sick. Being sick just wasn't part of who she was. Maybe that's why I didn't go back."

"What was wrong with her?"

"Cancer. Maybe she couldn't think of herself as being sick, either, because she let it go for so long that by the time she finally went to the doctor, it had spread to her bones. I remember when they called to tell me. There were three messages on my answering machine before I finally called back, and then, even though I'd been totally independent and separate from them for nearly twenty years, it was like I'd been hit in the stomach." He broke off. Self-loathing returned. "I recovered. She didn't. I kept myself busy. She got weaker." He swallowed. "Oh, I said all the right things about getting a second opinion, a specialist from New York, an experimental protocol from Houston. I might have wanted those things if I'd been in her shoes. But she didn't. She wanted to stay where she was with the doctor she knew. So I went back to my own arrogant life, thinking that I'd done all I could. Only I never visited."

"Never?" Bree asked in disbelief and, yes, disappointment. She couldn't conceive of having a mother—let alone a good one—and not treating her well.

"I did visit, just not enough. I went once in the beginning, another time about halfway through. It was painful. Easier to stay away." He looked Bree in the eye, challenging again. "That's the kind of person I was. I did what suited me. They used to leave messages saying that she was weakening, or that the cancer had spread more, and I'd send a card or leave a phone message, because it was easier that way. I always had an excuse. Either I was working on a book or off doing publicity. The pathetic thing is that I wasn't writing. I didn't have time to write. I was too busy being a star."

The line between his brows deepened. "I was vacationing with a group of equally famous and sybaritic friends when she died. We were on a boat on the Adriatic. My family had no idea where I was. They left message after message on my answering machine. When I didn't answer any of them, they had no choice but to go ahead with the funeral." His voice broke. "I showed up a week later."

"Oh, Tom."

He held up a hand. "Don't feel sorry for *me*. I got off easy.

Hell, I missed out on the pain of having to go through the whole drawn-out ordeal of a funeral." His Adam's apple moved. "The thing is, there's a purpose to the ordeal. Funerals are outlets for grief. I was trying to deny the pain and my guilt, and I didn't have that outlet. And suddenly the pain and the guilt and the grief cleared all the other nonsense from my head, and I had a clear vision of what my life had become. That answering machine I mentioned? While I was sailing merrily through the Adriatic, while my mother was being embalmed and my family was trying to reach me, no one else was. Once I erased their messages, there was nothing. I was in pain, and no one came around. And it was my fault. Absolutely my own fault. I was a lousy friend, a lousy person."

Without a second thought, Bree came forward and curved her hands around his neck. His pain was real as real could be. She was desperate to ease it.

He raced on, the dam broken. "I tried calling my father, but he wouldn't talk with me. Neither would my brothers. My sister did. We'd always had a special relationship, being the last of the six. But it was awkward with her, too. So I got on a plane and flew out there. I went straight to the cemetery." He took a shaky breath. Tears brimmed on his lower lids. "Looking at that grave with the dirt that hadn't had time to grow grass . . . looking at that stone that had just barely been carved . . . I thought . . . I thought that was the most awful moment in my life, but I was wrong. I hadn't been there more than ten minutes when my father arrived. He came up the hill with his head down and his shoulders huddled, like he was ninety years old. He couldn't have been more than twenty feet away when he looked up and stopped dead in his tracks. He straightened his spine, took a cold breath, and told me what he thought of me. Then he turned right around and walked back down the hill."

Bree held her breath. "Did you go after him?"

"I called, but he didn't stop, and it was weird, after all those years, but I just couldn't leave my mother, couldn't leave her alone in that place, so I stayed awhile. Then I went to the house. He was there. I saw him through the window. He was there, but he refused to open the door when I knocked, and he's right. Looking at me—knowing the opportunities I had that the others didn't have—knowing everything I didn't do when I could have —knowing all that I squandered—knowing how I let *my own mother* down at a time when there was literally no tomorrow . . . all that must be hell for him."

Present tense. "Still? You haven't talked with him since then?"

"I try. I call every few weeks. He won't talk." He looked down. "That was ten months ago. I went back to New York after that, but I hated it. Nothing fit me the way it had before. I didn't call people, they didn't call me. I sat alone in the loft that I had thought was so chic, and I hated the chrome and the leather and the gloss, and in the middle of that . . . starkness, all I could do was think about the people I wanted to be with, who I couldn't be with because, one by one over the years, I had picked them off and tossed them away like they were pieces of lint messing up my Armani tux."

He stopped talking. Slowly, he raised his eyes. They were bleak, challenging her to say what a worm he was.

But Bree couldn't. She didn't know the Tom who had done those things. The one she knew had been attentive to a fault. He had given up nights of sleep to see to her, had put his own needs second to hers. "You haven't tossed me away," she said, going at the tension in his jaw with small strokes of her thumbs.

She felt a faint easing in him. "Things are different here. The change has been good."

"Things here are basic. And you're basically good."

"I don't know as I'd go *that* far," he said, but she could see that he was pleased, pleased and so very close to her that when the first glints of warmth reached his eyes, she felt them.

Her thumbs slid up and back under his jaw. "What about writing?" It was time she asked about that.

In a reprise of disdain, he grunted. "I haven't written anything worth reading in four years."

"That's not true."

"Tell me honestly. Which of my books did you think were stronger, the first or the last?"

She thought back. "It's hard to compare. The last one was shorter—"

"And more shallow and less well plotted. I went through the motions of writing, but I wasn't involved. That last book was awful."

Bree wouldn't have used the word *awful*. But he was right about depth and plotting. "Still, lots of people read it."

"They sure did. It sat right at the top of the best-seller lists, so I told myself it was great. Now I can say that it wasn't. That'd be my second wish. To rewrite that book and the one before it."

"And the third wish?"

His eyes softened. A small smile touched his mouth. "A kiss."

Pleased, she smiled back, pointed to her lips, raised her brows.

"Yes, you," he said.

Something about the reality of what was about to happen caught a tiny train of her thought, and for an instant, just an instant, she wondered if she was buying trouble, playing with fire, with a man like Tom. Then the instant passed. It didn't have a chance against all he had come to mean to her.

"Consider this your lucky day," she said, and didn't have far to go, not with Tom meeting her halfway, but it wasn't his mouth she thought of first. It was his hands, one cupping the back of her head, the other threading through her hair in gentle possession, then both moving to shift her head, hold it, caress it with exquisite intimacy. She had guessed that his hands could do anything they tried, and she was right. His hands knew how to kiss.

Not that his mouth did a bad job. It was gentle but firm, soothing, challenging. It opened hers and ate from it, staying one step ahead in anticipation of her needs, and when those needs escalated to the point where her insides were humming and breath was scarce, it knew to withdraw.

*Too fast.* She clutched his shoulders and tried to steady herself. *Too hot, too fast.* He put his forehead to hers. There was heat there, too.

He dragged in a long, deep, shuddering breath and let it out with a tortured moan that said he wanted more but had no intention of taking it then.

Different. So different from other men. And sweet.

*What if he loved me?* Bree thought, then chased the thought away and simply enjoyed the moment for its closeness, which was so much more than she'd ever had that it was beautiful even if there wasn't love.

After several minutes' cooling, Tom pulled the pillows down from the wrought iron at the head of the bed and set them where they belonged. He switched off the light, helped Bree slide under the quilt, and stretched out on top of it. He lay on his side, facing her. Incredibly, given the pleasure of it, they weren't even touching when they fell asleep.

As November nights went, this one was cold. Had Bree's furnace gone on, Tom would have been fine. But the room was chilly when he woke up, and Bree seemed plenty warm, all bundled up. So he slipped under the side of the quilt where she wasn't, pulled it up to his neck, and went back to sleep.

Bree opened her eyes at dawn. Her head lay on Tom's arm, her cheek on his shirt just above his elbow. He lay on his side with his eyes closed, dark lashes resting not far from the yellowing remnants of a bruise and a fading suture line. She reached up to touch it but stopped just shy and drew her hand back. Holding it tucked to her throat, she looked more.

His hair fell onto his forehead from a mussed, off-center part. His ear was neatly formed and small-lobed, his sideburns neither short nor long. A day's growth of beard added even greater texture to his face than that already left by the sun. His tan was just starting to fade.

That tan had been the cause for much speculation. LeeAnn had bet it was from the jungle, Flash from a tanning parlor, Dotty—with a disapproving sniff—from a beach "for *naked* people." Bree had always figured that a man didn't have to be nude to get tanned on his face, throat, and arms, which was as much as any of them had ever seen of Tom, until now.

Now, with his shirt unbuttoned, Bree saw that the tan covered his chest—no surprise, since she knew that he had spent much of the summer in the yard behind his house, preparing the ground and laying stone for the terrace she so admired. She imagined that his chest muscles had grown while he was doing that work, though she assumed they hadn't been small to start with. But they were certainly impressive, tight and well formed, his skin dusted with tawny hair that spread wide before tapering. His entire torso tapered along with it, right down to a lean waist and hips that were angled slightly forward.

She let her hand go this time. The backs of her fingers brushed the hair at the center of his chest and found it surprisingly soft, but the warmth coming from the skin beneath it was no surprise. Even more than the quilt, he had kept her warm while the rest of the room got colder and colder.

The furnace needed another kick. One of these days, even that wouldn't work.

Then again, if she had Tom in her bed, the furnace could die for good and she wouldn't care. His warmth was a wonder. She could feel it stealing into her, stealing ever so slowly, deeper and deeper.

Fingers spread, her palm whispered its way down his chest to the tauntingly low point where the snap of his jeans lay open. She withstood the taunting for only a minute before, less steadily, folding her hand over the snap and holding on tight. The heat there was intense, his hardness unmistakable.

"Having fun?" came a thick voice from above.

Bree tried to find a reason why she shouldn't do this. Nothing came to her, except that life was too short for one to pass some things up. She had died and come back. Next time she could as easily die for good. So maybe Tom had a dark side, and maybe, just maybe, he would break her heart. But right here, right now, he had the power to make her feel loved. And right here, right now, that was all she wanted.

Was she having fun? "I *am*," she said, with a grin.

"Can I join in?"

She raised her mouth in answer, and in that very instant knew she had made the right choice. His kiss was everything she had dreamed a morning kiss would be. It held the sweetness of rest, the warmth of intimacy, the fire of awakening. Slipping fully into his arms was the most natural, most exciting thing in the world. It was where they had been headed since she had woken up in the hospital little more than a month before and found him there.

He fit her. Hands, chest, hips, legs—everything wound and pressed in its proper place as though it had been there dozens of times before. Only the arousal was new. It simmered through kisses, grew more heated through touches. It positively sparked when clothing came off, and when the freedom of that allowed for even greater intimacy, it burst into flame.

Bree had expected to feel twinges of pain when she stretched hard against him, but there were none. Nor were there any when his kisses moved down her body, because in this, too, he knew where she had been. His gentleness was a turn-on, as was the catch in his breath when he first saw her scars and the feel of his mouth there moments later.

If this was love, Bree had never even come close to receiving it before. If this was love, she never wanted to feel anything but.

He knew what she wanted and gave it, always in charge, ever careful. In a voice that was low but made rough by desire, he let her know that. *Can I? Does this hurt? Let me kiss you there.* He never gave her the brunt of his weight, not even when he made a place for himself between her thighs, and then, though the drive in him had his arms shaking as he held himself above her, he asked if he needed a condom.

Bree shook her head, a frantic no. Her men always wore condoms, but there was no need, no need at all with Tom. She urged him lower. For the care he took when he entered her, she might have been a virgin.

Emotionally, she was. For the very first time, her heart was involved, and the beauty of that was stunning. It enhanced everything she felt, made everything hotter and richer, drove her higher than she would have thought possible several weeks before. It made her feel that anything, *anything* was possible if she only dared take the chance. For a split second, at the very first moment of orgasm, her world was so blindingly bright that she thought she had died again. The realization that she hadn't only heightened the pleasure.

Tom felt pretty damn good. He had his favorite corner booth, a good book, a super turkey club with a double dose of Flash's curly fries, his favorite Sleepy Creek Pale, and Bree. She was moving from table to table, from the counter to the grill to the kitchen. Every time he caught her eye, she blushed.

Finally, she slid into his booth with her back to the rest of the diner and, trying to be stern, whispered, "Stop *looking* at me that way. I can't do my job. My hands start shaking. I forget what I'm supposed to be doing. It's embarrassing."

"You're doing just fine."

"You know what I mean."

"How do you feel?"

"Surprisingly good."

"Doesn't surprise *me*," he said. The second time around, she had made love to him in ways she couldn't have if she hadn't been healed. She was more woman than he had ever held in his arms.

Now she looked him in the eye, touched her tongue to the bow of her lips and left it there for a reminiscent moment, before pulling it back in, giving him a smart look, and sliding out of the booth. He imagined that her hips swayed as she sauntered away.

Moaning softly, he shifted on the bench. He was staring after Bree, thinking that redemption felt sinfully good, when a blond mess of hair surfaced on the other side of the table. It was a minute before Joey Little's face appeared.

"Hello," said Tom.

Joey stared.

"Well, hello back," Tom said.

Joey looked away for only as long as it took to settle himself on the bench.

"Have you had lunch?" Tom asked.

Joey nodded.

"What did you eat?" Tom asked. When Joey didn't answer, he said, "You have a macaroni-and-cheese mustache."

Joey sucked in his lips.

"Macaroni and cheese?" Tom asked.

Joey nodded.

Tom reached for the cap he had twisted off his beer bottle. He set it in front of him, took aim, and gently flicked it toward Joey. When it barely moved past the center of the table, he brought it back and tried again. This time it landed within inches of the table's edge.

Joey looked at the bottle cap, then at Tom.

Tom nodded, gestured that he should try.

A small hand came up and gave the cap a nudge. When the cap barely moved, the hand gave it a shove. There was progress this time, but not enough. Coming up on his knees, Joey gave the cap a wallop. Tom caught it on its way to the floor and held it in his lap.

Joey waited. When the cap didn't reappear, he stood on the bench seat, put his hands on the table, and looked down at Tom's side of the bench. Then, as quickly as he'd pushed himself up, he collapsed and disappeared. Seconds later, under the table, tiny fingers were prying Tom's hand open and retrieving the prize. Seconds after that, Joey was up on the bench again, setting the cap on the table, taking aim.

Tom figured it was a sign. It didn't matter that the child was two. Kids were wise. Instinctively, they knew friend from foe. Joey Little had decided that he was a friend. It was a start.

Once he was convinced that Bree was holding up well waitressing for the first time, that Flash was watching her closely, and that, in any case, she was having too much fun seeing all the regulars to leave, he settled his bill. Then he drove to the bungalow on West Elm, took a single-edge razor from the tool kit under the kitchen counter, and slit open the first of the cartons of books that hadn't seen the light of day since he left New York.

He was back at the diner at five to pick her up, drove her

home to the Victorian on South Forest, and gave her a full-body massage that put the foot warming he had given her at the hospital to shame. Later, in the claw-footed bathtub that barely, just barely, held two and was ideal for that reason, he told her that he loved her.

# chapter
# eight

Life was good.

No, Bree decided. Life was *great*. She was madly in love with a guy who loved her back, a guy whose main purpose in life seemed to be to please her. There were times when she was sure she was either dreaming or hallucinating, but when she pinched herself, Tom stayed right there, smiling at her like she was the answer to his prayers.

A few months back, she wouldn't have believed that she could have found a man who was as kind, as intelligent, as *famous*, as loving. That, though, was before she had seen the being of light.

The peace she had felt with that being was the same peace she felt with Tom. Same goodness. Same love. There were times when she wondered if Tom wasn't the incarnation of that being, times when she wondered if she had died and been sent back to earth for the sole purpose of being with him, times when she wondered if she *wasn't* the answer to his prayers. She was good for him. He needed laid-back, and she was laid-back. He needed open and sincere, and she was open and sincere. Though she was small-town, she read the books he read and could hold her own in any discussion he started. She gave his life a focus, something he hadn't had in too long a time. And she pleased him sexually. Oh, yes, she did. She could hear it in the sounds that came from his throat when she ran a hand down the center of his chest to his belly, could feel it in the tremors that shook him when her tongue found the smooth skin at his groin; and when he threw back his head and bared his teeth in the course of a long and powerful climax, then slowly sank down beside her with a look of pure love on his face, she knew it was true.

She hadn't told him that she couldn't have kids.

But if he loved her, that wouldn't matter.

If he would be gone by spring, it *really* wouldn't matter.

In any case, she had time.

Besides, she couldn't dwell on the future. The being of light had taught her that, though, like the three wishes, it was a lesson she had absorbed without hearing the words. More important, living for the moment was something she could *do*. It was something she could act on immediately.

She wasn't ready to act on the three wishes. Not yet.

Thanksgiving in Panama had been a communal affair since the days of the town's founding fathers. In those early days, the leading families, whose houses all circled the green, prepared grand turkey dinners and opened their doors to the town. As those families died or moved on and the town's population grew, things changed. The houses around the green still opened their doors, but now everyone chipped in with the work.

Bree had been assigned to the Nolans' house. She brought

two huge salads and Tom. After eating the main part of their dinner there, they strolled from house to house for dessert, as tradition decreed.

"Not great when it's raining," Bree remarked, remembering the mess of many another Thanksgiving Day. There was no rain on this one, though. From the start, the clouds were thick and white. By strolling time, it had begun to flurry. The town green became an enchanted place then, filled with townsfolk wearing brightly colored hats, jackets, and scarves, their faces flushed by good food and drink, and light white stuff falling innocuously around.

Bree couldn't have wished for a nicer day. From early morning to late night, she glowed. Tom rarely left her side, and then only to fill her dinner plate, refill her glass, or fetch her coat. He wasn't possessive. He simply doted on her in the nicest, most subtle of ways.

The significance of his presence beside her wasn't lost on the town. She hadn't come partnered to a town event since she had gone to her high school prom with Curtis Lamb. Nor, though, was Tom's presence beside her a surprise. It was common knowledge that he dropped her at the diner every noon, picked her up when her shift was done, and spent most nights at her house.

But something happened that Thanksgiving Day. A bit of the goodwill that the town afforded one of its own, and in even larger measure one as well liked as Bree, spilled over onto Tom. They didn't exactly open their arms. A wariness remained. But they included him in the talk.

More to the point, they questioned him. Curiosity took over where distrust had left off.

He was asked about being a lawyer. He was asked about being a writer. He was asked about his family. He was asked the same questions over and over again, first at the Nolans', later at other houses, and he answered with unending patience. Only Bree knew how hard the family ones were for him.

In a private moment's reminiscence, as they leaned against the warm brick of the Nolans' fireplace, he said, "Our house was always busy on Thanksgiving. My brothers played football, too, so there was always a game. Afterward everyone poured back to the house—friends, family, coaches, teachers. It was a little like this, actually."

He didn't have to say that he wondered what his family was doing this Thanksgiving Day. Bree had seen him lift the phone that morning and hold it to his chest for a long moment when he thought he was alone, before quietly putting it back. She could see the sadness in his eyes now when he looked at one family after another of parents, grandparents, aunts, uncles, in-laws, and kids.

If she had three wishes, she might wish for Tom to make that call. But it wasn't her place to suggest it. The best she could do was to help field his sorrow.

She was prepared to do that. What she wasn't prepared for was fielding a sorrow of her own, unexpected pangs at times when she saw those families that were larger by one child than they had been the year before. She looked at the runny noses and the hands greasy from turkey skin, and reminded herself that she hadn't wanted to have kids.

Still, the pangs came.

In the days following Thanksgiving, Joey Little became a regular at Tom's booth. At first he stayed on his side of the table, shoving the bottle cap toward Tom, slipping underneath to retrieve it from Tom's hand, and scrambling back to his own side. In time, he took to stealing under the table and coming up to sit beside Tom. Gradually, his silences gave way to giggles and shrieks.

One particularly high shriek brought Liz on the run. She found Joey scrunched under Tom's arm, making faces at his upside-down reflection in the soup spoon Tom held.

"Oh, dear," she said. "Is he bothering you?"

Tom gave the little boy a squeeze. "No way. We're best buddies, Joey and me."

"He can be a handful."

"I've got big hands," he said without a second thought. He had played this way with his nieces and nephews on the rare occasions when he'd visited. Children fascinated him. Their motives were clear, their instincts straight from the gut.

He was pleased when Liz slipped in across from him. "What did you think of Thanksgiving?" she asked. "Kind of different, huh?"

He had done Thanksgiving at the Ritz in Laguna Niguel, at a posh estate north of Manhattan, and on the slopes in Aspen. "Different from anything I've done in recent years," he told Liz now, then added, "Nicer. I liked it."

"So did Bree. I've never seen her look so happy. I wasn't the only one to think so. Lots of people said it. I guess we have you to thank."

The old Tom would have taken all the credit. The new Tom wasn't falling into that trap. "Bree's had an interesting fall. She sees things differently. She's happy to be alive."

"It's more than that," Liz said and sat back. "So are you going to break her heart and leave, or are you staying?"

"I won't break her heart." He couldn't do that without breaking his own, and he had never been a masochist.

"That's only half an answer."

Tom sensed that Liz was a friend. He liked her husband, felt an affinity for them both. They, too, came from the city. They, too, had professional lives independent of Panama. They, too, adored Bree.

So he confided, "I don't know the other half. I haven't decided that yet."

"Martin Sprague is convinced you're writing a book set in Panama."

"I'm not. I'm not writing, period."

"Martin wants to think you are, because the alternative is that you might just hang out a shingle and practice law on his turf."

Tom cleared his throat. "I sensed he was worried about that. But I won't."

Liz studied the table. She scrubbed at Joey's smudgy fingerprints with the arm of her sweater. "You could. There's a need."

"Martin handles it."

"Barely," she said, and raised her eyes to his. "Don't mistake me. He's a wonderful man. He's handled Panama's needs for years. The problem is that some of us who are new to Panama have needs that are new, too." She took a breath. "Ben and I design ad campaigns for small businesses. Last summer we made a presentation to one of our clients. The president didn't like it and hired a cut-rate firm instead. Suddenly now the company is running print ads that are identical to the ones we proposed. That's theft."

"Doesn't Martin agree?"

"He doesn't call it theft. He calls it an unfair business practice, and he says it'll cost us more to go after them than we'd have made in the first place. I'm not sure he's comfortable doing the going after."

"He isn't a litigator."

"No." She paused, looking him in the eye. "You are."

He had set himself up and been caught. Clever Liz. "I'm not practicing law."

"You could."

He shook his head.

"Why not?" she asked.

"First, I haven't practiced law in eight years. Second, I'm not a member of the local bar. Third, you said it: this is Martin's turf."

"Do you agree with him that this isn't worth going after?"

"I couldn't say that without knowing more. Intellectual law wasn't my specialty. Don't you have lawyers in New York?"

"We thought we did until we called. Apparently there isn't enough money at stake for their tastes, and they're right, in a way. With us, it's the principle of the thing. We don't have copyright protection. It never got that far."

"Then you may not have a case."

"We have the ads we designed. We have a copy of the ads being run. We know that the same things the president of the company said he objected to in our ads are right there in the ads being run."

"Can you prove it?"

"We have a tape of our meeting with him."

"Stating his objections?"

"Yes."

Tom was tempted. But there were still the three points he had ticked off.

"Don't say anything now," Liz said, clever in that, too. "Just think about it. Okay?" She looked around. "Where's Joey?"

Tom pointed down to his left. Curled up, pleasantly warm against him, was Joey Little, fast asleep.

Bree found new surprises each time she went to Tom's house. One day it was the family room with endless shelves filled with books and not a carton in sight. Another day it was cartons gone from the kitchen, their contents now in the cabinets. Another day it was oil paintings hung on the living room walls.

Most touching were the framed photographs that began appearing. Most were small, many were faded. Each had a story.

"There's my oldest brother, Carl," Tom told her. "And, in descending order, Max, Peter, Dan, and me. This is my sister, Alice, all dressed up for a sixth-grade dance. Notice that her date is nowhere in sight. He was scared of us."

"He wasn't."

"Well, only for a little while, and then he came back. He decided that he was more scared of what we'd do to him if he didn't. He lived right down the road. We'd known him all his life. He was a nice kid. Alice ran circles around him, though."

Bree picked up another picture. After checking back to the first and making allowances for the passage of time, she said, "This is Max?"

"And his wife, Sandra, taken on their wedding day. They'd been childhood sweethearts, but Sandra went off to school and married someone else. When the marriage fell apart, she came back home. Max had been waiting. No way could he have married anyone else. The kids are from her first marriage. They've had two of their own since this picture was taken."

"They look like a peaceful family."

"They are," Tom said.

"How many grandchildren are there in all?"

"A dozen at last count."

Bree heard pride. Looking up, she also saw longing. Touched, she set the picture down and lifted a third.

"That's my dad," Tom said, pointing to a large man who stood, shoulders back, with a proprietary hand on the hood of what must have been at the time a brand-new Chevrolet. Scattered over, in front of, and beside the car were Tom, his five siblings, two dogs, and one cat. "He saved for years for that car. It was the first new one he ever bought. We used to crowd around his chair and look at the dealer's brochure. He'd go back each year for a new brochure, he was that long saving up. He wouldn't buy it on time, had to have the whole amount saved. He finally bought the car in sixty-five. Carl and Max had their licenses, but it was months before he let either of them drive it. Max had an accident the very first time he took it out."

Bree caught her breath. "What did your dad do?"

"He yelled and screamed until my mother told him to keep still. Max drained his savings to pay for the repairs. Years later, he learned that Dad had paid for the repairs himself and banked Max's money for him. It paid for his honeymoon with Sandra."

That said something about the man, Bree decided. It said that regardless of how hard he looked, he had a soft spot inside. She wondered if any of it was left.

Studying the picture, she decided that Tom's brothers took after his father far more than he did. He and Alice were the different ones, resembling each other in coloring and smile. "You and Alice must take after your mom. Why isn't she in any of these pictures?"

"She's taking them."

"Do you have one of her?"

"Upstairs."

It was on the dresser that had previously been bare, a simply framed snapshot of a twenty-something Tom with a woman who was an older version of his sister, Alice. Bree looked at the picture for a long time. When she looked up at Tom, his eyes were still on it.

"My law school graduation," was all he said.

"She must have been proud."

He nodded and set the picture back on the dresser.

"Call them, Tom," Bree whispered.

Tucking his hands in the pockets of his jeans, he looked off toward the window. "I want to."

"Then *do* it."

He looked back at her with something akin to panic. "What if he hangs up?"

"Call Alice, then. You were closest to her."

"What if *she* hangs up?"

"What if she doesn't?"

Contacting his family was Tom's decision to make. But Bree knew she had given him something to think about when, after staring at her in amazement, he shook his head, chuckled, and hooked an elbow around her neck. "You're tough," he said, dragging her close.

"Maybe I'll wish for it, you know?"

"Don't you dare," he scolded. "Those wishes are yours."

So he had something of his father, after all, Bree mused. Hard voice, soft heart.

"What would I wish for?" she asked, filled to overflowing with the moment's joy. "I'm too happy to want a thing. There's absolutely nothing I need."

"You need a new furnace," he said. "Wish for that."

She screwed up her face. "I'm not wasting a wish on a furnace."

"Yours is on its last leg. Maybe I'll get you a new one."

"Don't you *dare*." She tossed his words right back. She wouldn't *allow* him to do it. After all, if things went the way she hoped they would, she wouldn't be living in the house on South Forest for long.

That was something to wish for, if she was into wishing.

Serious snow arrived the first week in December, with the cold air and ice that went along with the season. To say that life in Panama slowed down implied that it couldn't handle the snow, which wasn't the case at all. The town handled the snow just fine now that sand barrels were in place and plows were hooked up. What slowed life down was tradition, specifically the East Main Slide.

"Come again?" Tom asked, when Bree took a break from waitressing and slid into his booth, close beside him, to explain what the diner's buzz was about.

"The East Main Slide. It's a race. It starts at the town green and ends at the bottom of the hill. School lunch trays, cardboard boxes, trash can lids, chairs—anything unconventional can be used. There are prizes for the fastest, the slowest, the most original, the oldest, and the youngest. Actually, anyone who finishes gets a prize."

"Everyone wins?" Tom asked. "What fun is that?"

Bree smiled. Tom Gates might be a world traveler, but he had a lot to learn about Panama, Vermont. Pleased to be his teacher, she said, "You only win if you finish, and you only finish if you go from top to bottom without stopping. You can take a running start off the green at the top of the hill, but then you have to stay on for a single continuous ride. If you tip over, you're out. If you go off course, you're out. If anyone gives you a push or any other kind of help, you're out."

She could see Tom's mind starting to work. He suddenly looked very young.

"When?" he asked.

"If the snow stops? Tomorrow at noon. There are heats, six sleds per heat."

"One person per sled?"

"Any number per sled, as long as it stays the same from start to finish."

"Can anyone enter?"

"Uh-huh."

"Do you?"

"I did once, when I was in high school. Three friends and I took the legs off an old porch bench and waxed the bottom slats. We thought we could steer by shifting our weight around." She slowly shook her head.

"Went off the road?"

"Real quick."

"Did that turn you off trying again?"

"No. But my father kept saying I was crazy to risk getting hurt, and then once I started working for Flash, I was needed here. The diner is halfway down the hill. It's the only pit stop for spectators. We dole out hot chocolate all afternoon." At least that was what she had done for the past God-only-knew-how-many years, but it sounded boring as hell to her now. "I wouldn't be against entering. People don't usually get hurt." Certainly not as she had been hurt during an innocent walk home from work.

Tom was clearly interested. "Are you up for it?" he asked. "Physically?"

Bree straightened. Physically, she felt great. Emotionally, she felt great. She wasn't afraid of getting hurt this year. If she'd been meant to die, she would be dead already. And damn it, she *wasn't* pouring hot chocolate all afternoon.

"I'm up for it. Got any ideas?"

His idea, to which they devoted all that evening and most of the next day, involved cutting a four-foot piece from a wide tree trunk that had fallen in his woods, slicing it in half, hollowing out its insides, sticking a rudimentary rudder through a hole in its rear, waxing its bottom, and canoeing down East Main. They weren't the fastest or the slowest, weren't the oldest or the youngest or the most original, but they did finish.

Bree had never had so much fun in her life.

The next week, Tom had a glimpse of what winters in Panama were like. A second storm hit, dumping a foot of snow on top of the fourteen inches already fallen and frozen. The roads were quickly cleared and sanded, so he was able to drive Bree to work, but there was something confining about having that much snow on the ground. He was bored.

Just for the heck of it, he climbed up to the room he called his office. It was the only room in the house that wasn't unpacked, and he didn't unpack it now. He simply turned on his computer, plugged it into the phone jack, called up Lexis, and did some legal research.

Then, just for the heck of it, because Bree had another few hours of work and he had nothing better to do, he typed up some thoughts on the Littles' case as Liz had outlined it, suggested possible strategies, and, taking those, composed a prototype of the kind of letter that Martin Sprague might want to think of writing to the company president who had rejected the Littles' plan. He put everything in a five-by-seven envelope and slid it into the book he was reading.

Then, just for the heck of it, because he knew that Martin ate at the diner every Monday, Wednesday, and Friday, and this was Wednesday, and because he'd planned to go there anyway and eat with Bree when she finished work, he drove over. If Martin hadn't been there, he would have left the envelope in his book and disposed of it later. If Martin had had people sitting on either side of him at the counter, he would have done the same thing. But the stool on Martin's left was wide open.

"How're you doin'?" Tom asked, pulling himself onto that wide-open stool. He winked at Bree, who winked right back but instinctively knew to steer clear.

"Not bad," Martin said.

"I have a favor to ask."

Martin grew wary. "What's that?"

"I was talking with Liz Little about her work, and she mentioned the unfair-competition problem she has. That's not my field, mind you, but it interested me, so I did some research. I think there might be an easy solution to the problem, especially since Liz and Ben have that tape." He waved a hand no when LeeAnn arrived with the coffee carafe, and kept his voice low. "The right threats in the right kind of letter might be enough to get that company president to negotiate a settlement with the Littles."

"What kind of threats?" Martin asked.

Tom shrugged. "Threat of a suit under the Vermont labor laws. Threat of an audit. Threat of an injunction. Any one of those will cost a small business more money than it wants to spend. At least it seems that way to me. But I could be all wrong. Like I said, intellectual property isn't my field, and anyway, I'm not a member of the local bar. You'd be the person to handle this." He slid the envelope out of his book and across the counter until it was anchored under Martin's plate. "Want to take a look? Give me your opinion on whether you think the case has merit? As far as Liz is concerned, I forgot about it right after she mentioned it, so she doesn't expect anything. But she and Ben are good people. It doesn't seem fair that they shouldn't be paid for ideas that are theirs. If a session at a negotiating table can get them some cash, that's good." He slapped the counter and pushed off from his stool. "They're your clients. It's your call."

By the third week in December, the diner was decked out for Christmas. Place mats had been printed with a Santa hat topping the frying pan. Snowflakes hung from the ceiling tiles. A decorated tree stood by the jukebox, which was restocked with holiday songs that Flash kept playing at his own expense. The small black vases on each of the tables held bouquets of red dogwood stems, sprigs of holly berries, and mistletoe. Even The Daily Flash reflected the season. One day it offered "Santa sushi"; the next, "Christmas carbonara"; the next, "Niçoise Noël."

"Too tacky?" a cautious Bree asked Tom, knowing that he had seen grander and more sophisticated holiday touches.

"Definitely tacky. But *great*," he said, gilding a season that Bree was seeing through new eyes and loving as never before.

Christmases with her grandparents had been sober affairs. They had viewed the holiday as a day for prayers of gratitude for the Savior's birth and hadn't seen any connection between celebrating his birth and giving gifts to each other or to Bree. Her father had given her small toys when she was a child, justifying it to his parents by saying that he didn't want her to think that Santa didn't love her, too, but the practice stopped the very first year she had outgrown her belief in Santa.

Bree hadn't missed the presents. She had desperately missed the cheer.

There was that and more this year. The diner's festiveness was only the start. There was the annual clothing drive at the church, which was as much a Christmas cookie exchange as anything else. There was the annual dance celebrating the winter solstice, at which she learned the joy of slow dancing with Tom. And there was the approach of Christmas itself.

Tom surprised her on the twenty-third by decorating her house while she was at work, turning the sour-faced Victorian old maid into something surprisingly gay.

"But I wanted to help," was her only complaint, halfhearted at best, she was so touched by what he'd done, and even *then* she got her wish. After Tom dropped her at work the next morning, Flash ushered her right back outside.

"What are you doing?" she cried, when he wouldn't let go of her arm.

"You're taking the day off," he said, "and don't tell me there's work to do, because we both know you don't care as much as you used to. You don't give me lists of things to do anymore. Hell, you've even stopped crapping about Stafford, though his milk still goes bad. I don't want you at work today. I want you out here."

She was about to ask *Out where?* when she faced front and saw a grinning Tom. His truck was idling and warm. He was clearly in on the joke.

Bree went along without a fight, hiding her delight until there was just too much to contain. Tom took her into his snowy woods to cut a tree for his house, popped popcorn to string, opened packages of tinsel, little hanging doodads, and red velvet bows. When everything was in its place, he hoisted her up to place the glittery star on the top of the tree.

That night, they joined the rest of the town for midnight services, and there was something extra special in that, too. Though never before terribly religious, Bree felt blessed. Sitting in church beside Tom, with all the people she knew seated nearby, she experienced the same sense of belonging she had felt with the being of light.

In other respects, too, she was aware of the being of light. She didn't know if that being was God, Jesus, Saint Peter, or another figure entirely, but sitting in that church, she felt its warmth, felt its love.

In the oddest way, Bree felt like a newborn, which was probably why she indulged herself when, returning to Tom's house after church, she found a pile of gifts for her beneath his tree. With a child's excitement, she opened every last one.

"Don't you want to save a few for morning?" he teased, laughing.

She merely shook her head and slipped off another ribbon. She had gifts for him at her house. If she had been able to wait, they might have opened their gifts together. But it was out of the question.

She opened fun gifts—a hand-carved backgammon set, books that were on her list to read, a new Garth Brooks CD. She opened practical gifts—a cashmere sweater set that she would never have splurged on herself, a scarf and mitten set, a waffle maker.

Tom saved the best for last, and then, like the star at the top of the tree, the present he handed her glittered. It was a pair of earrings that looked suspiciously like diamond studs.

She swallowed, looked up at him, swallowed again, and even then only managed an awed whisper. "These aren't . . . they look like . . . are they?"

He nodded, grinned. "Real."

It took a long minute of trying to steady her hands before she fitted the posts into the holes in her ears, a long minute of ogling in the mirror, a long, *long* minute of hugging Tom in thanks when her throat was too knotted for speech, and a long, long, *long* time after that before they fell asleep.

Bree didn't need any three wishes. She decided that again on Christmas Day, and nothing in the days that followed convinced her otherwise. Tom made the week an unending celebration. He cooked a goose one night, took her to dinner at an inn outside Burlington another. On the weekend between the holidays, he drove her to Boston, where they saw *The Nutcracker*, slept at the Four Seasons, ate brunch at the Ritz, and browsed through Newbury Street shops.

Bree had been to Boston before, but never as lavishly, and never in the company of her dream man. During the drive home, she sat back, turned her head to Tom, and grinned. "I've died and gone to heaven. That's all there is to it."

"Again?"

"Still."

It did seem that way. Then came New Year's Eve and, after the champagne, a tiny pop in her bubble.

# chapter
# nine

"Do you believe in making New Year's resolutions?" Bree asked Tom. They were on their way home from a party thrown by the Littles. He held her hand but was quieter than usual.

"I don't know," he said. "I used to make them when I was a kid. I'd resolve not to fight with my brothers, or to clean my room without being asked. By the time I got to high school, I was resolving to get better grades. By the time I got to college, better grades weren't enough. I was resolving to get A's."

Disdain had crept into his voice. Bree hadn't heard that in a while. "What happened after that?" she asked.

"I got the A's. I got most everything I wanted without making resolutions, so I stopped." He shot her a look. "I was arrogant as hell."

"Was," she echoed, satisfied to hear the past tense at last. She raised his hand and ran her mouth over the scar that had healed to a thin ridge. "So do you believe in them?"

He thought about it. "I do. They imply a willingness to grow."

"So what are yours?"

He shot her another look. "You first."

"I asked you."

"I'm driving. I can't concentrate. You can. What are your New Year's resolutions?"

"Just one," she said. "To live life to the fullest."

She watched for his reaction. It was a small, pensive smile. "I like that."

"And yours?"

He turned onto West Elm and cruised over the snow-crusted road to the shingle-sided bungalow. Ice crunched under the truck's tires on the drive. He pulled up under the carport.

"Tom?"

"I'm thinking."

Bree felt a touch of unease. It was not that she didn't want him to think, just that something that was taking so long had to be heavy. She didn't have to be a genius to know that it was related to the future. New Year's resolutions always were.

Tom reached for the door handle. Bree reached for his arm.

He stared at the steering wheel, his lower teeth clenching his upper lip, then sighed. "My New Year's resolution is to figure out my life."

She caught her breath. He caught her hand.

"That came out wrong," he said. "I don't need to figure out you and me. It's the rest that's murky. I need to decide what's fitting in where."

It had been only a matter of time, Bree knew. Living in the here and now couldn't last forever. But it had been nice. She had been able to accept diamond earrings from Tom as a simple gift of love, had been able to live day to day without any expectation beyond seeing him after work. She had been perfectly content, *more* than content, living for the moment. Doing that, she had been free of disappointment.

Now, suddenly, she was afraid. For the first time in weeks, she wondered if Tom would leave town.

He opened the truck's door, drew her across the seat and out after him, and threw an arm around her shoulders as they walked into the house. They dropped their jackets in the kitchen.

Bree followed him into the family room and watched while he started a fire. When the kindling caught and the flames spread, she turned to the bookshelves lining the walls. Her gaze went straight to the books Tom had written. They were six in a row in an unobtrusive spot, off to the side and higher than eye level, and should have been lost among hundreds of other books. But they weren't. From the day he had put them there, she had been acutely aware of their presence.

"Do you want to write?" she asked.

He was hunkered down, stoking the flames with his back to her. "I don't know. I've been rereading what I've already written. The early ones aren't bad."

She folded her arms around her middle. "Do you have new ideas?"

"At first I didn't. But that's changed. Right now, ideas are the easy part. If I pick up a newspaper, I get ideas."

"What's the hard part? The writing?"

"No. Writing was never a problem for me."

"So what's the hard part?"

"What comes after."

Ahh. His nemesis. "Fame."

He dusted his palms on his jeans and pushed himself to his feet. Shoving his hands in his pockets, he looked at her. "I'm not sure I can trust myself to handle it well."

"Kind of like an alcoholic in a room with a bottle?"

"Kind of like that, and anyway, I don't know if I want to write. I know I can. I just don't know if I want to."

"How do you decide?"

He scratched his head. "Beats me." He left his hand on his

head. "You want to live life to the fullest. Well, so do I. There are times when I feel like I'm already doing that. I'd say nine-tenths of my life is that way, that happy. Then there's the one-tenth that says my father was right. I have skills that I'm wasting." He crossed to where she stood and hung his arms over her shoulders. "The thing is, I can't sit around here each day while you go to work. It isn't right."

"I don't mind," Bree insisted, afraid, so afraid. "I like working at the diner. Besides, I don't need fancy things. You could have given me beach stones instead of diamonds, and I'd have loved them just as well. If it's a matter of money—"

"It isn't. It's the principle of the thing."

A man of principle was one to admire, she reasoned, though it did little to ease her fear. What eased her fear was thinking of the being of light, which loved her and wouldn't let anything bad happen. And then there were her three wishes. If they were real, she would use one of those in a heartbeat to keep Tom.

Two weeks into January, Tom went to New York. He had made a lunch date with his agent and a dinner date with the lawyers with whom he had once practiced. Bree saw the sense in it. She knew that he needed to mend fences before he could decide if he liked what was inside. That didn't mean she wasn't jittery from the moment she learned he was going.

Tom insisted that she drive the truck while he was gone. "I don't trust your old car," he said, which annoyed her no end.

"Then let me buy a new one. You keep talking me out of it."

"You don't need a new one. You have the truck."

"It's *your* truck," she said. "I want *my* truck." She hated thinking that way. But wasn't he going to *his* New York, while she stayed behind in *her* Vermont? Weren't they from different worlds, after all? And hadn't she done just fine for herself before he came along? She resented the idea that she had become suddenly dependent, resented the idea that she had given so much of herself to a man who might, just might, throw it back in her face. "I can negotiate a deal on a car. I've done it before."

"Wait," he begged. "We'll go together when I get back."

Thinking of his return began to make her feel better.

Seeing him dressed in a suit, ready to leave, didn't. She stared at him for so long that he looked down at himself. He touched his tie, brushed his lapels, checked his fly.

Then he looked back at her and read her thoughts. "Weird, huh? I'm a stranger to me, too."

From the neck up he was fine. His hair was neatly combed, though longer, she wagered, than it had ever been when he had worn this suit. Add that to the slim line of the scar on his cheekbone, and he was the man she knew and loved. From the collar down was the problem.

"You look stuffy," she said, when what she was really thinking was that between that longer-than-lawyerly hair, the prominent scar, the suit and the stunning body beneath it and *everything* about his face, from his eyes to his straight nose to his squared chin, he would stop traffic, which meant that God only knew what possibilities lay open to him in New York, but in any case he would *never* come back.

"Two days, Bree. That's all."

She wanted to believe it, but there were so many possible glitches. "What if something's too good to resist?"

"Nothing will be. I just need to talk through some things. I need to see what's there and what isn't."

"There'll be women."

"I won't be looking at women."

"They'll be looking at you."

Suit and all, he gave her a bear hug. "I love you. I'm immune."

She grunted against his designer lapel. "That's what they all say. I'm going to wish for you to return."

"Bree." He held her back. "Don't. That'd be a total waste. I'll be back day after tomorrow. My tickets say it. I say it."

Bree took a deep breath and pictured the being of light. It was real. The mole on the back of Simon Meade's neck proved it. The being of light wouldn't let her lose Tom. Would it?

Worst case, there were still those wishes.

*     *     *

Afterward she would blame it on loneliness, frustration, and simply thinking about the wishes once too often. At the time, all she knew was that she had woken in her own ancient house without Tom, and she was cold.

Scrambling out from under the quilt, she pushed icy feet into slippers and trembling arms into her robe. Pulling the belt tight, she glanced at the clock on her way to the door. It was six in the morning. She hadn't slept well. She missed Tom, missed his bed, missed his warmth.

The house was dark, but her feet knew it well. They plodded with due speed and much annoyance down the stairs to the first floor, then through the kitchen and down a narrower flight to the basement, which was framed in stubbly cement and colder than cold. The furnace was at the far end. She pulled the light chain there, shivered, and scowled.

She jiggled one knob, then another. She made sure the pilot light was on. She checked to see that the dampers were open. She turned a dial and gave the furnace a shove. When nothing happened, she shoved it again. Her breath came out white when she swore.

Tom had warned her. Flash had warned her. She hadn't listened. She didn't want to listen even now, because the *last* thing she wanted to do was to pour money into this house. She didn't want to *be* here. She wanted to be with Tom. But Tom was living it up in New York, having all kinds of fun with his friends, maybe even making plans to return there and wondering how to break the news to her.

She needed a miracle, was what she needed. Right here. Right now.

Feeling desperate and cross enough to be brash, she squeezed her eyes shut, laced her fingers together with her knuckles by her chin, and dared the being of light to put up or shut up. "I . . . wish . . . for . . . heat." Picturing that being, she said it again, louder this time, to make sure it heard. "I . . . wish . . . for . . . *heat.*"

Opening her eyes, she tucked her hands under her arms, glared at the furnace, and waited for it to turn on.

It didn't.

She rocked back on her heels, tucked her hands in tighter, and waited longer.

Nothing.

Turning on her cold-enough-to-be-nearly-numb heel, she stomped back upstairs and lit the woodstove in the kitchen. By the time it was radiating warmth, she was wrapped in a quilt in a chair inches away, brooding over a mug of hot tea, telling herself that maybe, just maybe, wishes took time.

She arrived at the diner at ten, two hours before she was due to start work. If three layers of sweaters and two of socks hadn't given her away, her scowl would have.

"Aha," Flash gloated. "What did I tell you? If you'd listened to me, you'd still be lying in bed, nice and warm. How cold is the house?"

"Cold," Bree grumbled, though she suspected disappointment was as much behind her mood as the chill in her bones. She had waited at the house for nearly four hours, *four hours,* and her wish hadn't come true. Okay, she had money to fix the furnace. A new car could wait. But the thought of having three wishes had been kind of nice.

Flash wrapped her hands around an apricot bran muffin that was fresh from the oven and warm. "Sit and eat. The Wrights will handle the heating, and they won't charge you an arm and a leg. They'll be in for lunch. We'll give them the news then."

When the Wrights came in at noon, they were the ones with the news. "Can't eat now," Ned said. "Just got word on the scanner." As he spoke, the whine of the town's fire alarm began to sound from the top of the hill to alert the volunteer force. "There's a fire over on South Forest."

Bree had the worst thought. "South Forest?"

"Don't know whose house."

She saw Eliot turn into the diner's lot with his lights flashing and ran to the door. When he climbed from the cruiser looking straight at her, she knew. Grabbing her jacket, she joined him.

Horror was shaking her so badly that she didn't trust herself to drive.

Within minutes, they were at the scene. There wasn't much she could do but stand and watch. There were no flames shooting through the roof, only thick black smoke, but the flames were on their way. The second floor was fully engulfed, the first floor long gone. She imagined that the basement was nothing but a charred concrete shell.

Feeling helpless, discouraged, and quite personally at fault, she watched while the men she knew—plumbers, carpenters, and electricians transformed into firefighters—directed thick streams of water through the upper windows. Glass shattered. Water was re-aimed. The air was filled with the acrid scent of a burning past.

She didn't want to think about the damage, about the loss of a history, about memories that would never be the same, but she thought about all those things. She was the last of the Millers. This house was all she had.

"This wasn't what I meant by heat!" she wailed to no one in particular. "It wasn't what I meant *at all!*" Her voice held both upset and accusation. She wanted to blame someone else, some-*thing* else. But her cry was lost to the awful sound of fire and the thunder of water from yards and yards of canvas hose.

As word spread through Panama, friends arrived to stand with her, but they were small solace for the ravage she witnessed. By the time the flames were out, nearly half the town was there, and she was feeling completely alone.

"You'll rebuild, Bree."

"The house will be better than ever."

"You can stay with us. Our attic room is perfect."

"Take the room over our garage. It's yours."

Her eyes remained on the ruin of her house. She couldn't seem to drag them away, not even when they filled with tears.

Jane slipped an arm around her. Quietly, she said, "You'll stay with Tom?"

Bree nodded. She was practically living at his house anyway. That's where she would have been last night, if he hadn't been in

New York. She wouldn't have slept at her own house, wouldn't have woken up lonely and cranky and cold, wouldn't have dared the being of light to make good on its promise, wouldn't have forfeited a wish out of spite.

There was plenty of heat at Tom's house.

So had her wish come true in some perverted sense?

Many hours later, warm as toast under the down comforter on Tom's bed, she was no closer to an answer. Her stomach turned each time she pictured the blackened remains of her house. It had taken two showers before the stench of the smoke left her hair, and a bath filled with scented oils before her skin let her forget.

By that time, she was worried again. Tom hadn't called. He had said that he would, had *promised* it—his word, not hers. If he hadn't been able to get through at her house, he would have tried here, unless he was so wrapped up in being back in New York that he forgot. She was scared, so scared.

Sitting up, she hugged her knees to still the shaking inside. Fine. If he gave her up and went back to his life in New York, she would take the insurance money from the house on South Forest and buy this house from him. She had always wanted it. She could live here without him and go back to her own life, which had been just fine before him. Just fine. Yes, it had been. Just fine before Tom.

The digital clock turned. It was midnight. He should have *long since* called.

Grabbing for the phone at the side of the bed, she called information, got the number of his hotel, and, on the second try, pressed all the right buttons. A hotel operator answered. Bree asked for Tom. After a pause came word that he had checked out that afternoon.

She didn't know what to think or do. In a bid for calm, she tried to recapture the comfort of the being of light. For the first time, she couldn't. She could picture a great ball of light, but the picture was an intellectual one. She couldn't feel it. Emotionally, she was detached. And suddenly she was back in the world she had known before that October night, only it didn't seem as wonderful to her now as it had seemed then. Now it seemed programmed and parochial. It seemed lonely. It seemed boring. Ironic, but it even seemed *barren*.

Unable to sit still with those thoughts, wanting to recapture the present, she left the bed and began walking from room to room. That was how she found herself upstairs, looking out over the front yard from the spare bedroom, when a pair of headlights lit the street. Her pulse skittered when she saw that the head-lights belonged to a taxi, which pulled up in front of the bun-galow.

It was Tom, back home a day early. Because New York had been so good that his mind was made up?

Heart pounding, she watched him turn away from the cab and lope up the walk. She ran down the stairs, opened the door just as he reached it, and held back in fear for only as long as it took him to drop his bag. When he reached for her, she was there, holding tight to his neck, clinging in a way she would never have done in her other life but which was the only thing that made sense in this one. It was a long minute before she realized that the shaking wasn't all coming from her. He was holding her that tightly.

"I went by the house," he said, in a voice so raw she barely recognized it. "What happened?"

"Fire," was all she had a chance to say, because anything else would have been lost in his kiss. It was a kiss that tasted of fear and a desperate need for reassurance, as much of it his as hers.

When it ended, he took her face in his hands. "When?" His thumbs brushed at her tears.

"Lunchtime today." She wormed her arms inside his and touched his face right back, needing to know more, feel more, to prove he was there. "I called your hotel. They said you checked out."

"I had to get back here. Were you at work when it happened?"

She nodded and burst into tears. "Why didn't you *call*?"

"I tried, but your phone just rang." He pulled her close. "When I tried the diner, the line was busy, and then I was sitting in the airplane on the goddamned runway for three hours while the fuckin' air traffic control computers were down. Aw, honey, don't cry. Please don't cry."

She tried to stop—told herself that there was a message in his wearing jeans and a sweater under his coat and not his despicable suit—but it didn't work. "I was scared!"

"So was I," he said against her hair. "Scared in New York, scared back here. I love you, Bree."

She locked her hands at the center of his back and cried harder. She didn't want him to leave, didn't want him to leave *ever again*!

He held her for another minute, running his hands over her back, telling her he loved her, begging her not to cry. When he urged her inside and shut the door behind him, he leaned against it and pulled her tight to his side. "I bought you something."

She ran the back of her hand past her eyes. "I don't want anything. Just you."

"You heard me say that."

"Huh?"

"The exact same words. I was saying them the whole time I was in New York. I didn't like the traffic. I didn't like the crowds. I didn't like Nathan saying that he could get me good money for a three-book deal but *great* money for a four-book deal. I didn't like my law partners trying to measure in dollars and cents the kind of clients I could bring in from the entertainment industry. The hotel was pretentious, the restaurants overpriced, and the air polluted. I kept asking myself what in the hell I was doing there, when the only thing I wanted was you."

Bree raised her head. "It was?"

"Is." In the near dark, his eyes were fierce, his voice was compelling. "I was supposed to see Nathan again today, but I canceled. I walked up and down the streets and thought about the people I'd planned to stop in and see, and I didn't stop in and see a one. The only thing I wanted to do was shop." He reached into his pocket and drew out a box. It was small, square, and blue, and had a neat white bow tied around it.

Bree looked from the box to his face and back.

"Open it," he coaxed.

She released her hold of him and took the box from his hand, untied the ribbon, and lifted the top. Inside was another box. She looked at Tom again.

"Go on," he said, and took the outer box from her when she removed the inner one.

Afraid to hope, she held it in her hand. Then she lifted the lid. There, on a dark field, lay a pear-shaped diamond set in platinum, and slowly but surely the light returned to her life, radiating outward from the diamond, speaking of belonging and love, filling her with warmth. "This is . . . ?"

"It is."

She looked up. "Are you asking . . . ?"

"I am."

"Oh my *God*," she breathed, and she threw her arms around his neck. Seconds later, she was back looking at the ring. She had never owned anything like it, had never *dreamed* of owning anything like it. "You bought this in New York?"

"It's the only important thing I did the whole time I was there."

Bree was short of breath. Holding the ring box in her hand, she hugged Tom again. "Thank you," she whispered against his cheek, seconds before drawing back to look inside the box once more. The ring was still there.

"Put it on."

She was about to. Then she had a thought that wiped the smile from her face. Without hesitancy, because she knew it had to be said, she blurted, "I can't have kids, Tom. I can't. There's scar tissue."

He went still. "From the accident?"

She nodded. "You want kids. I know you do. I've heard you talk about your nieces and nephews. I've seen you with Joey Little."

He was shaking his head. "We'll adopt."

"It isn't the same."

"It *is*." He removed the ring from its box and slipped it on her finger. Then he raised it to his mouth, kissed it, and looked her in the eye. "I wasn't thinking about kids while I was walking around New York. I was thinking about you."

"But you want family. That's what you've missed."

"Right, and the root of family is a man and a woman. If the root stinks, the whole thing fails." He gave her a crooked grin. "There's no other woman I want to root with."

She could feel the sincerity in him. Tears welled again.

"Marry me, Bree?"

No matter that she had his diamond on her finger: hearing the words in the air stole her breath. She must have looked dumbfounded, because he laughed. The sound was full and rich, as she imagined life with him would be. "I thought for sure you'd decide it was New York that you loved," she cried. "I was lying here thinking it was all over, like a dream that ends in one second of waking up." The ring sparkled as she turned her hand. Its light brought a special kind of calm.

"I wished for heat," she told him, at three in the morning. They had made love, made pizza, and made more love. Now they lay in the sweet redolence of passion and sweat, Bree with her cheek over the strong beat of Tom's heart. Her hand lay nearby on his chest, fingers splayed. She flexed the third one to see the diamond sparkle. The excitement of it nullified fatigue.

Tom must have felt the same way, because there was nothing sleepy about his voice. "Wished for it?"

"Closed my eyes, pictured the being of light, and wished. Nothing happened. I waited and waited, then finally went to the diner. By noontime, the house was on fire."

He chuckled. "So here you are in a house with plenty of heat, and here you'll stay. You got your wish."

She raised her head. "Did I? I wished for heat, and there was a fire. Was it my wish or something more logical, like an erratic old furnace? I've thought about this, Tom. In the figurative sense, I did get my wish. But what about the literal sense? Did I actually cause that fire by wishing for heat?"

"If you're feeling guilty, don't."

"I can't help it. That was a *home*."

"It was a thing. It can be replaced." He stroked her cheek, suddenly serious. "I'm sorry about the business about kids, Bree. I'm sorry you had to hear that from the doctor and keep it all to yourself. If you'd told me, I could have shared the pain."

"You did. You came to my house that night and held me when I cried."

"You should have told me why you were crying."

"You'd only have felt more guilty about the accident. I don't want you feeling that. I don't want to think you gave me this ring because of guilt."

"Selfishness is more like it. You're the best thing that's happened to my life. Giving you a ring is the first step in tying you down. So. What do you think? We could get married next week, or next month. A Valentine's Day wedding might be nice."

Bree put her head down, smiled against his chest, and savored the moment. "We'll decide."

"When?"

"Soon. I've never been engaged before. I want to enjoy it for a while."

That night, she dreamed she had a baby. It was a little boy, a miniature version of Tom as he'd been in the family pictures she had seen. He was perfectly formed and alert, focusing startlingly clear eyes on them as though, right from that moment of birth, he knew exactly who they were. Paternal pride swelled Tom so that he grew a whole twelve inches, there and then. As for Bree, she was filled with so much love that she just . . . burst.

She awoke with a start, feeling that love still. And the sadness of knowing that the dream was only a dream? It was forgotten, first in Tom's arms, then in the excitement that filled the diner when her friends saw the ring.

# chapter
## ten

"**W**ho'd have thought it," Jane said, after oohing and ahhing over the ring. Her excitement was genuine. Since she would have given anything to be married herself, that was doubly meaningful. "I am so-o-o"—she hugged Bree—"happy for you. It's a dream come true."

Bree glanced at the put-up shelf, saw that no orders were ready yet, and took Jane's arm. "I have to talk with you." She led her through the diner's kitchen to the small office at the rear and shut the door. "I need your opinion."

Jane held up her hands. "I know *nothing* about weddings."

"Not about that." Bree hadn't begun to think about that. A wedding would be a while in the coming. Other things were more immediate. "You know me as well as anyone. You know that I'm sensible. You know that I'm levelheaded. Aren't I?"

Jane nodded vigorously.

"Do you believe me when I say I had an out-of-body experience?"

Jane opened her mouth, then closed it. After a minute, she said, "You wouldn't have said you had one if you didn't believe you had."

"But do you believe they're possible?"

"I might not if anyone else was saying it, but you don't dream things up."

Bree pressed her lips together. She debated for a final minute. Then, taking a deep breath, she told Jane about the three wishes. Jane's eyes grew larger and larger.

"You mean you can make things happen just by wishing them?"

"I don't know. I don't know if I did. That's the problem."

"How's it a problem? You got heat. You got an even better place to stay. You always hated your house."

"But the house is my inheritance. I didn't mean to burn it down when I made that wish."

"Did you go over there this morning?"

"No. I'm a coward. Tom went." It was gruesome, he said, and he urged her to wait until the shock wore off. One part of her wanted to know what remained and what didn't. The rest of her —the part that didn't want anything touching her happiness— was content to stay away. "He said that the fire inspector came in from St. Johnsbury. What if he says it was *arson?* Will they accuse me of it?"

"Arson means using matches and gasoline. You didn't do anything like that."

"No. I just wished."

Jane considered that for a minute, scrunched up her nose, shook her head. "That probably had nothing to do with it."

"Then the wishes aren't real?"

Jane looked doubtful, but Bree couldn't give it up. Simon Meade had a mole on the back of his neck. She could only have seen it from outside herself, which meant that her out-of-body experience had been real. If that was so, she didn't see why the being of light and his three wishes couldn't be real, too. "Maybe I should ask Verity."

"Don't ask Verity. Verity is crazy."

"Not crazy. Just eccentric."

"She thinks thunder is the sound of God bowling."

"So did I, when I was younger."

"Then you grew up."

And Verity hadn't grown up? Not so long ago, Bree might have agreed with Jane. That was before things had happened to her that she would have sworn were impossible. "Maybe I'm crazy, too. I swear I was told I had three wishes to make. I swear I was sent back to earth just to make them."

"Then try another," Jane suggested. "Something specific, so you'll know if it worked. Heat is too vague. It can be taken lots of ways. This time, wish for a *thing*."

"I don't want a *thing*."

"It may be the only way you'll know if the wishes are real."

"But if they are, that will be my second wish. And then what?"

"You'll make a third."

"And *then* what?" Three strikes and you're out, was what she was thinking.

Jane simply grinned. "Happiness forever after?" Her grin faded in the next breath when the office door flew open.

"Jane." Dotty gave a long-suffering sigh and a withering look. "I have been waiting outside for twenty minutes. You're supposed to drop me home if you want the car, and you need the car if you're going to Ashmont. They're expecting you at the community center in thirty minutes."

"It doesn't take long to get there," Jane said, though she quickly gave Bree a hug and moved toward the door.

Bree knew Dotty hadn't been waiting any twenty minutes. Jane had been checking the front lot until Bree dragged her back to the office, and that had been no more than five minutes before.

But arguing with the woman would only make things worse for Jane.

"Don't I get to see the ring?" Dotty asked Bree.

Bree would have liked to hide it. But that would have made things worse for Jane, too. And besides, mere mention of the ring made Bree grin. She held out her hand.

Dotty turned her ring finger one way, then the other. "It looks like a decent diamond."

"Mother."

Dotty frowned at Jane. "What?"

"It's a *perfect* diamond."

"You're a jeweler now? For all you know, this diamond is cracked or chipped or inferior or *fake*. 'It's a perfect diamond.' That shows how much *you* know. It would be *another* thing if you'd ever had a diamond of your own."

Bree took back her finger. "Jane's no fool. If the choice was between a lousy guy and no diamond, I'd pick no diamond, too."

"Ward Hawkins is a disgusting man," Jane said under her breath.

Bree agreed. He lived two towns over and had been married four times. He proposed to Jane on a regular basis.

Dotty snorted. "At least he offered." With an arch look at her watch, she left the office.

"Go," Bree urged Jane. "We'll talk later."

"I'm really happy about your ring."

"I know. Now go." She gave a gentle push. Jane was barely gone when Flash appeared. He was looking back at the pair.

"Why does Jane take it?" he asked. "Why doesn't she just leave?"

Bree had asked Jane that many a time. She answered Flash the same way Jane always answered her. "Where would she go?"

"*Anywhere* would be better than living with Dotty."

"On what? What's she got for money?"

"Same thing you have. The difference is that you work."

"So does Jane, only she doesn't get paid for it."

"She should charge for her artwork."

"She can't. The town won't pay."

"Neither will I, if you don't get back up front."

Bree left the office. "Food's up?"

"Not yet. But everyone wants to see your ring. Now that you're engaged to marry a celebrity, you're a celebrity yourself. It's kind of a fairy tale, y'know?"

Tom's celebrity status was reinforced, now that he was engaged to marry the town's own celebrity. Bree's popularity in Panama had people acknowledging him with a warmth that had previously been withheld. He was congratulated at the post office when he went for his mail, at the bank when he went to deposit royalty checks he had picked up in New York, and at the hardware store when he went to buy paint for the spare bedroom's wall. He was given thumbs-up by walkers as he drove around the green, and once he reached Bree's house, he was even congratulated by local men who were helping the fire inspector sift through the ruins.

"Just how fast does the grapevine work?" he asked Eliot Bonner after he returned to the diner to wait out the last of Bree's shift. They sat on adjacent stools, nursing beers.

Eliot chuckled. "When there's a diamond involved? Lightning fast. It's a nice ring."

Tom caught it glinting on Bree's finger as she worked around the diner. It wasn't the biggest diamond he had seen in Tiffany's that day, but bigger wasn't better. He had learned that the hard way and wasn't making the same mistake twice. He had spent hours picking just the right ring for Bree. This one had her brilliance, her simplicity, her grace. It was as beautiful on her hand as he had imagined it would be, and she looked beautiful with it there. Glowing from within. Radiant. They were clichés, but they fit.

"So now that you're marrying into the town," Eliot broke in, "I guess you're staying?"

Tom smiled. "I guess I am." It hadn't been a conscious decision. But the only pleasure he had found in New York had been in shopping for Bree, and once that was done, he couldn't leave fast enough. Heading back to Panama, he was heading home.

He loved Bree and he liked her friends. He liked the fresh air and the slower life. He even liked the physical exertion of shoveling snow twice a week. Okay, so gossip was a staple and he'd had enough of gossip to last a lifetime. But that was a small minus against lots of pluses. The town was like a large extended family, which wasn't a bad thing to have if one was estranged from one's own. Tom thought he couldn't find a better place to raise kids.

"What'll you do here?" Eliot asked.

"Finish unpacking. Paint a few rooms. Maybe build a garage." It wasn't productive in the way his father meant, but it satisfied him for now.

"Make it nice for Bree," Eliot ordered. "She deserves nice things." He shook his head. "Too bad about the house. It was old, but it wasn't bad. What'll you do? Rebuild and sell?"

Tom tipped the Sleepy Creek Pale to his mouth. He even liked the *beer* here. "That's up to Bree. It's hers."

"She'll get insurance money. She could keep that and just bulldoze what's left of the house and sell the land." He swiveled toward Tom, looking puzzled. "It's the damnedest thing. The fire inspector couldn't figure out what caused the fire. Couldn't find a thing. We all know she had a bad furnace, but she said the pilot light wasn't doing a thing when she left for work. So what happened? There could have been a spark. Only there wasn't much around the furnace but concrete. So what was it that caught so bad? The inspector couldn't find one thing burned more than another. It was all pretty even. He figures there was some kind of flukey explosion, you know"—he used his hands—"*pffff*, with flames hitting the ceiling rafters. That would have done it."

"I suppose," Tom said. He could picture an explosion, a sudden wild burst of light not unlike the luminous being Bree swore she had seen. He wasn't saying that he believed her wish had caused the fire, but he wasn't ruling it out. Bizarre things happened sometimes. Take his life. Five years ago, ten years ago—hell, twenty years ago—he would never have imagined finding happiness in a small town with a local girl. Even when he had been at the height of his fame he had never felt as good, as *full,* as he did now—even with the knowledge of what the accident had done to Bree. He would spend his life making that up to her, and what a nice, rich life it would be.

"Hi, guys," said Bree, but her eyes were all for Tom, which made him feel even fuller than before, which should have been impossible but apparently wasn't.

The weirdest thing was that he hadn't even noticed her the first time he had come to the diner. He had been too deeply mired in his own pain to be admiring a butt and legs. But Bree had nice ones. He had come to realize that in the months after his arrival, when the rawness of his situation began to ease and he started looking around him, but even then he wasn't consciously aware of being drawn to her. He just knew he liked her. He liked her hair, which was dark and thick and slightly disobedient, and her eyes, which were hazel and warm. He liked the way a smile lit her face, as though her pleasure was thorough. And yeah, he liked her butt and her legs.

Come late summer, he had begun looking forward to seeing her at the diner, but it wasn't until after the accident, when he watched her for hours on end, when he touched her and let her lean on him, that he felt the force of physical attraction. By then, the emotional attraction was established and strong. He supposed that was what had made the physical one so powerful.

And powerful it was, but not in the typical way. He didn't need to look at her mouth or her breasts or her belly to feel it. All he had to do was look into her eyes.

Eliot loudly cleared his throat. "Ah, kids, excuse me."

Tom jumped. He hadn't realized Eliot was still there.

Bree blushed. Sending Eliot an embarrassed grin and Tom a last look, she headed for the booths.

Tom took a steadying breath.

"You're hit bad," Eliot remarked.

Slowly, Tom raised his head. His eyes found the stainless-steel wall panel and, in the reflection of the diner, found Bree. The image was vaguely distorted and pretty even then. He took another breath. "Tell me about it."

"Nah-uh. Got something else to tell you. Martin says you helped him on a case."

Tom looked at him in surprise.

"Some business with the Littles," Eliot went on. "They'll be coming into some money that they didn't think they'd get."

"Hey, Tom," said LeeAnn in passing, "what an *awesome* ring."

Tom smiled his thanks but was glad she didn't linger. "Martin told you I helped?" he asked Eliot.

"Yup. Surprised me, too. I don't know if Martin took your suggestions because he thought they were good, or if he was afraid that if he didn't you'd do the work yourself, but the important thing is that the Littles are getting what's due them." He frowned at his coffee cup, tapped the rim with his thumbs. "Can I ask you something?"

Tom steeled himself for a warning about butting in on Martin's business.

"I got a phone call the other day," Eliot said, in a voice that was low and private. "Don't quite know what to do about it."

Tom didn't, either, if it was what he thought. "Media?" he asked, wondering if his praise of the discretion of the townsfolk of Panama had been premature.

"No. It was a call from the family of one of the people who recently moved to this town." Eliot ran his tongue over his lower lip, shot Tom a warning look. "Can I trust you won't talk?"

Tom was so relieved that he would have promised most anything. Confidentiality was a cinch. "Yes."

Eliot's back curved around his secret. His voice went even lower. "It was from Julia Dean's son. He said he thought she was in trouble. Thought someone was holding her hostage."

"Holding her hostage? I doubt that. I see her coming and going."

"I told him the same thing. He said he meant mentally. He thinks the woman's been brainwashed or is somehow else being controlled by another person. He asked me to investigate. So I made a point of dropping by the flower shop to talk with Julia, and she seemed perfectly fine to me. When I called the son back and told him, I thought he'd be pleased." Eliot shook his head no. "He wants me to charge her with theft."

"Theft of what?"

Eliot's eyes flew past Tom. Even before Tom could turn, his shoulder was clasped. "Hey, Chief, is this the guy?"

Four large men stood there. Tom recognized them as truckers who had been at the diner before.

"Sure is," Eliot said. "Tom Gates, meet John Hagan, Kip Tucker, Gene Mackey, T. J. Kearns."

Four beefy hands shook Tom's in turn, each one accompanied by a comment.

"You got a great girl. Bree's the best."

"One look at her face and we could see something was up."

"I'd'a gone after her myself, if I wasn't already married."

"Take care of her, man."

Tom watched them trail off. As he swiveled forward again, he felt the same fullness he had earlier. Celebrity status had never been so good.

"Money," Eliot said by his ear. "From the trust left by her husband. Seems she was supposed to use the interest only, but she went ahead and helped herself to more. When I told him she had the flower shop and a small house, he was surprised. He thought she was just working for a florist and renting a place. I thought it'd calm him to know where the money went. Just the opposite. He got more angry."

"How could he not know what she was doing?" Tom asked, but the minute the question was out, he realized its absurdity. *His* family didn't know much more about his current life than his address and phone number, which was all he had shared with them, and that by letter. He had hoped they might write back and ask. When they hadn't done so he blamed them for not wanting to know, which was probably a cop-out on his part.

Probably? Definitely.

For the second time in as many minutes, Eliot dragged him back to the subject at hand. "The son and a daughter live in Des Moines. Julia visits them twice a year, but she doesn't talk about them much around here, so I'd guess she doesn't talk about us much when she's there. It's like she's got two separate lives."

"There's no crime in that."

"That's what I told him. He said it'd be okay if it weren't for the money."

Tom didn't know much more about wills and estates than he knew about intellectual property law, but certain things were basic law school fare. "If there's a trust, there's a trustee."

"She's it."

"Then her husband must have trusted her."

"That's what I told the son. He said she changed after he died. The thing is," Eliot said, shifting awkwardly on his stool, "I could tell Julia about the calls, but I don't much care to. She's a nice lady, y'know?"

Tom did. She was quiet and pleasant, she worked hard, and she was talented. She had sent Bree four flower arrangements in all, one at the hospital, three others during her recuperation at home. He often saw her arranging fresh flowers in the small table vases here at the diner. Flash had told him that her prices were dirt cheap.

So she wasn't a businesswoman. So she needed to take money from the trust fund to survive. That wasn't a crime, either.

"Does the son have a case?" Eliot asked.

"You can't know that without reading the trust instrument. Many trust instruments allow for emergency disbursement of money. If this one does, it may be a question of the son differing with his mother's definition of emergency. In any event, there's nothing you can do. If charges are brought, they have to be brought in Des Moines, if that's where the trust was drawn up and executed. The son has to go to authorities there."

Eliot nodded. "I pretty much told him that. I just wasn't sure if I should be doing anything more on this end. I wouldn't want to be accused of shirking my responsibility."

"Will you look at her?" Flash interrupted to ask. Bree was serving an early-evening breakfast to the local boys Sam, Dave, Andy, and Jack. "She's on cloud nine. Didn't make a peep when another gallon of milk turned up bad." He moved on.

Tom watched Bree until she winked at him on her way back to the kitchen. Strengthened, he told Eliot, "I wouldn't worry about shirking your responsibility. There isn't much you can do in a case like this without violating Julia's civil rights." That was a field of law about which he did know a lot. Some of his most celebrated cases involved civil rights issues.

Eliot took a deep breath that uncurled his spine. "Good. I like the woman." He snorted. "If you ask me, I'd rather have Julia in my town than her greedy son, any day."

What stuck with Tom about the discussion wasn't Julia or her son; it was the fact that their lack of communication was so common a problem. Things happened in families. Angry words were spoken, hurt was inflicted. Oh, those things happened among friends, too, but that was different. People were more vulnerable where family was concerned. The angry words were hotter, the hurt was more painful. Silences grew to become as obtrusive as the most bothersome of family members.

Breaking the silence was the problem. It took strength, and in his instance it meant dealing with pride and with fear. He had been grappling with both for months. What made the difference now were his feelings for Bree.

She was sleeping soundly when he left the bedroom and picked up the phone in his office. It was eleven at night, ten in Ohio. With any luck, his father would be asleep.

He punched out the number and waited nervously, holding his finger over the disconnect button, wavering right up until the moment he heard Alice's voice rather than his father's.

"Hi, Lissa. It's Tom."

There was a stunned pause, then a soft "I know who it is. No one else calls me that anymore. No one else has your voice."

Compliment or complaint, he wasn't sure. "It's been a while."

"A long one," she said. She had never been one to beat around the bush. Spunky, was what she was called.

"How are you?" he asked.

"Okay. And you?"

"Not bad. Actually, I'm pretty good."

"Are you back in New York?"

"No. I'll be staying here in Vermont."

There was another pause, then a skeptical "Staying, as in permanently?"

"Funny, isn't it? I was in such a rush to see the world. Now here I am in another small town."

"They're good for some things." She sounded expectant, as if she was waiting for the second shoe to fall.

He let it. "I've met a woman here. Her name's Bree. We're engaged."

"Engaged to be *married?*"

He smiled at her astonishment. "Yes."

"Are you sure?"

He knew she was remembering the pride he had taken in being named one of the twenty-five most eligible bachelors by *People.* He had strutted around for days after the issue had come out.

"I'm sure. Bree's a remarkable woman. I've been wanting to tell you about her for a while. You'll like her a lot, Lissa. I'd love you to meet her."

Her voice hardened a touch. "Will you bring her here to visit?"

He wanted to. But if he went there now, it would be a nightmare of a visit. More quietly, he said, "I need to do some patching up there first."

"That's wise."

"They're still angry?"

"Shouldn't they be?" she asked. "They won't ever forget what you did, Tom, and it wasn't only when Mom died."

"I know."

"Dad doesn't want your money."

Tom knew that, too. Every check he sent was returned uncashed. More quietly, he asked, "How is he?"

"Old and mean and crotchety."

"More so than usual?"

"You could say that." There was a change in her voice then, a crack in the spunk. "He isn't pleased with me. I did the unthinkable."

Tom could think of only one thing that was unthinkable for a daughter of Harris Gates.

"That's right," she singsonged. "I'm pregnant."

His first response was excitement, his second was to think.

"Right again," she said in his silence. "Pregnant and unmarried."

"That's still great . . . I think. Who's the guy?"

"Someone I work with."

"Are you marrying him?"

"No."

"Why not?"

"I don't love him."

"Did he ask?"

"Yes. I said no."

"Do you want the baby?"

"I'm not on the witness stand," she protested, in a way that said Tom's grilling was the latest of many.

"I'm sorry," he said gently. "I just want to know if you're happy."

"I am. Yes, I want the baby. I love babies, and I'm not getting any younger."

"You're only thirty-eight."

"Thirty-nine next month."

And still living in her father's house, much as Bree had done until her father had died. In theory, that showed either great strength or great weakness. Tom knew it was the former in both women. They were a lot alike. "When's the baby due?"

"April."

Three months off. So she was six months pregnant. And he hadn't known.

He tried to picture his little sister with a round belly and couldn't quite. He imagined that wasn't the case to his father's disapproving eye. "Come live with us, Lissa," he said on impulse. "Have the baby here."

There was sadness in Alice's voice when she said, "And give up my life here? I can't do that, Tom. You left when you were eighteen and didn't look back. I've been here all along. I can't leave now. I won't do that to myself, and I won't do it to the people I love."

"But if Dad is making your life miserable—"

"He'll come around. If not before, then after. He may have gripes with his kids, but he loves his grandkids. If you'd spent any time around here, you'd know that."

Tom did know it. There had been grandkids aplenty before the estrangement. He had seen his father with them. At the time, he had attributed the softness to age. Now he realized that that was only part of it.

"Then will you just come to visit?" he asked. Even beyond introducing Bree to Alice, he wanted Alice to see Panama. He knew she would like it.

"That might be hard."

"Because of work?" Alice wrote for the local newspaper.

"Because of Dad. And Carl and Max and Peter and Dan."

The opposition was formidable. Tom took it step by step. "Would you come for my wedding?"

"When is it?"

"Soon, I hope."

"I can't promise anything, Tom."

But she hadn't hung up at the sound of his voice, which was something. "I'm happy about the baby, Lissa. If anyone will be a great mom, it's you. Do you need anything?"

"You mean like money?" she asked, with an edge.

Yes, that was what he had meant. It had been an automatic thing. Less automatically, more thoughtfully, he said, "Support of any kind."

"I have what I need."

"Will you let me know if you don't?"

She didn't answer.

"Can I call you again?" he asked, and this time he waited. After what seemed an eternity, she whispered a soft, "As long as he doesn't know," and quietly hung up the phone.

Bree woke up when Tom came back to bed. She assumed he had just gone to the bathroom and was surprised to find his hands and feet cold. When he drew her into the curve of his body, she shivered. "Where've you been?" she murmured against the pillow.

"On the phone," Tom breathed against her hair. "I called my sister."

Bree opened her eyes. "You did?" She turned in his arms to see him, though it was too dark to see much. "How was it?"

"Nice."

"She didn't hang up?"

He chuckled. It was a sweet sound, which said he was feeling pleased. "Only at the end. I told her about you. I invited her to the wedding. I said I'd get back to her with a date. So. What do you think?"

Bree slipped her arms around his neck. "I think it's great. I'm proud of you. You took the first step."

He gave her a squeeze. "About the wedding. What do you think?"

"I think I can't set a date until I get used to being engaged. Tell me about Alice. Was she friendly?"

"Mostly."

"Mostly?"

"She's between a rock and a hard place."

"Between your dad and you?"

"And my brothers and me. It won't be easy, reconciling."

"But you want it. I know you do."

"I do."

She beamed. "I'm *so glad* you called her."

He drew back his head. "You didn't wish for it, did you?"

"Me? No." When he continued to look at her, she said, "I swear I didn't. But I might have. That would have been something worthwhile to spend a wish on."

He sighed, relaxed, and drew her in tight. "I used to think family wasn't important."

"It is."

"I'm sorry I never knew yours."

"Don't be," Bree said. Her grandparents would have been scandalized by Tom's reputation. Her father would have positively faded into the woodwork beside him. "It's better this way."

"What about your mother?"

"What about her?"

"Do you ever think about her?"

Bree did. More often in the last few months. "Sometimes."

"Do you ever think about tracking her down?"

"I used to think about doing it. Then time passed and I let it go. Maybe I should wish for her," she said on a whim. "Y'know, make that one of my three wishes. It'd be a good one, don't you think?"

"It would. Hypothetically."

"I know, I know. You're afraid I'll set my heart on seeing her, and then if the wish doesn't work, I'll be upset."

"I don't want you upset."

"But it'd be a good wish," she reasoned, warming to the idea. "It isn't greedy, like for something material. And it isn't vague. If I wish for my mother, she either shows up or she doesn't. Then I'll know, one way or another."

"About the wishes."

"About the wishes." She snuggled closer, warm and suddenly sleepy again. "I'm happy for you, Tom," she whispered.

"Me, too," he whispered back.

The idea of wishing for her mother might have come on a whim, but Bree couldn't believe how perfect it was. Getting engaged was something to share with a parent, and this woman was the only parent Bree had left. If ever there was a time to try to reach her, it was now.

So while Tom was putting coffee on to brew one morning the following week, she came close to him at the counter and said, "I'm doing it, Tom. I'm wishing for my mother."

He stopped mid-scoop. "A real wish?"

"If that's what they are."

He finished measuring coffee into the filter. By the time he was done, she saw telltale lines between his brows and by his mouth.

"What?" she asked.

He turned to her. "I don't want you hurt."

"By what? The wishes not being real? Or her not being what I want her to be?"

"Either."

Bree had given both possibilities plenty of thought. "It's okay if the wishes aren't real. But I have to know one way or another, and I won't unless I try something else. The fire may have been caused by the furnace. It may have been a coincidence at the time that I made my wish. This is different. What would be the chance of the woman materializing after all these years at exactly the same time that I'm wishing her to appear?"

"Slim."

"Very. Her name was Matty Ryan. My father met her in Boston and followed her to Chicago. I was born there. He never brought her back here. So maybe she doesn't know where I am. This would help both of us."

Tom looked pained.

"Okay," Bree conceded. "Maybe she could have found me if she wanted to. But what if she was afraid I wouldn't want to see her after all this time?"

"Do you know for sure that she's still alive?"

"No. But she was twenty when I was born, so she'd only be fifty-three now. That's not very old. Think about it," she said, when he remained doubtful. "What do I have to lose? Worst-case scenario, no one shows up, so I can forget the business about the dreams."

"Worst-case scenario," he corrected, "she shows up and isn't what you want her to be." He took her face in coffee-scented hands. "As long as you recognize that that's a possibility, it's okay."

She wrapped her fingers around his wrists, wanting him to know how sure she was that making this wish was right. "My grandparents said she didn't want me, and my father never disagreed. So that's what I've believed all my life. Isn't *that* the worst-case scenario? That she doesn't want me?" Her eyes softened. She allowed herself to feel the excitement she had been trying to stem. "But what if she does? I've read stories about women who gave babies up for adoption and were reunited with them years later. What if I could have a reunion like that with my mother? What if there were *reasons* why she gave me up? My father loved her. I used to see a look in his eyes that I never understood until I met you. I feel it in me when I look at you, the same wanting I saw in his eyes. He never stopped loving her. But what if she didn't love him? What if his love frightened her? What if she felt *suffocated* by it? What if she had no money at all and thought I'd be better off with my father? What if she just assumed he would pour some of that love into me?"

A silence fell between them.

"He didn't," Tom said sadly.

"No. I wasn't her. She must have been special."

He folded her in his arms. "So are you."

She could feel his conviction in the way he held her. It gave her strength. "I want to do this, Tom."

He took her face again and kissed her this time. She imagined she tasted vulnerability, even desperation, in him.

"It'll be okay," she soothed. "Don't you see? I could have gone looking for her years ago, but I didn't feel strong enough then. I couldn't take the risk. I didn't have enough to hold me up if she turned her back and walked away. Now I do." She rose on tiptoe, stretched her arms way up past his neck, and held on tight. The sense of fullness was back, richer than ever. She breathed it in and smiled.

"And if it's the second wish?" he whispered. "What then?"

"No more wishes."

It must have been the right answer, because after another minute, he held her back and she knew she had won. The worry lines had left his face. Anticipation was in their place.

"So how do you do it?" he asked. "Is there a ritual?"

She felt a burst of excitement. "There were never any specific instructions. I guess I'll just do what I did last time." She laced her fingers and shut her eyes. In the next instant, they popped open again. "You won't laugh, will you?"

"Of course not."

"This must look pretty silly to someone who doesn't believe."

"Bree."

"Okay." She closed her eyes tighter this time, brought her laced hands to her chin, and said, "I . . . wish . . . to see . . . my mother." She conjured up an image of the being of light, waited until she felt the warmth of it and its calm, and said the words again.

Then she opened her eyes. They met Tom's expectant ones. Only their breathing broke the silence. Slowly, she unlaced her fingers, let her hands fall to her sides, and relaxed.

For the longest time, they simply looked at each other. Finally, Tom whispered, "What now?"

"Now we wait."

# chapter
# eleven

Bree sat on pins and needles through breakfast and a morning of stripping gray paint from the pine moldings in Tom's living room. Working side by side, she and Tom exchanged the occasional expectant glance. The slightest sound from outside brought their heads around, but the doorbell didn't ring.

Bree refused to be discouraged. "It could take a while. The fire didn't happen until six hours after the wish. Maybe I have to be at work. You know, thinking about other things."

She was grateful, though, when, rather than dropping her off at the diner, Tom parked and came in. He read in his corner booth while she worked, then switched to the counter when the lunch business picked up. His presence reassured her, as did the ring on her hand. They made her feel less alone than she might otherwise have felt.

Regulars came and went. Of the new faces that appeared, not a one was female.

Lunchtime passed. Bree grew more edgy. "What do you think?" she asked Tom, back in his booth now.

"She could be coming a distance. Let's give it more time."

His voice held no mockery. He was as into the wish as she was. She would have loved him for that alone, if she hadn't loved him already.

"What if it takes days?" she asked, impatient now.

He slid her an encouraging smile. "You've waited this long."

Yes. She had. Waiting now, she remembered those years. Bits and snatches of the old curiosity—questions about her mother's appearance, taste, and personality—had been distracting her all day, so that she had forgotten things like Carl Breen taking his scrambled eggs dry and Travis Fitch wanting his chili with cheese. But Tom was right. She had waited this long. A little longer wouldn't hurt.

She returned to work. After another hour of only locals walking through the door, though, she had another thought. "A watched pot never boils," she told Tom. "I think you should leave."

Tom shook his head. "I'm staying with you."

"What if she's waiting at the house?"

That gave him pause. "Do you think she might be?"

"I don't know," Bree said, feeling bewildered. "I don't know *anything.*" Pushing loose strands of hair back from her cheek, she eyed the door. "This is frustrating."

He closed his book. "What would make you feel best?"

She weighed the comfort of his being there against the fear that her mother might be looking for her elsewhere. "If she goes to the house on South Forest and sees that it's burned out, she might stop somewhere in town and ask. Most people would direct her here. Some might direct her to your place. Or she might just know to go there," she added more softly, because there wouldn't be any rational explanation for that. But then, there was no rational explanation for the idea of three wishes, yet here she was, having made a second one.

"I think," she said, "that we should cover our bases. Just to be sure."

He nodded. "I'll go back there and check. I'll check South Forest, too." He slid out of the booth. "Will you be okay here?"

She looked up at him and swallowed, pressed her face to his shoulder, breathed in the clean, male scent that was his alone. In that instant, she knew that she would never, *never* have been able to do this without his support. He was her safety net if the wish went all wrong.

"I'll be fine," she said. "I have ordering to do. I can set the computer up right here and watch the door. No one much is coming. Suppertime's still a ways off."

Promising to be back before then, Tom left. Bree opened the laptop at his booth, from where she could see both the diner and the parking lot entrance. Her eye kept wandering to the latter.

At half past three, daylight was waning, but it wasn't that as much as the late-January cold that reduced Panama to grays and whites. The ground was snow-crusted, the roads were dirty. The evergreens looked drab and withdrawn. Frost lined most everything in sight, from windows to truck bumpers to tree limbs to breath.

With the disposal of Christmas decorations, the job of providing color fell to the human population of the town. As Bree watched, a group of neon-jacketed students from the regional high school piled out of a souped-up red Chevy and came in for snacks. A truckload of telephone company workers, wearing orange reflecting vests and ruddy cheeks, ordered hot coffee and sandwiches. Angus, Oliver, and Jack shuffled in for sticky buns, wearing their plaid jackets and bright wool caps. Julia Dean pulled up in her yellow van, with a load of fresh flowers.

Bree always admired Julia's work, but never more so than in the dreary winter months. Julia saw color where others didn't. She could walk into the woods and return with armloads of shrubbery stems, fir fronds, and berry sprigs. Alone, they were beautiful. With the addition of a single hothouse flower, they were striking. Of all the bills Bree paid for Flash in a month, the one she did with the most pleasure was the one submitted quietly, almost apologetically, by Julia.

A car turned off East Main. Bree's eye was back on the window in time to see it pull up beside the front steps in the space reserved for the handicapped. Though the marking was hidden under the snow, regulars to the diner knew not to park there. That was the first thing to alert Bree. The second was the car itself, a sporty little Mercedes that should have had the same winter muck on its flanks as all the other cars in the lot, but didn't. The third thing was the driver. She rose from the car to an average height and ran a hand through hair that was shorter than Bree's, though just as dark. When the wind caught that hair seconds later, she turned and quickly locked up the car. Holding the lapels of a stunning navy suit closed against the cold, she trotted up the steps.

Bree's heart began to pound. She watched the woman enter the diner, straighten her collar, and look around, more curious than searching. Her gaze touched Bree and moved on. Bree was trying to decide if it had lingered a second longer on her than on others, when the woman strode toward her.

Bree didn't breathe.

The woman slid in two booths away, set a briefcase-type purse on the table, loosened the silk scarf around her neck, and studied the menu.

Her coloring was right, Bree decided. So were her features. Her skin looked young, and her hair had no gray, though Bree knew that both qualities could be artificially achieved. But the neck never lied. Nor did the hands. Judging from the two, this woman could easily be fifty-three.

LeeAnn rounded the counter, and in a flash Bree was up, waving her off. "I'll take this one," she said, fumbling nervously for her order pad. She was at the table before she managed to fish a pen from her apron.

"Hi," she said, with a breathless smile. "Welcome." She tucked a strand of hair behind her ear, wishing she had done something more with it, fearing she looked a mess. The wind might have caught this woman's hair when she had stepped from her car, but every strand had fallen back into place. She looked professional and sophisticated and smelled expensive, all of which was consistent with the car, the suit, and the large emerald ring on her hand.

She glanced at Bree and back down without a smile.

Bree wasn't discouraged. She figured that if the woman had any character at all, she had to be scared out of her wits, seeing her daughter for the first time in thirty-three years. She had taken pains to look nice. That much was clear. The diner hadn't seen anyone dressed as well in years. Nor had the town, for that matter.

Bree searched for an opener that was less threatening than just coming right out and confronting the woman. "Is this your first time in Panama?" she finally asked.

"Definitely."

"Are you just passing through?"

"God willing." She waved a negligent hand at the menu, put that same hand to her throat, and raised direct eyes to Bree. "I am parched. Could you bring me some Perrier, please? And I'd like to eat something hot but light. What do you recommend?"

The CEO of a large corporation, Bree decided. Being a take-charge type was necessary and commendable for someone in that kind of position. No doubt she had hundreds, even thousands, of employees on her payroll. No doubt she had more than one office and more than one home. No doubt she had frequent-flier mileage piling up right and left. She had been to exotic places and met exotic people. She had ambition.

Bree wondered if that ambition was what had made her decide to give up her child. And if she had decided the other way, what might Bree's life have been like? One thing was for sure. This woman—a onetime free spirit, if the story was right—had left Haywood Miller in the dust.

"Excuse me," the woman said. "You are here to take my order, aren't you?"

Bree dropped her pen. She bent to pick it up. "Yes. I'm sorry. You wanted Perrier. And something hot and light. Did you see the specials board?"

"No. Is there anything on it that's hot and light?"

Bree started to point to the board, then caught the woman's expression. Its impatience said that she didn't want to look herself but wanted a recommendation. Wondering if this was a test, Bree suggested, "Homemade vegetable soup. Flash purées the vegetables, so the soup is healthy and hearty without feeling heavy. He serves it with toasted Parmesan bread sticks."

"That sounds fine," the woman said, and turned to her purse. She drew out a pair of glasses, a pad of paper, and a thick fountain pen that looked luxurious to hold. She uncapped it, then looked up at Bree. "Is there a problem?"

Bree hurried off for the water, all the while telling herself that if the woman was short-tempered, it was nerves. Even the most skilled CEO would feel awkward in a situation like this. Running a business was one thing. Dealing with a sensitive family matter was something else. Bree couldn't imagine anything more sensitive—and intimate—than mother and daughter meeting this way.

"Here you go," she said, and set down a tall glass. Normally, she would have set the bottle of Perrier beside it. This time she did the pouring herself. When the glass was full, she carefully set the bottle behind it. "The soup will be right up."

The woman frowned. "I wanted a twist of lime."

Bree left. She sliced a fresh lime and returned. After setting the plate down by the glass, she smoothed the narrow band of her apron. It was an unconscious gesture, meant to ease the nest of knots in her stomach, but in the doing, Bree saw a side benefit. No thinking, breathing woman could miss her ring. It was just as stunning as this woman's emerald. Surely, it was an opener.

The woman didn't take it.

Casually, Bree asked, "Where are you from?"

The woman darted her a glance over the top of her glasses. "New York." Setting the pen aside, she took several lime slices, squeezed them over the water, dropped them in, and took a drink.

"Are you on your way there now?"

She shook her head. "Montreal." She picked up the pen and began writing.

"On business?"

A nod this time.

Bree would probably have been just as tight-mouthed, had she been in this woman's shoes. Nobody in her right mind would tip her hand too soon or put herself in a position of vulnerability unless she knew she would be well received.

"My dad had a friend once. Actually, more than a friend. He was madly in love with her. The way he described her, she could have been you." It wasn't quite true. Bree's father hadn't done much describing, despite Bree's pleas. But the fib was for a good cause.

"Hm," the woman said in acknowledgment but little else. She sounded unimpressed, even uninterested. Bree wondered if that, too, was a cover.

"Were you ever in Boston?"

Sighing, the woman set down her pen. "I grew up in Boston."

"You did? Not California?"

"No. Not California."

"Did you ever live in California?"

"No." She glanced toward the kitchen, then looked back at Bree. "Is my soup ready yet? I have to get some work done here."

"I'll check."

Bree dashed straight through the kitchen to the employees' bathroom. She brushed her hair, pinched her cheeks hard, reglossed her lips. Cursing softly, she brushed lint from her black jeans. Then she washed her hands, buffed her ring on her thigh, and went for the soup.

By the time she returned to the table, the woman was talking on a cellular phone. In the process of sliding the soup bowl onto the place mat, Bree caught phrases like "grand jury" and "show cause" and excitedly revised her theory. She left to give the woman privacy, but the minute the phone was set aside, she returned.

"I'm sorry, I couldn't help overhearing some of what you were saying. Are you a lawyer?" She was about to say that her fiancé was, too, which would give them a small bit of common ground, when the woman shot her a quelling look.

"No, I'm not a lawyer. Look, I've come a long way today, and I'm tired and hungry." She picked up her spoon and arched a brow.

Bree forced an apologetic little laugh. "Sorry," she said, and withdrew, discouraged for the first time. Tom had warned her that the mother she found might not be the one she wanted, and that was okay. She hadn't expected that they would fall into each other's arms and be inseparable. She didn't want it, didn't need it. She had her own life. She'd done just fine without a mother up to now and could do just fine again.

*If* this woman *was* her mother.

Feeling shaky and unsure, she returned to her own booth and closed the laptop. Flash was napping in the office, sprawled in the chair with his feet on the desk. She stole in, set down the computer, and stole out, then called Tom from the kitchen phone and whispered a frantic "She's here—at least I think it's her, but I don't know for sure. She's beautiful and rich, and so different from anyone who usually comes that I don't know what to say to her or how to get her to say whether she is who I think she is."

"What's she doing now?"

"Eating soup. But she isn't admitting anything, she isn't very friendly at all, and I don't know what to *say*."

"Hang in there, honey. I'm on my way."

Bree hung up, ran to the door, and peeked through the window. The woman was still there, looking elegant and out of place. It would have been worse if the diner had been full, but the predinner lull was in effect. LeeAnn was at the counter, talking to Gavin, Julia was arranging the last of her stems, the grillman and the cook were smoking out back.

Taking a damp cloth and a deep breath, Bree went out front

and began to wipe down unoccupied bench seats in anticipation of the evening crowd. It was a job that justified her looking from booth to booth.

The woman alternately jotted down notes and spooned up her soup. Her hand was steady, her movements were smooth. At one point, she made another phone call. She looked thoughtful, distant. From time to time, she glanced up. Each time, Bree averted her eyes and poured herself into her work, but the more she thought about what was happening, the more frightened she grew. Time was passing. Before long, the woman would finish her soup, pay her bill, and be gone. If this was Bree's wish fulfillment—this one brief meeting with her mother—she wanted to know.

She pictured the being of light and let the peace of it calm her, but there were no answers to be had in that calm. *Tell me she's it,* she begged. *Give me a sign. Just so I'll know I've seen her once, so I'll know my wish came true.*

Nothing.

*Then Tom,* she pleaded, peering through frosty windows to search East Main for a sign of his truck. *Bring him quickly. He'll know what to do. He can carry this off better than me.*

But Tom wasn't there. She was on her own, just as she had been for most of her life, and why? Because some woman—perhaps this one—had decided she didn't want to be a mother, well after the deed had been done.

Desperate to know the why of that, she tucked the damp cloth behind the counter and went to the booth where the woman sat. "I have to ask you something," she said, in a voice that surely betrayed her fear but was the best she could do.

The woman took a wallet from her large leather purse. "How much do I owe you?"

"Does the name Haywood Miller mean anything to you?"

A ten came out of the wallet. "I'm afraid not. Do you have my check?"

Bree took the pad from her pocket. "Thirty-five years ago, Haywood Miller was working in Boston when he met a woman named Matty Ryan. I was thinking you might be her."

"Me?" The woman shuddered. She gestured toward Bree's pad. "I have to be going. I owe you what—five, six dollars?"

"They fell in love, but something happened, and they had to separate. He never forgot her. He loved her until the day he died."

The woman set down the ten and reached for her purse. "This should cover it."

"Wait. I need to know. This may be my only chance."

But the woman was tucking the purse under her arm and starting for the door.

Bree caught her arm. "This sounds bizarre, but you may be my mother."

Cold eyes pinned her in place. "Your *mother?* Oh, please. Look, I don't know any Haywood Miller, and my name isn't Matty Ryan, and I pray that no daughter of mine would accost a stranger in a diner. Now"—she glanced at Bree's hand on the sleeve of her suit—"if you don't release my arm, I'll charge you with assault."

Bree let go. She watched the woman leave the diner, climb into her car, and speed off down East Main toward the highway. By then, her eyes were flooded with tears.

"It's all right," came a soft voice behind her. A tentative hand touched her shoulder. "She isn't your mother." Julia Dean was there, looking heartsick. "I couldn't help but overhear."

Bree looked at Julia, then beyond. Most everyone in the diner was watching her. She made an embarrassed sound, shook her head, and went to the end of the row of booths. Julia came right along.

Elbows on the jukebox, Bree pressed her fingers under her eyes to stem the tears. "It's okay. Really. I don't know what I expected." She grew angry. "A woman would have to be pretty cold to abandon her newborn baby. She'd have to be pretty selfish to go through life without ever calling on the phone or sending a card. She'd have to be *heartless* to just vanish." She blew out a shaky breath. "I used to wait on my birthday. I figured she couldn't forget that date. But she did. Every year. I thought she might come when my father died, but I guess that didn't mean anything to her, either." She turned pleading eyes to Julia. "What kind of a person *does* that?"

Julia didn't answer. Looking as pained as Bree felt, she moved her hand in small, light circles on Bree's shoulder. Finally, gently, she said, "There may be a reason. She may not have done all those things out of choice. She may have thought about you a lot."

Bree wanted to believe it. She almost could, hearing it in Julia's sure voice. Still, there was the lingering scent of the woman who had just come and gone. "That woman didn't look like she was even curious."

"She isn't your mother."

"How can I know that? How can I be sure?"

"Your mother wouldn't talk to you like that. She wouldn't sit here and order you around. She wouldn't come all this way just to hurt you."

"How do you *know?*"

"Because you're not like that," Julia said, with a small squeeze and more of that quiet confidence. "And everyone in town says you take after your mother."

Bree sighed. "No one here has ever met her."

"It makes sense, though, doesn't it?"

"I suppose." She sure didn't take after her father.

A winded Tom rushed to her side, with a dismayed "I missed her."

Bree leaned into him. "You did. Boy. She was something."

"Not your mother," Julia repeated, and left her with Tom.

"No?" Tom asked Bree.

"She denied it."

"What else is new?"

"She was really beautiful. That was always one of my dreams. But she wasn't very nice. Maybe I came on too strong. Maybe I scared her away."

"Maybe Julia's right and she isn't the one."

"Maybe. But how will I know, Tom? How will I know for sure?"

*       *       *

As miraculous as Tom's presence in her life was, he didn't have an answer. Back home that night, when he questioned her about the woman who had come to the diner, Bree told him everything she remembered, right down to the pale pink of the woman's nail polish. But Bree didn't have the number of her license plate, and Tom agreed that a sporty red Mercedes wasn't any more unique in New York than a woman who wore a smart navy suit and carried a briefcase-type purse with a cellular phone inside.

So the woman was gone. Left behind, ongoing, was the matter of the three wishes.

Tom disagreed with the ongoing part. "It's over, Bree. That's it. Two wishes, no more."

"But what if they weren't wishes?"

"What if they were? I won't take that chance."

"*I'm* the one taking the chance."

"No, no, honey," he said, with a firm head shake and as determined a look as she had ever seen. "It's my chance, too. I'm the one who loves you. I'm the one who needs you. I'm the one who wants to live with you for the rest of my life. It may have been your chance three months ago, but now it's *our* chance. I say forget about the wishes. You've made two, and we can't prove they didn't come true. I don't want you trying a third. Not after what you said to me in the hospital about your fear of your time being up once you spend that last wish."

Bree might have argued more if she had felt he was being controlling for the sake of having control, but all she saw beneath his vehemence was love.

"Let's set a date," he said.

She searched his eyes. They were a strong sterling gray in a season of grays, but warmer and more uplifting than any other gray in town. She wondered if they would stay that way even when the reality of her not being able to have a child set in. "You need to think about it more."

"What's to think about?"

"Kids."

"I've already thought about that. It's settled. Like the matter of three wishes. Over and done. A no-brainer. We'll adopt."

"*Think* about it, Tom."

"What do you think I do all the time you're at work?"

"Paint walls. Strip woodwork. Sand floors."

"And think about you." He paused, frowned. "Is there something else, something I don't know about, that's holding you back?"

"God, no. I love you."

"But you don't trust me."

"Of course I do."

"It's my track record, isn't it?"

"No! I've never trusted anyone the way I trust you."

"Then why don't you believe that I mean what I say? The issue of kids is okay. Before I met you, I'd given up the idea of having kids, period."

"You come from a big family. You want one of your own, I know you do."

"Small family, big family, we can have what we want, and *don't*"—he held up a warning hand—"don't say adopting isn't the same, because I disagree." He took a step back. "Adopting is a nonissue. I can say that a dozen times, but you don't seem to want to be convinced. So there has to be something else on your mind. Maybe when you figure out what it is, you'll let me know."

His face was a mess of anger and hurt that she didn't know how to address, and then it was too late. For the very first time in their relationship, he backed off.

It was a while before Bree found the something else that was giving her pause, and then it came only after she stepped away from the relationship and looked at the whole. Childbearing was an issue, but more for her than for him. She was the one who still had to come to terms with her body's failings. In the excitement of being with Tom, falling in love, and getting his ring, she hadn't done that. She had been happy to be swept up in a world as fantastic as anything she had ever seen in her private little dreams.

The deeper issue had to do with the whole of that fantastic world. Until last October, she had been a realist. Then the accident happened, and her life had changed. But threads of the realist remained. They were reminding her of where Tom had come from, what he had been, and the sheer improbability of his landing in Panama, let alone as her lover. They were tweaking the far reaches of her mind into wondering now whether all that was real. They were trying to reconcile the life she had thought was perfectly fine before with this new one, which seemed too good to be true.

Bree could think of only one person in town who could help her decide if it was.

# chapter
# twelve

No one in Panama knew exactly when Verity Greene had come to town. It might have been twenty years before. It might have been twenty-two, or eighteen. People simply started seeing her walking across the green or browsing in the library or the general store. If she attended town events, it was at a distance. Likewise, she came to the diner at odd times and only when the counter stool at the far end was free. She minded her own business and spoke only when spoken to, and then with a southern accent that charmed Bree but made others all the more wary.

What she said didn't help if endearing herself to the town

was her goal. She was forever contradicting popular sentiment. Though she did it with a smile—and often quite sensibly, Bree thought—she was considered odd. No one understood how her mind worked. No one had cause to find out.

Her house was as much a mystery as she was. It was a small cottage that stood about as far out of town as it could stand and still be in Panama. To get to it meant driving deep into the woods on a rutted path. No one seemed to have known the path existed, much less the cottage, before Verity had taken root there.

From the first, she was considered bohemian. She wore long skirts, vivid crocheted vests, and voluminous blouses. Her hair was long, dark, and wavy, and was held back by a bandanna that covered her forehead. She was always impeccably clean, though as far as anyone in town knew, she had neither hot water nor indoor plumbing. As far as anyone in town knew, she had no electricity, either. She grew her own herbs and vegetables, stripped the best blueberry patches before anyone else could find them, and was thought to eat small animals as they died in the woods. She had no apparent source of income. As for her name, few believed it was real.

Theories had abounded over the years. One theory held that she was an outcast from a commune that had thrived in the seventies in southern Vermont. Another held that she was the daft daughter of a southern billionaire. A third held that she was a witch.

Bree had never believed the last. She had talked with Verity, and while the woman had unusual views and no qualms about sharing them when asked, she seemed harmless. More, she seemed lonely, though when Bree suggested that to others, few agreed. The general consensus was that Verity chose to live as she did. Whether out of fear or respect, the town let her be.

Eliot was one of the few to have ever been to the cottage in the woods. He had described how to get there to Emma, who had told Dotty, who told Jane, who told Bree, who set off in Tom's truck first thing in the morning under the guise of shopping for clothes. She rarely shopped for clothes, *hated* shopping for clothes, and Tom knew it, but he didn't question her. He hadn't said much at all since their talk about setting a wedding date. He had held her, showered with her, made oh-so-sweet love to her. He had fixed her breakfast and eyed her longingly through the eating, but he hadn't said much. Nor had she. She just didn't know what to say.

After stopping at the diner to smuggle food from the back room reserves, she drove to the town line. Once there, she made a U-turn and drove very slowly back until she spotted the twin-trunked birch that was visible only from that direction. Beside it were the faint ruts that marked Verity's road.

The woods were surprisingly dark given the sun above and the snow below. Bree turned on her headlights and jolted along for what seemed an age. The jolting echoed the thud of her heart, which said she had no idea what she was in for. But she didn't stop and turn around. Verity was her last, best, whimsical hope.

When the road finally ended, it was Verity's old orange VW Bug that marked her arrival. The cottage itself was nearly hidden under a cluster of pines.

Uneasy, Bree knocked on the door. She waited several minutes and knocked again. She shifted the bags in her arms and was about to knock a third time, when she saw Verity's startled face at the window. Seconds later, the door opened.

The startled look remained, making Bree wonder when Verity's last visitor had come. Though she was dressed, she wasn't wearing her normal bandanna. Bree hoped she hadn't come at an awkward time.

She held out the bags. "For you."

Verity looked puzzled.

"It's not much, just soup and stew and some other wintry things. I'd have brought your usual," she added, with a tentative smile, "only it wouldn't travel well." Verity's usual was one hot dog, an order of fries, and a Coke. Bree had always thought it a sedate order for someone who was supposedly bizarre, though a perfectly sensible one for someone who normally lived on home-grown goods.

Verity's expression softened. Quietly, she accepted the bags and carried them into the cottage. Bree took a breath for courage and followed, though only enough to close the door. From there, she looked cautiously around. The whole of the place was a single large room, with a kitchen at its far end and a sleeping loft above. The walls were made of exposed logs, the heat was from a wood-burning stove. Baskets of brightly colored yarns were strewed around, a cozy touch. The fragrance that filled the room came from a window garden, where herbs were warmed by a string of sunbeams piercing the pines.

Bree wasn't sure what she had expected—incense smoke, the bodies of little creatures hung to dry, a world of dark corners and eerie sounds—but the cottage held none of that. It was simply furnished, commendably neat, startlingly conventional.

Verity returned to her. In the absence of the bandanna, wisps of gray hair glittered through darker strands. A long shawl covered her blouse and the top of her skirt. She wore thick socks but no shoes.

Bree tucked her hands in her pockets. "I like your place. I didn't know you had lights." She also saw a refrigerator and a television. "You must have your own generator."

"And a satellite dish," Verity said, in her light southern way.

"Ah. Shows how much *we* know." Bree smiled.

Verity looked around the cottage but said nothing.

Bree cleared her throat. "You're probably wondering why I'm here."

"You brought food."

"It's a bribe. I need your advice."

Verity's brows went up. When they came down, she smiled. "I don't think I'm one to be giving advice."

But Bree stood her ground. It was Verity or nothing.

Verity must have sensed her resolve. With a glance toward the back of the cottage, she asked, "Would you like some tea?"

Bree's hands were cold, perhaps from the outdoors, more likely from nerves. She rubbed them together. "That would be nice."

She followed Verity to the kitchen and sat at a scarred wooden table while Verity heated water, warmed a pot, and opened a tin of loose tea leaves. Bree smelled their scent as soon as they hit the air, even more when Verity spooned some into the pot and poured in boiling water. The smell that rose as the tea steeped was raw, rich, and sweet.

Settling in across the table, Verity folded her hands. "What advice do you think I can give?"

Bree had thought long and hard about what words to use. Convinced that her own clumsiness had turned off the woman in the diner and not wanting to do the same here, she had practiced scripts that gently and gradually related the problem. Sitting here, though, with a woman whose home held no pretense, she realized those scripts were misconceived. So, bluntly, she said, "Strange things have happened to me. You're the expert on strange things."

Verity's mouth twitched at that. "UFOs, CE5s, NDEs, OBEs, ESP. I'm not really an expert. Just an observer."

"And a believer."

"Sometimes."

"Do you believe in near-death and out-of-body experiences?"

"Like the ones you had? Yes." The word had two syllables.

"Why?"

Politely, Verity asked, "Why not?"

"Because there's no way to prove that they're real. They happen to people in the middle of traumas, and then they're over and done. Most of my friends think I imagined what happened to me."

Verity rose, took cups and saucers from the cupboard, and set them on the table. They were of fine china, white with delicate green leaves inside a bright gold rim, perfectly matched and unchipped. The stream of tea that filled one, then the other, was a deep shade of bronze. It smelled even richer than before.

Verity settled into her seat. She looked from one cup to the other, seeming to take in the whole picture. Then, sprightly, she raised her head and smiled. In the next instant, her eyes widened. Leaving the table again, she took a package from the bread bin, unwrapped it, cut several slices of whatever it was, and set them on a plate.

"A tea party isn't complete without sweets," she said, as she set down the plate and returned to her chair. "It's apple cake. The apples are from my own trees."

Bree wasn't hungry, but she took a piece of cake. Verity's pride was a tangible thing. Bree couldn't bear the thought of hurting her. Not that she needed to lie about the cake. It was moist, sweet, delicious. She told Verity so and took pleasure in her smile, then set to wondering how to return to the subject at hand.

Verity did it for her. After taking a sip of her tea, she said in a voice that was tea-party conversational, "Your friends think you imagined what happened, because they aren't open to the idea of a different dimension."

Bree blinked. A different dimension. "Am I?"

"Not the you who was raised by your father and grandparents. But the you who likes to stand in the woods and dream."

"How . . . ?"

"I've seen you. I'm a woods walker, too. I've seen the look on your face."

There was no point in denying it, not here, not to Verity, not when Bree's curiosity was whetted. "What kind of different dimension?"

"It's an energy channel. One step above man's everyday level of functioning. It consists of pure thought and feeling."

"Does it take a near death to reach it?"

"No. Psychics do it without. And many people who have near deaths don't reach it. Only the ones with open minds. The ones willing to believe. The others are weighted down by the physical world. They never rise."

"But I've always been a realist," Bree argued.

Teacup in hand, Verity sat back with a smug smile.

Okay, Bree reasoned. So she dreamed. But did that make her different from others?

"You believe in positives," Verity said. "You're an optimist. That's how you survived living with your father all those years. You made a life for yourself at the diner. You looked outward. You saw the glass as half full." She paused. "Those forest fairies stirred up by the wind?"

Bree's eyes went wide.

Verity smiled and shook a gently chiding finger. "Your face doesn't hide much. I've watched you watch them. Some people see drifting leaves. You and I, we see life."

*You and I.* Bree had a startling thought.

But Verity was speaking on, slowly and softly, with only the faintest of drawls. "You believe in a world of possibility. Not everyone does. Your friends don't, which is why they have trouble believing what you experienced. That, and they're jealous."

Of Tom? Of her diamond ring? "Of what?"

"Of the inner peace you found."

"What inner peace?" Bree cried. "I am totally confused. My life used to be sensible and predictable. Then the accident happened, and nothing's been the same since."

"Are things worse?"

"No." She hadn't meant to complain. Or maybe she had.

"Better?"

"So much so that sometimes I think it's too good to be true."

Verity studied her for a minute, then nodded. "Thomas Gates."

Bree sighed. "Oh, yes. Thomas Gates. Most of the time I forget that half the world knows who he is. Then I remember, and I can't believe he loves me."

"He seems happy."

"Well, he thinks he is now, but what if he should change his mind?"

"Are you going to throw away what you have on the chance that he will?"

Bree started to speak, then stopped. Put that way, the answer was obvious. It told only half the story, though. "If he had happened to me before all this, I could probably believe it faster. But first there was the accident, then the out-of-body experience, now the wishes. Put Tom in the middle of it, and I don't know what's real and what isn't."

Verity was frowning. "Wishes?"

Bree hesitated. Then she reminded herself that this was a woman who not only saw forest fairies but had argued more than once in favor of UFOs, psychics, and, yes, a bowling alley in heaven. So she told her about the three wishes, from her first awareness of them, to the fire, to the woman at the diner. She argued both sides, coincidence versus wish. "Do you see why I'm confused? And then there's the part of me that thinks the only reason I'm back here is for the wishes, and that after the third one, the being of light will reclaim me."

"Oh my," Verity said. "What makes you think that?"

"I don't know. Maybe it was the drugs I was on right after the accident. Maybe it's nothing but a human kind of fear." Most people feared death, didn't they? It was the most natural thing in the world, wasn't it? "Do you think the wishes are real?"

Verity considered the question. "They could be."

"Was that my mother who came to the diner?" When Verity shrugged, Bree again had that startling thought. Again she set it aside. "After the third wish, do I die?"

Verity raised both shoulders and kept them up this time.

"Can I risk it?"

The shoulders dropped. "That depends on what the wish is and how much it matters to you." She thought for a minute. "I probably would."

"Even if it means death?"

"What if it means life?"

"You mean a happier life?"

"Happier. Safer. Freer. Most people live like this." She drew a level line with her hand. "Some people live like this." She drew a higher line. "Having an open mind makes part of the difference. Risk makes the rest."

In a moment's frustration, Bree scanned the room. It held most every creature comfort. "This doesn't look too risky."

"Now it isn't. It was when I first came here. I had never lived alone. I had never taken care of myself. I didn't have a generator then, just the clothes on my back."

Regretful of her outburst, Bree brought the tea to her mouth. She let the nearness of the scent tease her taste buds for a minute, took a sip, and, in the smooth, rich heat, found a temporary balm. More calmly, she asked, "Why did you come?"

Verity smiled. "Not for the UFOs, though I do think this is where they land."

"What did you leave?"

The smile faded. "A man who swore to kill me if I left."

Bree gasped.

Verity waved a hand. "It's an old story. Not an uncommon one. It's nowhere near as exotic as the stories people tell about me in town."

"How many of them are real?"

"Not many. It may be possible to commune with the dead, but I've never done it. I have been followed by strange lights and do believe in UFOs, but I've never come face-to-face with an alien. I have come face-to-face with a bear. I was so frightened that I froze. The bear got bored and walked away. So people say I can control wild beasts with a single look. I let them believe it."

"Why?"

"Because it frees me to be and do whatever I want. For years I couldn't."

It sounded so sensible and unbizarre that Bree took the opening it offered. No hopes up, she told herself. Just curious. "Where did you live before you came here?"

"Atlanta."

"Have you ever lived in California?"

"No."

It was possible that Bree's father might have been either wrong or misled. "Have you ever been to Chicago?"

"Once. Fifty years ago. I was ten. We were visiting relatives there."

That would make her sixty, not the fifty-three that Bree's mother would be. In that, too, Haywood Miller might have been wrong or misled. "Do you have any children?"

"No. My husband wouldn't share me that much."

What if she had run away, had an affair with Haywood, and conceived Bree? What if that was the only way in the world she could have had a child? What if, years later, she had come to Panama to watch Bree grow? That didn't explain why she had never revealed herself to Bree. But what if Haywood had forbidden her to? What if that had been part of the deal? What if she had changed her looks so that Haywood himself hadn't recognized her?

Trying to stay calm, she asked, "What brought you to Panama?"

"I closed my eyes and pointed."

"Pointed?"

"I needed to leave the South. So I opened a map of the North, closed my eyes, and pointed."

"Did you know anyone here before you came?"

Verity shook her head. Then she tipped it and gave a small, knowing smile. "I thought you thought the woman in the diner was your mother."

Bree felt a stab of embarrassment. Throwing it off, she raised her chin. "I don't know that for sure. When I wished for heat, I got a fire. So I moved to Tom's, where I have heat. I got my wish, but in a roundabout way. My seeing the woman at the diner led to my confrontation with Tom, which led to my coming here."

Gently, Verity said, "I'm not your mother."

"Would you tell me if you were?"

"Yes. I believe in telling the truth."

"Verity."

"Yes?"

"Your real name?"

Her eyes twinkled. Her accent thickened. "It is. Right on my birth certificate."

Bree couldn't argue with a birth certificate. "Do you really think that God is bowling when it thunders?"

"Do you know otherwise?"

"When hot air hits cold air, there's lightning. The sound comes from that."

"Does air make noise? Do clouds?"

"Scientists say so."

"Does it make sense?"

Bree saw her point.

"Think back," Verity went on. "Did I ever say for sure that God bowled? Or did I say it was *possible?*"

Bree was caught. "Possible."

"Is it?"

"I guess."

Verity's smile was wide. "See? You do have an open mind, just like me, though not because we're blood kin. Both of us experienced a life threat. That freed us up."

Freedom was one thing, lunacy another, was what Bree was thinking.

Verity said, "Freedom is relative. So is happiness and reality and risk. Sometimes, in order to be free, we have to take risks. Sometimes, in order to be *happy*, we have to take risks. As for what's real and what isn't, it's like beauty, in the eye of the beholder. Reality is one thing for one person, and another for another. We make our reality. It can be what we want, or what we need."

"What if my reality is different from Tom's? What if he really is that other person, the famous one who lives in the fast lane?"

"And if he is? What would you lose?"

"The most wonderful thing in my life."

"Well, there you have it."

"Have what?"

"Your answer. The thing that brought you here, what's real and what isn't. If Thomas Gates is the most wonderful thing in your life, why question it? You're an optimist. Deep down inside, past that old inbred cautiousness, you believe in possibility. It doesn't matter if a *thing* is real. If the *possibility* is, that's what counts."

Bree's spirits rose higher with each jolt of the truck during the return trip on Verity's rutted path. At its end, the forest's darkness gave way to a near-blinding light that Bree took as her special being's approval of the visit. Waiting only long enough for her eyes to adjust, she turned onto the main road and, ebullient, headed for Tom.

The house was so quiet when she reached it that for an instant she feared she had waited too long. After searching the rooms on the first floor, she ran up the stairs. *"Tom?"*

"In here," came his voice from the end of the hall.

She went to the door of his office. He had yet to unpack the cartons there, but they were pushed aside, which was an improvement, and there was a lamp on the desk. He sat in its light with his computer open, gestured that she should wait, tapped at the keyboard. After reading from the screen, he jotted something on a long yellow pad, tossed down his pen, and pushed himself back.

There was an instant's hesitancy when he looked at her, an instant's reminder of their confrontation. Then came a slow grin and the sexiest "Hey" she'd ever heard, but he didn't leave the chair.

So she went to him. "Hey yourself." Stopping between his legs, she looped her arms around his neck and kissed him once with her lips, a second time with her teeth, a third time with her tongue.

He circled her waist. "Must have been one hell of a shopping trip."

She smiled down into his smiling face. "It was. Whatcha been doing?"

"Exploring the feasibility of obtaining a waiver of the ban on federal subsidizing of nonregulated growth material for the Allsworthys' farm down the road."

The only thing she could understand of his answer was the bottom line. "Another case?"

He shrugged, but his smile remained. Every few days something new popped up, some legal problem that Martin Sprague didn't know how to handle. Tom refused to take credit for the work, but the whole town knew what was what.

"I love you," she said.

He drew in a deep breath. It came out ragged. "I was hoping you'd say that."

"Let's get married."

He rolled his eyes.

She was more specific. "This weekend."

Slowly, he straightened. "Do you mean it?"

"Uh-huh."

"This weekend is three days off," he warned, but she felt his excitement.

"We don't need printed invitations."

"Are you sure?"

"About printed invitations?"

"About the date."

"Positive." She was making her own reality, tying Tom down, then giving him a last chance to escape. "Unless you'd rather wait."

The eloquent look he gave her was followed by another kiss. This one was longer and deeper than the three that had come before and tasted of commitment. Odd, but it made Bree feel free.

She smoothed his hair back and studied him, trying to see the brash and successful man whose face was on the books on the shelf. But there were no traces of that man here. This one was more handsome, more honest, more decent. His hair was longer and his coloring more healthy. He had a scar on his cheek that lent character, and wonder in his eyes. This one was the man who loved her enough to believe in her fantasies and wait through her doubts.

"You are the most wonderful thing in my life," he said, in a voice that was hoarse with emotion. They were the very same words she had used not so long before at Verity's house, and would have erased the last of her qualms if those hadn't already been gone.

All that remained was a world of possibility, one so large and bounteous that Bree couldn't have explored it all in an hour, a day, a year. But she tried. She touched Tom's face and his neck with her hands, then her mouth. She unbuttoned his shirt and touched his chest, unbuckled his belt and unzipped his jeans. She touched everything inside, stroked until she had created a new reality that was larger, harder, and so much more exciting than the old that she slipped to her knees.

Tom jerked at the touch of her lips. "Christ, Bree."

She didn't stop. The idea that anything in the world was possible gave her a certain freedom, which gave her a certain power. That power meant taking the thickness of him into her mouth while she held his thighs apart with her hands. It meant milking him to the point of release, then rising up, pushing aside her blouse and bra, and offering him her breasts. It meant watching his wonderful long-fingered hands knead them, then lifting her nipples to his tongue, and if there was brazenness in that, she had no regrets. The power was hers, the freedom, the possibility. All these were her reality with Tom.

With a sudden tousling of hands, clothes, and breath came the desperate drive toward consummation. There was Tom's hoarse "That's it, baby . . . lift . . ."

And her own breathless "Wait . . . there . . . oh, my . . ."

"Higher . . . wrap your legs . . . yessss . . ."

"Touch me . . . *there!*"

"You're so hot . . ."

"I can't . . . hold back . . . Tom!"

Her last conscious thought before her climax consumed conscious thought was that this was a reality she could live with.

The next morning, riding high on Bree's love and knowing that he would never feel bolder, Tom called his father. The older man's gruff "Hello" had him gripping the phone more tightly.

"Dad? It's Tom."

Silence.

"Dad?" His heart was beating up a storm, but nothing at all came from the other end of the line.

So he tried "How are you?"

When that didn't evoke a response, he jumped in with, "Something's happened here, something really exciting. I've been wanting to tell you about it for a long time—" He thought he heard a click. "Dad?" he tested, fearful. "Dad?"

When a dial tone came on, he let out a disappointed breath and quietly hung up the phone.

\*　　　\*　　　\*

If Bree hadn't believed that anything was possible, she would never have believed the kind of wedding that occurred three days later. When she set the date with Tom, she had envisioned something small, a simple church ceremony with a brief reception at either the diner, an inn in a neighboring town, or even Tom's house. That was before the townsfolk got wind of her plans.

Flash, who was the first to know, insisted that he was catering whatever, wherever. Jane, who agreed to be Bree's maid of honor, insisted that the whole of the town should be invited, since the whole of the town loved Bree. Jane called Dotty, who called Emma, who called Eliot and Earl, and before lunchtime of that very first day, the entire town was involved.

The pastor, who was thrilled with the idea of having a large and captive audience, promised to set up folding chairs in every available space in the church and perform the most beautiful ceremony Bree had ever seen. The organist secured a list of Bree's favorite songs and, insisting that the organ alone wouldn't do, called for a choir rehearsal that night. Emma, being as close to a mayor as the town had, insisted that the reception be held in the town hall, which had been newly painted in anticipation of the March town meeting anyway and was, after all, "the only suitable place for a town-wide event."

Volunteers began calling Flash to offer help in preparing the food. The owners of the Sleepy Creek Brewery pledged kegs of their best sellers. The owner of the local bread company announced plans for a huge four-tiered wedding cake.

By the time Bree dropped by the shop to talk flowers with Julia Dean, Julia had already gathered buckets of imported blooms. "I have people out collecting greens enough to decorate the church and the town hall," she said, with satisfaction. "All you have to do is tell me what flowers you want to carry, and I'll make up a bouquet. What are you wearing?"

Bree was feeling slightly breathless. "I don't know yet. I'm going shopping later. I don't think I can get a gown so late, but I should be able to find a pretty suit or a dress."

Julia set the stems she was clipping in a pail of water. Coming out from behind the counter, she stood back and studied Bree, up and down, for a quiet minute. Then, even more quietly, she said, "I have a gown you could wear."

Bree's heart tripped. "A wedding gown?"

"Can I show it to you?"

Too touched to refuse, Bree followed her out the back door and across the drive to the small house where Julia lived. Once inside, they climbed two flights of stairs to the attic. There, hanging in a small cedar closet, covered with wrapping that Julia carefully removed, was the wedding dress of Bree's dreams. It was ivory in color and Victorian in style, with a high neck, long sleeves, and a hem layered with ruffles and lace. Delicate beads dotted the bodice, right down to the fitted torso.

Bree swallowed. "It looks so slim."

"You're slim. Do you like it?"

"I *love* it."

"Try it on."

Bree tore her eyes from the gown. "Really?"

Julia nodded, looking pleased.

"Right now?"

"It'll save you a trip to the mall."

Bree knew that she could look for weeks and weeks and not find anything half as beautiful as this gown. Without another word—and only a brief thought to the scars Julia might see—she slipped off her jeans and shirt. By that time, Julia had tiny buttons unbuttoned and the back zipper down. Bree stepped carefully into the dress. Just as carefully, she drew it on. Julia helped her straighten the fabric and secured the zipper.

It fit. Perfectly. Amazed by that, and awed by the dress, Bree smoothed her hands over her stomach while Julia did up the tiny buttons, adjusted the shoulders, gently pulled at the sleeves. When Julia came around to the front and stepped back to look, Bree held her breath.

Julia's eyes teared. "At the time I wore this," she whispered, "I was sure it had been made for me and no one else. I was wrong."

"It looks okay?"

Julia's "Oh, my" said it looked a far sight better than that, and

Bree could feel it. Everything was right—the style, the fit, the length.

"When I sold my house in Des Moines and came here," Julia said, in a distant voice, "I thought about giving it away, but I couldn't. My wedding day was glorious. When my daughter got married, she wanted something new. So this has been wrapped up all that time. Something must have been telling me to take it along." Julia raised her eyes. Though they remained moist, her voice was clear. "I would be honored if you would wear it, Bree. It would mean the world to me."

"To *you*," Bree breathed, through her own film of tears. "It would mean the world to *me*." She imagined walking down the aisle of the church in this dress, imagined putting her hand in Tom's, imagined walking back up the aisle as his wife, and her throat swelled. Then she imagined dancing through a boisterous reception at the town hall, and had a thought that caught her breath up short. "What if I spill something on it?"

Julia laughed and brushed at her tears. "It'll clean."

"I'd feel *terrible*."

"I won't," Julia said, but she had turned away. Pulling a box from the closet shelf, she removed its lid and reached inside. It seemed that the magic wasn't over. She drew out a veil to match the dress and lifted it above Bree's head.

"My hair's a mess!"

"Just a quick look," Julia insisted. She set the band of the veil in place and, as though she were touching gold, arranged Bree's hair around it. Then she stood back and smiled.

"Yes?" Bree whispered.

"Yes," Julia said, and held up a finger. She went to the far end of the attic, bent her knees, moved this way and that. Then she motioned for Bree to come.

Bree walked on tiptoe so that the hem of the gown wouldn't touch the floor. The fabric made an elegant swishing sound as she moved. Once Julia had Bree positioned, she saw her reflection on the window. There were four pieces to it, where the mullions divided the glass, and while the image was remarkably clear, it was a total dream.

Bree could only stare.

"Quite something, isn't it?" Julia asked.

"Oh, yes."

"You look stunning."

"Tom will *die*."

"I certainly hope not."

"I look like a bride."

"You *are* a bride, or will be. Day after tomorrow. Oh, my."

"Too soon?" Bree asked, turning to her. "This is happening so fast I feel like I'm out of breath. Am I rushing it?"

"Not if you love Tom."

"I do."

"Then why wait?"

Good old commonsense Bree couldn't think of an answer.

"I was engaged for a week," Julia told her. "My husband was going into the army. We decided to get married before, rather than wait."

"Did you ever regret it?"

"Regret marrying Teddy?" Julia's smile was wistful. "No. I adored him. We had a wonderful life together. He's been gone three years. I still miss him."

"Is that why you left Des Moines?"

"It's one of the reasons. Everything there reminded me of him. And then there were the children. Not children any longer. Adults. A son and a daughter, both married, with kids. I was too close to them. Our relationship wasn't healthy. We needed distance between us."

"You must miss them."

"Not as much as I thought I would." She laughed. "That sounds terrible, but the truth is that I'm busier here than I was there, and then, each time I start thinking that it's family time, something happens here to make me feel as if the people here are family, too. Like this wedding. It's going to be special."

"It isn't the first wedding the town has put on."

"But it'll be the best. You're respected here, Bree. Loved."

Bree saw tears refill Julia's eyes. Her own throat grew tight. Laughing brokenly, she said, "Let's not start this again."

Julia nodded, wiped the corners of her eyes, straightened, and smiled. "So. Since flowers this time of year will have to come a distance, we can choose whatever we want." Thoughtful, she studied the dress. "What do you think? Would you like white tulips with baby's breath? Lily of the valley? Something with sweet alyssum or roses?"

Tom had been warned to wear a tuxedo, but he wasn't prepared for the sight of Bree when she appeared at the back of the church and began her walk down the aisle. She was a vision in ivory and lace, primly covered from neck to foot but provocative where the dress clung, and beautiful, so beautiful that she stole his breath.

She carried a bouquet of small white flowers and greens, and wore a veil that shaded her face, but he saw her eyes through it, saw her eyes and felt her love. When she reached him and he draped the veil back over her hair, the feeling intensified.

Incredibly, it just kept growing. If, a mere year before, someone had told him that he would be marrying a small-town girl in a wedding put on by her town, he would have laughed himself silly. But there was nothing silly about the wedding Panama gave them. It was the most touching wedding he had ever attended. From the church that was packed to the gills, to the town hall that wasn't much different, to Flash's food, to live music from a jazz band, a string trio, and a barbershop quartet, to the strobe lights of no less than four self-appointed photographers and two videographers, to smiles and wishes and handshakes that never stopped coming—he had never in his life been the recipient of so much sheer goodwill, and all because of the woman at his side.

He only wished that his family were there. He wished they could see Bree, wished they could feel the decency and caring in this room. He wanted them to be part of his new life, but his father had refused to talk to him, and when he finally reached his sister, she had declined his invitation to come. He offered to pay her way, to pay the way of any or all who would come, but she held firm. She had told his brothers that he had called, she said. She had argued in his defense, but the anger was still there. She begged for time. When he argued that a wedding was a onetime event, she argued that a mother's funeral was, too, and he had been silenced. His mother would have loved Bree, he knew, would have loved her spirit and her strength. At the drop of a hat, she would have become the mother Bree had never had.

On her wedding day, though, Bree didn't look to be missing a mother. She had dozens of mothers, dozens of sisters and brothers. Her face was wreathed in smiles from the minute he slipped a wedding band on her finger, through laughter and dance and food, to the minute she fell asleep against him in the wee hours of Sunday morning at the inn where they spent the night. Come morning, when they drove to Boston to catch a plane to the Caribbean, she was smiling still.

Tom had chartered a boat with a captain and a cook. It was the perfect way to island-hop without hassle. Their stateroom was luxurious, the food gourmet, and the schedule theirs for the making each morning when they arose.

He had done the Caribbean before, but this time was different. This time, he did it through Bree. Through her eyes he saw the brilliance of aqua water and the novelty of sun and warm sand in the middle of winter. Through her ears he heard the flap of sail against mast, the rustle of the palms, the laughter of native children on the docks. Through her hands he felt the beat of a steel band on Nevis, through her nose smelled goodies at a patisserie on St. Bart's.

Between the joy she took in each new thing she saw and the joy he took in her, Bree made his week. They returned to Panama tanned, happy, and rested. He was more in love with her than ever.

# chapter
# thirteen

Mud season in Panama wasn't attractive. With the last major melt of winter's snow, the ground grew sodden. Hillsides seeped onto hardtop and slithered down lawns. The half of Panama's roads that were unpaved became all but impassable for anything that didn't have chains, while the rest of the roads were just messy. Cars grew mud-spattered, shoes and boots caked. Those patches of snow that lingered in shady spots were edged with dirt. The town green became something to avoid.

The onset of mud season occurred anywhere from the fifteenth to the thirtieth of March. It lasted from two to three weeks. During any other time of the year, there were things to do outside. During these few weeks, there was nothing. Cabin fever raged. Tempers were short. The coming of spring seemed improbable.

The general assumption was that the founding fathers of Panama had held the town meeting at the end of March because, lacking snowplows, they couldn't mobilize themselves sooner. Modern-day Panama wasn't as concerned with snow as with creating a diversion in this bleakest, dirtiest, most boring of times. To that end, the town meeting was drawn out over three nights and sandwiched between parties before and after.

Bree was looking forward to the week, not because she was feeling bleak, dirty, or bored, but because she was happy. She was back working at the diner, which she loved. She had blissful memories of her wedding and honeymoon, and, still, healthy traces of a Caribbean tan, which she loved. And she was married to Tom, which she really, *really* loved. The fear that he would come to have second thoughts hadn't materialized. Nothing had changed with their marriage to dampen his ardor. He was as attentive, as protective, as interested and loving, as he had been before. She was deliriously happy.

So her reaction to the partying took her by surprise. Seeing families, seeing families with *children,* caused the same pangs she had felt in November. She thought she had come to terms with not being able to have a child. After the holidays and Tom's repeated assurances that it didn't matter to him, she thought she was comfortable with the idea. Then she saw Tom at the dinners and dances and fairs that brought the town together, only now he wasn't just looking at warm family groupings from afar. He was in the middle of them.

It started with Joey Little. But Joey had friends. When those friends discovered that Tom had infinite patience and kid-friendly shoulders, they were all clamoring to climb up. Tom loved it. He was large and physical. He could toss giggling children around with such care that anyone watching laughed, too. He removed little noses and held them between his fingers, could pull quarters out of ears or throw shadows of wolves, witches,

and turkeys onto the wall. He was a kid when he was with kids.
He was meant to be a father.

Bree needed to talk about that, but she couldn't talk with
Tom. She knew how he felt. He had expressed it often enough.
She needed to figure out what *she* wanted to do. So, as casually
as she could, she raised the subject with friends.

Flash was the first. "Do you miss having children?" she asked
one afternoon in the diner's kitchen. He was experimenting with
dessert presentations and had spread raspberry sauce on a plate.

"How could I have kids?" he asked, preoccupied as he dropped
a glob of white cream in the center. He took a knife and drew it
from white to red, one way, then another. "I'm a kid myself."

"I'm serious."

"Me, too. How could I take care of a kid? I can barely take
care of myself."

"That's not true," she scolded, though, thinking about it later,
she wasn't so sure.

So she drove out to see Verity. Verity was a perfect example of
someone who could take care of herself. Bree brought a piece of
wedding cake from those sliced and frozen, and scolded Verity
for having left the reception too early to get one fresh.

"It was better that I left," Verity said. She was crocheting,
working so nimbly that Bree had trouble following the in-and-
out of the hook. "You don't need people making a connection
between us. Besides, I don't do well in crowds."

"Because of the children?"

Verity's hands stilled, though her eyes remained on her work.
"Why do you ask that?"

"Children make noise. They don't allow for peace and quiet.
Or for privacy."

"I never wanted the privacy. The peace and quiet is part of
me. It has been so all my life. That was the only way I survived
my marriage as long as I did. I used to withdraw into myself."
Her fingers returned to activity. "I wouldn't have been able to do
that if I'd had children."

"Are you sorry?"

"That I didn't have children?" She didn't break the rhythm of her work. "Given the circumstances, no. I didn't want to have his children. With another man, maybe. In another life, maybe. But it's too late in this one. No herbal potion or alien encounter will bring it about. I'm well past my childbearing years. And yes," she added, "I've come to like the privacy."

The only other woman Bree knew who prized privacy as much as Verity was Julia. Indeed, she sensed that Julia told her as much about herself as she told anyone, and that wasn't much. But the wedding dress had created a bond between them. Bree enjoyed being with her. She had taken to stopping in at the flower shop to talk whenever she passed.

As fate had it, on this day Julia was tying a huge pink bow around the neck of a vase filled with pink and white tulips, a gift for the barber's son's wife, who had just given birth to a daughter. Bree watched for a minute, then asked, "When you do up arrangements like these, do you think back to when your own children were born?"

"Sometimes," Julia said. She gave the ribbon a twist. "It was a special time."

"Was it hard?"

"Childbirth?" She smiled. "No. The cause was good."

"Labor can go on forever."

Julia gave a negligent nose-scrunch. "The worst comes only at the end, and then there are drugs to help. Drugs hurt the baby, you say? Well, our kids didn't seem damaged any. In my day, mothers weren't as quick to martyr themselves. After the children were born, yes. Child rearing was our major occupation. We often put it before our own best interests. At the time of birth? No. Ignorance was bliss."

"Kind of like a reward for surviving pregnancy?"

"Oh, I liked being pregnant. I liked it very much." She held back the vase, looked at it, then turned it to Bree.

But Bree was trying to convince herself that she didn't want to be pregnant. "I've heard awful stories."

"You're talking to the wrong people," Julia said. She paused, raised hopeful brows, lowered her voice. "Are you pregnant?"

"Good Lord, no. I just got married. It's too soon to be having a baby. So much has happened to me so quickly that I need time to adjust. I like working, and I like being alone with Tom and anyway, he's still trying to decide what to do about *his* work, so it wouldn't be fair to impose kids on him yet."

"I don't think children would be an imposition with that one," Julia said.

Bree knew she was right, which didn't help things much. She trusted Julia's judgment. But she needed an ally. So she raised the subject with Jane, leaning in close across the counter after the lunchtime crowd had thinned. "Do you worry about getting older? Does that thing about the biological clock ever get you to wondering?"

Jane sighed. "All the time. But what can I do? I don't draw men like you do."

"The right man just hasn't seen you. Someday he will." Bree believed it. Jane was too good a person to go through life alone.

"Someday," Jane said, and sighed. "I may be too old for kids by then."

"You could adopt. Single mothers do. Michelle Pfeiffer did. So did Rosie O'Donnell. The way some men are, a woman's better doing it alone anyway."

"Doing what alone?" Dotty asked, taking the stool beside Jane.

Jane gave Bree a look that said You should have warned me she was there, but Bree hadn't noticed it herself.

"Having kids," LeeAnn put in, having caught the conversation in passing. "Look at me. I've done it alone, haven't I?" She left again before anyone could answer.

"Look at her," Dotty muttered under her breath. *"Don't* look at her. She's no example of motherhood, doing that thing to her hair. Besides, it's just fine for a pretty little Hollywood face to adopt a child. Those women don't have to worry about paying the bills."

"Neither do I," Jane said quietly. She was looking at Bree. "I have a home. The oil is paid for. So's the electricity and the phone."

Dotty drew back and stared at her. It was only when Bree looked at Dotty that Jane did, too. "Don't worry, Mother. I'm not having a child."

"*Having?* I *hope* not. Good God, Bree. Are you putting bugs in her ear now that you're married? Well, she isn't, for one thing, and for another, you shouldn't be having a child yourself. You just got married. You don't know if the marriage will last."

"It will last," Jane said.

"The voice of experience. She's an expert on marriage *and* on babies."

"Adoption was the subject," Jane corrected.

"Don't you dare do that, either. I'm not up for raising another child."

"If it was my child, I'd be doing the raising."

"Like you do the cooking?" Dotty asked.

Bree tried to defuse the situation. "Verity was saying—"

"Verity?" Dotty turned to her. "That woman has nothing worthwhile to say. You talk with her too much, Bree. You encourage her."

"To do what?"

"To come into town. Fine. We can't keep her out of town meeting. But she doesn't have to be lurking around at the crafts fair. People won't buy what she crochets. She makes us all nervous. And showing up at your wedding?" Dotty reared back. "I wouldn't have liked that one bit, if it had been me."

"Verity is harmless," Jane said before Bree could stop her.

Dotty picked right up where she had left off. "That shows how much you know. You've been here when she's been talking nonsense. Don't you *know* it's nonsense?"

"She says things to shock us."

"Oh, she does? Who told you that?"

"I did," Bree said.

Dotty sighed. "Bree. Why do you tell Jane things like that? She believes them."

Looking straight ahead, Jane said, "Verity makes sense when you talk with her alone."

"Is that what you've been doing? Is *that* where the talk about adopting a child came from?" She pushed out a breath. "God save us from idiots." She left the stool with an impatient "Are you coming?"

As she walked off, Bree touched Jane's arm.

In a shaky whisper, Jane said, "One day she'll push me so far that courage won't matter. I hate her." She put a fingernail to her mouth.

Bree pulled it down. "You don't. She's your mother."

Jane wrapped a remorseful arm around Bree's neck. "I'm sorry. I know you never had a mother. I am selfish, like she says."

"If you were selfish, you'd have moved out long ago." Bree set her back. "Apply to art school."

"Art school?" Jane looked suddenly panicked. "It's a dream, that's all."

"Make it come true. Apply. You'll get in."

"You've never said this before."

"I should have. It's *so possible.*"

"I'm thirty-five. I'd be the oldest in the class."

"I bet you wouldn't be. But even if you are, so what? Apply, Jane. You *will* get in."

"And then what? How will I pay for it? How will I live?"

"*Jane!*" Dotty called from the door of the diner.

Bree held Jane's arm when she would have fled. "Scholarship. Dorm. Job. You can get all of them. Then you'll be free."

Jane looked torn.

"Think about it."

Jane nodded quickly and ran after Dotty, only to stop halfway there and run back. Anger tightened her face. "Don't listen to what she said about having children. Have them now, Bree. You'll make the best mother in the whole wide world."

So Flash didn't want children because he was part child himself. That didn't apply to Bree, who had never really been a child at all.

Verity hadn't had children because the circumstances were wrong. That didn't apply to Bree, either. She was married at the right time to the right man in the right place, with the right amount of love and desire and money.

Julia, bless her soul, had not only loved being pregnant but loved giving birth, which shot a great big hole through the complaints Bree had heard. And Julia was right about Tom. Being a father wouldn't be an imposition on him. He wanted family more than anything. He would thrive.

So would she, Bree knew. Jane was right. She would make a great mother. It didn't matter that she had never had one of her own to learn from. She loved children. She loved Tom. She would love his child. It made sense.

What didn't make sense was how to do it, because if the doctor was right and she couldn't conceive, the only way to achieve it was through a wish. But she still didn't know if the wishes were real. The fire was listed as accidental. The woman in the diner was long gone. Two wishes spent? Or none?

So, okay. She could wish, and nothing might happen. She would know for sure that the wishes weren't real, they could adopt a baby, and that would be that.

But if the wishes were real and this was her third, what then? She could live happily ever after with Tom and his child, and thank God every day that she'd had the courage to take the risk. Or she could die.

A bizarre thought, that one. And totally unfounded. She had no proof that she would die. She didn't even know where she'd gotten the idea.

But given the possibility of it, no matter how remote, was wishing for a child an irresponsible thing to do? A child without a mother—she knew how *that* was. Tom would have the burden of raising it alone.

But Panama was filled with people who loved them. Her wedding had shown her that. And Tom wasn't Haywood. He was strong and outgoing and able. If he was left to raise their child alone, he would have plenty of help.

She didn't want to die. She wanted to be with Tom. She wanted to be with their child. But if she didn't risk a wish, there might be no child at all.

*What do I do?* she asked the being of light, but it didn't answer. *Are the wishes real? Do I dare?*

In the end it came down to greed. Having Tom's baby was the one thing that could make her life more complete than it was. She tried to talk herself out of it: told herself that what she had with Tom was so much more than most women ever had that she should be satisfied, told herself that they could adopt a baby, told herself that making a third wish wasn't worth the risk.

Then she saw Tom at town meeting, standing to discuss the pros and cons of keeping town positions under the civil service system, and all the while he was talking, his hands were behind his back, doing funny little things to entertain two restless children in the row behind, and she knew. She knew she could debate forever, but the truth was that her heart had already made up her mind. She'd had enough of being sensible and cautious. Expecting the worst was no way to live. These days, she was banking on optimism and hope. These days, she was squeezing the best out of life.

More than anything else, she wanted to give Tom a child. She didn't have to close her eyes to imagine that child. She could see it clear as day, just as she could feel her own joy. That joy justified the risk.

So she did it. That night, after town meeting adjourned, when she was in the bathroom before joining Tom in bed, she laced her fingers together by her chin, closed her eyes tight, and whispered, "I . . . wish . . . to have Tom's child." She pictured the being of light and repeated the words. "I . . . wish . . . to have Tom's child."

For long minutes she stood there, with her heart pounding at the gravity of what she'd done. But the wish was sent. She couldn't take it back. Trembling, she imagined it rising on a starbeam and finding the being of light. As she homed in on that being, its luminescence was as strong as ever before, and soothing. Gradually, the pounding of her heart eased, and her trembling gave way to an overall calm. She drew in a slow, deep, satisfied breath and let it out. Smiling, she combed through her hair, smoothed the silk of her negligee, and went to join Tom.

\* \* \*

It happened that night. She was convinced by the sense of fulfillment she experienced as she lay against him afterward. They were both bare and damp. From a microscopic near-nothing deep inside, her body glowed.

She didn't tell him, neither then nor the following week, when a home test confirmed what the tiny dot of heat that glowed more strongly inside her each day told her was true. Nor did she worry. She was committed. There was no turning back.

Between repairing winter's damage to the grounds, preparing the malleable ground for the garage he planned to build, and playing newlywed with Bree, a busy month passed before Tom asked about her period. She had figured he would ask in time. He was always attuned to those days when she was feeling bloated and crampy. "How did I miss it?"

"You didn't." She kept her voice low, her excitement in check, but barely. "It's late."

He was instantly on the alert. "How late?"

"Two weeks." Bits of excitement escaped. "What do you think?"

"I think you should do a test."

"I did. It says I am. But I'm not supposed to be."

Tom made no effort to control his excitement, which was precisely what Bree wanted to hear. "Doctors can be wrong," he said. "It won't be the first time. Did you call him?"

She nodded.

"Why didn't you *tell* me? What did he say?"

"I have an appointment two weeks from now. By then, he can decide it with a physical exam, and I didn't tell you because I don't want us getting our hopes up. He said it'd be a real fluke." She had clung to that thought. A fluke was something that was improbable, that happened rarely but happened nonetheless. It was something that defied the odds but might indeed have happened on its own, without any wish at all.

Tom took her arms. His eyes were wide and bright. "The test said you are. That's incredible."

She nodded again, grinning widely now.

He put a hand on her stomach and said in a hushed voice, "Do you feel it?"

The look on his face was precious, not to mention the awe in his voice. He looked as though he had been given the most precious gift possible, and in that instant, third wish or not, she was so, *so* glad she had done what she had.

She covered his hand. "It's too small to feel yet, but I swear I do. It's a little warm spot in the middle of everything else down there. I've been feeling it since it happened."

"You *have?* And you *didn't tell me?*"

"I thought it was just happiness. Love."

He made a sound deep in his throat, ever so gently took her face in his hands, and, moving his thumbs against her cheeks, said, "You've turned my life around, Bree. Whether you're pregnant or not, you've saved me from a whole other fate. How do I thank you for that?"

By way of answering his own question, he spent those two weeks making Bree the center of his life. He brought her breakfast in bed every morning, gave her flowers, spent his free time at the diner, told her many times a day just how beautiful she looked. When they were in bed, he was hungry, if solicitous, but she had no cause for caution on that score. Her baby had taken root and wasn't being dislodged, and she wanted Tom. There wasn't a time when he turned to her that she wasn't ready. Even when she emerged from a deep sleep to find him hard against her, she was quickly aroused. Her body was extrasensitive, her breasts fuller, her insides moist. She climaxed often and well.

He was spoiling her. She loved every second of it.

Mud season ended with April's lengthening daylight and a gradual hardening of the ground. Tom and Bree spent hours on the bench by the brook, listening to the rush of the water, smelling the promise of spring in the damp ground, watching the return of migrating birds.

Bree had been happy before, but those two weeks gave new

meaning to the word. She shared a joy with Tom that was inno-cent and complete. If, indeed, God had put man on earth for the purpose of procreation, He was smiling on them now. Their life together was rich in satisfaction and love. Bree was back to pinching herself, wondering if it all was real.

Tom didn't question the pregnancy for a minute. Everything that had happened since that October night had been unex-pected. This was just one more thing.

But what a wondrous thing it was! He thought he had been the happiest man in the world when Bree set a date for their wedding, but that happiness had been topped on their wedding day, when she appeared at the church looking like a dream, walked down the aisle only to him, and smiled up through tears when he slipped his ring on her finger. They had been married for barely two months, had known each other for barely six, but she was as much a part of his life as his heart.

And now this. A child. Bree's child. Bree's and his.

Paul Sealy was stunned. Returning to his desk after Bree's examination, he looked from one of them to the other, shook his head, blew out a breath. "How to explain it? I've specialized in gynecology for twenty years. Infertility is an increasing problem, often for very new reasons, but this wasn't a situation like that. It was an age-old case of an injury causing scar tissue that would interfere with conception. I've seen dozens of cases like it. In some, surgery solved the problem. Simon and I discussed it. We didn't think that would help here, or we'd have suggested it." He focused on Bree. "We never would have put you through the agony of thinking you couldn't have children if we hadn't thought the chance of it was better than ninety-nine percent." He frowned, puzzled. "I'm usually pretty good at prognoses."

"Is that what it was?" Bree asked. "Ninety-nine percent?"

"I'd have said ninety-nine point five, odds against."

"So I'm the one in two hundred people who got pregnant in spite of the scarring?"

"Looks that way."

"And you're sure she's pregnant?" Tom asked. He knew *she* was sure, could see the conviction in her eyes and her smile, could feel it in her hand, which he held so tight that her fingers would have choked had they been her neck. But he wanted to hear it again.

"Oh, I'm sure," the doctor said, still amazed. "The signs are all there. She's six weeks along. Whew. I'm sorry for the heartache we caused. We messed up."

*Damn straight!* Tom thought. Bree had come close to not marrying him, because her doctors had messed up. He could strangle them for that, either strangle them or sue them, though he doubted Bree would allow either. Sitting beside him, she was benevolence incarnate.

"No heartache now that a baby's coming," she said in a serene voice.

Tom would share that serenity once he knew a little more. "Is there no scar tissue, then?" he asked the doctor.

"Apparently not as much as I expected."

"Will it affect the pregnancy in any way?"

"It shouldn't. But I think we can plan on taking the baby by cesarean section."

"Why?"

"Her uterus has been cut and repaired. It hasn't had much time to recover. I wouldn't want to risk a rupture during hard labor. A cesarean is no problem, though. We won't even use general anesthesia. A spinal block will do it. Many a woman who delivers vaginally has that." He frowned, tapped a fist in the air, murmured, "I was so sure." With a final head shake, he brought himself back. "I don't foresee any complications with the pregnancy itself. You're perfectly healthy, Bree. You've had an amazing recovery from the accident."

She shot Tom a look that said he was partly responsible. His chest swelled.

Sealy reached for a prescription pad and a pen. "You'll take vitamins daily. Eat a balanced diet. I'll see you monthly until the seventh month and more often after that." He glanced at her record and pulled up a calendar. "As I figure it, you're due . . ." The tip of his pen counted out the weeks. "Too much," he said, with a chuckle, and raised his eyes. "As I figure it, you're due on or about Christmas. I'd say there's magic in that."

*I'd say there's magic in that.*

Tom heard those words over and over during the ride back from Ashmont, and with growing concern. If Bree shared that concern, she didn't let on. She was exuberant the whole way. The only thing to upset her was when he refused to let her sit close and belted her in on the passenger side, but she held his hand in both of hers, as though she would float away if she didn't, and she didn't stop beaming.

It was almost enough to make him forget. When she turned her smile on him, he felt the force of it deep inside. He lived to make her happy.

But he kept hearing those words. *I'd say there's magic in that.* And he had to know.

"Bree?"

"What if it's a boy?" she asked in a dreamy voice.

Helplessly, he smiled. "What if it is?"

"He'll look like you."

"He could look like you."

"No-o," she wailed, shaking his hand. "I want a little Tom."

A little Tom. The thought of it made him so proud that he thought he would burst. But there was still the other. "Bree?"

"We'd name him Tom, wouldn't we? Tom, junior?"

"Maybe he should have a name all his own. My mother's family name was Wyatt."

"Wyatt," Bree repeated. "That's a *great* name. If it's a girl, she can be Chloe."

"Chloe. Where did that come from?"

"Nowhere. I just like it. Chloe Gates. It flows. I used to dream of changing my name to Chloe, but I couldn't let go of Bree. It's one of the few things I have of my mother."

Tom knew that she thought about her mother a lot, more so since the incident at the diner. He had actually talked with the private investigator who had helped him on many a case in the past, but they had precious little to work with to decide whether the second wish had come true or not. "Her name wasn't Bree."

"No, but she chose it for me. My grandparents always hated it. Keeping it was one of the few things my father ever did against their wishes. That and going to Boston in the first place. I've always thought Bree was short for something. Brianna, or Brittany. Or Bridget. Can you imagine me as a Bridget?"

He couldn't. Shifting gears, he pulled the truck onto the shoulder of the road.

She twisted to look out the rear window. "What's wrong?"

He parked and faced her. "I need to know something, Bree. Did you wish for the baby?"

She started to blink, caught herself. "Of course I did. I wished ten times over. It's what I want more than anything else in the world."

"But did you *wish?* You know, do the ritual? Did you use your last wish for this?"

"You heard Dr. Sealy. He said my conceiving wasn't an impossibility."

"Bree."

She didn't say anything. She didn't have to. The look on her face said it all.

"Oh, baby," he breathed, feeling a deep, tingling fear. He hooked his arm around her neck, brought her face to his shoulder, and closed his eyes. "Why, Bree? *Why?*"

She clasped a fistful of his flannel shirt. Her voice came from his collar, words spilling fast in argument, as though she was trying to convince herself, too. "Because you'll be the very best father, and because I want your baby, and because if I was given three wishes, I was meant to use them. I don't know where I got the notion that the world would end once I used the last wish. We don't know that at all, and anyway, the more I think about it, the more I say that we're crazy to believe in three wishes. Life doesn't happen like that. When you pull a quarter out of Joey Little's ear, it's sleight of hand. That's all magic is, an illusion, but there's a rational explanation for it. So yes, I made a wish, but that's not why I'm pregnant. I'm pregnant because I love you, and because we wanted it so much, and because we'll be good parents, and because you turn me on so much that my body is entirely open when we make love. Scar tissue didn't have a chance against that."

Tom couldn't help it. He laughed. "Christ, what's medical school in the face of logic like that?"

"I'm serious."

"So am I." His laughter ended. Fear was suddenly a living, breathing thing inside him. "What if you're wrong? What if the wishes *are* real? What if the thing about the third wish is true? What if that really *does* mean . . ." He couldn't finish.

In a quiet voice, she said, "I'm not going to die."

Hearing the word loosed his fear. Wrapping both arms around her, he buried his face in her hair. "If something happened, I'd never forgive myself. I don't want to live without you. I *can't.* You're everything good that's come into my life, everything good that I've become." She was shaking her head no against him, but he believed what he said. "You are. You're my heart and soul. You're my conscience. When I'm with you, I feel more at peace than at any other time in my life. I don't feel driven. I don't feel competitive. I'm a decent person when I'm with you. A *caring* person. A *happy* person. I fell in love with *you*, not with the idea of having a baby. I don't need a baby. If we could go on living just the way we have for the last few months, I'd be happy. The baby's no good without you."

She pushed at him so suddenly that he couldn't hold her. The next thing he knew, her eyes were flashing. "Don't say that. Don't *think* it. That's pretty much what my father thought. I don't *ever* want a child of mine raised that way." She softened, grew pleading, touched his face. "Don't you see? This is what our love is about. It's what lives after *both* of us are gone. We all die, Tom. Sooner or later we do."

He saw her tears and was lost. It was like that every time. When she cried, her emotion became his. "Oh, Bree," he whispered.

"We do."

"But I want it to be later."

"It will be."

"I wish you'd talked with me first." He might have talked her out of it. He might have suggested they try to get pregnant without wishing for it. Of course, they had made love many dozens of times since November. He hadn't once worn a condom. Her body had been entirely open then, too. And she hadn't conceived.

That realization made him all the more fearful.

"You'd have said no," she said.

"Probably."

"So we'd have argued. I thought this all out, Tom. Really I did. I went over every argument, and the ones about *wanting* to have our baby were the best, but then there were the ones about not trying. About not trying and always wondering. About letting ten years go by and still wondering, and regretting, and then finding it was too late to try." She tipped up her chin in defiance. "Besides, it's my body."

Tom cursed liberated women then, but he felt the same little catch inside that he always felt when the bottom line was clear. He wanted to be angry with her, but he loved her too much for that. So he sighed. "Well, it's done. You are pregnant."

Her eyes lit. "I am so happy. Be happy, too."

"How not to be?" he asked. "As long as I don't think."

If he was nothing else, though, Tom was a thinking creature. More, he was a *deliberating* creature. It was the single trait most responsible for his success as a lawyer. He could look at a case from every angle, could analyze every argument and devise a strategy that, nine times out of ten, worked.

So he began deliberating. On trial was the validity of Bree's three wishes. The plaintiff was his own peace of mind. His goal was to prove, beyond the shadow of a doubt, that one of those three wishes had not been granted.

As he interpreted the testimony of the fire inspector, the cause of the fire could never be proved one way or another.

Likewise, given the doctor's suspension of disbelief, the pregnancy.

The one piece of evidence that hadn't been established as clearly, and therefore held the most promise, was the positive identification of Bree's mother.

# chapter
# fourteen

Tom had the best of intentions. He called his investigator friend and put him on the case. A few phone calls later, the investigator reported that the little bit of information on Bree's mother that was filed in records at the hospital in Chicago where Bree was born led nowhere, which meant that either the woman had given false information or the address she gave the hospital had been so tentative that no trail remained. Tom put him back to work checking out New York women who drove small red Mercedeses, women who were possibly involved in litigation and who traveled to Montreal on business.

Then life distracted him.

First, there was the weather. Mid-May brought clear skies and warm sun, fragrant apple blossoms, budding trees, and greening grass. Even beyond framing a two-car garage on the far side of the carport, there were chores to do, like replacing storm windows with screens, cutting back trees that were growing too near the house, cleaning the yard, and doing the season's first mowing. The year before, when he was alone and raw, these chores had been therapeutic. This year, they were a pleasure.

Second, there was Bree. How could he dwell on dark fears when she was so happy? She smiled through morning sickness, smiled through afternoon fatigue. She cut back her work hours to four a day and was right there puttering around the house with him, smiling all the while. If she ever thought about a less than happy ending to their story, she didn't let on. She was exhilarated and beautiful. His love for her grew with each day that passed.

Third, there was the phone. It rang more and more often with calls from people wanting legal advice. Those calls came from a growing circle of towns, from families and small-time entrepreneurs with problems that were novel enough to stump their local lawyers. In some instances, Tom shared thoughts off the top of his head. Others required research. He found the thinking a challenge, an easy return to law after a time away, but he never billed a client. That would have made the challenge a job rather than an intellectual exercise. If a case required follow-up, he referred it to Martin Sprague.

Martin proved to be a pleasant surprise. He was a plodding workhorse of a lawyer, making up in follow-through what he lacked in creativity. Tom was pleased to direct work his way, not only because of that, or because the man needed the work, but because Tom was a Panamanian now, and Panamanians supported each other.

Fourth, there was his family. He wanted to tell them about Bree and the baby, but he didn't think he could have borne it if his father hung up again, not when what he had to say was so close to his heart. So he bought a point-and-shoot camera and began writing letters. The first few were short and direct. They included pictures of Bree and him, and while he hoped for a reply, he didn't expect one. Each week, he sent a new letter. By the beginning of June, he was sending pictures of the house with its freshly painted porch and of Bree at the brook. He also dropped notes to his brothers, lighthearted, undemanding little things that said he was thinking of them.

He talked with his sister every few weeks. She had given birth to a boy and was doing well, and, yes, Harris Gates had come around. She thanked Tom for the large package of baby clothes he and Bree had sent. But she didn't invite him to the christening.

Tom didn't blame her. His presence would have detracted from the occasion. But he wasn't holding that against Alice. If anything, he grew more determined to check regularly on the baby and her.

By late June, the investigator had reached a dead end. He had amassed a file of information on New York businesswomen of the right age who owned sporty red Mercedeses, but Bree couldn't make a positive identification from the photos he offered.

"Not surprising," he said. "The car may be owned by the woman's husband or her boss. It may be leased. I've checked hotels and motels in Montreal, but I can't find the record of a car like that registered at any of the cheap ones on the day in question, and the expensive ones keep their records under lock and key. Times have changed, Tom. Thanks to guys like you suing the pants off them, places like that are locked up tight. And as for the litigation angle, *nada*. It could be she was talking about a friend that day."

Tom wasn't as disappointed as he thought he would be. He was coming around to Bree's thinking that the pregnancy had resulted from natural causes, which meant that the woman at the diner had been no one in particular and that the fire on South Forest had been pure coincidence. The natural-cause approach was the one that made sense, the one any levelheaded man would take.

Being a levelheaded man, though, Tom was cautious. He got second and third opinions from doctors in New York, who studied Bree's records and agreed with Sealy and Meade that while the chances of Bree's conceiving were slim, they had existed. The New York doctors also agreed, after seeing results of the tests Paul had run on Bree in May, that she was healthier than many an expectant mother. They assured Tom that her heart was steady and strong, and saw no reason whatsoever why Tom should drag Bree to New York for the birth.

So he pushed away the three-wish theory and espoused that of natural causes. Natural causes were easier to swallow than wishes. Natural causes were what he *wanted* to believe, because his life with Bree was rich. They were rarely apart, and then only for brief stretches. Many a day, he stayed at the diner while she worked, and he was seldom the only one in his booth. He had friends now, friends of hers, friends of his own. People looking for him knew to find him there. If the subject was law, he jotted notes on a paper napkin. If the subject was social, he sat back and relaxed. In both cases, he was more content than he had ever been, not to mention within easy reach of Bree.

She was his soul mate. He didn't know another word to describe it. She thought the way he did, felt the way he did. They were both small-town people at heart. She had known it all along. He had simply been longer in the learning.

Her quickness was only one of the things he loved about her. He had never been in a relationship that was so well balanced. When he felt like reading, she wanted to read. When she was hungry, he wanted to eat. When he wanted to walk in the woods, she was one step ahead. When she wanted to lie in the sun, he had chairs drawn up before she had changed her clothes. They went barefoot in the grass and deep-kissed under the lilacs. They talked and laughed and read each other's minds, and they rarely argued. She was his best friend. He would never have imagined a wife would be that, and it kept getting better.

July brought warmer sun and richer greens. Fireworks lit Panama's sky on Independence Day, marking the first of an endless string of summer celebrations. There were concerts on the green, warm evenings spent on nubby blankets, listening to the regional high school's marching band or singing along with Panama's barbershop quartet. There were cookouts in the lot behind the town hall, softball games in the schoolyard, a make-your-own-sundae orgy to introduce Panama Rich's twenty-fourth flavor, Oooey Gooey, which was a concoction of vanilla and mocha ice creams, caramel, fudge, marshmallow, and nuts. Even on evenings when nothing formal was planned, people gathered on the town green.

Tom bought a more sophisticated camera. It became a regular at his side, in his hand, at his eye. He photographed Bree in profile in the morning sun, with one hand on the new swell of the baby and a dreamy look in her eye. She had started wearing maternity clothes—early, she said, but her other clothes were too tight in the bust and belly, and besides, she admitted proudly, she felt pregnant and wanted to *look* it. He photographed her in every imaginable pose at home, photographed her in a huddle with Flash and LeeAnn at the diner and laughing with Jane and Julia on a bench on the green. He photographed the barber through the front window of his shop, the bread truck loading up for a day's deliveries, the bottlers at Sleepy Creek Ale taking a cool beer break in the parking lot of the brewery at day's end.

In its summer mode, the diner offered fresh lemonade and lime rickeys, soft-serve frozen yogurt, and iced cappuccinos. The Daily Flash listed two cold salads for every hot special and promoted Oooey Gooey. Picnic tables covered the grass in front of the diner. Sandwiches to go were the rage.

The sounds of Panama were of lawn mowers, sprinklers, and fun, the scents were of warm grass, hazy sunshine, and grilled chicken. For Tom, though, the essence of the season was captured by the Panama Rich ice cream truck with its jingle-jangle bell, its pied piper following, and the old-fashioned ice cream sandwiches it sold, meant to be eaten from the outer edges in.

The dog days of August had set in when Martin Sprague called and invited Tom to his office for a meeting. Ostensibly, the topic of discussion was a case Tom had referred. But he had never been asked to the office before.

On the second floor of the Federal that housed the bank, it consisted of two rooms overlooking the town green. One room was for a secretary, who wasn't there when Tom arrived. The other room was for Martin. It had the smell of old papers and the look of a man who was busier than he had expected to be. Folders lay in odd spots beside books that bulged where random objects had been inserted to mark a place. A standing fan, slowed by the heat, swiveled sluggishly from side to side. Only the computer that sat on a small side cabinet looked fresh, as much a guest there as Tom.

"It's not much," Martin said, with an awkward look around. "But it serves my needs."

He gestured Tom into one of two straight-back chairs and went to sit behind the desk. After pulling out a handkerchief and mopping his forehead, he jumped back up and opened the cabinet under the computer. It proved to be a small refrigerator. "Cold drink?"

"Sure."

Even with the fan, the office was warm. Four windows were open, two on either side of the wall behind the desk, but there was no breeze coming in off the green. Tom wore the T-shirt and denim cut-offs that were the summer uniform in Panama. Martin was the only man in town who wore a suit at any time of year. This day, mercifully, his shirt sleeves were short.

"You can have root beer or root beer," he said. Straightening, he handed one of two bottles to Tom. Then he returned to the desk and opened the nearest folder.

"The Ulrich business. I got your notes. You're right. It's a standard age-discrimination case, but the thing is that what you're suggesting involves going to court, and I don't do that. So I've been sitting here thinking that I could call Don Herrick over in Montgomery and he could take it to court, but then I said that that didn't make sense, not with you living right here in town and looking like you're going to stay. Are you?"

Tom could see that Martin was uneasy, but it seemed a different uneasiness from the one that, months earlier, had had the
man warning him off. There was more curiosity than resistance
this time.

"I'm staying."

Martin pushed the Ulrich folder out of the way and ferreted
another from the pile. He opened it and fished through the
papers there. Gruffly, without looking at Tom, he said, "I did
some calling. You practiced for more than five years in New York,
so you don't have to take any test to get admitted to the bar here.
You have to file an application and do a clerkship. That's three
months working under a local lawyer, someone like me. You're
pretty much already doing that." He raised his root beer but set
it back down without drinking. Both hands grasped the corners
of the papers before him. "So," he said, looking anywhere but at
Tom, "what do you think?"

Tom was stunned.

"And don't say you don't know local law," Martin grumbled,
"because you do by now. You've done as much work for me in a
handful of months as a kid out of law school does in a year. Local
law? Hell, it's *national* law, more and more. And *don't* say most
of this stuff isn't your field, because you did well enough with it
in spite of that. You were the one who hooked the paper company up with investors and helped them avoid a takeover. So
that's not your field. There's other stuff that is. Well?"

Tom held the cold drink can to the fast-beating pulse at his
wrist. "I wasn't planning on practicing law when I came here."

"That's what you said."

"It wasn't just words. I meant it. I'm not looking to take away
from your practice."

Martin waved a resigned hand. "They're going to you for
different things. Things I can't do. Things I don't want to do.
They'll keep coming to me for their wills and estates, and their
mortgage problems, and their lease agreements, but if I don't get
help on the rest"—his bewildered gaze encompassed the papers
on the desktop—"they'll go to someone else. It occurs to me"—
he shot Tom a skittish glance—"you could do your thing and I

could do my thing and we'd have a corner on the market. Know what I mean?" He sniffed.

"I think so."

"Hell, if we don't do the work, someone else will, and I'd rather the money be in our pockets. Course, the money's not like New York money. Nor's the practice. You already know the kinds of cases we get up here. Pretty tame, by comparison. Could be you'd be bored."

Tom doubted it. "I have a life besides law here. I don't want to work the way I did in New York." He felt no competitiveness, no driving hunger. Practicing law in Panama would be more fun than work.

"All these cases, and you never asked for a referral fee," Martin said.

"I'm not in it for the money."

"It isn't right. I say we make an agreement. You fill out an application to join the Vermont Bar and do your clerkship with me. You keep whatever money you bring in, after expenses." He sat back with a there-it-is, take-it-or-leave-it look on his face.

Tom found himself smiling. As agreements went, it was refreshingly simple.

Martin mopped his forehead. "I can put you in the next room and put Celia in a room down the hall."

"I have an office at home. I can work there." He glanced at the computer. "Is that functional?"

"It is. I'm not. And I won't promise to be. I don't trust those things. Look, this isn't the fiftieth floor of some skyscraper. It's the second floor of a building that's got no air-conditioning in a town that's got nothing but volunteers in its fire department. The clients don't come in wearing fancy clothes, and if you want to take them to lunch, it's Flash's or nothing. We're not fancy here, but we have legal needs, too."

"It's a deal," Tom said, feeling pleased.

Martin looked surprised. "You don't want to think about it?"

"Nah. It's good."

Martin scowled. "Don't think you can do your clerkship and then open up a separate office down the street from me, because

I'm putting a noncompetition clause into our agreement. And *don't* think you can move in here and take everything over yourself in two years when I croak, because I'm only sixty-six. I'm not croaking so fast."

"I hope not. The last thing I want to do is wills and estates and mortgages and leases. I'll handle the other stuff."

"You're satisfied with that?"

"Yes."

Martin rose from his seat only enough to stick out his hand. Tom shook it, and it was done.

Incredibly, Martin smiled. It was an odd smile, tight but pleased. Closing the Ulrich folder, he passed it over and sat back. "There's something else I need you to do." He took a swig of his root beer, set the bottle down, ran a hand back over thin hair. "It's a touchy situation. There's a woman in Des Moines wants to hire me. Her mother's living here. Julia Dean?"

At mention of Des Moines, Tom had immediately pictured Julia. "Yes?"

"Eliot knows about this. The son called him not long ago. He said he told you."

Tom nodded. "I told him that the son had to work through authorities in Des Moines if he wanted to claim mishandling of a trust fund."

"He's decided not to do that until he has evidence against his mother." He paused, made a face. "Evidence against his *mother?*" He grunted his disapproval. "The daughter's angle is to hire someone local to observe Julia and report on her instability."

"Instability?" Tom would have laughed if Martin weren't so serious. "Bree and Julia have become close. From what I've seen, Julia's entirely stable."

"I always thought so myself, but I figured if I didn't look into it, the daughter would hire someone else, and I'd rather give Julia an edge with me. Or with you."

"We're not psychiatrists."

"The daughter didn't ask for one. She said anyone with two eyes would do. She told me to hire whoever. I'm hiring you. So to speak."

*       *       *

Tom had defended many guilty people in his day. It had been his job to force the prosecution to prove his client guilty beyond the shadow of a doubt. Along the way, he had made mincemeat of witnesses who testified against him, had discredited the creditable, besmirched the innocent. In some instances, those witnesses suffered afterward. He knew of several who had lost jobs as the result of doubts he had cast on their testimony, others whose marriages were hurt—and those were only the ones he *knew*. During the first months of his self-imposed exile, he had given thought to those he *didn't* know and felt more than a little guilt.

Determined not to repeat his sins, he didn't skulk around watching Julia Dean. That wouldn't do in as small a town as Panama, where people saw things and talked. The mail Julia received created gossip enough. He didn't want to give fodder for more.

Julia was well liked. Flash wasn't the only one to rave about her work, though he did so on a regular basis—and she was regular herself, arriving like clockwork every Tuesday and Friday to arrange fresh flowers in the diner's vases. Tom had never heard a derogatory word spoken about her, had never seen anything to suggest mental upset, much less instability. He didn't want her hurt by even the hint of suspicion.

So he began by calling her daughter in the hope that a talking-to would appease the woman, but Nancy Anderson was upset. She proceeded to repeat much of what the son had told Eliot the first time around. "She hasn't been herself since my father died. When I ask her what's wrong, she denies anything is, but I know my mother, Mr. Gates. She spent a lifetime hating to travel. She always liked staying home. Then my father died, and she packed up and moved halfway across the country to a town where she knows no one."

"She knows people here now. She knows everyone in town. Maybe she just needed to make a change."

"She always hated change."

"Your father's death forced a change," Tom pointed out. He wasn't playing therapist, was simply expressing pure common sense. "It's possible that she couldn't bear to stay there doing the same things as always but without him."

"No. It's something else. She was so determined when she moved. It's like one day she just snapped. And then there's the trust fund."

"Do you or your brother need money? Is that the problem?"

"No, but what if we do someday? My father left that for us. There was enough so that she could live off the interest, only she isn't. But that's not the main reason we're doing this," she insisted. "We're worried."

Tom didn't doubt it. Judging from Nancy Anderson's voice, she was legitimately bewildered and more than a little hurt. "There's no cause for worry. She has a very nice life here."

"A *flower* shop?"

"Is that out of character, too?"

"No. She used to grow flowers in the yard. She used to *dance* out there. Flowers do something to her. They make her wild. You can understand why I'm worried."

Tom had seen Bree dance through wildflowers by the brook. He still held the image, clear as day and sweet.

"Does she have a man there?" Julia's daughter asked. "Because if a man is behind her taking that money, it *really* worries me."

"There's no man that I know of. The grapevine would have said if there were. Have you asked her about the money?"

"I can't. She'll think that's all I'm worried about, and it isn't. Really it isn't."

"What, exactly, do you want us to do on this end?"

"Watch her. The police chief wouldn't do anything. So I'm prepared to pay to have the job done. I want someone to look at her closely and see how she is."

"Why don't you? Why don't you fly out for a visit?"

"I wanted to when she first moved there, but she told me not to. Each time I mention it, she waves a hand and says it's easier for her to visit us here. I think she's hiding something."

"There may not be anything illegal in that."

"Or there may be. We want to know why she's doing what she is."

Tom suspected that a good mother-daughter heart-to-heart would solve the problem, but he was a fine one to talk. His father had hung up on him once, and he hadn't called again. Parent-child relationships involved great emotional risk, regardless of the ages of the parties involved.

"I have to tell you, Mrs. Anderson," he warned, "Julia has many friends in this town. She's known for being kind, talented, and reliable. I don't think you'll find anyone here willing to say she isn't stable." Mindful that the daughter might go elsewhere if she didn't get what she wanted from him, he bought time by adding, "I'll find out what I can. In the meantime, I want you to consider the possibility that your mother just needed to try something new. All right?"

Tom drove to the flower shop after he dropped Bree at work. A sign on the door said that Julia was weeding in the garden out back, and sure enough, there she was, sitting in the flower beds looking perfectly content, with a misshapen straw hat on her head and the occasional bee humming about.

She was an attractive woman, slim and of average height. Her brown hair was streaked with silver, but it remained thick. When she pulled it up into a clip, as she often did when delivering flowers to the diner, she looked a decade younger than the fifty-something she was. The peaceful look she wore helped.

Tom smiled. He liked Julia. More, he identified with her. She, too, had come to Panama knowing no one and had made a life for herself here. Unstable? Hell, from the look of her, she was rock solid and thriving.

When she spotted him, he glanced at the low ceiling of clouds. "You're taking your chances."

"Chances of what?" she answered, with a smile. "Getting wet? I won't melt. This time of year, it's cooler working under clouds than sun. How's Bree?"

"Fine. She's at the diner."

"She told me the morning sickness ended."

"Finally."

"It was worse on you than on her, I imagine. Men suffer during pregnancies."

"Thank you," he said appreciatively.

She tipped her head back to see him better from under the hat. "Are you here for flowers?"

"I'm here for you." He swatted at a hovering bee. "Can we talk while you work?"

"Of course," she said, but she set her weeding fork aside and tugged off her gloves. Her serenity wavered. "Is something wrong?"

He settled on a nearby patch of grass. "Martin Sprague got a call from your daughter. She's worried about you."

With a single definitive nod, Julia sighed. "Why doesn't that surprise me?"

"She doesn't understand why you're doing what you are."

"What did she want Martin to do?"

"Give an unbiased opinion of your mental state."

"For what purpose?" Julia asked, then said, "Don't answer. I don't want to hear." She pushed the hat back with her wrist. "I spent the better part of thirty years doting on Nancy and Scott. They can't understand why I'm not doing it still."

"Why aren't you?"

"Because they're adults. Nancy is thirty, Scott is twenty-eight. They're both married, both parents themselves. They don't need me. At least they shouldn't."

"Your daughter says she saw a change when your husband died."

"No doubt. Teddy died a slow, painful death. He was only fifty-two. I had been in love with him since I was ten. Then he was gone, and I needed to be someplace where I didn't see his face all the time."

"Why Panama?"

"There was no flower shop."

"Did you look at other towns?"

"I didn't have to, once I found Panama." A bee flew near. She gracefully waved it off. "My children think this was a sudden decision on my part. They might not understand the truth, which is that during the last months of Teddy's life, he was so sick and sitting by his bedside was so painful for me that the only way I could survive was by daydreaming. I studied maps and did my research and made my plans. I loved him with all my heart, and I buried a part of me with him, but the rest of me needed to move. Does that sound callous?"

It didn't to Tom. Nor did it sound like the voice of an unstable woman.

Reaching sideways, Julia bare-handedly tore a clump of weeds from the ground. She tossed the clump into a half-filled bag. Brushing off her hands, she asked, "Did she tell you about the trust fund?"

Tom nodded.

"That *really* has them hot and bothered. Oh, they don't come out and say it. They say things like, 'Isn't setting up a business risky at your age?' Like I have one foot in the grave," she drawled. "It's my fault, I suppose. When we knew Teddy was dying and were trying to get used to the idea, I kept telling them about the trust fund because I wanted them to know that Teddy had provided for them. Here, too, they may not understand the truth."

"Which is?"

"That Teddy meant for me to use as much or as little of that money as I wanted. He put it in writing. I have a copy of that paper. So does our lawyer. The children won't go to him, because he was a close friend of Teddy's and mine, and they're sure he'll side with me. But we both do have copies of that paper." She ran her palm over a pool of orangy-pink impatiens. "I bought the house here with what I got from my house in Des Moines, but I dipped into the trust fund to set up the shop. There's plenty left for my children." She turned beseeching eyes on Tom. "For years I gave them everything I could, even when there were things I wanted that I couldn't have. For years I put them first. Now it's my turn."

"Have you told Nancy that?"

"In gentler terms. But she doesn't hear, and her brother goads her on."

"Would you like me to talk to her? Explain a little of that?"

Julia grew hopeful. "Would you?"

"Should I mention the paper your husband left?"

"If you have to." She smiled a silent thanks. "You're a good man, Tom. Bree is lucky to have you. Unless people are right and her father became so withdrawn that he couldn't see beyond himself, he would have liked you, too."

"He was a tough man."

"Unsatisfied. From what I hear."

"Lovesick. From what *I* hear. He never got over Bree's mother."

A distant roll of thunder drew Julia's head around. "Maybe if he'd been a stronger man," she said when she looked back at Tom.

"Or if she'd been a stronger woman," he countered. "What would possess a woman to walk away and never look back?"

"She may have had good reason."

"*Good* reason?"

Julia arched a brow at his sarcasm. "Things aren't always as they seem, Tom. Take your reasons for coming here now. My children say that because I left them and moved away, something's wrong with my mind. But the reasons I gave you make sense, don't they? So maybe Bree's mother had reasons, too."

He scratched his head. "Yeah, well, it's hard for me to come up with a scenario that makes her a saint."

"None of us are saints. The truth usually lies somewhere in the middle."

He leaned back on the heels of his hands. "What's the middle ground here? What could possibly justify a woman's leaving her baby with its father and dropping off the face of the earth?"

Julia looked bemused. "Well, I don't know."

"Guess."

She frowned, shook her head, shrugged. "Maybe she had other ties, other responsibilities?"

"No tie could be as strong as the one between mother and child. Unless she already had a family. But if she did, she had no business carrying on with Haywood Miller in the first place."

Julia responded sadly. "You do sound like my kids. If I didn't know better, I'd think I was talking to one of them right now."

"Okay. So I'm being judgmental. I'm angry on Bree's behalf. If the woman wasn't free, she shouldn't have been with Haywood. If she was already married, she was cheating on her husband."

"So it would seem. But we don't know the particulars."

Tom's face hardened. "I've been trying to learn the particulars. I've tried to locate her, but I can't. She's done one hell of a job covering her tracks."

"After how many years?"

He conceded the point. Thirty-three years was a long time. With most of those years predating the age of computers, a track wouldn't need much covering. It would easily fade on its own.

Another roll of thunder came, still distant, but louder than the last. Julia raised her voice. "So focus on what you *do* know. See if any sense comes from that."

"All we know for sure is that the woman came from California, that she met Haywood in Boston, and that she gave birth to Bree in Chicago."

"Were they together the whole time she was pregnant?"

"The grapevine says they were."

"So where was her husband?"

Tom sighed in frustration. "You tell me."

Julia took him literally. "Somewhere else entirely, I'd guess. Maybe he was a traveling salesman. Or in the service." She frowned. "This would have been in the sixties?"

"Early sixties."

A furrow of pain crossed her face. "The first of our men were already lost in Vietnam by 1962."

Tom was drawn to her expression. "I thought it was later."

"No. It started then." She smiled sadly. "No great mystery how I know, Tom. My husband was among the first to be sent there. You can't imagine what it's like, the not knowing, the worrying. I knew women whose husbands were missing in action. That's a devastating thing. It leaves a woman feeling lost and alone."

"And vulnerable? Is that what you're suggesting? Vulnerable enough to fall into another man's arms?"

"It's possible. Don't you think?"

"But even so," Tom persisted, coming forward, folding his legs, elbows on knees. "Even allowing for the possibility of a war widow finding comfort with another man, why would she leave him once she had his baby?"

"Honestly, Tom, how would *I* know? All I'm suggesting is that you're doing just what my kids are doing. You're assuming the worst. Like the story between me and my kids, maybe there's more to this one that would make you see her choice differently." She waved a hand. "I mean, for the sake of the argument, what if a woman was told that her husband had died at war, and then it turned out that the report was wrong, that he wasn't dead and was coming home, just like in the movies. It happens, you know, and stranger things than that. Would you still be so angry?"

Tom softened, but only a tad. "Even so, even if there was something as far-fetched as that to explain it—thirty-three years without a word? We're back to square one. Even if she had reason to leave, how could she abandon the child without a trace?"

Julia nodded sympathetically. "You're right. We're back to square one. There are endless possibilities—we could speculate for days. Without more details, we can't ever know for sure why she left her child." She paused, seeming again to want to stick up for the woman, as she had done for herself minutes before. "Have you considered the possibility that this wasn't solely the woman's choice? Maybe the baby's father had a say. Maybe he made her leave."

"Why would he do that?"

"Hurt. Anger. You're a man. You tell me. Maybe refusing her contact with the child was his way of punishing her."

"But Haywood died three years ago," Tom argued. "If that were it, wouldn't she have shown up now that he's dead?"

"Maybe she's dead, too. Or maybe she *has* shown up."

"Ah. The woman in the diner. But you were there. You overheard what she said. You were convinced she wasn't Bree's mother."

"Maybe *she* wasn't. Strangers are in and out of the diner all the time. Bree's mother could have been one of them. For all we know, she's passed through here every summer since Haywood died just to look at Bree and see how she's doing. For all we know, she passed through here summers for years *before* that, too."

"Without identifying herself?"

"Sure. It'd be risky to come forward after all that time, don't you think?"

"Because of Bree? Bree is the kindest, most gentle woman in the world."

Julia replied slowly. "You didn't see her with that woman, Tom. She was very angry. I've never seen her like that before."

"Do you blame her?"

"Not at all. She missed having a mother. She has a right to that anger."

"I'll say," Tom avowed. With the first large, spattering drop of rain, he unfolded his legs.

Rising beside him, Julia brushed at the seat of her pants. "I don't envy the woman. It's a sad situation. Truly." She bent to retrieve her weeding fork.

Tom grabbed the bag full of weeds, and they set off for the shop. When the raindrops came faster, they quickened their steps, running at the end. They were laughing by the time they were inside.

"Look at it *pour*," Julia said, giving her hat a good shake as she peered through the rain. "But this is good. My flowers need it. I'm doing a wedding in Montgomery next week. I want the lilies to look their best."

"Business is good?"

"Business is fine."

"Do you enjoy it?"

"Yes. I've always been a flower person. Put me in a room with fresh roses, and I get a little high."

Free association took Tom from picturing Julia high on roses, to seeing her dancing through flower beds, to recalling the original reason for his visit. "I'll give Nancy a call and tell her we've talked. I can probably convince her to ease off a little. It would be even better if you two sat down together. If it's her brother who's getting her wound up, she needs someone giving her the other side. When will you be seeing her again?"

"Thanksgiving."

"Don't want to do it sooner?"

Julia shook her head. "I'll warn you now. She's upset because I told her I wouldn't come for Christmas, too. I have every other year. But this year I want to be here. I wouldn't miss the birth of your baby for the world."

Thinking of Christmas, Tom felt alternately exhilarated and terrified. "Bree's delivering by cesarean section. I thought the doctor might set a date, but he wants her to go into labor on her own. She could be late. Maybe you should rethink that."

"No. I want to be here."

Tom didn't argue this time. Something in her eye said she wasn't budging.

As soon as he returned to the house, Tom called Nancy Anderson. He described his visit with Julia and did his best to paint a picture of the contentment he had seen. When Nancy mentioned the trust fund once, then a second and third time, he told about the paper her father had signed. She seemed almost relieved. Tom imagined she was grateful to have an argument to give her brother.

A good lawyer never became personally involved with his client. It was a basic rule. But Nancy wasn't actually his client, since no money had exchanged hands, and he cared deeply for Julia. So he offered to meet her at the airport, if Nancy chose to come for a visit.

# chapter
# fifteen

*D*ear Dad, Tom wrote in early September.

    *Hard to believe that Labor Day has come and gone. I took the enclosed pictures at the town's celebration—a huge barbecue held in a pumpkin field. The pumpkins weren't quite ready for harvest, but that was the point. The whole town showed up to cheer them on. That's Bree in the first picture, with our friends the Littles and their kids. That's Bree in the second picture with the troika who run the town—left to right, the police chief, the postmaster, and the town meeting moderator. In the third picture, Bree is with her friends Angus, Oliver, and Jack, and her boss, Flash. Flash is a good soul.*

248

*You'd like him. He isn't thrilled with Bree right now, since she's cut back to working only a few hours a day, but I don't like her on her feet all day when there's no need for her to work at all.*

*She didn't want me sending the next picture. She says she looks fat. I say she looks pregnant and beautiful. She's just starting her sixth month. She's gained ten pounds and is feeling great. We love listening to the baby's heartbeat. The doctor is afraid we'll start making extra appointments just to use his stethoscope, and I don't rule it out. That heartbeat is something else. So's the baby's movement. We can actually see it now, a definite ripple. I guess after six kids you got pretty used to that, but this is my first.*

*You'll be pleased to know that I'm getting back to practicing law. A local lawyer and I are working together. It's an apprenticeship for me, since I'm not a member of the Vermont Bar. I've applied for that, though, and hope to be sworn in in another few months.*

*Practicing here is different from practicing in New York. The cases aren't blockbuster ones, but they deal with real people and real problems. In that sense, they're more rewarding. Also, practicing here allows for a gentler lifestyle. I'm working out of an office at home, which is a five-minute drive from my mentor's office in town. And I'm really only working part time, so that I can spend the rest of the time with Bree. I want to be involved in raising the baby. It'll work this way.*

*When I finally unpacked the cartons that were piled in my office, I found the family photographs that I framed when I first started to practice. Among them was one of all of us taken at my high school graduation. Do you remember it? We were on the front porch getting ready to leave, and Minna came from next door to take the picture so Mom could be in it, too. It's one of the few of all of us. I have it on my desk.*

*I hope you're well. I'll write again soon.*

*Love, Tom*

*Dear Alice,* Bree wrote in mid-September.
*Thank you so, so, so much for sending the picture of little Jimmy. He is precious. I see you in him, and even a little of*

*Tom. Tom stood looking at the picture for the longest time. He still keeps picking it up. So you know how much it means to him that you sent it.*

*Only three and a half months of waiting left for us. I go back and forth between being so impatient I can't sit still and being terrified. I don't tell Tom about the terrified part. It's silly, isn't it? I mean, doctors have childbirth down pat. What could go wrong? We had amniocentesis done, so we know that the baby's healthy, but we didn't ask for the sex. We want that to be a surprise. It's kind of neat that our kids will be less than a year apart, don't you think?*

*We've been working to get the baby's room ready. Tom sanded and lacquered the floor. He painted the ceiling white and the walls yellow. I made a clown border with stencils using navy blue, white, and red, so it'll be good for a boy or a girl. Believe it or not, Tom stood at the bottom of the ladder the whole time I was painting it. He was afraid I'd fall.*

*We've also started buying a few things. Thank you for the recommendation on the carriage. We bought it, and a crib. The crib is white. I start crying every time I look at it.*

*I know Tom has asked you himself, but I would love it, too, if you would come visit. I was an only child. The idea of having a sister-in-law is wonderful. We have a sleep sofa in the third bedroom, and a crib for Jimmy. I know that your father wouldn't like the idea of your coming, but if there's any way you can get around that, please consider it. It would mean a lot to me to meet you before our baby is born. It would mean a lot to Tom, too. Say the word, and he'll send tickets. You could fly into Burlington or Boston. We'll meet you in either place. Just let us know.*

*The trees are starting to turn. It's just beautiful up here. Please come.*

*Love, Bree*

*P.S. My stretched stomach itches something fierce. Any suggestions?*

*Dear Nathan,* Tom wrote in early October.

*I enjoy getting your little notes. Being out of the mainstream, I didn't know that my favorite publisher was fired, much less that the publishing house was bought. I didn't know that Ben Harps's book hit the lists, either. I'm pleased for him and pleased for you. Maybe someone like Ben can get you to stop E-mailing me. He's young and hot. If you haven't sold him to Hollywood yet, you will. His stuff is good.*

*I know I told you I'd think about writing again, and I have. But it isn't going to happen, Nathan, not now, maybe not ever. Drop all the hints you want, but you won't make me jealous of Ben or anyone else.*

*I've gone back to practicing law. Yes, up here. Don't be so startled. It's like going back to my roots. Very satisfying. Bree is expecting a baby in December, so there's plenty to keep me busy. I'm happier than I've ever been. Be happy for me.*

*Yours, Tom*

*Dear Dad,* Tom wrote in mid-October.

*Bree and I spent last weekend in Nantucket. These pictures are from there. The one of the two of us was taken by the owner of the bed-and-breakfast where we stayed. It was a charming place, small and quiet on a private way that led to the beach. We spent hours walking there and browsing through the shops in town. Bree had never been there. Her excitement made it like the first time for me, too.*

*A funny thing happened. When we stopped in at a little sandwich place, I was recognized by a woman who interviewed me several years back for* Vanity Fair. *She came right up and started asking questions. Two years ago, I would have answered. This time, I refused. I may have offended her, but I don't care. I'm done with that life. All I could think was that she was intruding on my time with my wife.*

*Bree is wonderful. She's starting to look very pregnant and has trouble keeping going endlessly the way she used to, but she doesn't complain. She's a trouper—the warmest, most interesting and loving woman I've ever met. Based on past performance, I don't deserve her. I'm trying to change that.*

*We had cause to celebrate in Nantucket. It was the first anniversary of the accident that brought us together. It scares me to think how close I came to losing her. Had she died that night, I never would have known this kind of love. Okay, if I hadn't known it, I wouldn't have missed it, but boy, it makes me think.*

*If you felt for Mom what I feel for Bree, I can understand why you were so hurt by what I did. If a child of mine ever did that to Bree, I would be angry, too. All I can say is that I didn't know, and that I'm sorry.*

*Enclosed is a small painting done by one of the local artists on the island. The view of the dunes is one that we saw each day. I hope you can get a feel for it through the oils.*

*Love, Tom*

*P.S. We're out of double digits. Only nine weeks until the baby is due.*

With eight weeks to go, Bree was sitting in the breakfast room, feeling lazy and replete in the morning sun, when the phone rang. Setting the newspaper aside, she rose to get it.

"Hello?"

"Bree?" The voice was tentative, new. "This is Alice."

Bree caught her breath. "Alice." There was only one person with that name. "Alice," she breathed, half relieved, half awed. "How *are* you?"

"Feeling like a traitor, but otherwise fine. I got my editor to send me to a seminar in Boston. I just landed."

"In *Boston?*" Bree's voice went higher. "Tom will be *so excited!* Can we see you? Will you come here? Where can we pick you up? How long do you have?"

"Three days. I have the baby with me."

"Oh my God! Tom'll *die* when he finds out. He just left to meet with his law partner in town. I'll call him there. We can be on our way in less than an hour. You should have called before you left. We'd have been there to meet you."

"I didn't know if I'd have the courage to call. I'm not sure I should be doing this."

"Of course you should."

"My father wouldn't be pleased."

"You're not making *him* come."

"This is pretty last-minute."

"Are you kidding? Tom's been dreaming of this for *months.*" So had Bree, more so of late. "Will you come back here with us?"

"If it's no trouble."

"None. Where should we meet you?"

They arranged to meet at the downtown hotel where the seminar was being held. While Tom and Bree were en route, Alice attended two lectures. When they arrived, she was sitting in the lobby, as petite as Bree had pictured her, with Tom's shiny brown hair and gray eyes. The baby was a sleeping wad strapped to her front.

Bree was entranced by the look on Tom's face when he first saw her. It combined longing and love with intense relief. He stopped just inside the revolving door. Alice rose. She didn't come toward them, but her unsureness ended his. He crossed the space in seconds, wrapped her in his arms, baby and all, and held them both for a long, silent time.

The forty-eight hours that they had together couldn't have been more perfect. As Boston fell behind mile by mile, so did the hard feelings that had kept them apart. By the time they reached Panama, all awkwardness was gone. The town was a pocket that the past couldn't touch.

Tom wanted to show Alice the town green, the church where he and Bree had been married, the office above the bank. Bree wanted to show her the town hall, where their wedding reception had been held, the general store, and the diner. Alice wanted to see the bungalow, the bench by the brook, the pumpkin field where the Labor Day barbecue had taken place.

They saw it all. The weather was perfect, the foliage vivid even a week past its peak. Townsfolk waved as they drove by and approached when they stopped. Alice's enthusiasm matched Tom's pride. Both matched Bree's happiness. She couldn't even be envious of Tom's intimate ease with his sister, because Alice was just as easy with her. In no time at all, she felt she had known Alice forever.

They spent time at the bungalow and time at the diner. Tom baby-sat Jimmy while Bree took Alice to meet Julia, and when they should have returned, they traded grins instead and went to Verity's cottage in the woods.

Alice was spirited and fun. Bree adored her.

And the baby? What could Bree say? He was smiley and sweet, wanting nothing more than dry diapers, mother's milk, and the occasional bit of attention. Tom gave him far more than that, uncle and nephew a sight to behold. If Bree had even the tiniest lingering doubt about having risked a third wish on their own child, it was dispelled by the sight of Tom stretched out on the floor, watching in fascination while the baby played inches away.

All too quickly, Alice's time in Panama ended. With Boston's approach, mile by mile, came threads of sadness.

"Will you tell Dad you saw us?" Tom asked.

"Not yet. But he isn't indifferent. He reads your letters, reads them more than once. And he studies the pictures."

"Will he talk if I call?"

"I don't know. He visits the cemetery twice a week. That's when he comes home all stoic and hard. I'll work on him, Tom. I can't promise anything more than that." She hugged him, then opened her arms to Bree with a what-can-I-say expression.

Bree held her tight. "Thank you," she whispered. "You've made him so happy by coming. Him *and* me." Alice would be a wonderful aunt to her child. Bree felt a profound sense of relief knowing that Tom and the baby would have family, should anything happen to her.

\*       \*       \*

By the end of October, Bree stopped waitressing. She went
to the diner every day, but what work she did was either by
computer or by phone. Before and after, she sat talking with
friends.

"Only two months left," Jane said. They sat side by side at the
counter, having late-morning muffins and tea. "Can you stand
it?"

"Barely."

"You look good."

"I feel good." She truly did—strong, energetic, and happy, so
happy sometimes that she burst into tears. Waking up beside
Tom each day was a dream, all the more so waking up *pregnant*
beside him each day. Julia had been right about the joy of pregnancy, though Bree figured the father-to-be made the difference.
Tom loved everything about her pregnant body. Rarely did a
night pass when he didn't remove her nightgown to run his
hands, ever so slowly, over the mound of her belly. He loved the
fullness of her breasts, loved the bump of her navel and the
vertical line beneath it. He loved putting his ear to the baby
and listening, and she loved pushing her hands into his hair
or rubbing his bare shoulders and watching them, father and
child.

If only there weren't that fear. It came and went, a scary little
shred. She was seeing the doctor twice a month now. He swore
all was just as it should be. The baby was bigger and more active.
But December neared.

"I want everything to go well," she told Jane.

"What's not to go well?"

She fiddled with the crumbs on her plate. "Remember I told
you about the three wishes?"

Jane nodded.

"I think this was one."

"The *baby?*"

"After the accident, the doctor told me I couldn't have kids."

"Oh, Bree. You didn't tell me that."

"I didn't tell anyone. I didn't want to think about it. I told

Tom before we got married. He was furious when I told him I wished for a baby."

"Why? What better thing to wish for?"

"It might have been the third wish." When the look on Jane's face said she still didn't get it, Bree added, "There's a part of me that thinks I was put back on earth for Tom and the wishes, and that once the third one is granted, I'll die."

"That's *crazy*," Jane scolded. She lowered her voice, but the fire remained. "Don't say it, don't think it, don't *breathe* it."

"I can't *help* it," Bree cried. Most of the time she believed that the pregnancy had happened on its own, but there was no way she could be absolutely, positively sure that the wishes hadn't been involved. She wrapped her fingers around Jane's arm. "Promise me you'll be there for Tom and the baby if anything happens."

"Don't even *mention* the possibility—"

"Promise me, Jane. You're my best friend. I want you to say it."

"I'll be there, but it won't be necessary. Nothing's going to happen. You'll fly through the delivery. Afterward you and I will sit here and *laugh* that you thought for even *one minute* what you just thought." She shivered. "God, Bree, that's *awful*."

But Bree felt better with Jane's promise secured. Dark images faded. Only bright ones remained. She smiled at those. "I'm okay now."

Jane eagerly changed the subject. "The shower's going to be at Abby's house. She insisted, and since the Nolans have the nicest house on the green, and since Abby's baby-sitter can watch the other kids, too, it seems right. Next Friday at five. Okay?"

"You guys don't have to do this."

"Yes, we do. Besides, it's already done. Everyone knows. We're not canceling." Jane's gaze shifted.

Bree looked around and smiled more broadly when she found Verity leaning against the edge of the next stool. "Hi. Sit and have a muffin with us?" She raised a hand to LeeAnn, but Verity drew it back down.

"I can't stay," she said softly. "I just wondered if you knew the sex of the baby. I'm crocheting something."

"Oh, Verity." Bree was touched.

"I want to make the color right."

"That's *so sweet* of you. But I don't know what the sex is."

Verity nodded. "Then I'll make it generic." She left the stool and was gone without another word.

Bree understood the rush when Dotty took her place, looking back at the door. "Good thing you didn't tell her. The last thing you need is something Verity makes."

"I would have told her, if I'd known the sex. I'd love to have something Verity makes. She's very talented."

"She's weird."

"She's my friend." Bree turned to Jane. "She's coming to the shower, isn't she?"

"I invited her."

"You did?" Dotty asked. "You said you wouldn't."

"You told me not to. I didn't answer."

Dotty made a guttural sound. "You're impossible." With a look of disgust, she left.

Jane kept her eyes on her tea. "I'm no more impossible than she is."

"You're not impossible. There's no comparison."

"I applied."

It was a minute before Bree understood what she meant. "To art school? That's *great.*"

"I don't know if I'll get in."

"You will."

"I don't know if I'll get a scholarship."

"You *will.*"

Jane let out a weary breath. "I hope so. I can't take much more, Bree."

"You won't have to. Oh, I'm *so pleased* you did it. When will you hear?"

"After the fifteenth of December."

That pleased Bree even more. It meant she would know before

the baby came, which meant that she would be able to lobby for Jane if Dotty gave her trouble, which she was sure to do. Dotty was a difficult woman.

Bree leaned close and, tongue in cheek, said, "Maybe your mom will have other plans next Friday at five?"

Dotty was at the shower. Verity was not. Bree kept thinking about that afterward. Worried, she drove to the cottage the next day.

Verity seemed unsure from the moment she opened the door. She invited Bree in and set about making tea, but she didn't quite look Bree in the eye.

So Bree said, "I missed you yesterday. Why weren't you there?"

Still without making eye contact, Verity said a breezy, "Oh, I hadn't finished making what I wanted to make," as though that were all there was to it, but Bree doubted it was.

"You could have come anyway. You didn't have to bring a gift."

Verity poured the tea.

"Dotty said something to you, didn't she?" Bree asked.

A plate of sliced pumpkin bread joined the tea.

"Why do you listen to her, Verity? She's one of those people you talked about who have a closed mind."

Verity slipped a slice of the bread onto Bree's dish. When Bree made no move to touch it, she sat back in her own seat, with her shoulders slumped. "She said you didn't want me to come. She said that you would never say anything to me, that you're too polite." She looked up. "You are polite, I know that."

"I wanted you there. I *told* Dotty that. I told her you and I are friends. I'm sorry, Verity. She's a witch."

Verity laughed at that.

It was a minute before Bree realized what she had said. Then she laughed, too. "She is. Not you. Her." She sobered. "I really did want you there. I want people to know we're friends."

Verity's smile turned sad. "No, you don't. You don't want that kind of stigma."

"There's no stigma. Not for me. I don't care what people think about our friendship."

"Your husband might."

"Tom? Oh, no. When I told him what I suspected Dotty did to you, he said . . . I won't repeat it—it was crude." And Verity was a southern lady, sitting there with her fine china and linen napkins. She still looked bohemian. But she was refined and sensitive.

"Dotty isn't alone. There are others who share her feelings. You have a baby to think about now. Maybe she's right. Maybe the baby would be better off sleeping under someone else's afghan."

Bree slid her arms across the table to touch Verity's hands. "I would be *honored* if my baby had an afghan made by you. It would bring luck."

Verity looked like she wanted to believe that.

"The baby may need luck," Bree said quietly, straightening. "If this is the third wish, I don't know what's going to happen." She wished Verity could read the tea leaves in her cup.

"You did the right thing," Verity said. "I've seen your husband's face when he's looking at you. That expression is as close to holy as we have here on earth."

"What if I die?" Bree asked. She couldn't ask anyone else quite as directly.

"You died once," Verity said. "Think back to how that was."

"I keep trying to, but I can't."

"Earthly images have come in the way."

Yes. She supposed they had. Swept up in the joy of life, she had distanced herself from the being of light. She had wanted to feel normal.

But she wasn't normal. She would never be normal.

"Take a deep breath," Verity said. "Close your eyes. Clear your mind."

Bree took a deep breath. She closed her eyes. She cleared her mind.

After a minute, Verity spoke again, but softly. "Now remember what happened that night."

That night. Bree recalled walking through the snow. She saw Tom's Jeep coming up the hill and, looking toward the far end of the green, saw the pickup barreling toward them. She relived the fear she had felt at the last minute, felt the pain of being hit, saw herself on the operating table, seconds from death.

Something took over her thought process then. Without a conscious effort to re-create it, she felt herself leaving her body and rising, rising past the room's ceiling. Her mind's eye looked up, drawn there by a light that grew brighter and brighter until it filled everything in its path. Love was there. Peace was. And happiness.

Bree grew stronger. Fear vanished, done in by the sheer beauty of the place where she was. Here, anything was possible. Every outcome was positive. Whatever happened was meant to be.

Calmer now, she drew in a deep, slow breath. Drowsy but renewed, she opened her eyes. They fell on Verity. "Thank you," she said softly, and smiled.

*Dear Dad,* Tom wrote on Thanksgiving night.

*I'm sitting in the family room with the fireplace lit and Bree curled up beside me, sleeping. We had a great day. Thanksgivings in Panama involve the whole town, so those of us without extended family don't feel so alone. That doesn't mean we don't think about what might have been.*

*I'm sorry we couldn't have been there with all of you. I'm sorry you wouldn't let us come. I respect the fact that you aren't ready to see me. Still, it's hard. Bree is at the end of her eighth month. The doctor doesn't want her flying after this, and once the baby's born, we'll have to stay put for a while. I wished she could have met you —and you her—before the baby's birth. She has no family at all besides me. She's hungry for it.*

*I know you're angry at Alice for coming to visit, but I want you to know that in all the time we talked, she never once criticized you. She never once said she thought you were wrong to be angry. Don't think that by her coming here, I got my way. If anything, her visit reminded me that I don't have all of you.*

*Bree loved having her here and wants her to come back. I wish you'd encourage her to.*

*I wish you'd come yourself, if not now, then once the baby is born. My offer of tickets is still open, for as many of you as will come. My house is small. Not everyone would fit here, but we have friends in town who will gladly house the overflow.*

*I was wrong, Dad. The way I behaved even before Mom got sick was wrong, and afterward, what I did was inexcusable. Mom's gone now. I can never apologize to her. I can never move past this with her. But I'd like to with you. I'm not asking you to forget. I'm not even asking you to forgive. What I'm asking is if we can bury the hatchet and maybe recapture some of the good times. You're the only grandfather my child will ever have.*

*Love, Tom*

Two weeks later, Bree was at peace. The doctor pronounced her in fine health, if still a ways from delivering, and she wasn't thinking about what-ifs. She had decided that nothing would get her down, and nothing did. Even eighteen pounds fatter, she was enjoying being a woman of leisure for the first and last time.

The season was perfect for that. She had the diner's best seat for watching the East Main Slide and got first crack at the cookie exchange during the annual clothing drive at the church. She spent hours reading before a blazing fire, and hours more at Verity's with yarn and crochet hook in hand.

Her joy was in spending time with those she cared most about. Tom topped the list, of course. Behind him came Jane, Liz, and Abby. Verity's spot was more private, Julia's more special.

She was with Julia on this day, watching her arrange greens in the diner's little black vases, when the front door opened. With the lunch rush over and the dinner rush yet to start, new arrivals stuck out.

Bree didn't turn. She was too bulky to do it with ease and, after the first seconds, too busy watching Julia's face. Her eyes had widened. Her skin had blanched. Her hands were suspended around the greens.

Slowly, she lowered them. "Oh, my," she said. "Oh, *my.*" She shot Bree a moment's frightened glance and slid out of the booth.

Only then did Bree turn. The newcomer was a woman, close to her own age, with thick dark hair spilling from a pretty wool hat, flushed cheeks, and a homespun look. Julia gave her a hug, then took her hand and stood for what seemed an unsure minute, before leading her back to the booth.

Looking as nervous as Bree had ever seen her, she said, "Bree, this is my daughter, Nancy. Nancy Anderson, Bree Miller."

Tom spent the afternoon in Montpelier, negotiating with federal prosecutors in an attempt to forestall a client's indictment for mail fraud. He carried a cellular phone, as Bree did. They had agreed she would call at the slightest hint of labor, but the phone didn't ring.

When he arrived home, Bree was setting the table. The instant she saw him, she dropped what she was doing and grabbed his shoulders. "You'll never guess what. Julia's daughter showed up, right out of the blue. It's the first time she's ever been here. Julia got so pale I thought she'd seen a ghost."

Tom hadn't heard from Nancy since he had suggested she come. "Julia's daughter? Nice. I take it Julia recovered?"

"It took a while. They've had some differences. Julia was cautious at first." She gave him a wide grin. "Hi, handsome. How was your day?"

He laughed. It was a joy, the way she did that each time he came home from wherever he was. He caught her mouth in a kiss and moved his hand on her belly. "Hard as a rock. Muscles contracting?"

"A lot. But I feel good."

"No pains?"

"None. Tom, they're coming for dinner."

"Who?" It took him a minute. "Here?" He counted the place settings. "Bree, you're not making dinner."

"That's what Julia said. But it's all made. Flash did it, three courses' worth. We just have to heat and serve."

"You won't. I will."

"I knew you'd say that." She unknotted his tie.

He unbuttoned his collar. "So what's the daughter like?"

"Very nice."

"You sound surprised."

"I was. Am." She frowned, then grew sheepish. "I think I was jealous. I've had Julia all to myself, then suddenly this stranger waltzes right in. Nancy looked even more nervous than Julia, though. I felt bad for her. We talked for a while at the diner, then Julia left to show her around town. They're coming at seven."

Something about the evening made an impression on Tom, but he couldn't put his finger on it. Neither he nor Nancy mentioned their earlier talk. She was entirely pleasant, apparently reassured after seeing Julia's life for herself. Julia seemed happy, even relieved, that her daughter had come. Bree was delighted to be doing something special for Julia, who had come to mean so much to her.

Three women, all smiling, talking comfortably, enjoying the night.

Naturally, Tom pulled out his camera. Nancy wasn't staying in Panama for long. Pictures of her visit would be special.

It wasn't until a full week later that he finished up the roll of film by shooting Bree at her heaviest and most lovely. He dropped off the film to be developed, but by the time he picked it up, he was so preoccupied between Christmas preparations and wondering when Bree's labor would begin, how they would get to the hospital in case of snow, and whether Bree would be all right, that he set the pictures aside without a glance.

# chapter
# sixteen

Snow came on the twenty-first of December. The flakes were large and nearly as thick as they had been on that fateful day fourteen months before. This time, though, the town was prepared. Roads were plowed and sanded throughout the day, particularly the ones near West Elm. Everyone knew Bree was about to deliver. No one wanted her stuck when her time finally came.

Tom wasn't looking forward to driving in the snow, but Bree had her last scheduled appointment with Paul Sealy that afternoon, and he wasn't having her miss it. Well before they reached

the medical center, he decided that if Paul said Bree was anywhere near delivery, they were staying.

Paul said she hadn't begun to dilate.

That made Tom nervous. He had read an Internet piece about
women dying from obstructed labor and figured that a failure to
dilate could cause that. Granted, those women lived in third
world countries. Still.

"Is it a problem?" he asked Paul, calmly so that he wouldn't
worry Bree, though she looked far calmer than he felt.

"No problem at all," Paul said. "Sometimes we know the exact
date when a woman conceived and still miss the delivery date.
Every woman is different. Every pregnancy is different. She may
not deliver for another ten days."

It occurred to Tom that Paul could do the cesarean now and
avoid the uncertainty of weather. But he didn't ask, because of
that other uncertainty. It sat like lead in the back of his mind.
He wasn't ready for the baby to be born. He wanted more time
alone with Bree.

Slowly, carefully, he drove her home through the snow. They
passed the town hall, where, despite the weather, the Winter
Solstice Dance was about to begin, but neither of them wanted
to party, not with others at least. Tom built a fire in the family
room, stir-fried a healthy dinner, popped popcorn, played music.
They swayed more than danced, rubbed against each other,
laughed. Then they lay in each other's arms on the sofa, watching
the flames.

"We have diapers," Bree said, running through the list for
the *third* last time. "We have a baby bathtub and towels. We
have baby powder and baby lotion. We have baby books. We
have baby clothes and a baby seat. We have a snowsuit. We have
formula just in case—"

Tom didn't like those words. "Shhh," he whispered, and held
her more tightly.

"In case I don't have enough milk," she specified.

"You will." How could she not? She was woman personified,
with her warm smell and the richness of a body ripe with child.
Her breasts had grown full, her stomach round and firm. During

the last few weeks, when intercourse would have been awkward, they had pleasured each other in different ways. Tom's orgasms had been intense. From the sounds Bree made, hers had, too. She was the sweetest thing he had ever tasted, the sexiest thing he had ever held.

His camera couldn't capture her spirit, though Lord knew, he had tried. But two-dimensional images were finite. They couldn't convey the heart of her, and her soul. She brought depth to his life, brought optimism and innocence and goodness.

Yet again he wondered if he should have insisted that she deliver in New York. But she was happy here. She had faith in Paul. Having come to know him well, so did Tom.

"I love you," she whispered against his mouth.

He hugged her but didn't speak. His throat was too thick to allow it.

On the twenty-second, Bree helped Tom decorate—"helped" being a relative term, since he wouldn't let her do much. She would have argued, had there been even a remote chance of her winning. But Tom had assured her there wasn't, so she settled for directing the goings-on.

Bree didn't miss out on the fun in the woods. She was all bundled up with Tom and Ben Little, picking the tree she wanted, cheering while they chopped it down, guiding them back to the house, and, once inside, steering them around corners until the tree was in place in the family room. She decorated the lower limbs, Tom the upper ones, with more tinsel, bigger bows, brighter decorations, than the year before. Come time for the star, he sat her right up on his shoulder and held her tight while she did the honors. It was a charmed time. Mistletoe hung in every doorway, big fat candles scented every room, and through it all, carols played, soft, sweet, and poignant.

Friends dropped by for eggnog and hot cider, starting the holiday early, a dream come true for Bree. She loved the sights, sounds, and smells of Christmas—all real now, as they hadn't been that October night fourteen months before when she had stood in the snow across from the diner and dreamed. Her life was rich and brimming. There was nothing she wanted that she didn't have. She felt blessed—and that was even before she saw Tom's gift to her. It arrived shortly before dusk, with a giant red bow on its shiny red roof—her very own brand-new luxury four-wheel-drive vehicle.

"With baby seat," Tom said, and there it was, belted into the back.

Bree was speechless. They never had gotten around to shopping together for her car. It simply hadn't been high priority, what with Tom's truck being right there and their going most everywhere together anyway. She hadn't dreamed he would do this on his own. For the longest time, she just stood there, looking at her gift, stunned.

"Do you like it?"

"I *love* it." She threw her arms around his neck and hugged him as tightly as she could, given the baby between them. Seconds later, she pulled back to lumber in behind the wheel, opening a palm. "Give me the keys. I'm going for a ride."

Tom shook his head.

"Tom," she protested. "Come on, Tom."

"After the baby's born."

"I won't hurt the baby. I'll go slow."

"You can't even reach the wheel."

"I can," she said, demonstrating. Her elbows were nearly straight, but no matter. "Just to the end of the driveway and back."

She finally wore him down. He actually allowed her to drive to the end of the street and back. She was in heaven.

On the morning of the twenty-third, Tom woke up in a cold sweat. He had dreamed that Bree's side of the bed was icy, and he put a fast hand there. She was warm and awake. He pulled her close.

"You're shaking," she whispered.

*She's here*, he told himself. *She'll always be here*, he told himself. "How long have you been up?"

"A while. I was watching you sleep."

He curved a hand to her belly. "How's baby?"

"All snug and settled in."

"Smart kid knows a good thing."

"What did you dream?"

"Nothing much." It hadn't taken much to cause the sweat. One thought. Just one. He could avoid it most of the time by obsessing over Christmas preparations, but he had less control over night thoughts.

Bree touched his face. "Things will be fine."

"I know."

Her eyes lit. "This time next week we'll be parents."

He brought her hand to his mouth, kissed it, held it there.

"We've done everything right," she reasoned. "For baby *and* me. We had all their tests—heart, lungs, blood—and they couldn't come up with a thing, not the *tiniest thing* that's wrong. We'll make it through this delivery just fine, all of us. I know it. I know it right here." She touched her heart.

What could Tom say to that? He couldn't tell her about the ominous feeling he had. It was the exact opposite of his utter conviction, in the waiting room with Flash on the night of the accident, that she would be fine. Okay, so he had more at stake now. But why such a strong premonition? And what could he say to Bree?

Not a damn thing, except "Wyatt for a boy, Chloe for a girl?"

She grinned and nodded. "I want a big christening, with everyone there and Julia as godmother."

"Not Jane?"

"Jane's going to art school. Dotty doesn't know it yet, but she is. She'll be a great visiting aunt, but Julia's *here.* She has the time and the love. It would mean a lot to her. . . . And I've been thinking: the land on South Forest? Let's sell it."

"Are you sure? We can wait longer. It's not going anywhere."

"I'm positive. You're good with money. Invest it for the baby. And call Alice as soon as the baby's born. She'll tell your father. He'll call us, I know he will."

"You sent them nice gifts."

She smiled. "It was easy."

"All with personal notes."

"What else did I have to do with my time? You won't let me do anything." She moved her lips over his, teasing, smiling. "I love the truck, Tom. Thank you. I can't wait till you see your gift."

"What is it?"

"I'm not telling. It's coming tomorrow morning."

"Give me a hint."

"If I do that, you'll guess."

"I won't. I promise."

She laughed. Her thumb found his chin, moved up his cheek to the scar on the bone, then over his temple, across his brow, and into his hair. She did that often—looked at him like he was the best thing to ever come down the road—and it never failed to both humble him and fill him with pride. If there had been a life before Vermont, he couldn't remember it. He had never felt so content, so satisfied, so fulfilled, so loved.

It was the morning of the twenty-fourth when his gift arrived, the large riding mower that he had sworn to buy in the fall, then forgotten in the excitement of everything else.

"I have this image," Bree said, "of you mowing the grass with the baby on your lap. Promise you'll do it?"

Tom promised. He had no choice. He shared the image and loved the gift. What he didn't like was the feeling he had—in this, in talk of godparents and christenings, in stocking the house with supplies enough to keep them for months—that she was making provisions for when she was gone.

"Don't do this," he whispered, pushing his hands into her hair and holding her face to his.

She didn't pretend not to know what he meant but clung to his wrists, her eyes bright with tears. "I just love you so much."

Words, tears, touch—all went straight to his heart. Fiercely, determinedly, he said, "That's why we'll be fine. You said it yourself. We've taken every precaution. The baby will be fine. *You*'ll be fine." He pressed her face to his chest.

"I'm tired of waiting," she said, in a moment's rare complaint. "I want it over, Tom."

"Soon, angel, soon."

The day alternately sped and dragged. Bree was calm one minute and shaky the next. She unpacked and repacked the baby's little bag, and unpacked and repacked her own. She washed the few clothes that she and Tom had worn since she had done the wash the day before, dusted tables that hadn't had time to gather dust, ran the dishwasher, made the bed. She checked the freezer for the tenth time to make sure it was packed with food. She called Flash. She called Julia. She called Jane. She called Alice.

Everything was done. It was barely noon.

She was in the family room, wondering what to do with herself, when Tom said, "Open your gifts." They were gaily wrapped and stacked under the tree—gifts for her, gifts for him, even gifts for the baby.

She considered it but shook her head. "Nah. I'll wait till morning."

"You didn't last year. Remember that?"

Grinning, she slid her arms around his waist. "Last year was my first Christmas. This year I'm more mature. But you can open yours, if you're impatient."

"I already got mine, even besides this one." He patted her belly. "Want to go to the diner for lunch?"

That was good for two hours. A movie at the mall was good for another two. It was dusk by the time they returned to town, blustery and gray, but Christmas Eve. Trees on the green were strung with bright lights. Every window in sight had a candle. The church at the head of the oval was bathed in white. The air was rife with wood smoke and pine.

Bree felt an odd unreality as they rounded the green, felt almost distanced from the holiday, though in its midst. She felt distracted. She felt *removed*.

Back at the house, Tom built up the fire. She napped against him and woke up feeling like a ten-ton load. She wasn't hungry for dinner. She felt stuffed even before she began. So she nibbled while Tom ate, and peppered the meal with frequent reassurances, lest he worry.

The plan was to attend midnight services with the rest of the town. She had showered and was standing before the closet in her robe, doubting that even her maternity clothes would fit over her pitifully swollen stomach, when her water broke. For a minute she just stood there looking down, knowing what had happened but paralyzed. Then she came alive with a long, broken breath.

"Tom? *Tom!*"

Tom was alerted by the alarm in her voice, well before he saw the puddle on the floor or the panic on her face. It was the latter that kept him calm.

"What do you feel?" he asked.

"Wet," she said, in a high voice.

"Any contractions?"

"Not yet."

"Okay," he said. He knew what to do, had been holding mental rehearsals for days. After guiding her to the bathroom and helping her dry off, he sat her on the toilet seat, with instructions not to move, and called Paul Sealy.

She was still on the toilet seat when he returned, which said something about her fear.

He took her face in his hands. "Paul's on his way." He kissed her eyes and her nose. "Let's get you dressed."

She nodded and did what she could to help, but she was shaking so badly her contribution was negligible.

Tom didn't mind. He had enough energy for both of them. "Left leg . . . I've got it; now the right . . . that's my girl," he soothed, and when the bottom half was done, he did the same for the top. "There . . . second arm, there you go. Now over the head. Good." He combed her hair with his fingers. "Okay?"

She nodded convulsively. "Okay."

By the time she was belted into his truck, she was feeling mild contractions. "What if it comes fast?" she asked. "What if we don't get there in time?"

"We'll get there in time."

"Drive fast."

Holding her hand the whole way, kissing it from time to time, he drove as fast as he dared. He wouldn't have minded being stopped by a cop and getting an escort, but it was Christmas Eve. He doubted cops were on patrol, in this neck of the woods at least. Houses were lit, people inside. The roads were quiet.

The last time Tom had made this trip at night, he had been terrified that Bree would die. A tiny part of him had the same fear now.

"I love you, Tom," she said in a tremulous voice.

"You'll be fine, Bree. This is our baby being born. It's the best Christmas gift in the world."

"Christmas. Oh, Lord." She took a shaky breath and smiled at Tom. "Last chance to bet. What do you think? Wyatt or Chloe?"

"I'll love either one."

"Bet, Tom. Just for fun. Loser does middle-of-the-night diapers for a week."

"I say Wyatt."

"So do I. What happens now?"

"We do diapers together." Tom liked the thought of that, but it left his mind seconds later. Pulling up at the medical center's emergency entrance, assailed by the fear he had tried to assuage, he wondered—again—why he hadn't taken Bree back to New York, where the best doctors in the world would have assured that she'd live. The answer came with the appearance of Paul Sealy and the nurses they both knew and trusted, running out to help Bree into a wheelchair.

Tom wouldn't be separated from her. He held her hand when they wheeled her inside and took her upstairs, letting go only to pull scrubs on. Then he was leaning over her, talking her softly through lengthening contractions, trying to calm her, trying to calm himself—all the while fearing that he was on a runaway train on a downhill track with no hope of stopping, no chance of regaining control. Too quickly, she was changed, prepped, and wheeled into the operating room. Too quickly, she was given a spinal, the anesthesiologist was monitoring her vital signs, and a drape was put up at the spot where her belly began.

"I love you," Tom whispered against her knuckles, taking heart in the strength of her fingers. Their eyes clung. When hers filled with tears, he kissed them away. Then he smiled. "You're beautiful. And so strong."

"What's he doing?" she whispered.

"Getting the baby out." He smoothed dark strands of hair back from her cheeks, which were pale but wonderfully warm.

"I can't feel it."

"Remember he said you wouldn't? That's the spinal."

"I love you," she mouthed.

He mouthed the words back, brushing more tears away with his hand.

Then, from the other side of the sheet, came a pleased, "Well, well. It looks like we have a healthy, perfectly formed little . . . *boy* . . . who is . . . getting . . . ready . . . to cry."

The cry came, lusty and long. Bree broke into a smile, but it swam through the tears in Tom's eyes. He touched her face, kissed her, touched her neck, kissed her, so relieved, *so relieved* that she was alive and happy and his. "A boy," he breathed.

"I'm *so glad,*" Bree cried, laughing.

Her laughter died on a fast, indrawn breath when the nurse appeared on their side of the drape with the loosely wrapped baby. He was red and wrinkly, clearly in need of something more than the cursory wiping they'd done, but he was the most beautiful thing Tom had ever seen. It struck him then, as it hadn't quite done during the months when process had overshadowed product, that this was his flesh and blood. This little thing was a human being. It was the little boy he and Bree had made.

His hand shook when he took the baby from the nurse, and his touch was awkward. But nothing would have kept him from it. Holding his minutes-old child had been a fantasy of his, but only half. He satisfied the other half by carefully placing the tiny bundle in Bree's waiting arms.

She was crying again, smiling as widely as he. He felt light-headed, and no wonder. A huge weight had been lifted from his shoulders. Bree was alive. *Alive.* And they had a son.

At right about the time when midnight services were in pro-cess, Bree was wheeled to a room not unlike that in which she had stayed the year before. This time, though, the air was festive, and she was wide awake and full of energy. The fact that once the spinal wore off she would feel the pain of the surgery didn't matter. She loved Tom. She loved the baby. And she was alive.

From where she lay, she had a front-row view of Tom's face as he stood by the baby's crib, at the foot of her bed. She loved his awe, loved his love, loved his excitement and pleasure and grati-tude. She loved life, even loved the *after*life that had enhanced her appreciation of all this. She felt bold and strong, felt so very happy that if she died right then, she would have died luckier than most.

It was a heartrending admission, but not one that she had time to dwell on. Julia and Jane arrived shortly thereafter. They had been tipped off when she and Tom hadn't shown up at church, and when a call to the house went unanswered, they'd headed here. Since it was the holiday, and since they swore they were next closest to Bree after Tom, the nurses let them in.

"He's beautiful, he's beautiful," Jane said.

Julia didn't speak, but the look on her face, in her eyes, said the same thing, and when she went to Bree, took her hand, and held it tight, Bree heard even more. Julia was happy. She was pleased for Bree and pleased for Tom. She was proud of the baby —though not even yet aware Bree wanted her to be godmother to Wyatt. That request was in the note accompanying the gift Bree had left at Julia's house for Christmas day.

Minutes later, Flash arrived. He was followed by Liz and Abby. No one cared about the hour. It was the holiday, and a nicer thing couldn't have happened. Bree lay in bliss, feeling no pain at all, with her husband sitting close by her side and their son asleep at the foot of the bed.

By two in the morning, the nurses shooed away everyone but Tom. By three, Bree shooed off him, too.

"You need sleep," she said.

"No, I don't." He had one arm over her head, the other holding her hand. Clearly, he didn't want to move.

"Well, then, I do."

"I'll stay and watch you sleep."

"I won't sleep if I know you're here, but if neither of us do, who'll take care of the baby tomorrow? I won't be able to do much, and I'll feel awful if I know you got no sleep at all. Besides, the baby won't be doing anything more for a while." She had already put him to her breast, though her milk wasn't in yet. Tom had changed his first diaper. They had oohed and ahhed over every inch of baby body, from tiny fingers and toes to Bree's mouth, Tom's eyes, and a thatch of auburn hair that came from God knew where. "Sleep for a few hours. Then call Alice and your dad. Load up the camera, and come back at eight. Maybe by then they'll let me up. You can help me to the bathroom, kind of like old times, y'know?"

He didn't budge.

She gave his hand a teasing shake. "I'll be here."

He breathed a sigh of relief. "You will, won't you." He kissed her, then went to the crib and kissed the baby. When he returned to kiss Bree again, there was a catch in his voice. "You are the most wonderful woman in the world." He sandwiched her hands between his and brought them to his mouth. "Know what I'm imagining now?"

She shook her head.

"Growing old with you," he said. "Watching the baby grow and have babies of his own. Walking down a lane, slowly when we can't go faster. Sitting on the porch in the sun when our creaky old bones need the heat. Aren't those incredible pictures?"

They were. They lingered with Bree long after Tom finally left, and they had her smiling into the night. Up until then, she hadn't dared think so far ahead. Now she could, and the thoughts brought a certain serenity. It swelled within her, as light, bright, and buoyant as the being of light that had started all this.

Were the wishes real? She believed that they were. She had conceived a child because she wished it, which meant she wouldn't have any more children, but that was fine, so fine. She had Tom and Tom's child, and a happiness that knew no bounds at all. The being of light had been good to her. She owed it deep, deep thanks.

Closing her eyes, she conjured it up. There was no waiting this time. It was right there, had probably been there all along through such a momentous night. She felt its love and approval, and the warmth of its smile. She smiled back when it opened its arms in welcome. Feeling radiant and ethereal, maternal and loved, she released a long, slow, satisfied breath and went up for a hug.

# chapter
# seventeen

Tom couldn't sleep. He tried to only because Bree had asked, but kept jumping up to check the clock, striding from room to room, bursting with pride and relief. He wanted to go right back to the hospital, but he knew Bree needed sleep. So he busied himself readying his camera for the first photographs of his son.

He was returning the camera to its case when he remembered the last roll that had been developed. The envelope lay unopened on top of cookbooks on the kitchen counter. He pulled the pictures out and went straight for the ones of a beatific Bree at the

height of her pregnancy. Helplessly, he smiled. She was something else.

Smiling now at the thought of photographing mother and
child, he absently flipped through the rest of the pictures, taken
during Nancy Anderson's visit. He was at the bottom of the pile
when his smile faltered. Flipping back a few, he looked more
closely at one picture, then another, and another. All were of
Nancy, Julia, and Bree together. In each, the three women wore
look-alike smiles—and suddenly, suddenly, it made total sense:
Julia knowing that the woman in the diner wasn't Bree's mother
. . . Julia offering Bree her own wedding gown . . . Julia in her
garden, defending Bree's mother to Tom . . . Julia offering encouragement and support as Bree's pregnancy progressed.

He might have felt a twinge of anger, if all hadn't been so
right with the world. But it was a time of forgiveness. And he
wanted Bree to know.

He picked up the phone to call, changed his mind, and raced
upstairs for a shower. He had just finishing dressing, intent on
driving to the hospital, creeping into Bree's room, and doing his
best to contain his excitement until she woke on her own, when
the phone rang.

It was five in the morning. He reached for it with a grin,
thinking it was his incredible wife on his brainwave again, but it
wasn't.

"Mr. Gates, this is Dr. Lieber at the medical center." His voice
was tense, the tone urgent. "I think you should come."

Tom went cold. "What's wrong?"

"We really need you here."

His heart started to pound. "What's wrong?"

"I'm afraid we have a problem."

"What kind of problem?"

"With Bree. She's had an attack."

For a minute, he couldn't breathe. "Attack?"

"Heart attack."

*Oh, God.* His voice rose. "Is she alive?"

"I think you should come."

"Is she *alive?*" he yelled.

There was a pause, then a quiet "No. We did everything we could, but she had been gone too long when we found her. I'm sorry."

The cold spread through him, ice in his veins.

"Will you come?" the doctor asked.

Tom swallowed. "Yes. Fifteen minutes." He hung up the phone and stared at it, pushed a hand through his hair, blinked.

Three wishes. One for heat, one for a mother, one for a child. And after the last?

It couldn't be, he argued with himself. There had to be a mistake. She had made it through the delivery, had been *fine* just two hours before. Besides, she couldn't have had a heart attack. She was too healthy for that. She was too *young* for that.

He swallowed again, feeling sick to his stomach. So was the call a joke? Not possible. No one, *no one*, would joke that way, especially not on Christmas morning.

If it wasn't a joke, though, it might be a mistake. Telling himself that was it, he lifted his keys from the kitchen table as he ran past. He was already in the truck when he thought to call Julia. Leaving the door ajar, he raced back inside and was nearly at the phone, when he changed his mind. He couldn't call her. Bree wasn't dead. There had been a mistake, that was all.

He drove through the predawn dark at the kind of speed he hadn't dared attempt the night before, but Bree wasn't in the car now, and time was of the essence. He had to get to the medical center to straighten things out.

Leaving the truck at the front entrance, he ran inside and up the stairs. One look at the somber faces gathered at the nurses' station, stark against a backdrop of tinsel and cheer, and the cold in him became dread.

Paul Sealy separated himself from the group. Looking devastated, he clutched Tom's arm. "The nurse checked at three-fifty. Bree and the baby were both sleeping. When she made rounds less than an hour later, Bree was gone."

Tom didn't understand.

Paul didn't seem to, either. "Her heart just stopped. There was no warning. No violence. The resident used defibrillators, but it was too late. She must have died right after that three-fifty check."

Tom frowned. He ran a hand through his hair.

"I don't know what happened," Paul said. "We tested her. Her heart was sound."

"Where is she?" Tom asked in a raw voice.

"In her room. We moved the baby to the nursery. He's doing fine."

Tom barely heard the last. He was already on his way down the hall to the room where he had left Bree alive such a short time before. He paused briefly at the door. She was sleeping. That was all. Sleeping. Three steps, and he was beside the bed, but the instant he touched her cheek, he knew.

It was cold as ice. He felt her neck, her arm, her hand. All cold, too cold.

He chafed her hand to warm it up and called her name in that same raw voice. Her face was pale and waxy, her lashes as dark on her cheeks as her hair was on the pillow. Her nose was delicate, her chin gently rounded. Her lips were curved in a soft, sweet smile.

She looked serene, even happy and beautiful, too beautiful to be dead.

"Oh, baby," he whispered, bringing her hand to his mouth. It smelled of the lilac bath oil she had used the night before, and of antiseptic, where the anesthesiologist had swabbed it for a drip.

As he stood there, the smell of the antiseptic faded, leaving only a lilac softness. Against it, he made a long, low, keening sound.

No joke. No mistake. Bree—his Bree—was gone.

Time ceased to count. He sat beside her on the bed, holding her hand, stroking her arm, kissing her cheek. He told her he loved her and breathed warmth into her cold fingers. Pressing them to his throat, he studied her face, tracing every feature, memorizing texture and shape. He struggled to accept that she wouldn't—wouldn't ever again—come awake and break into the smile that he loved.

At some point, Paul joined him. Quietly, he asked, "Is there anything I can do?"

Hit by a sudden insane fury, Tom turned on him fast. *What happened?* he wanted to scream. *She was in your care, so why weren't you here? Why didn't someone check her sooner? You knew she died once, man. You knew it! How could you have done all those tests and not known her heart was weak?*

His fury deflated with the realization that her heart hadn't been weak. The most he could manage was a stricken "Bring her back."

Paul ran a hand around his neck. "What I'd give to be able to. The few patients I've lost died because of accident, catastrophic illness, or old age. I've never lost someone like Bree before."

Neither had Tom. He touched her cheek. The chill of her skin went right through him, bottling things up somewhere deep in his gut.

"Is there anyone I can call?" Paul asked.

Julia. Tom had to call Julia. But he wasn't ready to share Bree yet. So he shook his head no.

Dawn broke after seven. Tom hadn't moved, other than to touch another part of Bree—her hair, her hip, her leg. Her feet were cold. Her feet were always cold, she had told him once. He remembered telling her what his mother had said about a woman's warmth being centered around her heart.

So was a man's, he thought now. His heart was broken. What warmth it had held had just seeped right out through the crack. He was nearly as cold as Bree.

"Tom?" came a frightened voice from behind. Julia was at the door, ghostly pale and visibly shaking. Her eyes were on Bree. "I woke up an hour ago with such an odd feeling. I couldn't shake it. So I drove over. They stopped me at the desk." She approached, still looking at Bree. She carried a small gift. It fell to the floor, unnoticed, when she put out a hand to touch Bree's face.

Then she covered her mouth. Her gaze flew to Tom.

"It was her heart," he said.

"No. She's just sleeping. Smiling at sweet dreams."

Tom shook his head.

"But she was fine," Julia protested. "Healthy. *Strong.* Women don't die having babies. Not here. Not anymore." She whirled toward the door, as if to summon a doctor to treat what ailed Bree.

Tom stopped her with a hoarse "It's too late. She's gone."

"*No.*"

"She is. I've been with her since a little after five. She isn't here anymore."

Julia shook her head in denial still, but when she looked back at Bree, she started to cry.

Tom held her, for his sake as much as hers. They shared something, Julia and he. They both loved Bree deeply. Julia's tears expressed his own grief in ways that the ice inside him wouldn't allow.

After a time, she drew back and pressed a tissue to her eyes. Her voice was ragged and low. "I was going to tell her today. I wrote it all out in a little book for her to read, everything that happened back then, my reasons and what I felt." She shot him a teary look. "You guessed the truth. After that day in the garden?"

"No. Not until a few hours ago. I was looking through pictures of you and Nancy and Bree. There's a family resemblance." He thought to correct the tense, but couldn't, couldn't.

Julia touched Bree's shoulder. She smoothed out the material of the hospital gown and ever so gently kneaded the skin beneath. Her smile was so sad that if Tom's heart had still been whole, it would have shattered right then.

"Beautiful Bree," she whispered. "Beautiful from the start." Her words began to flow, seeming appropriate, even soothing. "I was so frightened when I learned I was pregnant. But she was life, after months focused on death. I loved her the whole time I carried her, and Haywood loved me. He made me forget about

Vietnam. We built a make-believe life together. I was so happy when Bree was born. Somehow, I thought, somehow it would all work out."

She fell silent. Tom brought Bree's hand to his mouth and kissed it. Looking up, he wondered if she knew he was there. He wondered if she knew Julia was, too, and if she was listening to Julia's tale. He wanted that more than anything.

"Did your family know about Bree?" he asked.

Julia's sigh was rough. "God, no. We were Catholics. I had committed adultery. They wouldn't have understood. I had gone east to be with the wife of one of Teddy's war buddies, and they didn't even understand that. Teddy was an MIA. They thought I should be waiting at home by the phone. But, *Lord*, was it oppressive. I called home once a week to see if there was word. I couldn't bear calling more often than that. Bree was two weeks old when I learned that Teddy was found. They had brought him to a hospital in Germany. He had lost a leg and was going to need care. I didn't know what to do."

"Did you love Haywood?" Tom asked, as Bree would have.

"Like I loved Teddy?" Julia gave another sad smile before looking back at Bree. "Haywood was something to think about when I couldn't bear thinking about Teddy." Her voice shrank. "But I loved Bree. I did." Fresh tears slid down her cheeks. With near reverence, she drew a circle from Bree's cheek, over her forehead, past her other cheek, to her chin. "Bree," she whispered. "Oh, Bree. Maybe if I'd been older, or more sure of myself. I was convinced that Teddy was dead. When I found out he wasn't, I felt so guilty. I had betrayed my wedding vows while my husband was living a nightmare. The pain of leaving you seemed just punishment for that."

"Did you ever have second thoughts?"

"All the time. But Teddy was sick at first, and then Nancy was born, and Scott, and time passed, and it would have been even harder to tell them about Bree. Besides, Haywood had forbidden me to contact her. He threatened to expose me if I did. I had to wait until he died. Teddy died the month before." She shivered. "An eerie coincidence."

Nothing surprised Tom. Nothing at all.

"All this time," Julia said with regret, "all this time I've been here, and I didn't speak up. I was afraid she wouldn't want me. It was enough to just see her. So I didn't say a word until the day she thought that other woman was her mother, and even then I didn't tell the whole truth."

Tom was struck by the precision with which Bree's wish had come true. On the very day when she had wished to see her mother, Julia had come forward. The woman in the Mercedes had been a red herring.

"You were born in California?" he asked.

"Near Sacramento."

"Who was Matty Ryan?"

"Me. Ryan is my maiden name. Martina was my middle name. When I was little, everyone called me Matty. Everyone but Teddy. I was always Julia to him."

"Where did the name Bree come from?"

"My father. Bryce." She touched Bree's hair. "Haywood let you keep that at least. I wasn't sure he would. It meant so much to me when I found out. My father was a powerful man, with a shock of thick auburn hair." Her chin trembled. "Oh, Bree," she whispered, "I should have told you sooner." Softly, she wept.

Tom lifted the forgotten gift from the floor. It was small and compact, as a journal would be. He tucked it against Bree. "I think she knew. She told me how much you meant to her. She wanted you to be the baby's godmother."

Julia's sobs deepened. Her words came, broken and wrenched, from behind the tissue she pressed to her nose. "I was so happy —early this morning—couldn't sleep—so I opened Bree's gift— an album for baby pictures—along with this." She pulled a folded paper from her pocket and passed it to Tom.

*Dear Julia,* he read. *This gift is really from my baby, so you'll have a place to put pictures of him (I just know it's a boy). He's going to love you. He'll know that he can go to you when he has a problem. He'll know that you love him. Since I know all that, too, I'd be honored if you'd be his godmother. I'd be honored if you'd think of Tom and the baby and me as your family in Panama.*

*You've come to be special to me. I can't explain what happens, but something does when we're together. You always make me feel better, even when I didn't feel bad to start with. I especially needed you these past months. Being pregnant has been a little scary for me. You helped me get through it. I'm lucky you're here. Thank you for being my friend. Love, Bree*

Tom stared at the note for a bit, then carefully folded it and returned it to Julia. He held her shoulder, but it was a while before he could speak. "I didn't know she wrote that. I'm glad she did." But the poignancy of it left him feeling more hollowed out than ever.

When Julia quieted, sniffling, she glanced at the foot of the bed. "Where is the baby now?"

"In the nursery."

"Have you been there?"

"No."

"I'll help, Tom. Will you let me?"

What choice did he have? He couldn't begin to think about the baby. He couldn't think about the future, period. More than once he had been in the courtroom when a defendant was sentenced to life in prison without parole. He had truly tried to imagine what it would be like to face endless years of a cold and barren life. For the very first time now, he understood how it felt.

The thing about small-town life was that the choices were limited. Panama had a single undertaker and a single graveyard. Tom made the necessary arrangements from the hospital and stayed with Bree until the hearse arrived. Only when they took her could he leave.

Knowing she would have wanted it, he brought the baby home. The nurses dressed him in the tiny clothes that were in his little bag and wrapped him in blankets against the cold. Julia held him close, while Tom drove. Together they settled him in the crib Bree had picked out, and for the longest time, Tom just stood, looking around.

Bree was there—in the bunny lamp on the bureau, the framed clown prints, the turtle mobile over the crib. She had tested a dozen rocking chairs for comfort before buying one that was white, with a cushion of navy and yellow. She had placed it by the window with love.

*Where are you, Bree?* the panic in him cried. *I need you here. I can't do this. Not alone.*

Baffled, he wandered from room to room on legs that were wooden, muscles that were tight. Bree was everywhere—on the bedroom dresser, in the bathroom medicine chest, on his office walls, the family room bookshelves, and the kitchen counters. The scent of her led him, the echo of her voice followed. He kept turning to her and finding her not there. Aloneness closed in on him, barren and stark.

Then the doorbell rang. It was Flash, looking as lost as Tom felt. On his heels came a sobbing Jane, needing to be held. She was followed minutes later by her mother and Emma. In short order, as word spread, others arrived—Liz, Abby, Martin, and LeeAnn, Eliot and Earl and their wives, the minister who had married Tom and Bree not a year before. None seemed aware that it was Christmas morning. Their grief was heavy, their compassion heartfelt.

By midday, the house had filled with townsfolk wanting to pay their respects. Bree's childhood friends came, her father's childhood friends came, newer friends came, diner regulars came. They opened the door for each other. They answered Tom's phone. They brought food, though he couldn't eat a thing. They expressed condolences, shed tears, spoke about Bree in hushed tones. When they left, others arrived. Tom was hugged by friends and acquaintances alike. One and all, they were grief-stricken.

The baby was the only bright spot. Visitors who crept upstairs to the nursery returned smiling. "He's a handsome boy," one told Tom, and another, "Tall and strapping, like his daddy."

As for Tom, he didn't know how he felt about the baby. He was tired enough, numb enough, to confess it to Jane when she caught him in the kitchen alone. He had been rearranging foil-wrapped packages on the counter, needless busywork what with all the women taking charge of the food, but he didn't know what else to do with himself. He couldn't laugh, couldn't cry. Once a master of small talk, he couldn't handle it now.

Jane began with a confession of her own. "I know about the wishes, Tom. Bree told me. She was worried this might happen."

He thrust a hand through his hair. "She knew more than I did. I should have listened."

"She didn't *know*, not for sure. She just worried. But she was so excited about the baby. She wanted to give him to you. She wouldn't want you having regrets."

"How not to? She gave me back my life, so what did I do? I took hers."

"You didn't."

"She died because she had my baby."

"She *chose* to have your baby."

"Yeah, well." He rolled tension from his shoulders. "I wish she hadn't. I wish she'd asked me. I'd have chosen her over a baby."

"He's innocent, Tom. Whatever you do, don't blame him."

Tom kept telling himself the very same thing. It would be so easy to say that if it hadn't been for the baby, Bree would be there. So easy, so cruel, so morally wrong.

He sighed. "I don't know if I can do this."

"Do what?"

"Live without Bree."

"You lived without her before."

"And made a mess of things."

"You have the baby now. He'll keep you on track."

Tom stared out at the terrace that Bree had loved, toward the woods Bree had loved and the brook Bree had loved. "I wanted Bree. I wanted to be a parent with her. It won't be the same."

"Don't you love him?" Jane asked.

"I do." He drew in a breath. It burst from him seconds later. "But how do you swallow something like this? Who do you get angry at? Who do you blame? What do you do?"

A soft knock came at the back door. Tom saw Verity through the glass and, feeling an odd need to connect with her, opened the door. She was hugging a gift-wrapped bundle. When she hesitated, looking carefully past him to see who else would know she was there, he drew her inside.

She didn't say anything at first, didn't look capable of it. Her eyes were filled with a grief so intense that Tom understood why he wanted her there.

"It isn't often that people like Bree come along," she finally said. Her soft southern drawl was slowed by sorrow.

"She died too soon."

"I keep asking myself if I could have stopped this from happening."

"That's two of us."

"She died doing what she wanted."

Tom was moved to argue but couldn't. He recalled Bree's face in death. That smile, that serenity, would be with him forever.

"She wanted you to be happy," Verity said.

"Without her?"

"She didn't know that for sure, so she took the risk. She didn't regret it."

"But now I'm alone with her baby."

"It's your baby."

"He needs Bree."

"He can't have her. So who's going to love him and raise him the way she would have?"

Tom knew who. He just didn't know how.

Verity shot a nervous look at Jane, then beyond when Dotty and Emma suddenly appeared. "I have to leave," she whispered, and turned.

But Tom caught her arm. He gestured toward the bundle she clutched. "What did you bring?"

Still whispering, she said, "It can wait."

Jane was suddenly beside him. "You made something, didn't you?"

Verity looked uncomfortable. "It's not much. I wanted it to be ready for the shower."

"I'm sorry about the shower. Bree wanted you there. I wanted you there. Whatever my mother said was mean and dead wrong."

There was an indignant murmur from behind. Jane ignored it.

So did Tom. Bree had admired Verity. She would have wanted this gift.

With a brief spurt of feeling—defiance, as much as anything, at a time when he felt powerless—he said, "We'd like what you made, the baby and I."

Verity held the bundle for another awkward minute before finally unfolding her arms. There were actually two packages. The smaller of them, on top, had been hidden. As soon as they were in Tom's hands, she was out the door and gone.

From behind came Dotty's arch "At least she had the good sense to use the back door."

Tom looked at Jane, who was looking right back at him. In silent agreement, he lowered the bundles to the table.

"Why don't I just put those away for you," Emma offered.

But he was already opening the largest, the one with bright baby wrapping. He imagined Bree tearing at the paper in excitement and felt a vicarious thread of it himself. There was tissue inside the wrapping. Peeling it back, he lifted out an afghan. It was crib-size, navy, yellow, and white to match the baby's room, and more beautiful than anything he and Bree had seen in the stores.

"It's wonderful," Jane breathed, moving a hand over the fine crocheted wool.

Dotty sputtered. "Did she think the baby wouldn't already have a crib blanket?"

Tom said, "The one he has now wasn't handmade. I'd rather use this one. Bree would have."

"Bree would be *alive* if it weren't for that woman."

He looked at Dotty. "How do you figure that?"

"Verity Greene egged her on. Bree was too old to have children."

"Mother! That's crazy. Besides, *you* told her to *wait.*"

"Oh, hush."

"No, *you* hush," Jane said, drawing herself even taller than Dotty. "Bree did what she wanted. No one made her do anything. If she took chances, it was because she didn't want to live with the alternative. It's taken me a while, but I understand what she felt."

Dotty nodded. "So you're going to art school. If you aren't careful, you'll end up like Bree."

"Better that than living with the alternative."

Dotty gasped.

Emma led her from the room, saying, "She's upset. She'll come around."

Jane stared after them with her jaw set, then turned on Tom. "I *have* come around, and about time! Yes, I'm going to art school. Especially now. I'll do it for Bree as much as for me." Her eyes filled with tears. She pressed bitten fingernails to her mouth. Brokenly, she said, "I'm going to miss her so much."

Tom couldn't speak. The void in his life was gaping again, the emptiness of Bree's absence. He wished he could cry. The emotion backing up in him was painful.

Then Jane handed him the smaller package. It had Christmas wrapping and a card with his name on it in Bree's handwriting. His first instinct was to put it with the others under the tree. He couldn't deal with them yet. They were the last gifts he would ever get from Bree. Once opened, they would be gone.

But something had him taking this package from Jane and opening the card. *Dear Tom,* he read. *I had Verity teach me to crochet. I'm not very good at it, but this is the result. I was working on it all those afternoons I spent at her house these past few weeks. It's a scarf, in case you couldn't tell. Don't look too closely. It's got lots of mistakes. More love than mistakes, though. I adore you. Bree.*

Tom spent the night in the nursery, with the burgundy scarf wrapped around his neck. Pure exhaustion kept him asleep on the carpet while the baby slept. He awoke when the baby did, and changed him and fed him, as Julia had taught him to do. Then he sat in the pretty white rocker and rocked him back to sleep, as Bree would have done, and all the while her voice didn't call and her smile didn't show.

It hit him then that speculative talk about beings of light and three wishes was all well and good, but death was real. It was a hard, final, scientific fact.

He rocked harder now, seeking solace and finding none. With each passing minute, the pain of missing her grew.

Pain of missing her.

Fear of the future.

Dread. Sheer dread. They were burying her the following afternoon. He didn't know how he could stand there, cold all the way to his marrow and alone as never before, and watch.

But he wasn't alone. Crowds of people were already gathered at the graveyard by the church when he arrived, and then, while he waited at its entrance, the hearse inched its way through roads clogged with even more who had come. The whole town was in attendance, it seemed. As often as people reached out to touch the coffin as it was carried from the hearse down the narrow cemetery path, they reached out to touch Tom, who followed.

That kept him from being as cold as he might have been. It was a dreary day. Snow a foot deep lay over the graveyard. Though he wore a dark suit and a topcoat and Bree's burgundy scarf, his head and his hands were bare.

At the grave site, people closed in around him. He was barely aware of who was where, knew only that they were near and that they cared. The minister spoke simply. The choir soloist sang beautifully. Tom's eyes clung to the casket, to Bree. She was wearing the dress she had worn at their wedding. Julia had in-sisted on it. Tom would always remember her as she had been that day, his bride, his first and last, only truly innocent love.

When they would have lowered her into the ground, he felt a moment's jarring panic. Reaching out, he grabbed the wood and held it as though to keep her from the finality of death. But the wood was cold. What Bree was—her hope, her vitality, her love—wasn't there.

The reality of it pressed on his shoulders. Bereft, he stepped back. The coffin was lowered slowly into the ground. Watching it settle, he felt an ache so intense he began to shake.

Then, suddenly, a single ray of sun broke through the clouds and touched the wood, giving it a soft chestnut color and the warmth he sought. He closed his eyes, opened them again, and the warmth remained. His body steadied. His heart lifted. As surely as any dream he had ever had, he felt her presence. It began in the warmth of that improbable ray of sun and moved into the scarf around his neck, but it didn't stop there. He felt it in the people who wrapped their arms around him and held him, one after another, before leaving the graveyard. He saw it in the white-spired church where they had been married, on the town green where they had laughed, down the streets where they had walked. He even knew it would be in the bungalow on West Elm, where their son lay sleeping under his grandmother's watchful eye.

Bree was his soul mate. Her death couldn't change that. She was the ray of sun in a dark day, had been that for him from the first, and she was with him still, cheating death in her own imaginative way. Indeed, he felt her presence so strongly that when the crowd finally cleared, he half expected that she would be there.

Instead, standing a short distance across the newly tamped snow was his father.

Something inside Tom cracked. He was vaguely aware that Alice was there and that three of his brothers were, too, but it was his father who held his gaze, his father who drew his aging body up to Tom's height and started toward him, his father who didn't stop until he was close, then stood for a silent sad minute.

Tom wasn't sure what he saw then, because his eyes were filled with tears. But he felt things he had been too frozen to feel, felt love and grief and need. He felt regret and apology, felt acceptance, and suddenly he was ten years old, coming home to a place of unconditional love.

One open arm was all the invitation he needed. Wrapping both of his around his father, he buried his face in the collar of a coat where the scent of home was familiar and warm even after so many years away, and he cried as he hadn't been able to do before. He cried for Bree, cried for his mother, cried for things that had been lost in the morass of success. It all came out in low gulps that might have embarrassed him had his father made any move to set him back. But even when Tom was finished and held on still, his father held him right back.

In time, the others joined them. He embraced his brothers, holding each in silent thanks, and shared more tears with Alice, who had known Bree and felt her loss. He led them to the graveside, knowing Bree would appreciate that, and knew from the warmth inside him that she did. Then, finding warmth in this, too, he invited them home.

He felt a new urgency now. As short as the drive was, he grew impatient. Once there, he left his family with those closest friends who had gathered again at the house and ran up the stairs to the baby's room. Julia was leaning against the crib rail, rubbing the baby's back. Tom could see that she had been crying. He knew the exact instant when she saw that he had been, too.

"I just fed him," she said. "He's nearly asleep." She searched his face in relief and understanding, squeezed his arm, and left the room.

The baby lay under the afghan Verity had made. Tom drew it back and lifted him, one hand under his head and back, the other under his bottom. The baby didn't object. He didn't make faces or squirm. Little arms and legs barely left the fetal position. Eyes that had been nearly closed slowly opened.

Tom felt their warmth, and in that instant, Bree was with him again. The baby had her mouth, her neat ears, the shape of her face, her peaceful disposition. She had bequeathed him these things. He would wear them well. But he had other things, too, even aside from Tom's eyes. He had his own nose and chin, his own sweet voice, and a brain that made his tiny fingers move in gentle ways that were determined by no one but him.

Settling him in the crook of his elbow, Tom slipped a finger into those tiny ones. They promptly curled around it and held on. He lowered himself to the rocker and started it swinging slowly, soothingly, back and forth.

Bree approved. He could feel the force of her ear-to-ear smile. And if that didn't make sense? Tough. He felt it anyway. When she smiled that way, he felt strong. He felt that he could be a good father, that he could be a good *person*, that he could survive after all and make her proud. When she smiled that way, he *believed*.

"He's a fine-looking boy," came a gruff voice from the door.

Tom looked up. "His name's Wyatt."

Harris Gates came in for a closer look. "Definitely a mix of the two of you. Oh, I know. I never met her. But I saw those pictures. She looked like a good person."

"The best," Tom said. He drew in a deep breath, deeper than any he had taken since Bree had died. The pain was still there, but bearable now. "It's amazing. Two years ago, I didn't know she existed. We really only knew each other for fourteen months. Sometimes I think those fourteen months were preordained. Maybe they were all we were meant to have." He stroked the baby's silky auburn hair and swallowed. His eyes brimmed with new tears. Unembarrassed, he let them stay. "I used to think that she had come back to life solely for me to redeem myself."

"Haven't you?"

Had he? He had given Bree a home she loved, jewelry, a wedding, a honeymoon, a truck. He had been her cook, her waiter, her chauffeur. He had listened when she talked. He had been with her morning and night, taking pleasure from her pleasure. He had made her the center of his universe and had loved her with all his heart.

Could redemption have felt so *good?* Anything was possible.

"She wrote me a note," his father said. "It was with the gift she sent. She said you'd made her happier than she thought a person could be. Was she wrong?"

Tom studied the baby. His tiny cheek was against the scarf his mother had made. His eyes were closed, his little mouth pursing in sleep. Tom remembered Bree's mouth doing something like that, then spreading into a smile of delight when he woke her with a kiss. "No. She wasn't wrong."

"Did you do it only because of the accident? Because you felt you owed her?"

"No. It was because of her. Because I loved her. Because I

wanted to make her happy. Because making her happy made *me* happy." Which sounded selfish again. "So am I still the bottom line?"

His father shook his head no.

Tom studied his craggy face. Age had thinned it and added creases and marks, but it remained a solid face, one people admired. His mother certainly had. Tom had seen her searching for it out the parlor window at the close of the day, even that last time he had seen her, when he had refused to admit to himself how ill she was. "I made some awful mistakes."

"Yes," his father said. "You did." There was silence, then a rough flurry. "So did I. I should have accepted your apology sooner, should have met your Bree. I missed my chance. Now it's too late."

Thinking about that, watching the baby sleep in his arms, Tom remembered the words on the card that had come with his scarf. *Don't look too closely,* Bree had written. *It's got lots of mistakes. More love than mistakes, though.*

More love than mistakes. He supposed that was what life was about. She had been a wise woman, his Bree.

Gently, he touched the soft spot on the baby's head. The pulse beating there was little more than a whisper, but a sweet one. He tipped his head back to the ceiling. It was the crisp white that he'd painted it, made more brilliant by the beam of the lamp Bree had bought. In the shower of that light, he felt her nearness and smiled.

# epilogue

Photographs are wonderful things. They capture moments that would otherwise be lost and save them for all time. Some say photographs are flat, lifeless things. I say not. When the camera is in skilled hands, a photograph comes alive to capture a world of emotions.

Tom Gates's house is filled with photographs like that. I'm always amazed when I baby-sit Wyatt and find more on display. There are usually new ones of Wyatt, of course. Tom never tires of photographing him. But there are others that aren't newly taken, are only newly printed and framed. Those are of Bree.

You see, it's a two-way street. Tom documents Wyatt's life with him for Bree to see and Bree's life with him for Wyatt to see.

Oh, I know. You're thinking that Bree can't really *see* those pictures. Well, maybe she can't. Then again, maybe she can. I've seen Tom agitated over something one minute and, in the next, suddenly take a breath, draw himself up, and grow calm. He doesn't say it, but I know he's thinking of Bree. So is she present in his house?

I can't say she isn't.

She was actually the one to start the thing with photographs, and I don't mean the album she gave me. Among the gifts she left wrapped under the Christmas tree was a special one for Wyatt. It contained a double-hinged frame holding three pictures of her that Tom had taken during their all-too-brief marriage. No one looking at them can help but smile. They capture everything that was Bree—her warmth, her spirit, her love of the life that she found.

It took Tom months to open those last Christmas gifts. Long after the tree had been taken down, he kept them in a pile. He claimed that he had the only gifts he wanted, his son and the burgundy scarf Bree had crocheted. Only when spring arrived, and the daffodil bulbs that, against my better horticultural judgment, he had planted on her grave one bleak January day burst into glorious yellow bloom, did he feel strong enough to open the rest. There were books he had wanted, a legal print for his office, and driving gloves. There was a fine leather briefcase with his initials embossed. There was a small glass heart with multicolored swirls inside, good for nothing more than the thought it carried. Even now, five years later, Tom tucks it in his pocket every day.

Those first few months after Bree died were the hardest for him. Often I would find him in the rocking chair, with the baby asleep on his chest, tears in his eyes, and a stricken look on his face. As though she were an amputated limb, he kept feeling Bree there and mourned all over again when he found that she wasn't. In time, he adjusted to the idea that what remained of her was pure spirit.

That didn't mean he stopped missing her. He stayed home a lot that first year, bonding with Wyatt, yes, but unable to go out and just have fun. I had been the same after Teddy died. Feelings of emptiness, of guilt at being the one to survive, of fear of a future without, were overwhelming. Holidays in particular—the first this, the first that, without the person you loved more than life—were brutal. Occasionally, Tom strapped Wyatt to his chest and went through the motions, but anyone who looked could see his heart wasn't in it.

Two things changed that. No, three things. No, *four* things.

First, there was the town. If Panamanians were nothing else, they were persistent. They kept a close eye on Tom, bringing him food long after the funeral was over, calling often to see how he was, popping by to dote on the baby. They included him in their plans even when he resisted, protected him when the press finally found him, treated him as though he had lived in town for years. They let him know in dozens of wordless ways that he wasn't alone.

Second, there was Tom's family. His sister and brothers left two days after the funeral, but his father stayed on for a time. The end of their estrangement meant the world to Tom, all the more so as Wyatt grew bigger. Every few months, one Gates or another came to town. Whenever Tom felt too much time had elapsed, he packed Wyatt up, and the two of them flew home. Family had been Tom's backbone as a child. It was again now.

Third, there was work. Martin was the best partner Tom could have had. He might have felt threatened when Tom's identity first came out, but that feeling had disappeared entirely by the time Bree died. In fact, their roles reversed. Martin became more assistant than mentor. Under Tom's tutelage, he did the legwork that Tom couldn't do during those first dark days. By the time Tom felt up to returning to work, a thriving practice was waiting, so much so that he and Martin hired an associate. Even when he began to function well, Tom refused to work full time. He wanted to raise his son, Wyatt.

Yes, Wyatt. Wyatt was the fourth and probably the single most influential factor in getting Tom's heart working again. How *not* to smile and laugh with a child like that? I had worried that Tom's grieving would make Wyatt a serious child, but the reverse happened. Wyatt was an early smiler, an early tease, an early talker who loved being with people. Oh, he knew where his bread was buttered. He loved his daddy first and foremost, no doubt about that. But when his daddy took him to the diner, which he so often did, he was in his half-pint glory. By the age of three he had a killer smile and an uncanny sensitivity to people's moods. He had Tom's capacity to charm and Bree's outgoing nature, and was fearless, energetic, and imaginative. More than anyone or anything else, he led Tom back to the world of the living.

Tom has dozens of pictures of him scattered around the house and dozens more in albums—bulging, like mine—that are as popular bedtime fare as any story. *Remember this one, Daddy? Grammy, look at this one, it's you and me. Tell me again, Daddy, I want to hear about the time you took this one.* Some of the pictures are in color, some in black and white. Some show Wyatt alone, others show him playing with friends, at the diner helping Flash fix Earl his brownie sundae, picking blueberries with Verity, celebrating graduation from art school with Jane.

Jane has done well. She is working as court artist for a media group in greater Boston and is dating the detective who testified in one of her cases. Dotty says he's a thug who's only after her money, but since there isn't much of that, and since the detective in question comes from a family with *three* times as much, I doubt it's so. Besides, Tom's detective friend knows him and vouches for his character.

Tom is protective of Jane.

He is protective of Verity.

He is protective of me, too. Even back in those first days after Bree's death, he never betrayed me. My relationship to her was a secret we shared. He felt it was my job to tell people, my *right* to do it. He gave me time. And there was no rush. My presence in

Wyatt's life aroused no suspicion. People knew that Bree and I had grown close. As the baby's godmother, it was only natural for me to help out with his care.

A quick word here, before I go on. I *helped*. That's all. There was never any question about who Wyatt's primary caretaker was. From the start, Tom did all the things that men of my generation rarely did. He diapered and fed, bathed and played, taught and disciplined. He never walked away from a chore, no matter how dirty it was. He was more attentive than ever when the child was fussy or sick.

Wyatt knows that I'm his grandmother. He's known since he was old enough to understand, because the whole town knew by then. Did the grapevine have a field day with that one! Word spread like lightning, not all of it kind. For a short time I was an outsider again, the woman who had cheated Haywood and Bree, the one who had come to town with a "hidden agenda" and been less than honest for four years. I was honest then, though. I bared my soul and invited their censure as part of my penance. When understanding and forgiveness came instead, I knew that Panama was truly my home.

All that, though, came after another trial. Before I told the town, I had to tell Nancy and Scott. It was hard. I had kept secrets from them far longer than from Panama. Nancy was the quicker to come around, understandably so, since she had met Bree and liked her. Whereas she could identify with the despair I had felt thinking Teddy was dead, Scott identified with his father and had more trouble accepting my infidelity. Of course, Scott was nothing if not competitive. When Nancy began visiting me in Panama, he wasn't about to let her get a foot up on him, so he visited, too. By then the trust fund was reflecting a healthy stock market and beginning to grow. Scott was appeased.

I have a good life here in Panama. My work as a florist is only as demanding as I want it to be, which means that I can meet my little kindergartner at the school bus any day when Tom is in court. Naturally, Tom apologizes. He respects the fact that I have a business to run, and if I didn't love him for other things, I would love him for that. But it is a joy for me to be able to do for Wyatt in ways that I didn't do for Bree. I've been given a second chance. There's closure in that.

I see closure coming on another front, too. Tom needs a woman. Wyatt may be only five now, but soon enough, he'll be older and wanting to spend much of his time with his friends.

Tom knows that. He has taught Wyatt enough about Bree so that mention of her is a regular part of the child's existence. That will always be so, for *both* of them. But they need to move on.

Those times when I grow angry at the thought that Bree died too young, I think of the accident that snowy October night. She died then. Had she not been revived, she would never have known Tom or me. She would never have experienced the joy she had. She would never have left a piece of herself behind in Wyatt. So I see those fourteen months as a gift.

Finally, Tom does, too. He knows now that he can survive without Bree. He can be a good parent and a fine lawyer and live the kind of life that would have made Bree proud. She is an irrevocable part of who he is. But just as she willingly gave her life to give him a child, he knows that she wouldn't want him growing old alone.

A new woman has just moved to town, a widow with a teenage daughter and a successful statistical analysis business that she plans to run from her house. That house is a charming Cape newly built on the site of the old Miller house on South Forest. Yes, it took Tom this long to do anything with the lot. He held it for two years after Bree died, finally razed the burned-out old house and left the land empty for another two years before building the Cape, and *then* he was fussy about who bought it. He personally helped this woman secure a mortgage. Her name is Diana, shortened to Dee.

Too much of a coincidence, you say?

I might have said it once, too. That was before Bree's three wishes.

But were the wishes real? you ask.

It's a fair question. A fluke spark from a faulty furnace could have caused the house fire. Bree had seen me around town for three years before she wished to see her mother. And more than one doctor told Tom of the feasibility that intense emotion of the type she had felt at the baby's birth could have caused her healthy heart to stop.

So *were* the wishes real? I'll never know for sure. All I know is that Bree believed they were. In those last fourteen months of her life, she came to believe that anything was possible.

I like to think it is.